"Zeke, I Wasn't Going to Scream," She Pleaded . . .

Honey could see from the discernible rise and fall of his chest that he was breathing faster than normal, as though he had been running behind her instead of following so quietly that she hadn't known he was there.

"What's wrong, Honey?" Zeke asked softly, reaching out and closing his hands around her smooth, bare shoulders. He was hardly paying any attention to her words. It was her body language he was reading. She hadn't shrunk away from him. "Does everybody have to play the game according to your rules? You know this is what you want." He slid his hands down her back and then gathered her against him with a groan that came from deep inside. "It's what I've wanted for *years*. . . ."

Dear Reader:

Nora Roberts, Tracy Sinclair, Jeanne Stephens, Carole Halston, Linda Howard. Are these authors familiar to you? We hope so, because they are just a few of our most popular authors who publish with Silhouette Special Edition each and every month. And the Special Edition list is changing to include new writers with fresh stories. It has been said that discovering a new author is like making a new friend. So during these next few months, be sure to look for books by Sandi Shane, Dorothy Glenn and other authors who have just written their first and second Special Editions, stories we hope you enjoy.

Choosing which Special Editions to publish each month is a pleasurable task, but not an easy one. We look for stories that are sophisticated, sensuous, touching, and great love stories, as well. These are the elements that make Silhouette Special Editions more romantic...and unique.

So we hope you'll find this Silhouette Special Edition just that—*Special*—and that the story finds a special place in your heart.

The Editors at Silhouette

CAROLE HALSTON
Almost Heaven

Silhouette Special Edition

Published by Silhouette Books New York

America's Publisher of Contemporary Romance

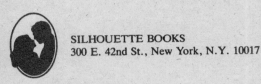

SILHOUETTE BOOKS
300 E. 42nd St., New York, N.Y. 10017

ISBN: 0-373-09253-9

First Silhouette Books printing August, 1985

10 9 8 7 6 5 4 3 2 1

America's Publisher of Contemporary Romance

Printed in the U.S.A.

Books by Carole Halston

Silhouette Romance

Stand-In Bride #62
Love Legacy #83
Undercover Girl #152
Sunset in Paradise #208

Silhouette Special Edition

Keys to Daniel's House #8
Collision Course #41
The Marriage Bonus #86
Summer Course in Love #115
A Hard Bargain #139
Something Lost, Something Gained #163
A Common Heritage #211
The Black Knight #223
Almost Heaven #253

CAROLE HALSTON

is the wife of a sea captain, and she writes
while her husband is at sea. Her characters
often share her own love of nature and
enjoyment of active outdoor sports. Ms.
Halston is an avid tennis player and a
dedicated sailor.

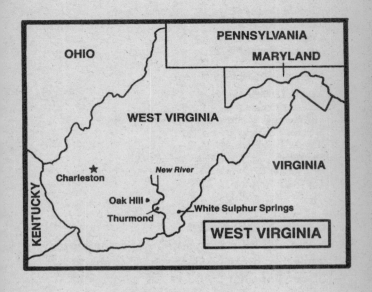

OHIO

PENNSYLVANIA

MARYLAND

WEST VIRGINIA

VIRGINIA

KENTUCKY

★
Charleston

New River

Oak Hill •

Thurmond

• White Sulphur Springs

WEST VIRGINIA

Chapter One

Honey Drake lay perfectly still on her poolside lounge chair, her eyes closed, feigning relaxation and pretending she didn't feel like an incredibly complex network of finely stretched wires. The conversation and laughter of her companions hummed and vibrated along the wires, intensifying her pent-up restlessness and sharpening the vague, illogical resentment of their carefree attitude. It wasn't the fault of her long-time summer friends that her world was in upheaval, that she felt miserable, betrayed, terribly alone.

". . . my history prof, you wouldn't *believe*—I mean, *really*, the man was a living, walking *dream*," DeeDee Maguire was declaring rapturously. *She used to sound the same way when she was talking about one of her precious horses*, Honey reflected sourly, and then waited irritably for Susan Levine's reply.

"Mine looked like a toad frog. He should have hopped into class." Honey had to stifle a groan during the brief pause Susan provided for DeeDee's obligatory giggle. Why did Susan *always* have to try for the witty remark? "My freshman comp instructor was another story, though. Every word out of his mouth was poetry, sheer poetry. I'd get positively weak every time he called on me in his deep, sexy voice: 'Miss Levine, could you tell us . . .'"

Honey shifted her attention to the male conversation over on her left. The guys were still hard at it trying to outdo each other with anecdotes about fraternity rush and initiation. The claims had progressed from doubtful to truly absurd.

"Come on, Copeland, you're putting us on. Four guys drinking a whole keg?"

"No kidding, man. I didn't sober up for days—"

How was she going to stand it here at the Greenbrier this year? Everything was so intolerably the same and, at the same time, so intolerably different. The ache of misery welled inside Honey's chest until she had to bite down hard on her bottom lip to keep from uttering a hurt, whimpering sound. The others sounded so normal and happy as they compared notes about their freshman year off at college. Honey should be joining in, the center of attention as she had always been. They all thought she was acting strange. She could feel their curious glances now and then. They all suspected what the problem was, but they didn't understand. Nobody understood. *Least of all, her father.*

"What a *boring* place this is!" The conversation on either side of Honey ceased as she sat up and made this vehement indictment. Sunlight glinted on gold as she rose and offered herself for censorious inspection once again, feeling a little thrill of disbelief at her own daring and a grim satisfaction in the general disapproval that came at her in waves from all over the spacious pool enclosure.

By Greenbrier standards, Honey's simulated-leopard-skin bikini was shockingly brief, but no one, not even the more corpulent of the matrons stuffed into latex one-piece suits, could honestly deny that Honey wore the suit well. At nineteen she was slim with lovely young curves, more girl than woman. Perhaps it was her underlying innocence that made the total ensemble all the more provocative. She had made an issue of her tanned bare flesh by draping herself in tasseled gold chains. One gleamed around her neck, another shimmered just below her waist, resting on the tender curve of her hips, and still another encircled her slender left ankle. She might have been play-acting as the pampered slave concubine of a jungle mogul.

The members of her own little group were eyeing Honey expectantly. She read the mixture of disapproval and envy in the eyes of Susan and DeeDee and then quickly scanned the faces of the three young men, reflecting open admiration, but also reserve. For all their boasting among themselves about their masculine prowess, Honey was more feminine challenge than they secretly felt themselves capable of meeting. For a brief moment Honey regretted the show of exhibitionism that had set her apart from her companions. She'd have given anything to simply be one of the group again. But then Susan spoke and, whether intentionally or not, put matters back into bitter perspective for Honey.

"My father would have twenty conniption fits if I came out in something like that. Wouldn't yours, DeeDee?"

"Mine would kill me," DeeDee murmured ruefully, glancing down at her own modest black one-piece as though trying to envision her stocky figure in leopard skin and gold chains.

"So would mine if he happened to *notice!*" Honey blurted out bitterly and then wished that she could cut out her tongue when instant comprehension leapt into the faces of her friends. "Don't *look* at me like that!" she cried out shrilly. "It's not some kind of tragedy just because my father's married again. I'm just tired of being dragged to this pokey old *boring* place year after year, where there's never anything exciting to do."

Feeling herself dangerously close to the humiliation of tears, Honey plopped herself down on her lounge chair and stretched out once again in a kind of repudiation of the sedate pleasures of one of the oldest luxury spas in the country.

An uncomfortable silence followed. DeeDee and Susan exchanged uneasy glances. Earlier they'd speculated on how Honey would be taking her father's remarrying after all these years. Her mother had died when Honey was only eight, and she and her father were extremely close.

"You're right. It is pretty boring here." Guy Bailey offered his agreement with a touch of apology, as though he were somehow at fault.

"Yeah," Arthur Copeland chimed in uncomfortably. "I mean, what is there different to do?"

Silence fell over them again as they all thought somewhat guiltily of the numerous diversions that usually filled up their annual two-week stay at the Greenbrier with their families, who came every year at this same time. There was golf, tennis, swimming, horseback riding, fishing, skeet shooting, bowling. The time always went by pleasantly, particularly since they had each other, and some kind of innocent devilry was usually afoot.

Honey lay there, humbled by their instinctive show of support, despising herself for having spoiled everybody's good mood and yet not trusting herself enough to speak and try to smooth things over. As soon as she had recovered her composure, she would make some excuse and go off by herself. In her state of mind, she wasn't decent company for anybody.

"Ever heard of the New River Gorge?" Johnny Marshall, the spectacled scholar in the group, was asking. Undeterred by the lack of interest in the negative replies and the impatient glances that met his seemingly irrelevant question, he went on in his slightly pedantic tone. "It's somewhere here in West Virginia. Several guys at school were talking about going there this spring and taking a rafting trip."

"A rafting trip?" DeeDee echoed contemptuously. Even to her that sounded tame.

"I'm not talking about floating in a swimming pool, smarty, I'm talking white-water rapids," Johnny retorted, and then shrugged. "It's probably too dangerous for amateurs, even if this New River Gorge happened to be anywhere close to here. These guys I heard talking had done a lot of white-water canoeing and rafting out west. They're pretty experienced."

"Our parents probably wouldn't go for it," Susan pointed out.

Everyone went still as Honey levered herself up on her elbows. "It sounds like a blast," she mused in a grim, faraway tone oddly at variance with her words. Mentally she was already relishing the idea of announcing such an excursion to her father. Maybe he'd tear himself away from his new wife, "Bev," long enough to notice Honey was alive.

"Let's go find out where this New River Gorge is

located," she said briskly, coming to her feet. "West Virginia's not that big a state."

Zeke McCade stuck his head in the open door of the tiny office and saw with a glance that his boss, Lee Baxter, wasn't there. Sally Baxter had heard his quiet tread, but she finished an entry on the page of the open ledger in front of her before she glanced around, her smile failing to mask her anxiety.

"Any problems getting the starter for the bus?"

Zeke shook his head. "No problems." Actually he'd had to run around all over Charleston, but he'd managed to locate a starter for the ancient bus that transported people and equipment from the base station to the "put-in."

Sally looked visibly relieved. "That's great." She glanced down at her watch. "I don't know what happened to Lee. He promised to be here around noon so that I could run home and grab some lunch."

"You know Lee. He probably got sidetracked somewhere." Zeke made his boss's unpredictability sound like an admirable trait. "Why didn't you just take off for an hour or so?" he suggested reasonably, knowing that's what Lee would have done.

"Because the season is too short to risk losing out on a reservation. Somebody in this operation has to take White Water Adventurers seriously, Zeke." The kindness in Sally's tone took some of the bite out of the reproof. "It isn't just a hobby, you know. It's the way Lee and I earn our livelihood." As if to signal "end of subject," Sally rose briskly from her chair and began to straighten the surface of the desk. "If you'll stay here and answer the phone for me, I'll go now."

"Sure, Sally, I'll be glad to," Zeke agreed in a chastened tone.

Sally Baxter was sympathetically aware of the complex nature of the young guide's discomfort. Observant and highly intelligent, he'd surely noticed that Lee, for all his white-water expertise and his likable temperament, wasn't the greatest businessman in the world. But because Zeke idolized Lee, he couldn't acknowledge any defects, a fact that Sally found rather endearing.

Lee Baxter was indisputably a living legend in his own time. Anyone with any interest in white water had heard of him since he'd charted some of the most treacherous rivers in the country. But, damn it, she and Lee couldn't exist on admiration. They had to eat and pay the bills. Somebody had to get that point across to the guides and Sally found herself by necessity elected to the job.

"Here's the reservation book." She waited until Zeke had come over to stand beside her. "As you can see, we're booked solid the next two weeks, but after that, there're some openings." She sighed. "I wish now I'd insisted on buying those extra rafts. We have the manpower. Oh, well, hindsight is always great, isn't it? Thanks a million, Zeke. I won't be long."

After she had gone, Zeke dropped down into the chair Sally had vacated and sat sprawled full length, staring glumly at the tattered canvas tennis shoes on his feet. He wore his usual guide's attire: disreputable cutoffs and a T-shirt. Part of the charm of this summer job was the utter casualness of the life-style. It didn't pay much, but he and the other guides would have worked for Lee Baxter for nothing because he was such a great guy and a genius on white water. It was something hard to explain with words, this passion for the white-water experience. When you shared it with another person, a special kind of bond was forged because that person knew exactly how you *felt* going through the rapids, that person understood the exhilaration that couldn't be matched by anything else Zeke had ever experienced.

Vaguely Zeke resented Sally for dragging the reality of dollars and cents into his pleasant summer world, but he was too fair a person not to recognize that his attitude was selfish. After all, he lived the insular life of the professional student. At twenty-four, with his master's degree in his pocket, come September he would be returning to the University of Virginia and entering the doctorate program in history. Thanks to a fellowship that would provide his basic needs, which were minimal, Zeke had no worries about money. All he needed was enough to get by, enough to allow him to do what he enjoyed. In his scale of values, what one did in life was little influenced by the prospect of earning money. It mattered not at all to him that his years of scholarship and study would, in all likelihood, earn him a low-paying history professor's salary. He was doing what he loved.

So engrossed was he in these thoughts, faintly tinged with guilt, that Zeke jumped when the telephone he'd been commissioned to tend came shrilly to life.

"H'lo," he spoke conversationally into the receiver, remembering almost as soon as he had spoken Sally's forceful little lecture a few minutes earlier. Coming bolt upright in the chair, he would have amended his greeting, made it more businesslike, but the caller didn't give him the opportunity.

"Is this White Water Adventurers, Inc.? Or has the operator rung the wrong number?" The voice was female, young, and imperious. It put Zeke on the defensive at once.

"No, er, I mean, yes, you have the right number.

This *is* White Water." The stammering quality of his reply brought a self-derogatory grimace to his features, an expression that turned to annoyed disbelief as he heard the female voice say quite clearly, apparently to a companion nearby, "I'm not too sure about this outfit. Some hillbilly fellow's answered the phone. He doesn't sound very bright."

"Can I help you, ma'am?" Zeke said loudly, overcoming the urge to hang up on the nervy little broad, whoever she was.

"Who are you?" came the impudent reply.

Zeke held the receiver away from him and regarded it distastefully before he brought it back gingerly to the side of his face and spoke shortly into the mouthpiece. "Zeke McCade." A little muffled sound suspiciously like a snicker made Zeke's face grow warm. Then, without even bothering to cover the mouthpiece, she was carrying on her dialogue with her friend, or "friends," as he was able to surmise.

"You guys won't believe this." Another snicker. "This fellow says his name is Zeke McCade. Sounds like some character out of "The Beverly Hillbillies," doesn't it?"

Zeke heard several voices, male and female, all obviously youthful. His irritation eased as he realized it was silly of him to let a bad-mannered little high school or college girl get his goat, when she was only playing to her friends. On the other hand, he had no intention of staying on the phone all day for her benefit.

"Look, honey, what can I do for you?" he inquired briskly and then felt the blood creeping back into his face when she burst into peals of laughter.

"How did *you* know my name was Honey?" she demanded gaily. "Seriously. My name is Honey. Honey Drake." The friendly tone was faintly patronizing, more offensive to Zeke somehow than her earlier arrogance. "My friends and I want to take a rafting trip on the New River. We're staying in White Sulphur Springs, at the Greenbrier. Looking at the map, the Thurmond area is several hours away, but that's no problem. We can arrange for a limousine to drive us."

Zeke rolled his chair up close to the desk and picked up a pencil in readiness for making the reservation, the set of his mouth reflecting distaste for his task. This rich, spoiled little brat and her friends would arrive here at the base office in their chauffeur-driven limousine and think that the money in their pockets gave them the right to special treatment. Well, if Zeke happened to be their guide, they'd have a surprise coming. He'd treat them just like anybody else.

"We're already booked for the next two weeks. It'll have to be after that."

"But we *have* to take the trip in the next two weeks!" Honey wailed. "We won't *be* here after that!"

Zeke relaxed a little, dropping the pencil. "I'm sorry—" he began complacently and got no further.

"I'd like to speak to the owner," Honey cut in haughtily. "I'm sure there must be some way we can be accommodated. We're willing to pay extra, if necessary."

Zeke's hand gripped the receiver tighter as he fought his irritation, reminding himself that this outfitting company *wasn't* his source of income, but it was Sally and Lee's, as Sally had just reminded him. He couldn't tell this little rich bitch what he thought of her and hang up. Looking down at the open pages of the wirebound notebook Sally had neatly set up as her reservation book, he double-checked the number of parties scheduled for each day. Every raft White Water Adventurers, Inc. owned would be in use the next two weeks.

Zeke noted his name written under Wednesday, the day after tomorrow, and circled in red. He was off that day. Sally was right. They had the manpower to take more parties, but not the rafts. . . .

"Well? Are you going to let me speak to the owner— or not?" Honey sensed what might be a weakening in her adversary and pressed her advantage. "One way or the other, he's going to hear from the manager of the Greenbrier about this," she bluffed.

"Believe me, I'd be more than happy to let you speak to the owner, if he were here," Zeke snapped, his tone completing the thought: Anything would be preferable to talking to Honey Drake himself. "His wife handles the reservations, and she should be back here soon. Leave your number and she can return your call."

"I'll call back in exactly one hour," Honey countered threateningly and winked broadly at her friends, who were all hanging on to her every word.

"Suit yourself." Zeke slammed the phone down and yelled, "Bitch!" for his own satisfaction. Almost immediately he felt better, if also a little foolish. By the time Sally returned, he had the whole little episode in perspective and was able to give her a humorous account. But Sally was only fleetingly entertained.

"If only we had an extra raft," she commented regretfully. "This is our first party from the Greenbrier, and we have to turn them down. If we could have accommodated them, just think how good it could be for business next year. They might have gone back to school and told all their friends."

With all his heart, Zeke wanted to protest that Sally was wrong in her thinking. Those shallow, spoiled little teenagers at the Greenbrier were just out for a superficial thrill. They weren't the kind Zeke wanted to guide down the river that was one of nature's most spectacular and compelling gifts to mankind. They could never appreciate the total white-water experience, which involved body, mind, and soul.

But how could he communicate such thoughts to Sally, who had already turned her attention to the day's mail and was murmuring, "Bills, bills, bills . . ." as she ripped open a long envelope. "What's that, Zeke?" she asked absently when his reluctant suggestion didn't sink in the first time he offered it.

"I said we can probably borrow a raft from some of Lee's friends." With hope blooming in Sally's face as she now fixed her full attention upon him, Zeke had no choice other than to finish what he'd started, against his deepest instincts. What was one wasted day in his life, if it lightened her load a little?

"I'm off Wednesday—and I don't have anything planned. I could take the group from the Greenbrier."

As he left the office minutes later, Zeke's mind was full of gloomy thoughts about fate. Lee *could* have shown up, as he was supposed to, and relieved Sally for lunch that day. Then she would have been in the office instead of Zeke when the call came in from the Greenbrier. Zeke would have been spared the irritation of Honey Drake's existence. More importantly, he wouldn't have found himself opening up his big mouth and volunteering to waste a whole day. Too late now to retract his offer, but, as he'd reflected earlier, what was one day putting up with a group of rich, smartass kids? In the language of the river, it would be a minor disruption, a pebble sinking quickly to the bottom, not a boulder crashing down from the mountain and diverting the whole course of the stream.

Zeke was whistling "She'll Be Comin' Around the Mountain When She Comes" by the time he had walked halfway across the graveled parking lot toward the barnlike building where they stored the rafts and equipment. There were always some chores to do there. When Lee showed up, Zeke would give him a hand installing the new starter in the bus. Maybe the man wasn't gifted with business sense, but he had a million other talents.

When the group of teenagers spilled out of the dark green limousine, Zeke was able to pick Honey Drake out at a glance, before any introductions. *Honey*. The name was perfect. She was slim and golden brown from the glossy cap of hair to sandaled feet with lacquered toe nails. Had the wide-set brown eyes been lit with animation and the pretty mouth been curved into a smile, Honey Drake would have been adorable in any young man's eyes, but there was no sparkle and no smile. For someone who'd insisted upon a rafting trip and gotten her way, she looked anything but happy. Whatever the reason for her dejection, any possibility of Zeke's feeling any sympathy for her was destroyed when she glanced around at the base station with its rustic buildings and muttered, "What a dump."

In Zeke's eyes, Honey may have succeeded in forcing her will upon others, but in her own heart of hearts, she knew she had failed miserably in her real purpose, which wasn't altogether clear in her mind but had something to do with getting her father's attention. From the first, she hadn't really cared about going rafting on some old river. Certainly, she hadn't dreamed that he would allow it. She'd expected him to forbid her to go on the trip, after which there would be a confrontation that would allow her to get her feelings out into the open. If she didn't manage somehow to do that soon, she was afraid she would explode into a million pieces. She was beginning to hate herself, hate everybody, hate everything.

But there had been no confrontation, not over the rafting trip or over the sensation she'd created at the pool. Once again her father had given her the "kid gloves" treatment he'd been giving her ever since he'd remarried, actually ever since Bev had come into his life.

"You're my Honey-With-A-Capital-H," he'd said lightly. "If something happens to you, I won't be able to get a replacement. Let me make some phone calls and check out this rafting thing to make sure it's safe for novices."

"Thanks, Daddy-With-a-Capital-D," she'd managed somehow to quip, when what she wished she could do was throw herself against his chest and cry out all the horrible feelings that tormented her and, at the same time, made her ashamed. *I don't want to be jealous of Bev. I don't want to hate her, but I can't seem to help it! I feel like such an outsider now! I don't want to share you with her, Daddy!*

Warren Drake had gone off to make his phone calls and ascertained that the New River at its summertime level was safe for novices as long as they had a skilled guide and that White Water Adventurers, Inc., owned and run by one of the foremost white-water technicians in the country, was a small operation with an impeccable safety record. Given those assurances, Warren Drake suppressed his gut instinct, which was to protect his little girl. As Bev kept reminding him, Honey wasn't his "little girl" anymore. She was growing up and would be moving beyond his sphere of control soon, very soon. He had to let her develop her fledgling's wings, but, damn, it was hard.

Honey had been stunned when her father not only gave her his permission but swayed the other parents with a report of his findings. *He doesn't even care what happens to me now that he has her,* she thought wretchedly. Searching desperately for some other explanation of her father's inexplicable behavior, she decided that he must have been influenced by Bev, who surely would be happy to get rid of Honey for a day. *Maybe more than a day, maybe forever!* she reflected bitterly.

On the morning of the rafting trip when Honey climbed out of the Greenbrier limousine with the others, she was a mass of turmoil inside. The hurt, angry child inside her said, *I don't care if I get killed today. It would serve both of them right!* The nervous tension in her middle contradicted this infantile suicidal urge. She looked around the base station, noted the unpainted buildings, the battered VW van with a raft tied on top of it, and the grim-jawed young man who wouldn't have been permitted to mow the grass at the Greenbrier dressed as he was in rags, his hair, longer than hers, held back out of his eyes with a red bandana. Honey had never felt more out of her element. Dear God, what had she gotten herself—gotten all of them—into?

Zeke tried to look friendly as he approached the group. "Glad to see you made it." They were more than an hour late. Didn't they realize you didn't want to be running the New after dark? "I'm Zeke McCade. I'll be your guide."

The name made an immediate impact. Zeke didn't have to guess why.

"Our *guide.*" Honey Drake stepped forward, her expression unbelieving. "You're our guide?" Her eyes started at the thick brown hair that hadn't known a barber's scissors since several weeks before the spring graduation ceremonies when Zeke had been handed his Master's diploma, traveled down the cropped T-shirt past a flat, muscled belly to cutoffs that could still be in one piece only by some miracle strength of frayed thread, paused at discolored tennis shoes, and came back to Zeke's face, which was frankly hostile by now. He didn't know what she'd expected. A member of the Park Service in dark green uniform, no doubt.

"That's what I said." Sounding out each word as though he were talking to a kindergarten class, he pointed to himself. "I'm your guide." Then he pointed to the VW van that they'd be using instead of the bus, which had already departed with the other rafting parties. "That's a van. On top of the van is a raft. These are insurance waiver forms that all of you must sign." He gestured with the clipboard he held in one hand. "Any more questions?"

Honey's face had turned scarlet under the mockery in his tone. Her friends had all gone into the pillar-of-salt routine, waiting to see what would happen next.

"Very funny." She stuck one sandaled foot forward and jutted a slim hip sideways as she held out her hand for the clipboard, took it from him, and then proceeded to read the form, which was phrased in legalese. "This looks okay," she told the others with the offhanded confidence of a Harvard law school graduate, and scrawled her signature on the top form with a ballpoint pen. The others quickly followed suit. Guy Bailey, who was last, started to hand the clipboard back to Zeke, who had his hand extended for it, but before Guy knew what was happening, Honey had taken the clipboard from him and handed it to Zeke herself.

"We'd better get started before half the day's gone," she said briskly. "And we're not riding in that dilapidated old van, either. We'll follow you in the limousine."

Now Zeke's color deepened. Not that he cared a damn whether they rode in the van or not, but Honey Drake might as well get one thing straight. Zeke was the guide, and on a rafting trip, the guide was boss. That was the only way it could be. "How you get to the put-in is your business, but from that point on, what I say goes. Is that clear?" He deliberately let his gaze rest equally on each countenance, ignoring Honey's leadership. "You'll be issued helmets and life jackets, and you'll wear them *at all times*"—each word enunciated grimly—"*unless* I say it's okay to do otherwise. Understood?" There were murmured words of agreement from everybody except Honey, who cast her eyes skyward and emitted a loud sigh. "Expect to get soaking wet. If you're wearing your swimsuit underneath your clothes, you'll be comfortable in it. The weatherman has promised us a great day." With the mantle of authority firmly in place on his broad shoulders, Zeke was sounding more like his usual self when he greeted a group he would be guiding down the river. "I see most of you have tennis shoes on. As you were told on the phone, that's one of our safety requirements. Now, if nobody has any questions, time's a-wasting."

Zeke conferred briefly with the Greenbrier chauffeur and was about to stride away to the van when he noticed that his young charges for the day had gone into a huddle and were arguing in low tones. "You've got to *tell* him, Honey!" he heard one of the girls insist in a stage whisper. He couldn't hear Honey's reply, but rebellion was etched in the set of her head and the posture of her slim body.

Now what? Zeke groaned mentally. "Something

wrong over there?" he called, taking a step toward the group and stopping.

"Honey doesn't have any tennis shoes," DeeDee Maguire volunteered apologetically, wriggling uncomfortably under the dagger of Honey's gaze.

"Big mouth," Honey muttered under her breath, and then squared her shoulders and lifted her chin a notch as she faced Zeke. She hadn't deliberately not brought along the required tennis shoes. She had forgotten them until she had met the others at the front portico of the big main hotel, where the limousine was parked in readiness. By then they were already running late, and she didn't see any necessity for wearing tennis shoes in a raft, anyway. But she had no intention of explaining all this to Zeke McCade, who apparently thought being a river guide gave him the power to boss people around.

"I don't care if my sandals are ruined," she said airily. "I can buy some more."

It wasn't the first time somebody had shown up without tennis shoes. More than the situation itself, Honey Drake's attitude irked Zeke. She seemed bound and determined to be uncooperative. What she needed was somebody to give her a good, hard spanking. Zeke would gladly have volunteered.

"I don't care if you can afford to buy fifty pairs of sandals," he retorted cuttingly. "The fact remains that you're not getting into that raft," he jabbed a thumb over his shoulder toward the van, "without tennis shoes."

Honey elevated her chin a little higher, pursed her lips, and studied the raft for long, irritating moments before she shrugged. "Well, I don't know what you expect me to do. I forgot to bring the tennis shoes. I can't just produce a pair like *that*—" sunlight gleamed on pink lacquered nails as she snapped her fingers "—out of thin air." It was only with the greatest of effort that Honey kept from smirking her triumph as she made eye contact with her friends, her expression telling them not to worry. Not for a second did she believe Zeke McCade would cancel the whole trip over such a minor issue as a dumb pair of tennis shoes. So caught up was she in this battle of personalities and wills, she had completely forgotten her earlier apprehension about the unknown dangers of rafting. She'd even temporarily forgotten about her father and Bev.

When Zeke McCade walked off without a word toward the building over on their right, Honey's confidence faltered a bit. Fortunately, no one took notice since they were all following Zeke's progress until he had stomped up the steps and disappeared inside the building, unleashing a flood of joking comments and speculations, all with an undertone of nervousness, about what would happen next.

"He's probably gone to get the owner. . . ."

"I bet he's telephoning some country sheriff. You're probably going to get us all thrown in jail, Honey."

"I think he's *cute*," DeeDee offered dreamily. "Don't you, Susan?"

"Cute!" Honey ridiculed before Susan could answer. "Cute! DeeDee, you'd think an Eskimo squatting in front of his teepee was cute."

"Igloo," Johnny Marshall corrected, and then they all turned their attention to the sight of Zeke emerging from the building. General comprehension expressed itself in DeeDee's murmur, "Look what he's carrying. A pair of shoes . . ."

Zeke marched purposefully toward the group, well aware of the gathering suspense. When he reached them, he stopped in front of Honey and held out toward her a pair of stiff, dirt-grimed tennis shoes discarded by a female rafter earlier in the season and retrieved from the refuse barrel for just such an emergency as this one.

"Here. These should fit you." Zeke wouldn't have been human if he hadn't taken some delight in the real horror that flashed over Honey's face as she shrank back, eyeing the shoes in disgust.

"I'm not going to wear somebody else's old shoes!" she declared, her outrage genuine. "You can't make me!"

"You're right, Honey," Zeke agreed evenly, managing to resist the temptation to taunt her. "I can't force you to do anything. But if you don't put on these shoes, you're not coming along with the rest of us. Now why don't you stop acting like a spoiled brat and be a sport? Otherwise, you'll just end up missing a lot of fun."

Before she had any chance to react to his deliberate implication that the others would go along without her, Zeke handed the shoes to the sandy-haired youth who stood next to Honey, wheeled, and headed for the van. To give them a minute or two, he double-checked the number of life jackets, paddles, and helmets in the back, then closed all the doors loudly, jumped into the driver's seat, and started up the engine, the nerves in his belly tightened with suspense. *Would they follow him or head on back to the Greenbrier?*

The limousine was loaded up and followed behind the van as Zeke drove down the steep, winding driveway and turned left, heading in the direction of Thurmond. He eased out a sigh of relief when he saw that he wasn't heading to the "put-in" alone. Thank God he had read the situation accurately and gambled on his instincts. The other Greenbrier kids were basically just normal teenagers, even if they had been indulged more than the average. Zeke had seen in their faces a hint of embarrassment that their ringleader was going too far. He'd counted on their peer pressure to bring Honey Drake into line, and apparently it had. Hopefully, things would go smoothly from here on.

Zeke wasn't proud of the way he had handled the little minx. He didn't know what had gotten into him that he'd ever lowered himself to a battle of personalities with her in the first place, except that she was ten times more irritating in the flesh than she had been over the phone. Still, that was no excuse. It was part of his job as guide to cope with all kinds of personalities, to impose his authority without making enemies. There could be no enemies in a white-water raft, not without endangering lives. Fortunately, Zeke had reminded himself of that fact when he went to get the shoes. He didn't intend to step out of role again.

As he made this well-intentioned resolve, Zeke had no way of knowing that, while Honey had been spoiled and had always been a natural "ringleader," her rude, rebellious behavior today wasn't typical. What he had read as embarrassment in the faces of her friends was partly that, but it was also the recurring disbelief that adventurous, good-natured Honey had undergone such a personality change, apparently as a reaction to her father's remarriage.

Zeke didn't know that by activating peer pressure, he had only made matters worse. Now, more than ever, Honey felt totally alone and misunderstood, her pride ripped to shreds. As she sat, silent, in the limousine on the bumpy, interminable ride to wherever that big bully was taking them, she was seething inside. All the hurt and confusion and resentment of the past few months merged, in the most illogical fashion, into a hatred of Zeke McCade. He was her enemy. She would fight him to the death. Such terminology might be absurdly exaggerated for the actual situation, but not for Honey's emotions.

When he pulled up at the launch site, with the limousine right behind him, Zeke's first concern was getting the raft off the van and the equipment unloaded. It wasn't until he was handing out the life jackets that he noticed the girls had all shed their outer clothes and were wearing their swimsuits, as he had suggested they might want to do. Most of the girls who came along on the rafting trips were fairly athletic types and, more often than not, wore their Speedo racing suits. Few wore bikinis and certainly none in his guiding experience had ever worn a leopard-skin string bikini so brief there wasn't much room for the leopard spots. Taken off guard, Zeke couldn't help taking a hard look any more than he could help admiring what he saw. Honey Drake's name seemed even more uncannily perfect with the exposure of those smooth golden-brown limbs and female curves. Recognition of a potential new threat made his voice a little brusque as he held out an orange life jacket to Honey.

"Here you go." His whole body tensed, and not just from annoyed expectation, when she just stood there, looking startled and unsure, staring into his face.

At nineteen, Honey was no stranger to male admiration, but it was the last thing she had expected from *him*. With the disapproval briefly erased from his clear blue eyes and blatant male recognition in its place, she had felt naked and vulnerable as his gaze moved over her body. How dare he humiliate her in front of her friends and then look at her like that! Intensely conscious of hard-muscled shoulders and chest that were bare now—he'd taken off that shapeless, faded old cropped T-shirt—Honey concentrated on not looking at Zeke as she took the life jacket from his hand, and held it gingerly out in front of her.

"You don't really expect me to wear this old thing? It's dirty—just like these awful shoes." She raised one slim leg in a ballerina kick and sent the life jacket skyward and then leapt up to catch it, the whole graceful exhibition earning her the giggles and guffaws of her friends.

Zeke's pulse rate had doubled. Against his will, he was stimulated, as well as annoyed, and frustrated that he couldn't deal with her on a personal level because there was nothing he'd have liked more. *Come here, honey girl, and I'll help you put on that dirty ole thing.*

"Afraid so," he said aloud, banishing the sensual allure of touching her skin. "Okay, everybody, let's get those life jackets on. They have to be tight. If you feel like you can't breathe, all the better."

Honey's pride had been somewhat reinstated by the little incident. As the moment of actually launching the raft neared, she began to experience some of her earlier trepidations about the possible dangers ahead of them, and offered no further resistance to Zeke's instructions. She donned the life jacket and the helmet, listened as he pointed out the various rowing stations where they would sit along the inflated tubular bulwarks of the raft, and tried to conceal the anxiety that rose inside her when he explained techniques for staying inside the raft when they were hitting the major rapids, most of which would come the second half of the day.

When he gave the order for everyone to grab a ring and help carry the raft down to the water, Honey grabbed the closest one and lifted with all her slender strength. Once the raft was afloat in the shallow water, there was laughter and a great deal of awkward clamboring about as they boarded the raft and jockeyed for rowing positions. Guy Bailey and Arthur Copeland claimed the two front spots that, Zeke had warned, caught the worst brunt of the waves. DeeDee and Susan had scrambled into the positions just behind Guy and Arthur, leaving Johnny Marshall and Honey no choice but to sit farther astern. Honey found herself on the right-hand side, immediately in front of Zeke. She sat stiffly erect and faced forward, fearful that he might think she had ended up close to him by design.

Zeke tried to ignore the tantalizing proximity of slim hips and thighs and a pert bottom only partially concealed by leopard spots. He was frankly grateful for the top cover the bulky life jacket provided. Following his usual starting routine, he introduced several rowing formations and had them practice each one, emphasizing over and over again how essential it was that they respond instantly to his commands.

"If I call for 'Hard Ahead,' that means give it everything you've got. If I yell 'Relax,' that means stop rowing immediately. Okay, you've done great. I think we've got a good crew. Now you can 'Relax' and enjoy the scenery."

They floated slowly along, the river broad and calm, on either side of them a thickly wooded slope. The sun was bright in Honey's eyes and hot. Sweat trickled down her rib cage beneath the bulky, uncomfortable life jacket, which, according to Zeke's orders, was strapped tight. She wiggled her toes in the clammy, unfamiliar cavern of the tennis shoes and grimaced with renewed disgust at the idea of wearing some stranger's discarded old shoes. Why had she been forced to wear them and this smelly life jacket and this stupid helmet? To float down some perfectly harmless river. It was absurd.

"This is boring," she complained to the world at

large, but the words were really directed to that presence behind her. With no provocation in mind, she lifted her bottom and splashed a handful of river water on the hot plastic tubing, then settled back down, moving her hips from side to side and feeling the refreshing coolness. The disapproval she felt emanating from him made her feel even better than the water.

"You can all roll over the side and cool off, if you want to," Zeke announced with a forced pleasantness, his eyes firmly directed toward the front of the raft, *not* at the sinuous side-to-side movements of her hips. "Life jackets, helmets, and shoes stay on," he added authoritatively, as Honey reached down to untie a shoe lace.

She froze momentarily, not believing her ears. Slowly she sat up straight again and swiveled around to face him, brown eyes wide with outrage, tanned cheeks rosy with angry color. "You have to be kidding me. Why would anyone wear tennis shoes in the water? I'm going to swim, not walk on the bottom."

Zeke locked gazes with her, provoked, amused, titillated, determined to show that he was none of those things. "Shoes, life jackets, and helmets stay *on*." He clamped his lips together to keep from adding, *unless I say otherwise,* but he might as well have said it. He thought for a second Honey was going to launch herself at him. The exhilaration that prospect raised inside him made him yield on the staring contest and direct his gaze forward, sight of the other spellbound members of the crew reminding him again that he had to resist confronting Honey Drake on a personal level. He was the guide, responsible for everybody's safety.

"There are seven people in this raft. That means seven life jackets, seven helmets, seven oars, *fourteen* shoes, not to mention the first-aid kit and the lunch container." Zeke was honestly making an effort *not* to sound as though this explanation was totally unnecessary unless one happened to be dealing with nitwits. "Altogether, that makes—"

"I can *count!*" Honey broke in furiously. The reasoning behind his refusal was sound. Admittedly, she hadn't stopped to think about all the clutter in the small raft if they all shed their safety equipment and shoes. What galled her was his evident pleasure in wielding power over her. She had to act quickly to retaliate as best she could and save face with her friends, who once again had stood on the sidelines and watched her go down in ignominious defeat by this West Virginia bully.

"Would anyone like to join me in a 'waddle' in the pool?" she inquired sarcastically, standing up and sweeping her arms wide in a graceful gesture that bespoke years of ballet classes. "Ladies and gentleman, the latest in sexy swim wear."

DeeDee giggled. "Too bad you didn't wear your gold chains, Honey."

Genuinely amused, Honey threw back her head and laughed along with the others. Zeke was captivated by the sound of her laughter, by her spontaneity, by this first glimpse of what she might be like if she weren't alternately sulking and openly rebelling. He also had an eye-level view of slim, bare hips and small shapely bottom beneath a taut scrap of fake leopard skin.

"You should have seen Honey at the pool." DeeDee started to explain to Zeke the reason for their merriment, since he was excluded from it.

"Zeke doesn't want to hear about me," Honey cut in quickly, not solely because she thought Zeke deserved to feel like an outsider after the high-handed way he had acted. She didn't want to give him a chance to make some critical remark at her expense. "Do you, Zeke?" she taunted over her shoulder, uncomfortably aware that he might sense both those reasons for her interruption of DeeDee's explanation.

By now Honey's Greenbrier friends had grown weary of Honey's antagonism toward Zeke and wanted no part of it. Guy Bailey and Arthur Copeland exchanged eloquent glances up in the bow and acted upon the basis of their unspoken communication, partly to create a diversion and partly because the temptation to cool off in the water had become too strong to ignore.

"Last one in!" Guy yelled, and rolled over the side to set off a laughing, awkward evacuation of the raft. Intent on Zeke's reaction from behind her, Honey was taken off guard. With the sudden removal of weight toward the front of the raft, she lost her balance and fell backward, right on top of Zeke.

Instinctively he reached for her to help slow her descent and soften the impact. As she sprawled on top of him, the life jackets they both wore provided some cushioning, but the weight of her lower torso coming hard to rest on Zeke's groin brought a grunt of pain from him. He grasped her by the hips to ease her to one side and then left his hands there. As the haze of weakness cleared, he was aware of her bare flesh beneath his palms. Moving his fingers ever so slightly at first, Zeke explored the texture of her skin and found that it was as lovely to his touch as it was to his eyes. *So smooth, so resilient, so like honey-colored satin.*

The jab of Honey's elbow in the side of his chest as she struggled to lever herself upright brought Zeke painfully back to reality. He had been lying there contentedly underneath her, stroking his fingertips up and down the lovely curves of her hips, oblivious to the circumstances. "Are you okay?" he asked gruffly, taking her by the upper arms and helping her in her efforts to pull free of him.

Honey didn't answer. She scrambled awkwardly a little distance forward and plunged over the side into the water. "This feels great!" she yelled, making a great production of splashing and kicking until she was safely in the midst of her friends. Even as she joined in their conversation, her hands crept down to her hips and rubbed abrasively, as though to remove the imprint of Zeke's fingers. The delicious tingle he had awakened lingered to remind her that she had lain there and let him put his hands on her. A complete stranger whom she detested! And how could his touch have been so gentle, so *reverent*, when he so strongly disapproved of her? Honey wouldn't have been nearly so confused and disturbed if Zeke had pawed at her, like one of her college dates who'd had too much to drink.

When Zeke announced that they would soon be coming upon a "ripple" and should get back into the raft, Honey informed DeeDee that she wanted to trade places with her. DeeDee, who would have loved to sit closer to Zeke from the beginning but was too shy, didn't put up a struggle.

Zeke let the transfer of seats occur without comment, thinking that it would probably be for the best. Later when they got into the big rapids, he would need to concentrate fully upon his task of steering. Honey's proximity had definitely been a distraction earlier.

In her new position behind Guy, over on the left-hand side of the raft, Honey was more intensely conscious of Zeke's presence than she had been when she had sat right in front of him. It seemed to her as she chattered with determined gaiety that she could feel his eyes boring into her. On and on she talked and made her friends her unwitting accomplices in the instinctive effort to shut Zeke out as she entertained them with anecdotes about her freshman year at college and drew them into spirited exchanges about sororities, fraternities, dormitory pranks, and off-campus parties.

As the river narrowed and they came to several minor rapids, she offered no blatant resistance to Zeke's command of the raft, paddling when he called for paddling, and coming to rest when he bade them "Relax." But no sooner were they through a rapid than she was making lightly derogatory comments, such as, "After this trip is over, we might want to try something *really* dangerous, gang, like riding a roller coaster." And, then, instead of letting the river weave its spell around them and draw them all together into a single unit, she would launch them into more conversation. When the subject of college was exhausted, there were Greenbrier stories to dredge up, but those backfired on her, bringing a chilling reminder of her father and Bev, together back at White Sulphur Springs.

"God, this is a *bore!*" she exclaimed vehemently, taking them all by surprise with the sudden change in mood as she lapsed into a tense silence that she couldn't sustain. Then she was talking again, driven to pelt with words that silence coming to her now like a judgment from the stern.

Far up on the steep, wooded slope to their left, Zeke noted the weathered remains of an old coal tipple. Usually he pointed it out and sketched in a little of the colorful mining history of the gorge. If there was time enough and sufficient interest, he might stop and lead a party up through the woods to one or another of the old mining ghost towns, draw from his store of knowledge to make it come to life for them.

Today he didn't even mention the tipple. He kept his

silence, listened to the sound of Honey Drake's voice, felt the undercurrents of her animosity toward him and her desperation. His dissatisfaction with himself deepened as he acknowledged his utter failure in dealing with her, based on the snap judgment that she was just a spoiled, willful brat. Now he sensed that she was deeply disturbed about something and was driven to this constant talk and unflagging inner resistance in order to fight whatever was bothering her.

Zeke knew he also had underestimated her, wrongly assuming that he could ride roughshod over her pride and her will. She had proved herself a formidable adversary, using her intelligence, wit, and quick insight into those around her to her own advantage. Zeke might have coped with her better if he hadn't appreciated her perverse cleverness. And if he hadn't been so receptive to her physical allure. Deep down, he suspected that this whole day would have gone differently if Honey Drake were more like the other two girls, cute and fresh but lacking that devastating combination of innocent and sexy.

Even now, as he regretted his failures, he felt his eyes being drawn to her slender golden hips and thighs. His fingers tightened on the paddle that lay across his knees as he remembered the feel of her skin. It was an effort to clear his mind as he announced that they soon would be coming up on the first big rapid.

"After you've been through it, you'll know why we call it Surprise. There's a five- or six-foot drop, and then suddenly it's all over. A little later on, we'll be stopping for lunch. Then—"

"I can hardly wait!" Honey sang out, interrupting him. "What are we having, anyway? Soggy peanut butter and jelly sandwiches?"

The same joking question had been posed dozens of

times on previous rafting trips and never caused Zeke such effort to keep his voice clear of any personal message as he gave a typical rejoinder. "How did you guess? As I was about to say, after our soggy peanut butter and jelly sandwiches, we'll be getting into what you came for today, some class IV and class V rapids."

"I can't wait," came the sarcastic retort from the front, left-hand side of the raft.

Zeke had to quell a renewal of his earlier conviction: Honey Drake needed a good, hard spanking. He couldn't think of such things now. He had to concentrate fully upon the narrow band of foaming, churning white water that had just come into view. Mentally, he relived running the rapid and then began to give clear, terse orders.

"We'll head straight for that big rock over on the left. When I give the order, Left Back, remember, everybody on the left paddle backwards, everybody on the right keep paddling ahead. Got it? Now give me Easy Ahead."

Honey had been lulled much earlier into deciding that there really wasn't much to rafting through rapids, after all. She wasn't prepared for the feeling of being sucked into a giant, roaring whirlpool. When the supple raft hit the hole Zeke had warned them about, the front of it dipped out of sight, leaving Honey prey to a huge wave that came at her like a moving white wall instants before the whole world dropped out from beneath her. A scream of sheer terror was ripped from her throat as she felt her body propelled skyward, torn free of the force of gravity. Forgetting everything but survival, she let go of her paddle and hurled herself sideways, landing down on the floor of the raft, where she cowered and stayed.

And then as suddenly as they had found themselves

in the middle of the maelstrom, they were out of it and floating in a calm pool. Honey lay where she was, trembling. By the time she felt strong enough to get up and return to her position, the others were all in place. It seemed to her that Zeke's lecture was directed solely at her.

"Remember to hook one foot underneath the tubing. And hang on to the paddle at all times. Don't let go of it." Fortunately, Honey's paddle hadn't flown out of the raft. She picked it up and held it across her lap. The weakness in her limbs was gradually going away. "It's important to keep paddling unless I tell you to stop. Number one, there isn't room for everybody down on the floor of the raft. Number two, if you don't all do your part, we'll more than likely end up on a rock." During the pause, she tensed for his next words, sure they would be a scathing condemnation of her. "Actually, you guys did a pretty good job. We usually sacrifice at least one victim to Surprise."

His light tone released chuckles and giggles and excited comments from everybody except Honey about what it had been like, going through their first big rapid. She felt personally humiliated and more alone than she had ever before felt in her life. They had all deserted her and rallied around Zeke. Sitting with her back to him, her head a little downcast as she watched the fingers of her left hand trail in the water, she could feel his gaze on her and bitterly resented him.

From Zeke's viewpoint in the stern, Honey hadn't done any worse than anybody else. A novice couldn't be expected to do much more in the middle of Surprise than hang on. The rapid served a valuable purpose, though. It aroused respect for the sheer power and treachery of the New as it narrowed and gained momentum. Of the three girls present, Zeke would have expected Honey to be the most fearless, but it appeared to him that she had been shaken up and, typically, was too proud to admit it to the others. Or to him.

By the time they reached the lunch site, Honey had recovered somewhat, but fears about what lay ahead that afternoon tightened into a knot in her stomach and destroyed any appetite for food. Added to the physical danger of being thrown from the raft was the almost certain prospect of disgracing herself in front of her friends and Zeke.

When the raft had been pulled up on shore, Zeke gave his permission for them to remove the helmets and life jackets. He was prepared for a sarcastic remark from Honey, but she only muttered "Thank God" in a heartfelt tone as she immediately stripped off her helmet and life jacket. Surprisingly, she didn't even raise the issue of whether they could take off their shoes, too. He'd been expecting that.

Honey stood a moment in indecision as DeeDee and Susan crowded around Zeke with offers to help. Then she made her way over to a broad, flat rock in the sunshine some distance away and sat leaning back on her hands, head tilted back and her eyes closed. The warmth of the sun brought a fine sheen of perspiration to her skin but it failed to relax her. If possible, she felt a thousand times more tense and tightly strung than she had three days ago lying beside the pool at the Greenbrier, chafing under the sound of her friends' happy conversation, desperate to think of some way to get to her father.

Now she wished with all her heart that Johnny Marshall had never mentioned the New River or white-water rafting. Her father and Bev were safe and sound at the Greenbrier, probably having the sumptuous buffet lunch out on the terrace at the Golf Club, glad to be rid of her presence, not knowing or caring that she faced real physical danger and total humiliation. No, that wasn't true. Her father cared deeply about her. He'd always given her everything she wanted, including his time and interest. He'd made every effort to make up for the absence of a mother. Now that she had started college and was gone most of the time, busy with her own friends even when she was home, he had every reason to want a companion. But how had Honey rewarded his years of being a loving, devoted father? By causing him embarrassment and being rude and unfriendly to his new wife. No wonder Bev didn't like her. Honey didn't like herself the way she'd been lately.

"Come and help yourselves," Zeke's voice invited. Honey stayed precisely as she was, wanting nothing but to be left alone in her misery.

"Honey, Zeke was just fooling us. It's not really peanut butter and jelly sandwiches," DeeDee called over to her. "It's ham and cheese and potato salad. It looks delicious."

The knot inside Honey's stomach rocked gently on a wave of nausea. "Thanks. I'm not hungry." She could sense the curious glances thrown her way, the looks exchanged, and then the shift of attention away from her and back to the food.

As he stood to one side, Zeke's gaze might have been directed toward the five young people loading food on paper plates, but he was seeing Honey stretched out on that rock, a picture that was sleek, tawny perfection except for one wrong note: the clumsy, ugly tennis shoes he had forced her to wear. He had a ridiculous, fierce urge to go over there and take them off, as though by doing so he could make amends, start all over with her, draw her out of her splendid isolation into the group. Instead, he just stood there, knowing that there was little point in urging her to join them and eat.

Guy Bailey had managed to be first in line and came to stand next to Zeke with his amply loaded paper plate and cup of lemonade. "You know, Honey's really not like this," he said in an apologetic undertone. "She's usually the life of the party and real easy-going. I guess she's feeling some kind of rejection now that her father's remarried. She thinks the sun rises and sets on him. She cooked up this whole rafting trip, the same way she's been doing other things—like shocking all the old ladies at the Greenbrier pool by showing up in that leopard-skin bikini with gold chains draped all over her—just to get his attention." Guy shook his head at the memory and then added in a male tone Zeke well understood, "Boy, she looked like something else. But I just wanted to say, Zeke, we're all—except for Honey, that is—having a great time."

Zeke clapped Guy on the shoulder and said something appropriate before he went to fix himself a sandwich and take a dab of potato salad, despite the fact that he didn't have much of an appetite. As he sat on a piece of driftwood and ate, he mulled over what Guy had told him. Honey had evidently been resorting to atypical, outrageous behavior in order to force a confrontation with her father. Zeke had an intuition that she hadn't met with any success and probably was spoiling for a fight that morning when she arrived at the base station. It would explain her immediate strong antagonism toward him and resistance of his authority, but it gave him no clue as to how he might approach her now and win her trust and cooperation before they set out again.

"Okay, everybody, last call for grub." There was a

note of resignation in Zeke's voice as he rose to his feet and made this announcement. Just as he had suspected, there was no movement over on Honey's rock. "Remember that whatever we brought to shore, we take with us," he reminded, shaking out a garbage bag and dropping his paper plate, plastic fork, and paper cup into it. DeeDee and Susan came to help him pack the uneaten food into the water-tight plastic canister. The garbage bag of refuse was compacted and placed on top, and they were ready to go.

"In case anybody has need of the 'facilities,' ladies can take upstream and guys downstream." Zeke was tying the canister back in place in the raft and saw the movement of golden limbs out of the corner of his eyes.

Honey headed into the woods in a kind of panic, purely and simply to delay the moment of departure. She wished now that she had at least taken a sip of something to drink. Her mouth felt parched. The undergrowth was too dense for her to go far. She halted and braced one hand on the trunk of a small tree, stood there with her head bent, drawing in a deep breath, when something cool and dry slithered across her hand. She snatched it away and then clapped it over her mouth, too late to keep a high-pitched shriek of terror from escaping. Almost immediately there was the sound of running footsteps.

"I'm okay!" she managed to call out breathlessly in a fruitless effort to stop them. She didn't even have to turn around to know that it was Zeke. "It was just a lizard," she told him over her shoulder. "You can go back. I'm all right."

"Honey—" Zeke involuntarily took a step closer, reached out a hand to touch her, and then quickly drew it back. He had reacted with instinctive concern to the sound of her scream. Now that he was here and had the opportunity, he wanted to start all over with her, one human to another. But he didn't trust himself to touch her. "Honey, I know I've come down a little hard on you today. . . ." he began awkwardly and faltered for words as she turned around to face him, her chin high.

Zeke stared into her eyes, great dark pools of unhappiness mingled with defiance and another emotion he was having difficulty reading. Uncertainty? Shame? Was she so proud that she couldn't bear to have him think she had a weakness?

"Honey, why don't we just strike a truce?" he cajoled softly. "We've got some big rapids out there this afternoon. I need you with me in that raft, not fighting me every step of the way."

To his disappointment she broke the eye contact, looking away across his shoulder. Her response, spoken in a small, proud voice, took him utterly by surprise and raised inside him a tenderness and a protective instinct, the power of which he had never known before.

"I'm scared."

"It's perfectly all right to be scared, Honey," he chided gently. "I've been through these rapids at least a hundred times, and I'm always a little scared deep down in the pit of my stomach." Her eyes came abruptly back to his face and searched it with skepticism.

Zeke unconsciously closed his hands into fists. The urge to take her into his arms, hold her close, ease away all her fears with the reassurance of his own body was a compulsion he could just barely control. He had to use words instead.

"You're going to be fine, I promise. All you have to do is listen to me and concentrate on doing exactly what I tell you."

"But I *can't*!" she blurted out desperately. "When we went through the one you called Surprise, I tried to paddle, but I lost all control and almost fell out." Her voice lowered in shame, but her eyes held his so that she could read their expression. "You saw what happened to me. I dropped my paddle and fell down on the floor of the raft." To her amazement, he smiled.

"Honey, everybody in the whole raft, except for me, fell down, and almost everybody dropped the paddle. Didn't you realize that? It's what usually happens. No matter how much a guide tries to prepare a group of novices for what a major rapid is going to feel like, they have to experience it firsthand for themselves. After being knocked flat on their faces, they can realize what a power they've come up against and that it's going to take all their combined courage and strength to measure up." The passion of his own words embarrassed Zeke, but he kept going because she was listening raptly, an uncertain hope dawning in her eyes.

"I wasn't lying to you a minute ago when I said there's always that little undercurrent of fear when you head right into a big rapid, but you feel superhuman, too, everybody all together in the raft yelling and fighting like hell. And when you make it through, you feel on top of the world, ready for the next one." He shrugged in self-disparagement and, feeling the need of understatement, added, "It's really great. I think you're going to like it."

Honey stood there an instant after he had finished speaking, caught up between the anticipation he had raised with his fervor, and self-doubt. She wished she could feel for herself what going through the rapids was like for him, but she didn't know if she could measure up. The specter of failure was more awful than ever now that he had made her see herself as not just accountable for herself but responsible to the others in the raft. Responsible to Zeke.

"Honey, it's *fun*," Zeke urged lightly to counteract the deepening discouragement in her face. He held out his hand. "Ready to give it a try?"

She drew in a deep breath and made an effort to match his tone. "Guess I don't have too much choice, do I?" She reached out and touched her hand to Zeke's palm, as though sealing a pact with him, and then drew it away, disconcerted by the intimacy that had grown between them.

"Smart girl." Zeke turned abruptly to lead the way back, aware of his heartbeat. After working so hard to build some basis for her trust, the last thing he could afford to do was take her into his arms and kiss her.

Honey followed along behind him, composing her face in readiness for the curiosity that would inevitably be lying in wait for them. But Zeke handled the situation with ease, declaring that he had rescued Honey from a twenty-foot python, strangling the monster with his bare hands. Then he was all business, giving orders and getting them afloat again.

"Johnny, I think we can make better use of our manpower by putting you up there behind Guy. Susan and DeeDee, you're fine where you are. Honey, you sit here opposite DeeDee. You two guys up front, remember to dig in hard when I give the order and make your strokes parallel to the raft. Don't follow the contours. Now, all together, give me some Easy Ahead."

Honey quietly took the place he had assigned her, grateful both that he had brought her back closer to him and that he had done it so adroitly that no one seemed to take any special notice. As she dipped her paddle into the water, she adjusted her timing so that her strokes coincided perfectly with Johnny's. The instant Zeke called for them to Relax, she lifted her paddle from the water and rested it on her knees. He had promised that if she concentrated totally on doing what he told them to do, everything would be all right. She had no choice other than to trust him.

All Honey asked was somehow to rise to what would be required of her during the remainder of the day. She blocked every other consideration out of her mind. The world consisted of herself and six other people afloat on this river that narrowed and rushed along between sheer constricting banks, tumbled madly over rocks, swirled and roared and foamed and kicked up great sheets of white spray, only to settle down again like a docile giant before going into a rage again. She braced herself against it, fought for balance, and put every ounce of energy into obeying Zeke's shouted orders. And at some point—she didn't even know when—the screams coming from her throat and mingling with the yells and screams of the others were not screams of terror but of the purest exhilaration.

Never before in her life had she yielded herself so utterly to a common effort. They were all one body, one spirit, instantly responsive to Zeke's commands, utterly dependent upon his expertise and unerring judgment, riding together to impossible heights that would forever defy expression.

During the quiet times between rapids, Honey would join in the conversation occasionally, but mostly she was silent, not sulking now or brooding or even thinking. It was as though her soul had been opened up to the wild beauty of the gorge. She took into her pores the sense of vastness and timelessness that diminished her importance and yet brought a deep sense of peace in the recognition that she was a part of it all.

The whole time, during the furor of the rapids,

during the serenity of the pools interspersed between them, there was Zeke just behind her. She was intensely aware of him in the most strange, and yet companionable, kind of way. It was as though he shared her perception of things, making speech unnecessary. As they approached the final rapid, he had to be aware of her sadness that the day ever had to end. Wasn't there a corresponding note of regret beneath the matter-of-factness of his voice when he called their attention to the bridge spanning the river up ahead of them.

"That's Fayette Station. We're getting close to the end of the line. Past the bridge is one last humdinger of a rapid. Then the take-out station. Your limousine will be waiting for you there. Let's do this one right and call it an all-around good day." *One of the best days of my life on the New.* He had never concentrated so totally. Never felt any greater technical mastery. Never felt quite the same thrill in sharing the total white-water experience with another human being as he had felt today, sharing it with Honey. Her triumph over her fear had been his own. Her ecstatic pleasure had raised his own exhilaration to a new high. *And the Greenbrier limousine will be there at the take-out station, waiting to take her away.*

As she climbed out of the raft in the shallow water, grasped a ring, and helped carry the raft ashore, Honey couldn't quite believe it was all over. The sight of the dark green limousine and uniformed driver brought back the reality of returning to the Greenbrier and her father and Bev. Strangely, the prospect didn't fill her with dread. She would go back to the Greenbrier a different person on the inside, thanks to Zeke and what he'd helped her to experience today. She felt purged and cleansed and at peace with the world, humble and thankful and yet strong, full of pride in herself. Such feelings were far too complex and private to express with either language or gesture and to communicate anything less to Zeke seemed a compromise. When her friends crowded around him, uttering sincere but inadequate words of thanks, she hung back and stayed silent, telling him only in her heart, *Thank you, Zeke. This has been one of the most special days in my whole life. I'll never forget it . . . never forget you.*

Normally the take-out station was a scene of hectic activity, the rafts arriving one after the other and everyone piling into the ancient bus for the ride back to the base station. Today, though, Zeke's party was behind all the others. The take-out site seemed intolerably quiet to him. His breast was crowded with emotions far more powerful than those he usually felt at parting with a group he'd guided down the New.

"You're one of my best groups," he told them sincerely, looking from one open countenance to another and coming last to Honey. "How about same time next year?"

The suggestion eased to some extent the poignant sense of finality, and at that moment Lee Baxter drove up in the battered van Honey had refused to ride in just that morning, eons ago. Zeke was grateful that he didn't have to stand there and watch the group from the Greenbrier climb into the limousine and drive away.

"How did it go?" Lee asked conversationally as the two men set about securing the partially deflated raft to the top of the van.

"No problems," Zeke replied. He could hear the engine of the limousine revving up, then the crunch of tires on gravel. "No problems at all," he said a full two minutes later, when he could no longer hear the faint engine sounds. The hollowness of his voice brought a quick glance from Lee but no comment.

As he loaded life jackets, helmets, and paddles into the back of the van, Zeke wondered how long it would be before he could hand out life jackets and not see a living-color replay of Honey Drake kicking her life jacket high into the air and then leaping up gracefully to catch it. *An adolescent Eve in a leopard-skin bikini.* The memory speeded up his pulse, brought a fleeting smile to his lips, and helped to ease the strange sense of loss. *How could he feel so empty about losing something he'd never had?*

Chapter Two

*H*oney answered the telephone in the faintly bored tone of voice that had grown habitual with her of late. It was indicative of a state of mind that caused her some concern. Nothing seemed to rouse any enthusiasm any more. Perhaps her friends were right: After a year maybe she hadn't fully recovered from the failure of divorce.

"Honey Drake, is that really you? This is Deirdra Anderson—better known to you back in our Greenbrier days as DeeDee Maguire. What have you been doing with yourself all these years?"

"DeeDee, what a surprise. Why, it's been . . ." Honey paused to count.

"Almost ten years!" DeeDee finished the sentence for her. "We haven't seen each other since that summer after our freshman year at college. We went on that wild rafting trip, remember? The next year you didn't come to the Greenbrier with your father. Maybe that was why the rest of us were all bored to death. I didn't go myself the following year, and after that, well . . ." DeeDee's voice trailed off sadly.

"We all had to grow up, DeeDee," Honey put in wryly. "I did run into Susan Levine several years ago. Naturally, she'd married and her name wasn't Levine anymore. I can't recall—"

"Angelo. She's Susan Angelo now." DeeDee promptly supplied the forgotten information. "Susan and I have kept in touch, more or less. I hadn't seen any of the guys from the Greenbrier, though, since my last summer there until a couple of weeks ago I literally ran into Guy Bailey in a shopping center in Chicago. He's on his second marriage. Arthur Copeland was best man in both of Guy's weddings, but Guy claims that's as close as Arthur will ever get to the altar! Neither one of them has kept track of Johnny Marshall. Do you happen to know anything about his whereabouts?"

"Why, no, I don't," Honey denied politely. Had DeeDee located her whereabouts and called just to catch up on what had happened to the members of their old Greenbrier group? Those days seemed a thousand years ago now.

"I hope we can track him down—but, wait, I haven't gotten around to the purpose behind this phone call, have I? Guy mentioned that it would be fun for all of us to get together again at the Greenbrier. I thought it was a great idea and so did Susan. We could bring along our husbands and kids and have a great time together, just like our families used to have in the old days."

Honey's reaction was mildly negative. She had neither a husband nor a child to bring with her to the

Greenbrier and no desire to encounter a lot of curious questions about what she'd done with the past ten years of her life.

"I really don't think—"

"Honey, please consider it! Come for at least a couple of days. It wouldn't be a Greenbrier reunion without you. You know you were always our ringleader. Wait, maybe this will sway you. Guy thought we should take another rafting trip—with that same outfit if it's still in operation. Wouldn't it be just too good to believe if we could get that same guide! What was his name, anyway? I've been wracking my brain. . . ."

"Zeke." The name came without any difficulty from wherever it had been stored away for years. Along with it came a clear picture of a young man with a fit, rugged physique and blue eyes. "Zeke McCade."

"That's it! Do you remember what a hard time you gave that poor young man, Honey? He hardly knew what to do with you!"

Oh, yes, he did. "Please don't remind me, DeeDee. I acted like an insufferable spoiled brat. But it's been almost ten years. White Water Adventurers, Inc. has probably long since folded. It wasn't a very prosperous-looking operation, as I recall." *He probably has a wife now and three or four kids that he supports, working at some ordinary job.* The unspoken reflection was accompanied by a sensation in Honey's breast that took her totally by surprise. It had been like the prick of a tiny, sharp needle, felt and then gone. Yesterday she had looked across a restaurant, seen Phil, her ex-husband, lunching with a beautiful girl, presumably his latest romantic interest, and felt nothing except concern that there hadn't been any emotional reaction. The pang of regret that had just struck her unawares meant that she still had the capacity to feel.

"You even remember the name of the rafting company!" DeeDee exclaimed, the thread of satisfaction in her voice suggesting that she considered Honey's excellent memory a good sign that Honey might cooperate. "What do you say, Honey? Will you make plans to join the rest of us at the Greenbrier the second week in July? In the meanwhile, you could set up a rafting trip for all of us just like you did before, only this time the group would be a little larger. Besides you, me, Susan, Guy, and Arthur, there would be Susan's husband and mine, plus Guy's wife, and possibly Johnny Marshall, if we can locate him."

DeeDee's failure to assume that Honey would be bringing along a husband went unremarked. Obviously DeeDee knew about Honey's divorce. Finding that she was swayed by DeeDee's urging, Honey let her mind go back to that last summer at the Greenbrier. Her father had married Bev only a few weeks earlier, plunging Honey into an abyss of emotion more intense than anything she had felt before or since. It was as though she established lifetime boundaries of feeling during that brief period, sinking to her lowest low and rising to her highest high. Never again, not even when she knew for certain that her husband was unfaithful to her, had she felt such utter rejection and despair. And on that happiest day of her life in the intervening decade, her wedding day, she hadn't come close to the rapturous heights she'd reached on that trip down the New River. God, what she would give now to resurrect the ghost of her younger self and have again that feeling of grabbing onto life and not letting go, no matter how much it hurt or how good it felt! One sacrificed so much for emotional survival and didn't even realize the cost until the bill was paid.

"Maybe it would be fun to go back to the Greenbrier

for a few days," she mused aloud, more to herself than
to DeeDee, who immediately seized upon her words as
a definite agreement not just to participate in a "reunion" with her former summer companions but also to
take responsibility for arranging another rafting trip.

Afterward Honey was neither particularly glad nor
particularly sorry that she had permitted herself to be
included in the plans for a Greenbrier get-together. She
did note, though, that times had definitely changed. In
the past Honey had always been the one to originate or
at least to "shape" plans for the whole group. Now she
was perfectly content to go along with whatever the
others wanted to do.

A call to the long-distance operator elicited the
surprising information that White Water Adventurers,
Inc. was still in operation. Honey had a vision of
unpainted buildings and graveled parking lot full of
potholes as she punched the digits of the number the
operator had given her, using the eraser end of a pencil
to spare her long, perfectly manicured nails.

This time a girl answered the phone. "White Water
Adventurers. May I help you, please?"

Honey's pause was involuntary. Surely she hadn't
been expecting a casual masculine "H'lo."

"I'm calling long distance from New York City," she
informed the girl crisply and then stated her business in
the same tone.

The girl repeated the date Honey had given her and
then began what sounded like a refusal, "That's a
Saturday, ma'am—"

"Weekends are undoubtedly your busiest time,"
Honey cut in sympathetically. "Fortunately, this is well
in advance. I'm sure the owner of White Water Adventurers will find some way to accommodate our group
when he learns that we're driving all that distance from

the Greenbrier, just for sentiment's sake." In ten years she had refined her technique for applying pressure, but the same basic elements of intimidation she had used against Zeke were still there.

Rose Jennings gazed helplessly down at the reservation book. It was hard to make heads or tails of some of the scribbled entries. She didn't honestly know whether they were fully booked on that Saturday or not.

"Why don't you give me your name and number—"

Once again Honey graciously cut her short to take control. "My name is Honey Drake." She'd taken her maiden name again after the divorce. "Why don't we go ahead and confirm the reservation. You can take down whatever information you need and charge the deposit to my Visa account. If there proves to be a problem, the owner can contact me personally."

Having been politely divested of all power to do anything but comply, Rose picked up a pen and wrote what she was told to write. It was in this robotic state of mind that she replied to Honey's question, "I don't suppose you still have a guide named Zeke McCade around?"

"Zeke McCade? Why, yes, he's still around, but—"

"He *is*." Honey couldn't believe the way her heart had begun to pound. "In that case, we'll insist upon having him as our guide again."

"But, ma'am—"

"It doesn't matter if he's already been assigned to another party. That can be changed." Feeling the gathering resistance at the other end of the line, Honey fell back upon the old standby that had seldom failed her, the power of money. "We'll pay him a five-hundred-dollar bonus to guide our party. Just tell him that and make sure he decides for himself."

Before the girl could make any reply, Honey thanked her cordially for her efficient service and hung up.

"But he isn't a guide!" Rose protested weakly, the dial tone buzzing in her ear.

"Five hundred bucks!" Zeke echoed with amused skepticism. With his hands clasped behind his neck, he leaned back in the homemade rocking chair, denim-clad legs stretched out in front of him. He'd spent all afternoon working in his study and was glad Lee Baxter had dropped by. "Who'd pay that kind of money for a river guide?"

"Obviously somebody with a lot of it." Uncomfortable with the telltale note of feeling behind a remark he had meant to be jocular, Lee took a deep swig of cold beer and shifted to rest his back more comfortably against a square-hewn post. Refusing Zeke's offer of a chair, he had chosen to sit on the edge of the front porch. "You must have made one hell of an impression on this broad, Zeke, who sounds like the kind who's hard to please. Rose said she'd never run up against anybody so dead set on having her way. She had to have a certain day, whether there was an opening or not—and she had to have you."

Zeke grunted his bemusement. "She must have a good memory for names. I haven't worked as a guide in eight or nine years. I don't guess you remember her name?"

"You know me and names, Zeke." Lee was digging into the right front pocket of his jeans. "I wrote it down. The first name was something sweet, like Sugar." He pulled out a slip of paper and unfolded it. "Here it is. *Honey*—" The sound of Zeke's voice speaking in unison with his own brought Lee's head up in surprise.

Zeke shrugged. "Your clue must have jogged my memory. She's the only person I've ever met named Honey." A smile touched his lips and made his blue eyes gleam with amusement. "Apparently her personality hasn't changed. She was determined to have her own way when she was eighteen or nineteen, too." *She had remembered his name?* "Did you write down her last name?" *It would be different now. She was certain to have married.*

Lee glanced down at the paper again. "Drake. Honey Drake." He looked back up in time to note the startled expression of recollection on Zeke's face.

"That's the same last name," Zeke mused, his mind full of images whose clarity utterly amazed him considering how long he had retained them. She must have married, divorced, and taken her maiden name again. The way he remembered her, she would have had no shortage of marriage offers. In one day's time she had raised powerful yearnings inside his manly young breast, not to mention his loins, and invaded his dreams for several years afterward.

"I didn't think you'd be interested in doing it." Lee stuffed the piece of paper carelessly into his pocket, lifted his bottle of beer to his mouth and drained it in several deep swallows.

Zeke came back to the present and eyed his old friend with concern. "How are things, Lee?" he asked quietly, the vague phrasing deliberate so that Lee's answer could be as personal or as general as he chose to make it.

Lee Baxter's shoulders sagged, and his weathered face looked at least a decade older than his forty-five years. "Not good, Zeke. Not good at all." He hesitated, and for a moment seemed uninclined to say more. "It's more than just all the hospital and doctor bills piled sky high. Nothing's the same anymore, with Sally gone. I think it's time for me to find a new scene. The only thing that holds me back is the fact that she put so much into building up the business." Guilt clouded his downcast features.

Zeke had to contend with his own mixed emotions before he could speak. Deep down he suspected that the best thing for Lee might be for him to sell out and go somewhere else, where he could start off fresh and recover from the death of his wife, who had waged a long, costly battle with cancer and lost. Here Lee would be reminded of her at every turn. But Zeke would miss Lee if he did move away.

"Sally would want you to do what was best for you, Lee. You know that." Zeke hesitated, choosing his next words with care. "What she wouldn't want you to do is let the business go downhill. I think she'd rather have you make some profit off all the years of hard work and leave it in good hands, don't you?"

Lee nodded soberly. "I know what you're trying to tell me in a very tactful way, Zeke. I'm one hell of a poor businessman. I always was. You hit on dead center, though, when you said Sally would want me to leave the business in good hands. The two of us started off White Water Adventurers with five rafts and my reputation. I couldn't sell out to just anybody. It'd have to be somebody who loved white water . . . somebody like yourself, Zeke." Lee sat up straight, the notion taking hold. "You know, that's not a half-bad idea. You've got all the practical know-how, and a man with a Ph.D. ought to be able to handle the business angle. We could work out the terms—"

Zeke's hands came down to clasp the arms of his chair as he rocked forward. "Come on, Lee, I'm a historian, not a businessman!" he chided. "I've got my hands full with this oral history project I'm working on, not to mention expanding my doctoral treatise into a book. Besides—" Zeke grinned ruefully. "Selling out to me would prove just how bad a businessman you really are. With the kind of down payment I could make with my savings, you'd be a hundred years getting all your money."

"Say, man, I know how you could earn yourself an easy five hundred bucks." This latter exchange had taken Lee's mind off his troubles. He looked and sounded more like his old happy-go-lucky self.

Zeke didn't need five hundred bucks. The grant to do an oral history study of the coal mining and lumbering era of the New River Gorge provided enough money for his modest living expenses. When that was finished, he would probably go back to teaching in a university. But Lee could well use all the money he could get his hands on. The medical bills from Sally's hospital treatment were astronomical. Still, it wouldn't occur to Lee to put any pressure on Zeke to guide Honey Drake's party, even if she threatened to cancel it unless she got her way.

"What puzzles me, Lee, is why Rose didn't explain that I'm no longer a guide."

"She tried to, but this, er, Sugar character—"

"Honey," Zeke corrected him automatically.

"Right. This Honey just rode right over her. She insisted the guide had to be none other than yourself, threw out her five-hundred-dollar bribe, and hung up. How long ago was that, anyway, Zeke?" he added curiously.

Zeke had counted up the years by this time. It had been the summer between finishing up his master's and starting his Ph.D. "Ten years. That was that first group from the Greenbrier, remember?" He shook his head.

"I guess what intrigues me more than anything else, Lee, is the assumption that I would still be right here, working in a seasonal occupation. Tell you what. I'll take that party down the New for you, free of charge, but you be sure to charge Honey Drake the five hundred bucks. I'll try to make sure she gets her money's worth."

True to his open nature, Lee Baxter didn't argue. Nor did he question Zeke's motives. He assumed that Zeke was acting partly out of friendship and partly out of curiosity. After all, what man wouldn't be flattered to have a five-hundred-dollar-a-day price tag put on his services?

When Honey received written confirmation of her reservation, it was accompanied by a slick brochure, obviously not the work of amateurs. Despite this sign of prosperity, she wasn't expecting the physical changes that had taken place in the outfitting company's base station, nor its expansion into a large-scale operation.

Gone was the ramshackle building into which Zeke McCade had disappeared to return with the awful tennis shoes. In its place was an attractive cedar structure with angled roof lines. The parking lot, much enlarged and thickly covered with gravel, was crowded to capacity with vans, four-wheel-drive vehicles, and conventional automobiles. The whole place seemed to have been inundated with college students. The scene was one of organized confusion.

A pigtailed girl in her early twenties, wearing hiking shorts over her one-piece swimsuit, met the limousine with a clipboard in her hand, showing no signs of being impressed. "Ten o'clock party?" she inquired briskly of the chauffeur, who glanced over his shoulder and then passed along the affirmative answer. "There's parking space in our rear parking lot. The bus leaves in fifteen minutes. Life jackets and helmets are being issued over there." She pointed to the new building and then motioned the driver to move on. Hesitating, he glanced back over his shoulder again.

Honey saw that everyone was expecting her to take charge, just like in the old days. "You can turn off the engine," she instructed the driver firmly and waited while he obeyed. "Tell this young person, whoever she is, that we will wait right here for our guide." There was a pleased stir among Honey's companions, the additions to the original group having all been given enthusiastic accounts of the first rafting trip, including Honey's role as their rebellious leader.

The Greenbrier driver quite obviously took some satisfaction in relaying Honey's message. He wasn't used to Greenbrier guests being greeted in such a disrespectful manner.

"But you can't just *park* here!" the girl sputtered indignantly. "I have no idea who your guide will be—" She looked around for help, but the only person in sight was her boss's history professor friend, Dr. McCade. He raised a hand in salute and smiled reassuringly as he headed toward her.

"It's okay, Mary. I'll take care of this."

Mary flashed him a smile that was more than thanks before she hurried off to make sure that the lunch canisters were ready to be loaded onto the bus. She shared with the other female guides at White Water Adventurers the general opinion that Zeke McCade was a "hunk."

With Zeke's appearance the doors of the limousine swung open and its passengers climbed out to gather around him with friendly greetings. Several of them looked vaguely familiar but struck no sharp recognition.

"Guy Bailey." A sandy-haired man with "sales executive" stamped all over him stuck out his hand. "Zeke, I want you to meet my wife, Amy Lou. You'd never guess from her name that she's a southern belle, now, would you?"

Zeke shook hands, smiled genially into one face after another—the ones he was supposed to remember and the ones he wasn't—and made appropriate responses to promptings so detailed that they really required no memory. "Remember me, I was the one . . ." *She must not have come, after all.* The dawning realization was accompanied by sharp disappointment.

"Of course, the one in our group that Zeke couldn't possibly have forgotten is Honey," the short, plump, black-haired woman named DeeDee declared to her husband, whom she'd introduced as Walt, a big-boned gentleman a generation older than the others.

Mention of Honey's name caused everyone to look around. Through some instinctive parting of the cluster of people, Zeke finally saw her where she was standing by the limousine. Swiftly he took in the similarities and the differences. The hair color and skin tone were the same as he remembered. Her figure was still slim, her facial features delicately molded and feminine, dominated by the large brown eyes that regarded him calmly. She had matured into a strikingly pretty woman, poised, flawlessly groomed, with not a single jarring note in her entire appearance. *Brittle*, Zeke found himself thinking and was taken aback by his sense of regret at what had been lost.

"Hello, Zeke." She held out a slender, manicured hand as she stepped toward him, the gracious hostess in control. "You haven't changed much at all." The faint cynical inflection on *you* told him his feelings must have shown in his eyes.

"Hello, Honey." Zeke clasped her hand briefly.

"Well, here we all are." Honey broke the eye contact with Zeke, finding his gaze as direct and penetrating as it had been ten years ago. Even though he did look amazingly the same, he *had* changed, of course. She'd noted the difference from inside the limousine when he came striding over toward them. Ten years had added assurance, the kind that took away the need for asser-tiveness, and beneath his easy, genial manner, there was a detachment that hadn't been there before. It presented an unexpected challenge.

"This place certainly has changed." Honey's glance took in the busy compound and came back to Zeke, a glint of amusement in her brown eyes. "With all these people, there must be dozens of pairs of discarded tennis shoes for you guides to foist off on unsuspecting souls." As she expected, there were appreciative guf-faws and giggles. "You'll be glad to know that I'm a totally reformed character, Zeke. This time I brought my own tennis shoes, which I'll wear at all times, of course, especially in the water."

It was a perfect chance for Zeke to mention that he wasn't a guide anymore, but the members of the original rafting party had to reconstruct once again the famed tennis shoes scene between Honey and Zeke. Before they had finished, one of the bona fide guides came up and told Zeke in an aside that the throng of college kids would shortly be boarding the bus. If Zeke wanted to avoid a lot of confusion at the put-in site, he should take his party on ahead.

"We need to get started," Zeke told the group pleasantly. "The river gets crowded this time of the year on weekends, so the outfitting companies cooperate to try to space out the parties. The equipment has all been transported to the put-in site and is there waiting for us. I'll lead the way in my jeep—"

"Say, why don't you just ride with us?" Guy Bailey broke in to suggest. "There's plenty of room."

Zeke shrugged in ready agreement. "Fine with me." Without waiting for any discussion of seating arrangements, he walked around the front of the long, dark green vehicle and climbed into the front passenger seat.

For the first five or ten minutes, there was no conversation behind Zeke. Everyone seemed to be keeping a respectful silence while he gave the driver directions. When they were headed along the narrow mountain highway that would bring them to their destination, Susan Angelo, formerly Susan Levine, spoke up cheerfully.

"These mountain roads haven't changed, have they?"

"Actually they're in a lot better shape than when you were here last," Zeke put in, talking over his shoulder. "Now most of them are paved. You must have driven over our spectacular new bridge over the gorge. Wait until you float under it and you'll really be impressed."

"This is my first time in West Virginia," Amy Lou Bailey volunteered in her soft drawl. "It's so poor looking. I haven't seen hardly any real nice houses. And house trailers everywhere you look. Of course, the Greenbrier is lovely, honey, just like you said." Amy Lou offered the last to her husband, almost by way of apology.

Zeke was very sensitive to the fact that the driver was probably a West Virginia native. But he would have felt obligated to address the tactless remarks anyway, out of a sense of personal loyalty. There was just a hint of the college professor coping with ignorance in the classroom as he spoke sternly over his shoulder.

"You won't find a more sturdy breed of people than these, and when you know some of the history of West Virginia, and this area in particular, you understand why. Their fathers and grandfathers logged the virgin forests and took coal out of the New River Gorge virtually with their bare hands and a few crude implements. There are still a few old-timers around who can give you firsthand accounts. And some of these quiet little communities that you ride through—Thurmond is one of the best examples—in their heyday were as exciting and dangerous as any western boom town during the gold rush. Thurmond was known as "the Dodge City of the East," for good reason."

"Say, that's really interesting, Zeke," Arthur Copeland put in with a bit too much enthusiasm, hoping to smooth over the awkward moment. Guy had really picked a pea-brain for a wife this time. "You sound like quite a local history buff."

Here was Zeke's opening to mention that he was more than a "history buff." He was a historian with a doctorate from a highly respected southern university, but Honey's voice immediately captured his attention.

"It's fine for a lot of old people to sit around and talk about the 'good old days' when times were exciting, but what does this area offer to young people? Why would anyone with ambition and intelligence stay here, when the outside world offers so much more?"

"Such as what?" Zeke snapped back, without a second's hesitation. "Jobs with big money to spend at bigger shopping malls?"

The limousine had gone dead silent, and Zeke could understand why. There had been nothing of the college professor in his reply to Honey's remarks, which hadn't been any more offensive, at least not on the surface, than Amy Lou's had been. It both amused and irritated him that she had been able to needle him so expertly when her assumptions about him were all wrong.

"Nothing personal, Zeke," Honey apologized sweetly.

Like hell. "You're undoubtedly right, Honey. An ambitious, intelligent young person probably wouldn't choose to stay here in Fayette County, West Virginia."

Honey picked up the private amusement in his openly ironic agreement and wondered at it. She also wondered at herself. Amy Lou's comments might have been in poor taste, but they were not calculated to affront, as Honey's remarks were. *I wanted to bring his attention to me!*

"To each his own." Guy Bailey offered this trite bit of wisdom in the expansive tone of a practiced peacemaker. Conversation then resumed along less spontaneous lines, with no further contributions from Honey. Zeke found himself waiting for the sound of her voice, looking forward to the time when she would level another potshot at him. In the process of acquiring that hard polish of sophistication, Honey Drake hadn't lost her wit or sharp intelligence. She still knew precisely how to get under the skin of an adversary. Zeke found the whole situation highly stimulating, particularly when he reminded himself that she had been willing to pay dearly to have him along.

"We're almost there," he announced as the limousine drove through the quiet streets of Thurmond. "This is Thurmond, the coal mining town I mentioned earlier. At one time it was accessible only by railroad, and yet it had mail delivery three or four times a day. A man could spend his week's pay in his choice of several saloons, visit the houses of prostitution, or join in a poker game at one of the back-room gambling dens. His odds for staying alive weren't good, no matter what he did. Thurmond probably would have died out like some of the other coal boom towns if a road hadn't been built to it before the coal mining industry declined."

"What do you mean, 'might' have died out. It looks dead to me," Honey said feelingly. "What do people do in a place like this?"

There was a little nervous stir as everyone waited for Zeke's response. Honey had spoken what all of them were thinking.

"That's hard for me to say," Zeke replied humorously. "You see, I live in the Thurmond 'suburbs' and don't get to town that often to see what's going on."

This earned him some appreciative laughs and put everyone at ease so that they didn't feel as if they would have to watch their every word for fear of offending him.

At the put-in site, their raft had been unloaded from a large flatbed truck and was waiting for them halfway down the steep slope, life jackets, helmets, and paddles piled inside. Zeke walked on down to the raft and checked to make sure there was enough equipment while the others made last-minute preparations, those who hadn't worn tennis shoes having to put them on now and those who chose to wear just a swimsuit shucking the outer clothing.

When he straightened up, they were all coming down the slope. His eyes went automatically to Honey Drake, who wore a sleek burgundy one-piece swimsuit that, despite being cut fashionably high on the hips, would easily meet Greenbrier standards for decorous attire.

On her feet were thin-soled canvas sneakers, obviously brand new and the same color as her swimsuit. The brown eyes that met his gaze were not full of angry rebellion, nor did they widen with shock at his male inspection. Instead they were coolly amused and challenging.

"Everybody grab a life jacket and a helmet," Zeke instructed, feeling his senses jangled keenly to life. "Those of you who are old-timers at this remember that the lifejacket has to be tight. In the unlikely event that you are thrown out of the raft, you don't want your life jacket up around your head." Even though it had been years since he had worked as a guide, the introductory routine came back easily to him.

"Okay, are we all set?" He glanced around to affirm that they were all wearing the ungainly orange life jackets and white helmets.

"All set, Zeke," DeeDee assured him cheerfully. "Even Honey. I guess she really is a reformed character."

Zeke's eyes sought Honey's. *Reformed only on the surface.*

"I wouldn't want anyone to be disappointed," Honey declared, raising her eyebrows ever so delicately in question. "I'll be happy to take my life jacket off and make a scene, just for old times' sake." She dipped her head to sniff and then lifted it high, her nose wrinkled in disdain. "Actually, I suspect this is the very same jacket I wore before. I'd recognize that smell anywhere."

"Everybody grab onto this thing and let's get it afloat," Zeke ordered, cutting into the general stir of amusement. "There'll be plenty of time later for acting out old scenes."

Honey reached obediently for a plastic handle and ran alongside the raft with the others, a little smile on her lips. Zeke might have been talking to everybody in general just now, but there had been a private challenge directed just to her. *Be my guest, Honey. Play out your "old scenes" and see what happens this time.* What amazed Honey more than anything else was how titillated she was at the thought of taking him up on that challenge.

But, once the raft was launched, they all settled into their rowing positions, and Zeke, following precedent, put them through basic drills. Honey felt boredom set in, just as it had ten years ago. Only now it went much deeper. In the intervening years, she had tested out life and found it ultimately flat and disappointing. In the process she had learned not to blurt out her honest feelings, but to put on a polite face and make whatever social effort was required of her.

The present situation, which brought together old acquaintances and new, lent itself to endless conversational possibilities. Honey, who had arrived too late the night before to join the others at dinner, found herself the object of curiosity that she had fully expected to encounter on the drive there, but all the talk had centered around the first rafting trip.

"Honey, what have you been up to since we saw you last?" Guy Bailey demanded genially. "The rest of us kind of caught up with each other last night."

"Would that I had a more interesting tale to tell," Honey apologized lightly. "I did everything by the book, just the way I was supposed to do. Finished up my degree at Vassar with the prerequisite engagement ring on my finger. Traveled around Europe for a year with a couple of girl cousins and an aunt as chaperone.

Married my Princeton man and lived happily ever after for four and a half years until we were bored to death with each other and got a divorce. That was a year ago. Since then I've been testing out occupations and so far have failed to come up with anything interesting. And that's my story," she finished brightly, scooping up a handful of water and raising up a hip to splash the water on the hot plastic tubing.

Zeke noted the movement closely and responded to it as he had done a long time ago, on that day when he had stored up enough sensual memories to keep fantasy alive for years. Her hips were still slim and wonderfully curved to tempt a man's eyes and his hands, her bottom pert and firm, her thighs slender and rounded. They showed no imprint of a man's possession, but she had slept with this vague, faceless "Princeton man" for four and a half years. Zeke found that he didn't like the idea at all.

"What kinds of occupations have you tried?" Susan wanted to know. Privately she was thinking that only Honey could give the most noncommittal account of her background possible and manage to come out sounding glamorous.

"Oh, I worked on the staff of a women's magazine for a few months and then a friend who owns a decorating firm in New York talked me into doing some work for him." Honey shrugged carelessly. Both jobs had been all right. Both had been dumped into her lap by well-meaning friends.

"It seems like everybody these days gets divorced, sooner or later," Amy Lou commented sadly in her liquid cadences. "It's so fortunate, under the circumstances, that you and your ex-husband didn't have any children, isn't it?"

"Very fortunate."

Zeke picked up the ironic undertone and wondered about it. Honey took him off guard when she turned and looked back at him. For a moment his eyes probed hers questioningly, but there were no answers in her carefully guarded brown gaze, just the cool suggestion that he mind his own business.

"Isn't it about time for everybody to go overboard, in full dress, of course?" she inquired with light irony.

"Time for a 'waddle in the pool,' you mean?" The rejoinder was not premeditated. Zeke was as disconcerted as she was by the startling fidelity of his memory. "Honey's got a good point, everybody," he said quickly, adopting a public tone. "Why don't we all get wet and cool off a little. Just kind of roll over the side."

"It's better not to stand up," Honey cautioned the world at large to make sure Zeke knew her memory was working well, too. "Unless you want to land on top of somebody." *And have that somebody slide his hands up and down my hips. . . .*

Before she could give in to the incredibly powerful urge to reenact the very mishap she warned against, Honey slipped over the side into the water and moved her arms and legs vigorously to dissipate the sexual tension in her lower torso.

"Coward," Zeke said in an undertone nearby.

She looked around to see that he had come into the water, too, and was guiding the raft along with one hand.

"I would think you'd be appreciative," she taunted lightly. "At the time, I was too young and ignorant to realize that the way I landed on top of you, the impact might be doing permanent damage. I hope I didn't impair your male performance. I'd hate to know I'd robbed you of being a father." This last was more than just provocative repartee; it was blatant curiosity about his marital status.

"It's hard for a man to be the judge on his 'male performance,'" Zeke shot back swiftly before he readily volunteered what she wanted to know. "To the best of my knowledge, I am not a father. But since I've never been married, that's probably—in Amy Lou's opinion, anyway—a 'fortunate' state of affairs."

Zeke was doing a little indirect probing of his own, without any intention of hitting a live nerve. The flash of bitterness in Honey's face brought a quick apology to his lips. "I'm sorry—"

"Don't be," Honey ordered curtly. "Actually, that asinine woman is right. It is 'fortunate' Phil and I didn't have any children. If we had, we'd still be married."

Zeke waited for some explanation, but there was none. Honey slipped her smooth mask back in place, her only emotion a cool amusement that she had whetted his curiosity with her cryptic remarks and then left it unsatisfied.

"I'm surprised you're not married, Zeke," she mused. "How has a man who's obviously such good husband material managed to escape all the local girls? I expected to find you fifteen pounds heavier with a wallet full of pictures of your wife and kids."

It was Zeke's turn to be cryptic. "A man in my line of work can hardly expect a woman to want to share his life." It was an honest answer, even if she was guaranteed to misinterpret it.

"But being a guide isn't that dangerous . . . you mean because of the income, I suppose." Puzzlement brought a little distracted frown to her face. She shook her head. "I just don't understand—"

If Honey had completed the thought and asked Zeke

point-blank why he hadn't done something with his life besides working as a guide, Zeke would have answered her honestly. But she kept her puzzlement to herself, and he left her faulty assumption intact since the real facts about his life were irrelevant anyway. This was a day that had nothing to do with reality, and Zeke was thoroughly enjoying himself.

Chapter Three

We have our first big rapid coming up. Those of you who made this trip with me before might remember Surprise."

Zeke paused to allow for the inevitable exclamations and the warnings to the uninitiated to be ready for something they couldn't possibly imagine until they actually experienced it for themselves. He noticed that Honey had nothing to say. She clenched her paddle tighter and pushed her front foot further up under the inflated tubing running athwart the raft just in front of her.

"Don't listen to all these alarmists," he scoffed. "Surprise is over almost before you know it. Just do what I tell you as long as you can and then hang on. You'll be fine. Okay, let's all paddle nice and easy together, straight for the middle."

Honey could have sworn he was talking solely to her, but then undoubtedly every person in the raft was grabbing onto the confidence in his voice and holding fast to it as the raft came closer and closer to the white water ahead and the roar grew louder, filling her ears. Nervousness sent the blood coursing through her body so that her pulsebeat competed with the din of the rapid. Zeke's voice sounded far away as he shouted, "Paddle *hard* ahead! *Hard*! Give it all you've got!"

Suddenly they were in the middle of chaos. The great wave of white water hit her full in the face, tearing a scream of mixed terror and exultation from her throat as the bottom of the world dropped away. Then just seconds later the raft was bobbing along on a gentle cushion of water. Honey came out of her crouched position, paddle clenched firmly in her hands. The smile on her lips was an irrepressible reflection of the jubilation inside. God, how incredible it was to feel herself merged with the unharnessed power of the river and then set free of it again! There was also a definite element of satisfaction that she hadn't been nearly thrown from the raft this second time through Surprise.

Zeke saw the smile and the expression on Honey's face and felt an ache somewhere deep inside. His voice sounded strangely brusque to his own ears as he prodded his dazed crew into regaining their rowing positions and then delivered a stern lecture that came automatically from his memory. *God, she is beautiful with her face drenched and uplifted, illuminated from within, her eyelashes all stuck together in spikes, mouth soft and tender with elation. . . .*

By the time everybody had settled down, Honey had collected herself and added her own reassurances to those of the other "veteran" rafters as they calmed the fears of the novices, the most vocal of whom was, not surprisingly, Amy Lou.

"I'm just shaking like a *leaf*! I've never in my *life* been so frightened, I promise you!"

"We all know exactly how you feel, Amy Lou," Honey spoke up kindly. "Nobody could have been more scared than I was after my first trip through Surprise." Honey felt the quickening of interest among her companions, but she was most keenly aware of the attention that came from behind her. Zeke was surprised by her admission and waiting to hear what she would say next.

"You, scared?" DeeDee murmured disbelievingly.

"Scared to death. It seemed a certainty that I would either be killed or permanently maimed by the end of the trip." A self-protective tinge of humor had crept into Honey's voice. "You'll get over most of the fear after we've been through a few more rapids and you find that you can stay in the raft." She paused, but nobody interrupted. They all seemed to be waiting for her to continue. Zeke was waiting, too. "Just blot everything out of your mind except the sound of Zeke's voice. Concentrate on doing what he tells you to do, and you'll be all right. Zeke's a great guide. That's why we insisted on having him again. Right, DeeDee? Susan? Guy?"

The chorus of agreement gave Zeke a moment before he had to make any reply. "Thanks for the vote of confidence." *And is that the only reason you insisted?*

Honey didn't miss the undertone meant just for her, but chose to ignore it and Zeke, who was being a little presumptuous. He needn't act as if she had come back here after ten years just to seek him out personally and satisfy some deep-seated desire. Apparently he had put his own interpretation upon the five-hundred-dollar bonus.

"Arthur, tell me how you've managed to escape the

bonds of matrimony all these years when the rest of us haven't?" she demanded lightly, changing the subject.

"Now the truth comes out. I've been waiting for you, Honey," Arthur rejoined theatrically. "All these years I've been haunted by the picture of a suntanned goddess in leopard skin and gold chains."

"Well, here I am," Honey invited huskily, amid the chuckles and comments. "I just hope I'm not too big a disappointment after the years of waiting."

Zeke sat in the stern, listened, and watched, completely aware of what was happening. She had deliberately led the conversation into territory that would exclude him. Yet her remarks to Arthur just now were more for Zeke's benefit than anyone else's, and the message was mixed. On the one hand, she was making it clear that things hadn't changed that much in ten years. She was still out of his class. Zeke could buy that, but why the defensiveness? Why should it matter whether he found her a disappointment or not, since he was only a "great guide"?

"Okay, folks, we have Upper Railroad coming up ahead," Zeke broke into the conversation some minutes later and instantly commanded everyone's complete attention.

Honey listened along with the others, hearing the same general information about what lay ahead, the same friendly encouragement and advance instructions. There was nothing in what Zeke was actually saying to make her pulse quicken, but the message was there in the cadences of his voice. *You can't ignore me, Honey, any more than I can ignore you.*

The feeling of suspense grew inside Honey during the next hour and a half as she and Zeke carried on a strange kind of duel. She didn't question his authority or try to undermine it when he took command of the raft as they approached a rapid, but no sooner were they floating along peacefully than Honey immediately took charge of the conversation with all the skill of a maestro directing a symphony orchestra. *You see, I am ignoring you, Zeke.*

"Anybody hungry?" Zeke called out when he saw the original lunch site ahead and unoccupied.

The question raised a whole chorus of affirmative replies and brought on the inevitable reminiscences. "Are we having the same soggy peanut butter and jelly sandwiches?" DeeDee wanted to know, giggling and casting a knowing look at Honey.

"What else?" Zeke replied cheerfully. "That's standard fare for rafting trips. Remember?"

"Peanut butter and jelly sandwiches," Amy Lou echoed distastefully. "Is that what we're having for lunch? Ugh. I don't think I'll be able to eat anything, anyway. My stomach feels queasy."

Her remarks brought laughing reassurances from all the members of the original rafting group except for Honey, who climbed out of the raft in the shallow water and helped carry it up on shore. The painfully vivid memory of the last time she had been in this spot brought back the aching misery and the terrible aloneness. She had come to West Virginia to thaw out the emotional numbness, but a return to this place where she had come face-to-face with despair reminded her of why she may have dispensed with feeling in her life.

"You can take off the life jackets and helmets while we're here." Zeke's voice as he made this cheerful announcement was strangely comforting to Honey. The words were an echo out of the past, and yet very much a part of the present.

"Sweetheart, could you help me? I feel weak as a kitten," Amy Lou implored of Guy, who quickly came to his wife's aid and removed her helmet and life jacket with solicitous care. "You're a dear," she murmured. "I think I'll just go over and sit on that big old rock in the sun."

Honey was in the process of removing her own sodden life jacket, but in her impatience to be rid of it, she was having trouble with the fastenings. Amy Lou's statement of her intentions made Honey's fingers falter momentarily, and then they were covered by Zeke's.

"Here, let me help you."

Taken off guard, Honey looked up into his face and saw the remembrance in his eyes at the same time that she absorbed the impact of his nearness. He had already shed his life jacket and helmet. His dark brown hair was wet and yet it had an unruly vitality. His chest and shoulders were bare and just inches away. His fingers were strong and sure as they brushed hers aside and dealt with the metal clips. There was something incredibly protective and supportive about his coming to her aid, that far surpassed the actual act itself.

"Thank you," Honey said softly as he lifted the life jacket free of her shoulders and then slipped it down her arms.

"You're welcome." The words were part caress and part frustrated protest. At that moment Zeke would have given almost anything if by a snap of his fingers he could have made the rest of the group vanish, but DeeDee and Susan were demanding his immediate attention about the serving of lunch. There was no opportunity for him to say any of the things he wanted to say to Honey, about the way she had drawn him ten years ago when she sat alone and miserable on her rock or the way she drew him now as she dealt with her memory of that other time. Zeke would have liked to spend the rest of the day right here alone with her, talking and touching, getting beyond the barriers. But once again circumstances didn't allow for that.

Honey stood there a moment after Zeke had walked away, running her hands through her wet hair and fluffing it up while she put matters in perspective. She was a grown woman fully capable of taking care of herself, a divorcee of some means having a weekend in West Virginia with some old friends. This place was simply a small clearing on the bank of a river, used time and time again as a lunch site by groups of rafters. Zeke McCade was a river guide. True, he was virile and attractive and surprisingly perceptive for someone who'd settled for so little, but still a river guide, not some ideal of male strength and integrity as she may have unknowingly built him up in her mind. The attraction between him and Honey was elemental and purely physical. It was sex, nothing more.

With that settled, Honey took in the immediate situation. Guy was sitting with Amy Lou over on the same rock that had been Honey's solitary domain ten years ago, talking to her in low, soothing tones. Honey felt no inclination to join them. The others were grouped around Zeke, either helping to set out the lunch or standing back, waiting. DeeDee's husband Walt was in this latter category. Honey walked over to stand next to him.

"Did I hear DeeDee mention that you breed Thoroughbreds?" she inquired and knew at once that instinct had served her well again. Walt's kindly, weathered face lit up as he answered in the affirmative and then willingly went into some detail about his Virginia farm.

Honey managed to look interested, put in appropriate words and questions here and there, without really listening. She was intensely aware of Zeke's every movement and the sound of his voice, which was terse to her ears. He was irritated with her. That perception gave her faint satisfaction and made her feel she was in control.

"Okay, everybody, let's eat." Zeke was briskly matter-of-fact, clapping his hands. "We don't have all day. The parties behind us will be coming along any time now." *Today won't last forever. No day does.*

Suddenly not nearly so pleased with herself, Honey made herself a sandwich and took a meager helping of fruit salad. With her plate in one hand and a paper cup of lemonade in the other, she went down near the water and sat cross-legged on the hard-packed ground before Susan or DeeDee could summon her over to sit with them and their husbands. Arthur followed behind her.

"May I join you?"

"Of course." She tried to sound inviting as she looked up at Arthur and summoned a smile. Zeke had waited until last to fix his plate and was taking a cup of lemonade.

"Zeke, we've saved a place for you over here," DeeDee called out.

Honey would have expected at least a slight hesitation, a regretful glance from Zeke down in her direction, but instead he responded quite readily to DeeDee's invitation, and Honey could hear the sound of his voice as he joined in the conversation. The sharpness of her disappointment was quite overwhelming. This one opportunity that she would have had to talk to Zeke was being wasted. Soon they would be back in the raft. The afternoon would go quickly as they passed through the big rapids ahead. At the take-out site, the limousine would be waiting. . . .

"Arthur, tell me what it's like being a big stock broker." Honey deliberately made her voice loud enough to be heard by everyone. To her own ears, the gaiety sounded as forced as it was and didn't quite cover up the urgency of her own thoughts that destroyed her appetite for food as nervousness had done ten years before. *He's only a river guide, remember? Not some rare opportunity.*

Arthur could hardly be blamed for responding to Honey's smiles and expertly placed questions. At such close range he was half-inclined to believe that he had been waiting for her all these years. It was heady stuff, even now, being the focus of Honey's attention. She seemed too intent upon listening to bother with eating her lunch.

"Say, you've hardly eaten a thing," he declared, getting up to go back for seconds.

Honey's heart suddenly was pounding so hard that she felt a little light-headed as she rose to her feet.

"I guess I'm not very hungry," she announced quite clearly, the tone of her voice capturing general attention. "These rafting trips seem to destroy my appetite." She walked to the garbage bag Zeke had shaken out and left draped across a piece of driftwood. As she dropped her plate, cup, and plastic fork inside it, she was aware of Zeke rising and coming over to her, but there was nothing personal in his manner as he dropped his refuse into the bag she was holding open.

"Okay, everybody, last chance for seconds. We need to get packed up and on our way."

DeeDee came up, followed by Susan. Honey thrust the garbage bag out at them and didn't bother to notice who took it.

"Are the 'facilities' still upstream for ladies?" she inquired of Zeke's back and saw him go alert at what he heard in her voice. "Or was it downstream for ladies and upstream for gentlemen?"

There was complete silence. Even those who hadn't been on the first rafting trip sensed the drama of the moment. Honey didn't give a damn about the audience. There were only two actors, herself and Zeke, and the play was strictly ad-lib, to be acted out now or never.

Zeke turned around and looked at her. "Upstream for ladies." He didn't care about the audience, either.

She held his eyes a moment longer and then started walking toward the edge of the woods, dimly conscious that her movement had broken the spell holding her companions in rapt silence. There were giggles and the sounds of voices as explanations were begun for the sake of the uninitiated.

"You could always depend on Honey—" DeeDee's voice followed behind her and was joined by Guy's male cadences. ". . . never a dull moment."

Honey picked up the pleased undertone that had always been there with her Greenbrier cronies, even when they were shocked or irritated or jealous. They had always looked to her to add the zest of the unexpected, never quite sure whether she was just trying to be the show-off or being true to a strain of originality they lacked. They weren't sure now.

At this particular moment Honey couldn't honestly have said whether it had been her assumed obligations as leader of the pack that had led her to dream up pranks and practical jokes, all of them ultimately harmless. She did know for sure that her flight into the woods at this very spot ten years ago hadn't been for their entertainment. It had been prompted by a very real, private desperation. Nor did her actions right now have anything at all to do with them, although they would probably think otherwise. Right now they were filling in all the ten-year-old details for Walt and

George, Susan's husband, and Amy Lou and waiting for a bloodcurdling scream that would send Zeke crashing into the woods to see what was the matter.

What was Zeke thinking right now? Did he think she was putting on an exhibition for her old friends? What had begun spontaneously in answer to an urgency she didn't really understand suddenly seemed cheap and farcical. Honey wouldn't scream today. She couldn't take the chance of demeaning what had taken place between herself and Zeke ten years in the past. It had been one of those special transactions between two human beings.

Quite without realizing it, Honey had gone farther into the woods than she had before. Coming to that realization, she stopped, thinking of how ironic it would be if she got herself lost and had no choice other than to yell for help. A sound behind her made her freeze momentarily and then whirl around, panic flaring up inside her. She stared at Zeke as he came toward her.

"You—you followed me . . ." she murmured stupidly, trying to come to terms with his presence. The panicky feeling was still there, but it had changed.

"Wasn't that the idea?"

Honey saw with dismay that he did think she was acting out the old scene. There was cynicism in his blue eyes, mixed with open desire and his clear intention.

"Zeke, I wasn't going to scream," she pleaded with him earnestly as he came up close. She could see from the discernible rise and fall of his chest that he was breathing faster than normal, as though he had been running behind her instead of following so quietly she hadn't known he was there.

"What's wrong, Honey?" Zeke asked softly, reaching out and closing his hands around her smooth, bare shoulders. He was hardly paying attention to her words. It was her body language he was reading. She hadn't shrunk away from him. "Does everybody have to play the game according to your rules? You know this is what you want." He slid his hands down her back and then gathered her against him with a groan that came from deep inside. "It's what I've wanted for years. . . ."

"Oh, Zeke," Honey murmured, as much in surrender as protest. His embrace was a strong, warm haven she might have been seeking her whole life. It felt so totally right to lean into him and hug him tight around the waist, and yet it was terribly important that he understand the decision she had made just now.

"Zeke, I'm serious," she said, pressing her cheek a little firmer against his shoulder and absorbing through her pores the warm pulse of his skin. "I wasn't going to scream because I was afraid the others would think I was just clowning—" His hands were moving over her back in what didn't seem at all like a new exploration, as it was, but a reclaiming of familiar, prized territory. "Zeke, please, you've got to let me tell you—" she breathed out desperately as his hands slid down to shape her buttocks, like a sculptor adoring his handiwork.

Honey felt his chest swell with a deep, indrawn breath and then he was clasping her by the shoulders and pulling her a little away from him. Her head felt too heavy for her neck to support as she looked up into his face and saw the passion there before she heard its raw resonance in his voice.

"Honey, I don't give a damn about the others. You must know that. You're the only reason I'm here today.

This is the only reason." He cupped her face in his hands and took her lips with tenderness and deep, restrained hunger.

Honey kissed him back because her sole purpose in being at that moment seemed none other than to attend to his need. For just a fleeting second, before she was much too involved in what was happening to think, it occurred to her again that there was no element of trial and error in Zeke's kisses any more than in the touch of his hands. As his tongue went searching for hers, it was urgent for the intimacy and yet fully expecting the sweetness.

Zeke could have explained the odd impression of familiarity. He had made love to Honey in his fantasies many times. Now as his hands delighted in the feel of her body, they were repossessing each part of her: the warm satin of her skin, the pliant firmness of her buttocks, the small, round perfection of her breasts, her slim thighs that came apart for him as he fitted his palm to the softly mounded feminine juncture. A fierce sensation of ownership rose up inside him at the sound of her soft moan. It startled him and brought him partly to his senses. Zeke McCade could never own the likes of Honey Drake except in his dreams. Due to circumstances, he couldn't even realize the real-life culmination of his youthful fantasy and make love to her.

"Who says we grow wiser as we grow older?" he murmured against her lips and took what was intended to be one last taste and then another and another. His hands came up to lightly clasp her shoulders, in preparation for that time when he would have the strength of character to put her away from him.

"Why do you say that?" Honey asked softly, between kisses. She was aware of his struggle with himself to bring an end to things, and yet she gave him no help.

Her arms were wound around his neck and she leaned the entire length of her body against him.

Zeke moved his hands on her shoulders, feeling the texture of her skin and then, with a quick intake of breath, tightened his grasp and held her firmly in place while he stepped back.

"Because when I was twenty-four, I had sense enough not to start something I couldn't finish," he said ruefully, reaching up for her hands and taking them from his shoulders, but then holding them to prolong the physical contact.

The soft haze on Honey's face was quickly gone as she rejected what Zeke was implying. "It wasn't like that at all," she protested, pulling her hands free. "You didn't even touch me. In the state I was in that day, you could easily have taken advantage of me, and you didn't." Honey realized that she sounded as if she were defending some innocent person who wasn't present, but she had to continue.

"I was like some awful, trapped little animal, with no hole to hide myself in. I'd been spiteful to you all day, caused you every kind of problem. I hated myself, hated you, hated everybody." She looked away from him, remembering. The lift of her chin caused Zeke's memory to pull out an old image and lay it over the real vision in front of him, girl from the past and woman in the present merging into one.

"I'll never forget the way I felt when I looked around and saw you," Honey said in a low voice. "I knew I deserved every mean word you could say to me, deserved whatever you would do to me to get even. And you were so kind and gentle." She paused, bogged down in awkwardness, but unable at this point to retreat from her task of expressing thoughts she'd never said aloud before. "You made me want to be a nicer

kind of person because you were who and what you
were. I wished I could be someone you could like."
Honey switched her gaze to his face and was vaguely
surprised at how uncomfortable he looked. "I know it
sounds as though I'm magnifying a small incident into
something of immense importance, but that whole day
was important to me, Zeke. Afterward, when the
rafting trip was over, I wanted so badly to thank you
somehow, but, of course, I didn't—I couldn't. There
wasn't the opportunity, and I didn't have the courage
or the words." She laughed self-consciously. "I don't
have the words now, actually."

Zeke was aware of the distant sound of voices and
laughter. Other parties of rafters had caught up with
them. There wasn't time to stand here and talk about
the past or the present. The sober realization that there
would be little point in verbalizing their feelings further
and venturing even deeper into an intimacy without a
future didn't keep Zeke from resenting that wisdom.
Suddenly he was angry at her for slipping in and out of
his life like this, raising unwanted yearnings that
couldn't be satisfied, angry at himself, angry at the
situation.

"We have to be getting back to the others," he said
brusquely. "Before we do, I want to make one thing
clear, Honey. You may remember me as some model of
male honor, but I wanted your body ten years ago the
same way I want it right now." *You're lying, pal. You
want her more now, a whole hell of a lot more.* "You
drove me out of my mind that day in that skimpy little
leopard-skin bikini. I slept with you in my dreams for
weeks afterward." *Weeks, hell. How about months and
years?*

"Too bad *I* missed out on it!" Honey snapped,

reacting to his tone rather than to his actual words. "I hope I was good."

"You were incredible," he gritted out curtly.

They both held their breath as they stared at each other, antagonism making the attraction between them flare up so strong that it was agony for them not to touch each other. Zeke shook his head slightly.

"I shouldn't have said that," he muttered apologetically. "Come on. We have to get back."

Honey followed along behind him, trying to sort out her reactions. He hadn't denied that what he had said was true. He had simply apologized for having said it. The thought that Zeke may have made love to her in his waking or sleeping fantasies brought a sensation that was odd but not at all unpleasant. If he had made the admission in a different tone, her answer would probably have been the same but sincere: *I'm sorry I missed it.* His imagined intimacies with her body might explain that strange sense of "rightness" in being in his arms and having him kiss and caress her, as though it were not the first time.

Why had he seemed to become angry at her fumbling efforts to express her gratitude for his kindness years ago? That made no sense at all to her. No matter what he said to the contrary, she knew there had been more than lust involved in his treatment of her. There was more than lust between them now.

"That must have been a *big* python you had to rescue Honey from today, Zeke," Guy called out in a jocular tone when Zeke and Honey emerged into the clearing.

Zeke didn't trust himself to answer. He was sick of the river guide charade and furious at himself that he had given in to this crazy impulse to pretend he was something that he wasn't. Ten years ago it had been fate that caused him to be the one to answer the telephone when Honey Drake called from the Greenbrier. Today he had only himself to blame for being here. He ought to be in his study working instead of following her around in the woods and letting himself in for a whole lot of frustration.

"Let's get those life jackets and helmets on," he ordered tersely. They all obeyed him without a further word.

Once the raft was floating down the river again, the rawness inside Zeke eased, and he was able to regain his perspective and regret his earlier irritability. It wasn't anyone's fault but his own that he had succumbed to curiosity or whatever other impulses had led him to agree to leading this group once again. Besides, he wouldn't have missed this for the world, anyway. Anticipation awoke every nerve in his body and made him feel intensely alive as he looked forward to the afternoon ahead, when once again he would pit all his human resources against the treachery and the wiles of the New, with the added stimulation of sharing the total experience of the river with Honey, not only the challenge and the excitement but the serenity and wilderness loveliness, as well.

"Okay, folks," he called out as they approached Upper Keeney. "Up ahead you see Whale Rock. That means we're coming up on the Keeneys Creek Rapids. There's three of them with just barely enough room in between to take in a deep breath and get ready for the next one. Listen to me and do exactly what I tell you, and we'll sail right through. Now let's all paddle ahead nice and easy."

The reckless anticipation in his voice was infectious. There were smiles on all the faces, even the nervous

Amy Lou's, but Honey read the private message that was for her and no one else. *I'm glad that I'm here. That you're here. That we're here together. Let's forget everything else and go for it!*

Honey needed no further urging. She held back nothing, feeling all the while the incredible intimacy of knowing that Zeke was aware of her every second. He was there for all of them, shouting orders, using his strength and his expertise to guide them through the rapids, urging them to rise with him to a level of exhilaration no human could hope to withstand for long periods. But, most especially, he was there for her.

When they had successfully executed the passage through a difficult rapid or series of rapids, Zeke would praise them all as a crew working together. The approval in his voice affected Honey like a caress, making her feel warm inside. *You are wonderful,* he seemed to be saying, just to her. To banish the skepticism that she was only imagining things, she would look back at him and catch her breath when his eyes would meet hers, dispelling any doubt. How could there be this searing intimacy between a man and a woman who had never made love? she asked herself wonderingly and then supplied the answer. *But he has made love to you, many times—in his dreams!*

For Zeke it was different from any time he'd ever been through those same rapids before, different even from that first time with Honey in the raft, ten years before. Then, too, he had felt his technical mastery and sensed himself to be more than human in confronting head-on the enormous power and complex dangers of the river with its dips and holes and hydraulics camouflaged by rolling, churning waves. But today there was no culmination, no release. The ache inside him wouldn't be satisfied. It was like making love with a woman and almost reaching the crescendo time after time.

Zeke found it hard to believe that at age thirty-four he could be this susceptible to sexual frustration, which was the only label he could give to what ailed him. At least he was old enough to know that it wasn't a permanent malady, and there was the intense pleasure of sharing Honey's jubilation as well as the general satisfaction of knowing that he was doing his job well, for her, for all of them.

But then the ache inside Zeke seemed like something other than just sex at times, especially as the end of the trip drew near. All of his passengers in the raft were overwhelmed by the magnitude of the new bridge when they floated underneath it, but he found himself straining for her murmured words and scouring her features hungrily for her expression.

"You're right, Zeke." She glanced back and smiled at him. "I am impressed with your new bridge."

He nodded and held her gaze while he made an announcement that managed somehow to be general and yet personal.

"It won't be long now and we'll be coming up on the new take-out station. Your limousine will be waiting for you there."

"I can't believe it's already over!" DeeDee lamented. "Wasn't it great?" she demanded of all of them at large and then focused in upon the members of the original Greenbrier group. "Aren't you glad we decided to do this again?" Taking their agreement for granted, she smiled warmly back at Zeke. "It wouldn't have been the same without you, either, Zeke. It was just plain luck for us that first time that we ended up with the best guide on the river."

Zeke felt as though he were writhing in his discomfort as DeeDee's words brought forth an enthusiastic chorus of agreement, even from those who hadn't been on the first trip. He could still tell them the truth, that he wasn't really a river guide anymore, but in a few more minutes the deception wouldn't even be a factor in their lives. They'd be headed back to the Greenbrier, and he'd just be a character in their mental scrapbooks.

He wondered if anybody besides himself was noticing how little Honey was contributing to this end-of-the-trip camaraderie. The sense of déjà vu was absurdly strong for him. He was consumed by the same sense of urgency and helplessness he had felt ten years ago, knowing that the take-out site and the waiting Greenbrier limousine were just ahead. Once again there would be no opportunity for a private word with her. But, then, what was there to say?

Don't go.

Honey gazed off to the right at the place where the raft would land. There were people and vehicles everywhere. It looked almost as busy as the base station had been. The Greenbrier limousine was there waiting. God, how could this all be so much the same? It was crazy. She was ten years older now, had been married and divorced and was well in control of her life, and yet she felt the identical sense of helplessness she had felt at the end of the last trip, as though the New River were washing her up on its shore and pushing her along on the course of her life before she could stop long enough to make a meaningful "statement." Well, she would not stand for it this time. She simply would not be rushed.

Soothed to a measure by this vague resolution, Honey climbed out of the raft with the others and helped to carry it up on shore, where all responsibility for stowing it onto a large flatbed truck was assumed by several brawny youths. The pigtailed girl who'd greeted them that morning was on hand, helping to collect life jackets and helmets.

"Have a good trip?" she asked Zeke with a warm smile.

He nodded. "Fine."

The terse reply brought Mary's eyebrows upward in a quizzical expression, but she didn't have an opportunity to question him further because the members of his party were crowding around. From the looks of them, it would appear that everything had gone well. By now the news was out that this group from the Greenbrier had paid an extra five hundred dollars to get Zeke McCade to guide them. But he definitely looked tense.

For Zeke all the handshaking and the exchanging of pleasantries seemed interminable. It was a relief when one of the guides came up and announced apologetically, "Hey, Zeke, the limo's got traffic kind of blocked up over here."

With that it suddenly occurred to several of them that Zeke had ridden with them in the limousine to the put-in site.

"We can talk on the way back to your main station," Guy Bailey declared. "We'll need to make a stop anyway and change out of these wet clothes."

"I have a few things to take care of here," Zeke said firmly. "I'll get a ride back." *Let's get this over with, for God's sakes.*

They didn't argue. Fatigue was setting in. It was time now to change into dry clothes, sit back, and talk on the drive back to their luxurious accommodations at the Greenbrier, where arrangements had been made in advance for a late supper. Today had been a good day, but it was over.

"So long, Zeke. How about next year?"

Zeke didn't have the heart to answer. He stood there and watched them walk away. She was a little apart from the rest and walking more slowly, her head a little downcast. Perhaps it was his imagination, but he could almost feel her steps begin to falter, as though she planned to come to a standstill. Suddenly he knew he had to stop her, had to have at least a last, private exchange.

"Honey—"

She was stopping and turning around the same instant he was speaking her name.

"Zeke—" There was faint accusation, impatience, yearning in the one syllable.

Zeke walked quickly toward her and came up very close, but he didn't touch her.

"Honey, I wish you didn't have to go with them." It wasn't a proposition or even a suggestion, just a fervent expression of what he felt.

"I know. I'm not ready to go, either."

"Then don't."

They looked at each other searchingly for a long moment, a little overwhelmed at what they both were considering. Honey brushed aside the feeling that she was making some crucial decision and put the situation in perspective for herself. There was absolutely no reason she shouldn't stay here and spend an evening with an attractive man, if that was what she wanted to do. It was nobody's business but hers. She was an adult in charge of her own life this time, not a confused adolescent. Let the others talk, if they wanted to.

"I can rent a car around here, I suppose?"

"You don't need to rent a car. I can drive you back to the Greenbrier." There was a faint note of relief in the ready offer. Consideration of practical details changed the issue before them from *Stay with me* to *Spend the night with me*.

"You sure?"

"I'm sure."

Honey glanced around and saw that the others had reached the limousine.

"How long will you be?"

Zeke considered for just a moment changing his mind and riding back to the base station in the limousine. Then he rejected the idea.

"Not long." *Long enough so that you can still change your mind. Long enough so that there won't be another farewell scene, one way or the other.*

Honey read the rest of the answer in his eyes, turned, and walked rapidly toward the limousine.

Chapter Four

$\mathcal{I}$n the women's dressing room at the base station, while she peeled off her wet bathing suit and put on the soft, dry underwear she'd brought along, it occurred to Honey that she really hadn't come equipped to stay the evening. She had the tailored khaki shorts and white blouse she'd worn this morning and left in the limousine for wearing on the ride back, a pair of flat sandals, and the very minimum of makeup in her handbag. But she did have money and credit cards.

"I'm not going back with you," she announced to the women when she was combing her hair.

They acted surprised and faintly shocked at first, but Amy Lou said what they were all really thinking. "You lucky thing, you. That Zeke McCade's a good-looking man."

Wanting to avoid the masculine reaction to her decision, Honey didn't go outside to the waiting limousine. Instead she wandered into the combination shop and snack bar, mentally ticking away the time. Five minutes must have passed. The limousine would be gone by now. It was too late to change her mind. Zeke should be here soon. He would be taking her . . . where? Honey had no inkling of what sort of place Zeke lived in. Did he rent an apartment? A room in a boardinghouse? Perhaps he shared a house with some other guides or even lived with his family.

What on earth had she gotten herself into?

Growing more panicky by the moment, Honey looked through the poorly organized racks of clothing that seemed to have been just jammed into the available space without any regard to style or size. If she could find a halfway decent pair of slacks and a long-sleeved pullover, she'd buy them since the weather would probably get much cooler in the evening. But the colors were all terrible, and every garment seemed stamped or emblazoned with the name of White Water Adventurers.

A river guide, Honey! You're actually staying behind in this godforsaken place with a man who makes his living guiding people down a river!

When Zeke walked into the shop, Honey didn't see him because she was holding a pair of cotton knit drawstring trousers against her. The shade of pink brought to mind a cheap plastic doll, but it was the only pair she'd found that would come close to fitting her. Draped over her arm was a matching pink and white pullover with White Water Adventurers written in large script down the length of each long sleeve.

Zeke paused just a second, adjusting to the reality. She had stayed; he hadn't been sure at all that she would. Even with her hair still slightly damp and not the sleek tawny perfection it had been upon her arrival that morning, she still looked terribly out of place amidst the sweatshirt-clad college students buying garish T-shirts. A Bloomingdale's patron in the five-and-dime.

Honey looked up and saw him across the room. For some reason, it was infinitely reassuring to read the unguarded expression on his face. *He wasn't any more sure about this than she was.*

"Do you think this is me?" she asked jokingly when he had come over to her and was eyeing the garments she held questioningly.

"No."

"I think I'll take them anyway. If you'll just wait a minute, I'll pay for them."

Zeke didn't want to wait a minute. The place was filling up with guides and White Water employees. There were curious looks in his direction. Lee Baxter would probably be walking in any minute, and then there'd have to be introductions, delay, offers of going somewhere for a drink to turn down. Zeke wanted to get the hell out of there fast.

"That's okay. I'll take care of it later." He took her arm to convey his sense of hurry.

Honey resisted for just a moment as she glanced around, becoming conscious for the first time of the attention they were getting from over in the snack bar area, where the draft beer taps were getting a workout. The same faces and voices that had been all business at the base station this morning and the take-out site this afternoon were relaxed now, and the room was filled with laughter and banter. The guys were mostly in their early twenties, quite a few of them with beards. The girls were young, too, and fresh-looking, athletic types.

Those were Zeke's co-workers.

"I think you're embarrassed to introduce me to your friends," she murmured, yielding to the pressure he was exerting upon her arm and walking quickly beside him toward the door.

It didn't seem as though Zeke would answer, but when they were outside and half-running across the parking lot, he said, "They're not my friends. Over here."

Honey gave the mud-spattered black Jeep a summary inspection before she climbed up into the passenger seat, her trepidation returning full-force. *Honey, what on earth have you gotten yourself into?*

The Jeep engine was noisy and the suspension stiff, so that Honey found herself bouncing up and down in the seat. She looked over and giggled when she saw that Zeke was grinning at her.

"This is quite a car you have!" It was necessary to shout in order to make herself heard.

"It's great on mountain roads," he shouted back. "Especially when it's raining or snowing and they're not paved."

Were those the kinds of roads he had to drive over to get to where he lived? That morning he had told them he lived in the "suburbs" of that dreadful little town they had driven through. Before she could summon the courage and figure out just how to ask him what sort of a place he was taking her to, they were out on the main highway, and wind and tire noise coming through the open sides of the Jeep, added to the roar of the engine, made talking even more difficult. As they approached the New River bridge, Zeke began shouting out information about it.

"Largest single-arch bridge in the world, by fifty feet. Highest bridge east of the Mississippi, 876 feet above the water. Quite an engineering project since it couldn't be built by cranes from down below."

Honey leaned her head over closer to him so that she

could hear as he elaborated upon the construction of the bridge.

"You have a mind for facts and figures, don't you?" she remarked some miles farther on, when he had concluded. They had turned off the main highway and were going slower, so that it wasn't necessary to shout quite so loud.

Zeke didn't answer at once, and when he did, his eyes were on the road. "Yes, I guess I do. Maybe that's why I always liked history in school and decided to major in it in college. But facts and figures are only interesting to me when people are involved."

It was the first mention of college, but Honey found that she wasn't surprised, just a little curious at the rather self-conscious way he'd dropped the information. She couldn't see much point in pursuing the subject. Either he hadn't completed a degree in whatever college he had attended—probably one here in West Virginia—or else the degree hadn't led to a good job. After all, what could one do with a bachelor's degree in history except teach on the high school level? That probably paid less than being a river guide part of the year.

Zeke had been expecting some questions that would lead him quite naturally into a disclosure of his real occupation as a historian, but Honey didn't follow up on his mention of a history major in college. If she wasn't interested enough to ask, why should he volunteer information about himself? he reasoned a little irritably as they rode along in silence until they came to Thurmond.

"This is that town we went through earlier, the one you said was like Dodge City." They both heard the uneasiness in her voice.

She's wishing now that she hadn't stayed. The realization did nothing to relieve Zeke's own feeling of strangeness as he drove through Thurmond and a mile or two beyond it, turned off the paved highway onto the steep winding road that led to his cabin.

"We're almost there."

"I'm beginning to think you live in some abandoned coal miner's cabin." Honey didn't care if she did sound nervous. She was having horrible visions of driving up to some rundown shack with maybe an old woman and an old man sitting out on the front porch smoking corncob pipes.

"I do live in a coal miner's cabin." Zeke reached over and gave her hand a reassuring squeeze. "But it has indoor plumbing and hot and cold running water, all quite civilized."

Despite his effort at lightness, Honey could sense that he wasn't casual. "And do you live alone in this civilized coal miner's cabin?"

He gave her a quick, sharp look. His voice was dry as he replied, "Quite alone. Put your mind at rest, Honey. You're not about to be greeted by my whole tattered Appalachian family."

Honey felt her face grow hot with a combination of embarrassment and defensive anger. "How was I to know? I don't know anything about you, Zeke."

"No, you don't," he returned shortly. He pressed the accelerator and sent the Jeep spurting ahead into a small clearing where he braked to a jolting stop and killed the engine. In the sudden quiet Honey gazed at the cabin perched on a gentle incline among the trees, looking as though it belonged there quite as much as they did. It was sturdy and plain and neat, with no visible sag anywhere, not even in the little corner porch. She could hear the distant babble of water, the

rustle of leaves, and nothing else. All her fears suddenly seemed so silly.

Looking around at Zeke, she met his eyes, noted the
reserve in the clear blue depths, absorbed the impact of
his nearness, and knew again why she had stayed. It
made no sense at all, but it felt so right.

"Aren't you going to invite me into your civilized
coal miner's cabin?" she coaxed with a smile.

Zeke had been waiting tensely for her reaction,
prepared to engage in an exchange that would bring his
identity and circumstances out into the open. For just a
second he was resentful that once again she wasn't
giving him that opportunity, but the feeling quickly
faded as he met her eyes, softly alight with apology and
invitation. What the hell did it matter who and what she
thought he was? The primary and quite incredible fact
was that she was here with him.

"Sure thing," he said, relaxing visibly as he leaned
over and took her lips in a lingering kiss that had his
blood surging through his body in a matter of seconds.
When he tasted her sweetness like this, nothing else in
the world seemed to matter.

They were both breathing faster than normal as they
got out of the Jeep and walked over to the steps leading
up on the porch.

"Was this really a coal miner's cabin, Zeke?" Honey
asked the question simply to generate conversation and
set them both more at ease. She had little interest in the
historical background of the cabin, but a great deal of
interest in its present occupant.

"The front part of it was," Zeke answered readily,
bringing them to a pause on the porch. "The original
cabin was three rooms in the shape of an *L*, with this
porch filling out the square. That's a very typical

layout. The rooms on the back of the house are all more recent. They were added by the present owner."

"So you don't own the house."

"No, I just rent it." There was a door in each of the two walls flanking the corner porch. Zeke opened one of them and waited for Honey to precede him inside. The room they entered was small and cozily furnished as a sitting room. "This, of course, is one of the original three rooms. The other two—" he gestured over toward the side interior wall "—are exactly the same size. A small house like this one might accommodate as many as fifteen or eighteen people."

"Fifteen or eighteen people!" Honey repeated incredulously, looking around her as though reaffirming the modest dimensions of the room.

Zeke nodded but didn't otherwise address the interruption. "One room would be a kind of combination kitchen, dining, and living room where the food was prepared and eaten and whatever socializing was done would take place. A second room was for the miner, his wife and children to sleep in, while the third one might have as many as six or eight cots or stacked beds for single miners. The coal miner's wife did the cooking, cleaning, and laundry for all the men living in the house."

Honey was plainly aghast at such a spartan life-style. "How could people live like that? It must have been awful."

Zeke had given the little historical rundown partly because he was somewhat ill at ease bringing her into his habitat and partly because it came as second nature to him to connect the present with the past. He liked the sense of living in a house that reverberated with the voices and footsteps of earlier generations. It would be impossible for someone of Honey's background to understand the way he felt. He knew that and yet her response put him on the defense.

"I suppose it all depends on what your minimum expectations are and also what you're used to. A very small percentage of the entire world lives up to Greenbrier standards."

Honey's mouth fell open with astonishment. "I wasn't being *critical*," she protested. "I was merely expressing my personal opinion." Her tone grew indignant. "Surely even people who stay at the Greenbrier do have a right to an opinion."

Zeke's shrug was sheepishly apologetic. "Sorry. It's just that there always seems to be an element of censure in the reaction of the privileged to a standard of living lower than their own. The very existence of a lowly house trailer is an affront to the Amy Lous of this world."

"I'll thank you not to include me with the Amy Lous until you have reason!" Honey informed him hotly. "It's rather unfair, I think, to condemn someone automatically for having been born into a wealthy family. I couldn't help who my mother and father were any more than you could."

"And you are here with me, in my humble abode," Zeke appended, his voice edged with sarcasm.

"I am here," Honey agreed belligerently, pressing her lips together.

Suddenly they both were grinning at each other and intensely conscious that there were other reasons for being there besides carrying on a silly argument.

"So much for the old part of the house," Zeke said jokingly, slipping an arm around her shoulder and easing her toward a hallway. "Back here is the kitchen, dining room, bathroom—"

Honey leaned into him, letting her arm wind naturally around his waist. "What's in those other two 'old' rooms?" She really was rather curious. Through the door she'd been able to glimpse a portion of wall covered with framed photographs and what appeared to be documents and an ancient black typewriter on a small, old-fashioned table.

"I use those two rooms as a study," Zeke answered absently, bending his head and kissing her. He wasn't interested in getting into explanations now. There'd be time for that later.

A study? As her lips softened and clung to his, Honey tucked the answer away in her brain. It was one more thing about Zeke that just didn't fit. He was a virile, attractive man who had never married, obviously very intelligent but content to work year after year in a seasonal job with no future, living in a mountain cabin with a study. She was halfway reluctant to solve the mystery for fear that he would lose his fascination, become just an ordinary man and bore her. The thought made her vaguely guilty.

"Zeke." Honey pulled her lips free of his to speak his name with a soft urgency that arrested Zeke's attention.

"What is it?"

"I just wanted to tell you I'm glad I stayed."

Zeke searched her face, sensing that she hadn't spoken all that she was thinking, but what she had said was convincing and enough to make him forget everything else now but the need to assuage that ache he'd been carrying around inside him all day.

"I'm glad, too, Honey." The way he spoke her name, like a caress that brought him pleasure, caused a warm tingle of happiness inside her. It spread as he picked her up in his arms and carried her toward the rear of the house, down a hallway and into his bedroom. There he stood her gently on her feet again and undressed himself with savage impatience, ripping his T-shirt over his head, tossing it aside, jerking open the snap of his cutoffs and stepping out of them.

His sense of urgency as well as the sheer pleasure of seeing his body revealed to her made Honey's pulse hammer. Her fingers moved of their own accord to the buttons on her blouse as he took off his one remaining garment, navy briefs distended with the shape of his arousal, and stood naked in front of her.

"No, let me." His fingers covered hers and moved them aside. Honey found herself holding her breath as he stood so close in front of her she could feel the heat from his naked body. Apparently no longer in a hurry, he took his time unbuttoning her blouse, freed it from the waistband of her shorts, and slipped it off her shoulders. For a moment he contemplated her breasts, nestled in thin silk and lace and rising and falling noticeably, but he didn't touch them right away. His fingertips caressed the curve of her neck and smoothed along the shape of her shoulders and upper arms.

"Your skin feels so beautiful," he murmured and then smiled a little sheepishly, letting his gaze meet hers. "I don't suppose I'm the first man to think your name is perfect for you. Honey. The warm color, the smooth texture . . ." His attention switched to the slow, sensual trail his fingers were taking, from her shoulders down to the tops of her breasts. Lightly he followed the tender upper curve of each breast back and forth several times, his fingertips meeting as they dipped into the center cleavage. Then tenderly and possessively he finally cupped both small, round breasts in his hands.

Honey leaned toward him, murmuring his name in a lover's tone that required no translation.

"*Zeke—*"

A little spasm tightened his features as he slipped his arms around her and drew her tight against him so that she could feel his male hardness pressing into her. "I want you so much it hurts like hell, but I don't want to hurry," he muttered fiercely.

When he eased her away from him and bent, his attention focused on the front clasp of her bra, Honey ignored his earlier remonstrance and unfastened her shorts. When they dropped down around her ankles, she kicked them aside with so little fuss that Zeke, absorbed in his task, seemed hardly to notice. She wanted to be naked with him, to feel the intimacy of her bare flesh pressed against his, but she went no further in undressing herself because he was lifting the cups of her bra away from her breasts, aching mounds of sensitivity, and kissing them.

Honey grasped him by his waist as she tilted her head and arched her back, thrusting her chest toward him and moaning his name softly as he took one breast into his mouth and sucked. The pleasure shooting through her body made her weak and also made her long to press her lower body against his in intimate contact. When he intensified his warm, general suction and concentrated on the hard, aching peak of her breast, her need became too desperate just to stand passively and endure the exquisite pleasure.

Taking his head between her hands, she lifted it and brought his lips up to hers for a kiss that was instantly deep and hungry. Then she circled his waist with her arms and leaned her hips into his, feeling his jutting hardness. Languid, weak pleasure flooded through her and quickly sharpened as she made slight sideways movements, as though to accommodate the different shapes into which nature had molded them, man and woman, and yet was prevented from doing so by the triangle of lace and silk separating them.

The silken friction she was applying with the back and forth motion of her hips was Zeke's total undoing. He went rigid for a moment, summoning all of his control to stop the swift upward surge of his passion. Then he grabbed her close and held her against him, but she wouldn't cooperate. Her hands were sliding along his back, her palms pressing into him, and her voice was urgent as she spoke his name, begging him with its tone to hurry up and make love to her.

Zeke hadn't wanted it to be like this, and even as he succumbed to the sensual torrents sweeping him along, he clutched at his resistance to loss of control. Making love was like navigating a class V rapid; it required a certain amount of discipline and skill in order to bring the highest level of pleasure to both people. This was like riding straight into the Double Z, the most treacherous rapid on the New River, without so much as a paddle. But it was too late to pull back now. The ache inside his loins had reached the state of near-explosion.

Honey could feel the tremor in Zeke's fingers, the lack of gentleness, as he grasped the fragile material of her bikini panties and dragged them down from her hips. For a moment she thought that he would enter her with the two of them standing there, straining against each other in a sexual battle with a common purpose. But then he picked her up and carried her the several steps to his bed, laid her across it and stripped the panties free of her legs.

His face was a study of turbulent emotions as he lowered his body to hers and thrust inside her with his full strength, the way he'd never entered a woman before. Honey cried out with the initial shock and the piercing pleasure, arched her body upward and wrapped her legs around him, welding her hips to his and hanging on for dear life. Any glimmer of hope that Zeke might have nurtured for grabbing onto control was extinguished by the wild abandon in her face and her voice, even before she urged him on with her body, straining her hips upward.

He plunged straight into the maelstrom, letting it gather him up on giant waves, spin him helplessly around and around, suck him under and then spew him upward, higher and higher and higher. It was a feeling of unspeakable helplessness and unspeakable pleasure, unlike anything Zeke had ever experienced before. He made violent, desperate love to Honey, rushing along with her toward destruction without any sense of control.

His climax exploded him into a million pieces and brought a yell of ecstatic pain. The shudders rippling through Honey's body brought him no male satisfaction as might have been the case if he could have taken some credit for seeing to her pleasure. Instead she had just been a foolhardy companion on a dangerous adventure.

Lying slumped on top of her and totally spent, Zeke slowly returned to his senses. "God, I'm sorry," he mumbled, rolling over on his back beside her. "I'm not usually such an animal when I make love to a woman."

Honey let out a deep, satisfied breath and turned on her side, pressing her length along his. "Maybe I bring out the animal in you," she murmured complacently, stroking with gentle, relaxed fingers first his chest, then his shoulders and arms, and finally the planes of his face.

Her touch brought a subtle delicious warmth that Zeke allowed himself to enjoy for just a short time while he mustered his resistance. "Maybe you do," he agreed noncommittally and then captured her hand and held it still. "I know one animal who's starving for something to eat. How about you? Hungry?"

"A little," Honey replied agreeably. "Before we go somewhere to eat, though, I'd like to take a shower. It'll have to be a casual place," she added, remembering her limited wardrobe. "I don't have anything decent to wear."

Zeke chuckled. "You could wear either one of your two outfits to our local eating establishments and not cause a raised eyebrow. But I really wasn't planning to go out anyway. If you don't mind taking a chance on my cooking, I'd just as soon stay here."

"Suits me fine," Honey assured him contentedly.

"Good." He sat up and then climbed over her to get out of bed. "I'll take a quick shower first and then leave the bathroom to you."

Honey lay there and watched him while he gathered up his scattered clothes. "Neat, aren't you?" she teased softly.

Zeke looked around. She was all soft, satisfied femininity, lying there naked in his bed, surprisingly just the slightest bit self-conscious under his gaze. Tomorrow she would be going back to the Greenbrier, back to her friends and the luxury to which she was accustomed. Tomorrow night his bed would be empty. All would be returned to normal. *A few facts for you to keep in mind, pal.*

"I have to be neat," he said casually. "There's nobody around to pick up after me."

With his soiled clothes bundled under one arm, he got clean clothes from the drawers of a bureau and then left the room with the cheerful promise, "I won't be more than five minutes total."

Honey studied the empty doorway a moment before

getting up reluctantly. She did feel a little hungry, but she would have been more than content to linger there with Zeke a while longer. Was it her imagination or had he been rather in a hurry to get beyond the desultory intimacy that follows making love?

As she took her time about picking up her clothes, shaking them out and arranging them over the back of a chair, Honey looked around Zeke's bedroom with intense curiosity, as though searching for some clues to give her insight into the man. It was simply furnished, masculine, and orderly without being fussily neat. The bedroom of a man who was used to living by himself.

The bedroom of a confirmed bachelor?

Honey was shocked to discover that the question seemed to be something more than just idle curiosity. Surely she didn't want to make a serious conquest out of Zeke? They were both obviously very attracted to each other, but it was the pull between people who were totally unlike in every way, background, values, 'expectations,' to use Zeke's own term. Theirs was definitely not a relationship that held any promise of permanency. Honey must be careful not to allow herself to be too challenged by Zeke's detachment. It wouldn't be fair to him, to either of them.

"I'm out," Zeke called from the hallway outside, his voice bringing Honey back to reality and making her realize her apprehensions were farfetched.

"Okay," she sang out cheerfully and went to take her turn in the bathroom, which was functional and clean, as she'd expected. Zeke had laid out a large, fluffy man's towel in a no-nonsense shade of blue. Honey smiled as she reached out and touched it lightly. The thought of being here in Zeke's bathroom, showering in his tub, wrapping herself in his towel—it was so novel . . . and yet so nice.

"That's what I like. A man making himself useful in the kitchen," she declared twenty minutes later, walking into Zeke's kitchen wearing the pink knit trousers and pullover, which looked, she'd decided when she saw herself in the mirror, like an oversized pair of child's pajamas.

Zeke looked up from his task of chopping shallots and grinned when he took in her appearance. She didn't look at all like the chic woman she'd been that morning, makeup impeccable and every hair in place, but he liked the transformation. She looked cute and young with her hair wet and her face clean-scrubbed with no makeup except a touch of lipstick.

"Like my outfit?" she inquired with feigned archness, self-conscious in the ridiculous costume. Tilting her chin haughtily, she turned around and then halted in a model's pose.

"Sexy," Zeke complimented, turning his attention back to chopping seasonings for the dinner he was preparing. He hadn't really been kidding. The knit material of the pullover clung lightly to the shape of her breasts, giving him just a suggestion of the nipples underneath. The baggy pants made him want to slip his hands down inside them and feel the slim curves of concealed hips and buttocks. The truth was that Honey Drake would probably look sexy to Zeke's eyes no matter what she wore.

"Hey, don't get too close to the cook," he warned when she came up beside him to watch what he was doing. Teasingly he brandished his knife at her and then kissed her lightly on the nose. "You'll distract me and I'll chop a finger off."

Honey backed away a few feet, sensing that he was only half-kidding. "You look very professional at that," she commented, watching his practiced movements.

"What are we having, anyway?" When Zeke had said he would rather stay here and eat, she had assumed they would be having the usual masculine fare, steak and baked potatoes, but there were no steaks in evidence. On the stove he had an open flame going under an enormous pot large enough to cook food for twenty.

"Spaghetti," he answered, raking the chopped shallots over to join a little pile of finely diced garlic and fresh parsley. Skillfully he peeled the skin from a ripe tomato, seeded it and chopped it up coarsely before reaching for a second one. "And don't worry about the calories. You didn't eat any lunch, and I bet you didn't eat breakfast, either. It was probably too early for you."

"You're right. I didn't," she concurred readily, finding it most pleasant to watch him. He looked so clean and masculine in jeans and a gray sweatshirt, his hair wet and combed flat against his head, his feet bare. "Isn't that an awfully large pot to be using for just two people?" she asked idly as he took off the lid, inspected the boiling water inside with a satisfied expression and then got a package of spaghetti down from a top cabinet.

"You have to have a large pot to cook spaghetti," he explained patiently. "It has to continue boiling throughout the whole cooking process. The larger the pot, the less likelihood of having a mess to clean up."

"Makes sense." Honey watched as he added the brittle spaghetti to the boiling water a little at a time and then took out an iron skillet, melted a block of butter and sautéed the chopped seasonings at the same time that he made a tossed salad of lettuce and cucumber. "Hmm, my mouth is beginning to water," she said quite sincerely and then added so belatedly and in such an unconvincing voice that they both laughed aloud, "Can I do something to help?"

"Sure. You can tell me if the spaghetti's done." He fished out a strand with a large cooking fork and carried it over to her. Her heartbeat speeded up as he came very close and dangled the limp spaghetti in front of her mouth. Intensely conscious of his gaze, she opened her lips, took the end of the spaghetti in her mouth, bit off a piece and chewed.

"I think it's done, but you should try it, too." Silly to sound breathless talking about a strand of cooked spaghetti! "How do you usually decide—when there's no one around to perform the taste test for you?"

There was a heartbeat of silence while Zeke's eyes probed hers to discover what she was really asking him. Then he moved away, laying the fork on the counter without tasting the spaghetti for himself.

"It doesn't matter then," he pointed out carelessly. "I can eat spaghetti *al dente* or overdone."

While he drained the spaghetti in a colander, returned it to the huge pot, and then tossed it with the sautéed seasonings, butter, and olive oil, Honey stood there and wondered how many of his Appalachian neighbors had any concept of cooking spaghetti *al dente*. He grew more a puzzle to her with every passing hour, this wary, attractive man.

"Sorry I don't have any wine to offer you," Zeke apologized as he served the meal, the salad having been dressed under Honey's interested gaze with a free-handed blend of olive oil and vinegar that turned out to be perfect. "I have some cold beer in the refrigerator, but other than that, it's water."

For the first time it occurred to Honey that he hadn't

offered her a before-dinner cocktail, obviously because he didn't keep liquor on hand.

"Water's fine," she insisted, diving into her food hungrily. "Zeke, this is really fantastic spaghetti," she complimented when she slowed down enough some minutes later to speak. "If this is any example of what you can do in a kitchen, you must be a gourmet cook."

He looked pleased. "Don't you enjoy cooking at all?"

Honey shook her head without even hesitating to think. "I have no instinct whatever for cooking. It would never occur to me to start chopping up ingredients and put them together without the first measurement the way you did. I have to follow a recipe, step by step, and then the finished product *never* looks like the picture in the cook book. Fortunately—"

"You don't have to cook," he finished for her.

She shrugged an affirmative answer.

"When I was growing up, my father and I always had a live-in housekeeper who cooked for us—my mother died when I was eight years old." Strange to feel so intimate with someone who knew almost nothing about the facts of her life. "When I was married, my husband Phil and I mostly ate out. There were dinner parties several nights every week, either social, business, or a combination of both. Then, of course, clients expect to be wined and dined at expensive restaurants, and New York has no shortage of those. When we entertained guests at our home, I always hired a caterer. Number one, I wouldn't have dared risk doing the cooking myself, and, number two, my main purpose was to look pretty and mingle. If I must say so myself," she added with a light tinge of sarcasm, "I was good at playing the hostess game." It had just gotten very old and boring after a while and hadn't been enough to offset her failure to produce the royal heir Phil was pressured constantly by his parents to give them, practically from the day of his wedding to Honey.

As much as he wished that he could hear the unspoken part of the explanation, which had brought that tense, unhappy expression to Honey's face, Zeke wouldn't permit himself to probe. Instinct suggested that it would be better to keep things light and superficial.

"People who live in New York City don't have to know how to cook. If I had a good delicatessen right down the road, I'd be a steady customer," he declared, getting up to clear the table.

Honey found it easy to shove the past back into its dark mental cubbyhole as she watched Zeke carry their plates over to the sink and rinse them with easy, practiced movements. How could a man look so consummately masculine doing woman's work? She felt an odd blend of arousal and tenderness that made her want to go over and hug him from behind.

"I'd help you clean up if I had the strength to get up," she said complacently, sinking a little lower in her chair. In truth she was suddenly extremely tired, in a most pleasant kind of way. "I'm not used to getting up at dawn. Then all that fresh air and exercise followed by passionate sex and a wonderful meal . . ." The yawn came upon her unexpectedly and wouldn't be suppressed. It almost split her jaws with its force.

Zeke turned around with a teasing smile. "I didn't think New Yorkers ever folded under before midnight. Here it is only ten o'clock and you're falling asleep on me." He came over to stand behind her and massage her shoulders and neck with a gentle thoroughness that only deepened Honey's state of relaxation. Suddenly she didn't know if she could make it to his bed before falling asleep.

"I'm sor—ry!" she mumbled, giving in to another yawn right in the middle of the apology. "Maybe some coffee—"

"No reason to be sorry. I'm tired, too." But only physically. He had some doubts about falling asleep at all tonight. "You go on and get into bed. I'll be there in just a few minutes."

He grasped her by the upper arms and helped her to her feet. Feeling like a rag doll, Honey turned into his body and cuddled against him, sleepy and docile. "You're so nice," she murmured.

Zeke held her for a while, enjoying her warmth and softness even while he worried about the little ache that was back, deep inside his gut. It didn't feel sexual.

"Go," he ordered with feigned sternness, turning her around and giving her a little push in the right direction. She obeyed him, stopping at the door to blow him a kiss. When she was gone, he dropped down into the closest chair, the one she had been sitting in, and drew in a long, deep breath, disturbed with his own uneasiness.

What's wrong with you, pal? You're just lucky enough to have a night—and there's tomorrow morning, remember—with a good-looking, sexy woman. Enjoy it for all it's worth.

Zeke finished cleaning up the kitchen, mulling over his present life-style. He didn't exactly live in solitude, since he saw people almost every day, but he did live inside his own thoughts more and more, for the lack of anyone to share them with. Was he becoming so set in his ways that any deviation from the established routine upset his whole system? Admittedly that "established routine" hadn't included women and sex during the past months since he'd moved here to Fayette County and settled into this isolated mountain cabin, but that was more a matter of the lack of opportunity rather than any monastic tendencies.

Was it really lack of opportunity? Zeke had a quick vision of a pigtailed young woman's smiling face. He didn't even know Mary's last name, even though he must have heard it. According to Lee, she was one of his best guides and bright, too, all set to begin work toward a graduate degree in microbiology in the fall. So maybe there had been some opportunities, but it wasn't a crime for a man to become more selective as he grew older, was it?

With that irritable reflection, Zeke realized he couldn't stay in the kitchen all night. He had a woman waiting for him in his bed. To his relief, the thought of Honey, drowsy and soft and naked, stirred to life sensations that were definitely sexual in nature.

But she was deeply asleep, lying curled up on her side facing the place where he would have been had he been lying beside her. The sheet was pulled modestly up over her bare shoulders. Zeke stood beside the bed a moment listening to her slow, regular breathing. Despite the fact that he wasn't in the least sleepy, he contemplated undressing and easing into the bed carefully so as not to wake her. He could gather her up close to him, nuzzle her silky, fragrant hair, absorb into all his pores her warm, sweet vulnerability. . . .

Turning silently on his heel, Zeke left the bedroom and made a beeline for his study. Normally he didn't close the door behind him, but then normally there wasn't anybody in the house he could disturb, he told himself reasonably, settling behind his desk and clicking on the tape recorder.

It took five minutes or so for his pulse to settle down and his mind to clear of anything except the cracked but still vigorous old voice on the tape. Josiah Bedford was ninety-five, lucid, and, to Zeke's ears, wonderfully eloquent as he talked of his youthful years working as a coal miner in the gorge. It all came alive for Zeke. He could see the town of Kaymoor as it must have been, hear the sounds, feel the atmosphere with its excitement, danger, hope, and despair.

This was his reality, his work as a historian. It brought him deep personal satisfaction as well as a sense that in his own small way he was making a contribution to human knowledge and understanding. In return he was awarded the recognition of fellow historians and enjoyed the relative certainty that between teaching in a university and doing scholarly research, there would always be enough money to support himself.

In the familiar, secure confines of his study, Zeke was able to reaffirm that this life he had chosen was right for him. It was enough, even though it quite likely wouldn't ever include a woman on a permanent basis. Women wanted more out of life than he was able or willing to promise.

Especially a woman like Honey Drake.

Chapter Five

*H*oney didn't know where she was for just a second or two upon waking. She was in a strange bed in a strange room, and it must have been very early, since the light filtering through the windows wasn't sunlight. A sense of well-being told her that wherever she was, it was all right.

Then immediately she knew it was Zeke McCade's bedroom. Yesterday and last night came back. Her last memory was of taking off the awful new outfit and climbing into bed. That old cliche about falling asleep before your head hit the pillow had been true in her case.

Drowsily Honey turned on her side toward the unoccupied side of the bed and explored the spot with her hand. Had he slept in the bed with her at all? The feather pillow provided some positive proof that he must have. It was dented with the shape of a head.

Where was he? She couldn't hear a sound of anybody moving around. No radio or TV. He was probably one of those get-up-at-the-crack-of-dawn-full-of-energy people and was out for a morning run. Maybe he was out catching some mountain trout for their breakfast, she reflected only half-kiddingly, remembering the sound of water yesterday when they stopped outside the cabin and sat there in the Jeep. What a horribly awkward moment that had been, and mostly her fault, caused by all her unfounded fears.

Sitting up in bed, Honey stretched and yawned before flinging the covers aside, noticing that a blanket had been pulled up over the sheet some time during the night. She shivered and rubbed her arms as the chilly morning air struck her skin. What she needed was a warm robe to slip into before she dealt with the problem of clothes. Honey had never been able to stand jumping out of bed and putting on clothes before she was even fully awake.

"Zeke?" Her first try at calling out his name ended up more like a hoarse whisper. She cleared her throat and made another attempt, this one louder. There was no response. She sensed that the house was empty, but that perception in no way dissipated her feeling of general well-being. Wherever Zeke had gone, he would be back.

Hugging herself and shivering, she walked over to his closet, opened the double bi-fold doors and contemplated his wardrobe, searching for a robe. At first, she was too intent upon her immediate purpose for the fact to sink in that these weren't the kind of clothes she would expect to find in Zeke's closet. There were several suits, quite nice ones in sober, conservative colors, a variety of sports jackets and slacks, and a couple dozen shirts, mostly the long-sleeved, button-down-collar variety.

It was more the wardrobe of a man who has to get dressed and go off to work each day than the wardrobe of a river guide in rural West Virginia. Another piece of the Zeke McCade puzzle to put into place. Where did he wear all these clothes?

When Honey finally came to a robe, hanging all the way to one side where people usually put wardrobe items they don't use very often, it wasn't at all what she expected to find in Zeke's closet either. Lush navy velour and monogrammed, it was definitely expensive. Only a man of means and ego, who pampers himself with luxury, would buy such a robe for himself, not a man like Zeke. The robe must have been a gift.

Probably a gift from a woman.

As little as it pleased her to wear what instinct suggested some other woman might have given Zeke, Honey put the robe on since it was the only one in the closet. There was no lingering masculine scent to make her feel intimate wearing his garment. Probably he never wore it, she told herself with satisfaction as she knotted the tie.

"Zeke," she called out in the hallway, on her way to the bathroom. Just as she'd expected, there was no answer.

After she had finished in the bathroom, she went into the kitchen to verify that he wasn't there. No coffeepot was in evidence, much to her disappointment. For just a moment, she deliberated as to whether to search through his larder for a jar of instant coffee, but suddenly she knew there was something else she wanted to do first.

The door to Zeke's "study" did not stand ajar this

morning. Was it possible that he was in there, so immersed in a book that he hadn't heard her?

"Zeke?" She knocked on the door and listened to the answering silence before grasping the knob and turning, aware of her heartbeat. Silly to feel like Sherlock Holmes investigating a mystery!

Inside, she looked around, taking in the general impression that the room did indeed look like a "study." Bookcases lined one end and were filled with books, whole shelves of sober hardbound volumes as well as some paperbacks. In addition to the typewriter she had glimpsed yesterday, there was a large mahogany desk that gave every indication of being used. There were manila folders, papers, and correspondence arranged in an orderly manner on its surface. Also a tape recorder.

On closer inspection, she saw that the black-and-white photographs, simply framed and covering most of the wall space that wasn't bookshelves, seemed to be enlargements of old-fashioned snapshots and the subjects were men and women of earlier generations, many of the former identifiable as miners and lumbermen because of their garb and setting. There were pictures of old buildings and towns. Among the photographs were also documents, reproductions of the originals, she assumed.

Zeke hadn't been kidding when he admitted he was a "history buff," she marveled, taking another swift look around before she went into the next room. He had created his own pictorial archives on the walls of his "study."

The adjacent room apparently had taken the overflow from the previous one. There were several filing cabinets, more books on simple shelves that had been assembled with cement blocks and painted planks, some unpacked cardboard boxes and nothing much on the walls except the answer to Honey's puzzle—three black-framed diplomas.

Three! She registered the number even as she walked over closer and studied each one. Zeke had "majored" in history all right. He had not just a Bachelor of Arts degree but a master's degree and a *doctorate!* The undergraduate degree was from Duke University and the two graduate degrees from the University of Virginia, Thomas Jefferson's pride and joy.

Honey stood there, staring at each of the diplomas in turn and trying to assimilate her discovery, which still left many questions unanswered. With all his learning, why was Zeke living here in this cabin, working as a guide? Why wasn't he teaching in a university or doing something that would make use of his knowledge and intellect?

Why hadn't he told her he was a Ph.D.?

The engine sound she had been hearing in the recesses of her consciousness grew louder. Through the window she saw the black Jeep enter the clearing, pull up near the cabin and stop. Zeke climbed out with a paper sack in his arms and started briskly toward the porch, whistling a little tune.

Honey moved fast, emerging from his study the same moment that he came through the door to the sitting room from the porch. Zeke stopped short, taken by surprise on two counts. He hadn't expected to find her out of bed so early and certainly not coming out of his study swallowed up in the rich velour folds of the robe he'd forgotten he had.

"Good morning. You're up." *And busy exploring in my absence,* the light tinge of irony in his voice added.

"I woke up and couldn't find you anywhere." *If you'd been here, I wouldn't have had to go exploring,*

Dr. McCade. "My first thought was that you might be out catching fresh trout for breakfast. That was before I knew what highbrow company I was keeping, of course, and realized that you might have forgotten how to fish during all those years you were busy getting degrees. Why didn't you tell me you were *Dr. McCade?* I might have been more respectful."

Zeke was amazed at his own quick adjustment to the fact of her presence inside his study, which was more than just a working habitat, but the place where he could make contact with the most essential part of himself. His main thought was not that she had violated his privacy, but that she'd taken the necessity for explanations out of his hands. Now that she'd seen the diplomas and knew he wasn't what she'd thought he was, he could just savor the pure novelty of having her here, waiting to greet him when he walked in the door.

"Respect? Who needs respect?" he queried teasingly as he walked over to her and bent down for a kiss. "Hmm," he murmured, ignoring her lack of response, and took another one, letting his lips linger softly against hers until, against her will, she kissed him back. "You were halfway right." He rustled the paper sack. "I was out getting your breakfast. Hungry?"

Without waiting for her answer, he headed back for the kitchen, talking cheerfully, leaving her little choice but to follow along behind him.

"Lucky for you that country stores are open early. I was low on breakfast supplies. As for depending on my fishing ability for sustenance, I'm afraid we'd starve. I never was much of a fisherman, and I really can't imagine stomaching something you've just caught with treachery and slaughtered. If meat weren't packaged so that you don't ever have to think about where it came from, I guess I'd have to be a vegetarian."

Honey followed him right up to the counter and stood beside him while he set the bag down and started taking out its contents.

"Bacon, sausage, eggs, pancake mix—I didn't know what you'd rather have for breakfast, so I just got all of it." He turned toward her, the little smile on his lips matching the gleam in his eyes. "But maybe I'll just have you for breakfast instead." His hands caressed her shoulders through the thick velour while he studied the stubborn expression on her face. "You are in there somewhere, aren't you?"

Honey stiffened under his humorous inspection of her slim figure shrouded in the robe. The thought that it might be touching off memories that didn't include her existence, memories of other mornings with another woman, perhaps the same one who had given the robe to him, brought a sense of outrage.

"I hope you don't mind my wearing your robe without your permission." The terse words held far more accusation than apology.

Zeke assumed that she was still irritated that he hadn't told her about his real profession, but at the moment he really couldn't see that it mattered whether he was a river guide or a Ph.D. Either way, their time together was short. They should simply enjoy those few hours remaining before he returned her to her own world and came back to his own.

"I don't mind in the least." The caress in his voice complemented the touch of his hands as they kneaded her shoulders and then slid down her back, drawing her a fraction closer despite her resistance.

"I really was surprised to find it in your closet," Honey persisted doggedly. "It doesn't look like something you'd buy for yourself."

It still didn't enter Zeke's mind that the robe itself

was in any way an issue. She was obviously resentful of what she construed to be a deliberate deception on his part in keeping his educational credentials secret; his ownership of such a costly, luxurious garment was just further evidence that he was not to be trusted.

"I didn't buy it," he assured her soothingly, tightening his arms around her and drawing her up closer so that her ramrod stiff body was against his. "It was a gift." His eyes were lighted with questioning humor as he lowered his head to kiss her. *Isn't this all a silly waste of time?* was the message he meant to convey.

Honey gave her own interpretation to his amusement. He had the nerve to think it was funny that she didn't like the notion of wearing another woman's gift to him! Shoving hard against his chest, she took him by surprise and twisted free of his embrace.

"I knew all along some woman had bought this and given it to you," she announced with what she intended to be royal unconcern. "Now, if you'll kindly excuse me, I'll go and change for this breakfast you've promised." She wouldn't wear this damned robe a second longer than necessary, nor would she give him the satisfaction of any further prying about its donor.

Zeke watched her flounce toward the door, stirred by amazement, delight, and a strong urge to follow after her. She would be all slim, warm curves underneath the heavy folds of the garment in contention. Her heated emotions warmed his blood and made his heartbeat pick up its tempo. Was she actually jealous at the thought of a woman in his past?

"Honey?"

Unfortunately for Zeke's purposes, beneath the lover's cajolery in his tone there still lurked a faint amusement at the whole situation.

Honey whirled around, furiously aware that she

made a ridiculous figure. Her glare warned him not to come one inch closer.

"I'd rather have bacon, and—please—no pancakes, not after spaghetti last night."

Zeke couldn't keep the grin from spreading across his face, even though he knew it meant he would have to control his passion until later. He shook his head and watched her make her exit with navy velour flapping around her ankles.

Honey took her time about dressing, having little choice but to put on the same white blouse, khaki shorts, and sandals she had worn yesterday. Her dignity couldn't take the risk of wearing the pink trouser outfit. There was little she could do with her hair except comb it, but fortunately she did have some touch-up makeup in her handbag. She used it to make herself as presentable as possible before returning to the kitchen.

Zeke was whistling as he moved about the kitchen, tending bacon in a large frying pan, whisking eggs in a bowl. The delicious aroma of brewed coffee met her nostrils.

"Hmm, coffee," she said from the doorway, announcing her presence. "Can I have a cup before breakfast?"

Zeke turned around and looked her over in detail. It was an effort not to grin when this light, happy feeling was bubbling over inside him, but he didn't want to take the chance of offending her again.

"You can have anything you want, before, during, or after breakfast," he said feelingly.

"I'll settle for coffee right now," she replied pertly, feeling in control as she moved over to take the mug of steaming coffee he poured for her from an enamel drip pot on a back burner of the stove. Taking her coffee over to the table, she sat down.

"I don't understand why you kept your education such a deep, dark secret." Actually that was the least among those things about him that she didn't understand, but it was a starter.

"I didn't intentionally keep it a secret," Zeke disagreed good-naturedly, lifting crisp slices of bacon out of the skillet to drain on a cushion of paper towels. He deftly emptied the hot grease into a metal container and then poured the eggs into the skillet. "The subject just never came up." He took two slices of bread out of a loaf and popped them into the toaster.

"Of course, it never came up. Who would expect a rafting guide to have a Ph.D. in history?"

It wasn't a matter Zeke had any interest in pursuing. He decided to put it to rest as quickly and tactfully as possible.

"Normally it takes a group of people in a raft about fifteen minutes to get around to asking a guide all about himself, but that wasn't the case with your group, not the first or the second time. Nobody was the least interested in my personal background, educational or otherwise. It really didn't matter to me. I was there to do a job, not tell my life's story." So maybe it had mattered a little.

He buttered the two slices of toast, put two more slices of bread in the toaster and turned back to scrambling the eggs.

Honey sipped her coffee, mulling over his answer, unable to dispute its truth, aware of what he had carefully not said. Her little group from the Greenbrier had been too snobbish or, at the least, too absorbed in themselves to be interested in a mere guide.

"It was all my fault," she said reflectively. "The first trip I was too involved in my own personal little crisis to spare any interest for anyone else. My father had just remarried and I was terribly hurt and angry and totally frustrated that there was nothing I could do to change things back to the way they had been, with just him and me together.

"The others—DeeDee and Susan, the guys, as well —all were aware of what the problem was and sympathetic, too, I think, but helpless to know what to do to help or even how to cope with me. If I hadn't been along, I'm sure they'd have asked you questions about yourself. The whole trip would have been perfectly normal. But, then, without me, there wouldn't have been any rafting trip," she added with wry honesty. "I was the one who pushed the whole idea, just to upset my father."

Zeke set a plate of scrambled eggs, bacon, and toast in front of her. "Now, none of it matters, anyway," he pointed out philosophically. *You're here. I'm here. For the moment, that's all that matters.* "More coffee?"

"Please."

She waited while he refilled her mug, brought it back to the table, and then sat down.

"Eat," he ordered, sensing that she still wanted to hash it all over.

Honey picked up her fork and ate a bite of scrambled eggs without really tasting them. "How can you say that none of it matters? Doesn't everything that happens to us 'matter' in some way? We end up being who and what we are because of all the people we've known—" She stopped as Zeke put his fork down resignedly and sat back. "Well, can't we talk and eat, too?" she demanded. As though to prove her point, she picked up a bacon slice with her fingers, crunched off a bite, and chewed it noisily.

"Sure," he agreed, picking up his fork again. "But do we have to wrestle with heavy topics over breakfast?

It's too early in the day to discuss how we came to be who and what we are, don't you think?"

She thought that what he was really telling her was that he didn't want any depth. Theirs was strictly a transitory relationship.

"Well, what would you like to talk about?" The hurt note beneath the recalcitrance caught at Zeke's attention and brought dismay. Damn, he must have a knack for unwittingly offending her.

"Anything," he told her with a warm smile. "Anything at all. We can discuss God, international politics, the aftereffects of nuclear war or whatever."

Honey felt an answering smile tugging at her lips. "Why don't we talk about you?" she suggested lightly. "Tell me the answers to all those questions my friends and I were too self-centered to ask."

"Okay," Zeke agreed with alacrity, glad that he could humor her and lighten the atmosphere at the same time. "The Zeke McCade story begins in a small mountain town in North Carolina."

"Oh, so you're not from here."

Zeke had to fight a smile at the mild accusation that he had deceived her once again. "No, but I do have roots here. My grandfather, Ezekiel McCade—after whom I was named, obviously—came with his young wife to this county to work in the coal mines in the gorge. Fourteen hard years and four children later, he was killed in a mining explosion. My grandmother made the sensible decision of moving herself and her children back to her home state of North Carolina, where her relatives could help. The oldest of her children was my father, who by this time had spent several years working in the mines himself and had vivid memories. I always loved hearing his anecdotes about those early years, which weren't nearly so grim as my grandmother's memories." Zeke realized he was rambling on more than he had intended and decided to streamline his life story.

"My father married a local North Carolina girl. They settled quite contentedly in their hometown and had the usual large family, three boys and a girl, all still living. I'm the second in line. I attended public schools, managed to make my parents proud of me both on the football field and at graduation ceremonies. Got a scholarship to college and discovered the easy life of being a professional student." Seeing Honey's puzzled little frown, he accommodated her with a pause.

"But how did you get to be a river guide?"

"In my freshman year at Duke, I got to know some guys who were white-water enthusiasts. They talked me into coming up here and rafting the New River. Lee Baxter, who was something of a legend among white-water people, had started White Water Adventurers— it was the first outfitting company in the whole area. I don't know if I'd have come along except that I wanted to visit the area, where my grandfather and father had worked in the coal mines. I was immediately hooked on the white-water experience and fell in love with the gorge.

"Before I left that first day, I talked Lee Baxter into letting me work for him that summer, doing anything he'd let me do and for whatever pay he could manage. He and I had hit it off on first sight. He trained me to be a guide, and I came back every summer to work for him, mainly because I enjoyed it. By the time you and your group showed up from the Greenbrier, I was an old hand."

"You were pretty sure of yourself all right," she

accused fondly, remembering him the way he had come striding across the parking lot to their limousine, snapping out orders.

"I knew I had to be forceful," he countered feelingly. "You had bossed me around unmercifully on the telephone. One look at you and I knew I had my hands full. Which is the way I'd like to have them now," he added, rising from the table.

Honey was instantly receptive to his innuendo. As brief and casual as he had been in telling her the routine facts about himself, she felt closer to him and more interested than ever.

"Are you suggesting that we clean up the table?" she teased, getting up, too, and offering no resistance when he took her into his arms, an appreciative grin on his lips.

"No." He tightened his embrace and lifted her up off the floor, holding her tight against him so that their eyes were on a level. "I'm not suggesting we make up the bed, either."

Honey felt a bubble of joy swelling inside her as they smiled at each other, sharing their mutual attraction.

"You're not going to send me off into the bedroom this time and then not show up?" she blustered threateningly.

He shook his head. "I'm not going to send you off into the bedroom at all. I'm going to take you, the way a mountain man takes his woman."

Honey shrieked and pretended to fight him as he hoisted her up on his shoulder and headed for the bedroom. She was giggling, and he was convulsed with laughter by the time he tossed her down on the unmade bed and then threw himself down next to her, on his stomach. His mirth quickly subsided as he combed his fingers through her hair, smoothing it away from her happy, relaxed face. Honey was fascinated that she could see the growth of passion in his eyes. It ignited the blue depths with a more intense light than his laughter and made a responsive warmth spread through her and then grow quickly hotter. But there was more than passion in the words he spoke to her. There was a simple, unquestioning gratitude for what life had unexpectedly given them.

"I'm glad this happened, Honey. I'm glad you're here."

"I'm glad, too, Zeke."

It was an intense, utterly joyful moment as they looked into each other's eyes. Then by some unspoken accord, she reached her hands up to his face at the same moment that he began lowering his head to bring his lips to hers for a kiss so long, tender, and intolerably sweet that Honey thought the ache inside her breast would break her wide open. Parting her lips, she moved them against his in restless circles, tempting him with the hot moistness of her mouth.

"Easy, easy," he murmured, rising up on his elbows to halfway cover her body with his, as though to tame her passion. But then, despite the call for restraint, his kisses quickly deepened into a raw, hungry aggression. He held her face between his hands as though to keep her from escaping the bruising pressure of his lips or the plunging intimacy of his tongue, while in truth she was urging him onward with her response.

Suddenly he stopped and pulled away.

"Not this time," he announced abruptly. "I won't make love to you like a raging bull." He rolled onto his side and lay next to her, propped on an elbow, his free hand stroking the side of her face. "Let me take my time, Honey," he pleaded. "I want to look at you, touch you, *taste* you . . . all of you."

Honey's little movement was pure sensual response to the seductive promise in his words and voice. "And do you want me to look at you, touch you, *taste* you, too, Zeke?" she tormented him softly, feeling incredibly desirable.

He smiled a willing acknowledgment of her power over him. "As much as I can stand. Nice and easy ahead?"

She reached up and tousled his hair. "Nice and easy ahead it is. You'll give me the signal when it's time to go for it?" she couldn't resist adding impishly.

Zeke slid his hand down the front of her body, gliding over a mounded breast but not pausing, even when a sudden intake of breath made it rise against his hand. Lightly he continued a path down to her waist, hip and thigh. It was a little power demonstration of his own that charged the atmosphere between them.

"I'll tell you when it's time." The sensuality in his tone and in the expression in his eyes reinforced the promise. "But I think you'll probably know."

Honey gave him her cooperation, teasingly at first, stopping to inquire if it was all right to touch him here or there, in this way or that. But the teasing rapidly came to an end as she gave herself over to the mastery of Zeke's touch. He made love to her his way, unhurriedly, taking delight in the sight and touch and taste of her body. It wasn't so much a matter of skill as controlled interaction, because everything he did gave him as much pleasure as it gave her.

Honey discovered for herself the same dual stimulation in touching him intimately with her hands and her lips. His indrawn breath or low groan caused her own heart to beat faster and the need inside her to sharpen. Then suddenly the restraint was no longer pleasurable or endurable. There was no other certainty in her life other than that she would die if he didn't possess her at once.

"Zeke—"

Almost before the anguished sound of his name had escaped her lips, he was murmuring, "Now, sweetheart, now," and was inside her, taking away her breath with the incredible relief and the exquisite pleasure of his swift, deep entry.

But he wasn't ready yet to take her into total abandonment. With a slow, maddening rhythm, he built her up to a new crisis of stimulation until she was grabbing onto his shoulders to urge him onward and thrashing her head and shoulders from side to side.

"For God's sake, Zeke, it's got to be now!" she cried out.

The desperation in her voice might have been a hair trigger, turning him loose, for suddenly he was holding back nothing. Gone were rhythm and control. Gone was any consideration of safety or holding back reserves to meet the hazards up ahead. Gone was the distinction between the most intense pleasure and razor-sharp pain. Together they were whirling and plunging through the center of a maelstrom they had created with their passion, and the exhilaration was more wonderful than a mere human could bear.

Honey felt the same total lack of inhibition that she had felt on the river with Zeke when she reached the height of her jubilation in the midst of a powerful rapid. He had made it seem right, perhaps by his example, not just to feel the power and helplessness, the excruciating blend of joy and fear, but to cry it out. And cry out her feelings she did now, as she reached a climax before him and then absorbed the explosion of his body into hers while she thrilled in his own unashamed outburst.

Clasping her arms around his moist, inert body as he

lay on top of her, she hugged him close in a paroxysm of tenderness and felt all the pride and humility of having survived the most dangerous rapid on the New River.

"From now on, we'll always make love your way, Zeke," she murmured contentedly.

Her words must have penetrated and made him aware of lying heavily on top of her. He rolled over on his side and lay with one arm thrown loosely across her. Honey turned toward him and eased closer, realizing what she'd just said. In that short time the quality of his silence had changed: He was no longer just too insensible in the aftermath of passion to speak, but quiet.

"What are you thinking about?" she asked softly.

The arm lying across her suddenly wasn't lax anymore, but it didn't gather her closer, as she would have liked.

"About taking you back to the Greenbrier."

"Oh." It was surprising how much disappointment could be in a single word. "Do I have to go back today?"

Now the arm did tighten around her, and she nestled closer, assuming that he was granting her oblique request to stay at least another day.

"I think it would be better if I did take you back today," he said reluctantly, rubbing his cheekbone against her hair.

Under the circumstances, Honey couldn't take his words seriously. "Why?" she demanded complacently. "Are you tired of cooking for me?" She was struck suddenly by a practical obstacle that surprisingly hadn't even occurred to her before that moment. Zeke had a job to consider. "That's right—this is your busy season, isn't it?" Without waiting for him to agree to her disgruntled observation, she followed it up in a frankly wheedling tone, "Couldn't White Water Adventurers get along without their best guide for a couple of days?"

Zeke raised up and looked into her face. Honey gazed back at him, not comprehending the reason for his obvious surprise and then disbelief.

"What's wrong?" she asked uncertainly.

"You still think I'm a guide for Lee Baxter's outfit."

Honey blinked up at him. "Aren't you?"

Zeke's ironic little shake of his head wasn't an answer. It was a dialogue with himself. How could two people be so intimate on one plane of experience and yet be unfamiliar in every other way?

"No, I'm not one of Lee Baxter's guides anymore. I haven't worked as a river guide for nine years now. The summer following the one I took your Greenbrier group down the river was my last summer to work for Lee, although I've rafted the river with him every year since."

The faint reproof underlying his even-toned explanation made Honey instantly defensive.

"How was I to know you weren't a guide? Nobody—including you—mentioned the fact." Her aggrieved tone suggested that if anybody had been wronged in this current misunderstanding, it was herself.

"And, after all, you were paying enough money that you deserved a 'real' guide."

Honey felt her face grow flushed under his shrewd gaze. "I didn't say that. You did."

Zeke sat up on the edge of the bed, conceding not just that point but the whole issue of who had been at fault. What difference did it make, anyway?

"I guess I didn't take my autobiography far enough. When I met you coming out of my study this morning, I just assumed—wrongly and stupidly, I can see now—that you knew I'm a full-time historian."

Honey refused to accept the terms of truce he was offering with this casual assumption of blame. She didn't want to dismiss the whole matter as inconsequential.

"But what do you *do?*" she asked earnestly. "I saw your diplomas and all the books and old photographs, but I figured that you had to be doing something to earn a living." She thought suddenly of the clothes she had seen hanging in his closet, an academician's conservative attire. "You were teaching in a college or university before you came here, weren't you?"

Zeke nodded. "I taught for four years at the University of North Carolina." A fine institution that didn't offer a teaching position to just any new Ph.D. But Honey wouldn't know that, and Zeke didn't tell her. "Right now, I'm working on two related projects, both involving the New River Gorge during its coal mining and lumbering era. I'm expanding my doctoral treatise on that subject into a book and working on an oral history study that is funded by a grant. I'm interviewing old-timers and recording their actual memories of those bygone days. It's really quite fascinating—" Honey's little frown of concentration made Zeke realize he had supplied the essential information and should cut himself off before he warmed to the subject that he could talk about at length. He would only end up boring her to death.

"You're just not at all who I thought you were," Honey marveled aloud. Yet it all made a crazy kind of sense, didn't it? Hadn't her ignorance been only a "surface" kind of ignorance? Her assumption that Zeke was just a local man, born, reared, and educated in this backwoods area, was totally unsupported by any realistic notion of what such a person would be like. The "real McCoy" probably wouldn't have appealed to her at all. She'd been attracted to Zeke because of who and what he really was. Now suddenly it wasn't so incredible that she had stayed here yesterday afternoon. Her old acquaintances back at the Greenbrier wouldn't be nearly so shocked by her behavior when they learned that Zeke wasn't a river guide, but a scholar.

"But if you're not a guide, why didn't the girl who answered the phone the day I made reservations two months ago tell me that—and how is it that you were our guide?"

"From the report I was given, you used the same telephone technique on her that you'd used on me ten years ago," Zeke replied with a wry grin. "She apparently wasn't given a whole lot of opportunity to speak, and then you intimidated her into total silence when you started throwing around talk about five-hundred-dollar bonuses." He stopped and watched Honey nibble on her lower lip.

"You're dying to ask me if I did it for the money, aren't you?" he mused. "In a way, you could say I did, although I didn't get paid anything personally. Lee Baxter is in some financial trouble because of a personal tragedy, and I knew he could use the money. But it wasn't just that. I have to admit I was curious." His eyes went from Honey's intent gaze briefly down her nude length, making her aware for the first time since the discussion began that she was naked. That they both were naked. "I'm not really sorry at all," he added softly and then quickly stood up and began picking up his clothes. "That brings us right up to the present. And even though I don't have a 'boss' as such to ask for time off, I do have important work to do."

Honey didn't need a translation. He was telling her in a polite, regretful way that she couldn't stay. It had been great having her here last night and this morning, but she had to go back to the Greenbrier.

Chapter Six

*B*lind instinct made Honey want to cover herself up while she dealt with disappointment and a pain she assumed to be injured pride. Reaching down for the sheet, she curled herself sideways as though to protect her vulnerable inner parts. By the time she had the sheet firmly anchored beneath her upper arm and a pillow hugged up to her chest and propping her a little upright, determination had set in. He could force her to go, but she wasn't budging an inch from this bed until he was at least honest with her.

"That's not the reason, is it?"

The grim resolution in her tone drew a questioning look from Zeke. While he sized up the situation, Honey took full advantage of his momentary surprise at the realization that she intended to oppose him from a horizontal position in his bed.

"This is just a one-night stand for you, isn't it, Zeke? Now you want me to go back to where I belong and leave you to your books and tape recorder. Well, what's the big hurry? Haven't I been worth the interruption of your peaceful schedule?''

During the long moment that Zeke's gaze was locked with hers, Honey sensed that he wasn't dealing with her words, but with the response he would make to them.

"You know it hasn't been like that," he rebuked quietly. "Cheap expressions like 'one-night stand' don't apply, at least not as far as I'm concerned. But if you want me to put into words what we both know to be the situation, then I will." He paused while he buttoned the cuffs of his long-sleeved cotton flannel shirt and then started talking again as he pulled on his jeans.

"What has happened between us will always be very special to me, a kind of realization of a young man's fantasy. But that's all it can be." The snap of his jeans coincided with the last word. Working his fingers down into the side pockets, Zeke looked at her and wondered if she had any inkling of how hard she was making this for him.

"I'm a very selfish man, Honey. I live a simple life with just the basic necessities because it allows me to do what I want to do. My kind of work isn't lucrative, but it gives me satisfaction. One of the drawbacks is that I simply can't afford a woman to share it with, and certainly not a woman like you, who's used to every luxury." Honey's eyebrows shot up and her lips opened, but before she could speak, Zeke quickly pulled one hand out of a pocket and silenced her with a defensive gesture.

"I know what you're about to say: You never had any intention of moving in permanently. The point is that this place is going to be empty as hell for a while when I come back here later on today, alone. And you've only been here a few hours." Zeke moved his shoulders and made a visible effort to lighten his expression. "You don't want to make a poor, hardworking historian dissatisfied with his lot in life, do you, Honey?"

Honey wouldn't be coaxed into smiling. She sat up on the edge of the bed, giving the sheet a vicious yank, and wrapped it around the front of her body, leaving her shoulders and her legs bare.

"I can certainly agree with you that you're a self-centered man, Zeke McCade. It seems that the only person you're considering in this situation is you. What about me? Doesn't it matter at all how I feel when you drop me at the Greenbrier and drive off? What if I feel empty and dissatisfied with my life?" She eyed him belligerently.

Zeke didn't know what to say. This reaction hadn't figured at all into his thinking.

"Honey—" he began uncertainly, shuffling his bare feet.

"Don't 'Honey' me." She gave the sheet another little yank and arranged its folds more securely up under her arms. "And another thing. For an educated man, your attitude is unbelievably chauvinistic. Why does a woman necessarily have to fit into your life? Why can't you make some changes yourself? You don't have to be a pauper and a hermit in order to be a good historian, do you?"

Zeke felt the need to sit down, especially since he wasn't having much success at thinking on his feet. He looked around behind him to double-check that the chair was where it was supposed to be and then backed up and dropped down into it.

"Honey, what's the point in this?" he asked with a touch of pleading. "You know I'm right. We live on different social and economic planets."

"But even people on different planets can *visit* each

other and be friends," she pointed out stubbornly. "I feel perfectly comfortable here on your planet." She opened up one arm in a sweeping gesture to take in the room, the cabin, and the mountain location, then had to grab the sheet, which dropped to reveal one breast, and anchor it under the arm again. "I think you ought to visit mine." Her expression was absorbed as she started to make concrete plans in her mind.

Zeke watched, intrigued in spite of himself. When her face suddenly lit up with enthusiasm, he knew he was going to have a hard time saying no to whatever it was she was going to suggest.

"I know! You can come to the Greenbrier with me and stay for a couple of days! You'd find it terribly fascinating, from the historical viewpoint. There's a museum on the grounds and even a historian."

Zeke closed his eyes briefly to shut out her eager, pleased face. When he opened them, he shook his head slowly from side to side to forewarn her that refusal was unavoidable.

"You've just proved my whole point," he said patiently. "I can't afford to spend a couple of days with you at the Greenbrier."

The objection obviously made no impression on Honey, who waved it carelessly aside and seemed unaware that the sheet had dropped again, giving a provocative three-quarters view of a pink-tipped breast.

"I didn't mean that you'd pay," she corrected, matching his patient tone. "I haven't paid a cent here, have I? I've been your guest, and you'll be mine at the Greenbrier. You don't have to worry about being embarrassed, either, because nobody actually pays 'money' for anything. You just sign your name."

Zeke threw back his head and laughed.

"What a wonderful way of life where you don't have to pay for anything! Just sign your name!" He chuckled, shaking his head.

"You know what I mean," Honey said accusingly. "Of course, you get a bill later on."

"Of course," Zeke said more soberly. "I wasn't making fun. But, Honey, you must know that I can't go to the Greenbrier and freeload on you for a couple of days."

"You see?" she retorted indignantly. "That's exactly what I meant when I said you're a male chauvinist! Why can't you come to the Greenbrier as my guest if I invite you? What law says that a man always has to pay?" Her expression changed and became softly pleading. "Please, Zeke. I don't want to go back there by myself. It would be so much more fun with you—and you might enjoy it. If you didn't, you'd be that much gladder to come back here by yourself." To Honey, her logic seemed unassailable, but she mustered the entire force of her combined will and longing and focused them upon Zeke while he wavered.

"Please?"

Zeke threw up his hands in a gesture of surrender.

"How can I refuse such an offer?"

Honey's answer was to throw aside the sheet and come at him wearing just a wide, delighted smile. Zeke pulled her down on his lap, certain of only one thing: He had been a little hasty in putting on his clothes. They'd have to come off again.

Several minutes later Honey pulled her lips back a little from his, just long enough to say in a softly teasing, happy voice, "We can make love 'your' way at the Greenbrier, too, even if you are my guest."

"The perfect hostess always thinks of her guest first," Zeke murmured back and got caught in the middle of a half smile when she pressed her lips to his again.

It was only a matter of time before they made the transition from the chair to the bed. This time after they had made love, they lay together, holding each other very close and not speaking for several minutes, simply because there was no need to speak. It was one of the few times in Honey's entire life that she had ever rested contentedly instead of leaping up restlessly to get on with whatever would come next.

"I could stay right here forever," she whispered finally and rubbed her cheek against his chest, inhaling his warmth and the pleasing muskiness of his flesh.

Zeke's arms tightened and before she guessed his intent, he had rolled over on his back and brought her along with him so that she lay on top of him. Lightly he spanked her bare bottom.

"We can't stay in bed all day, woman. Not when you've promised to put me up in luxury at the Greenbrier."

Honey raised up and looked down at his face. He seemed as relaxed as he sounded, his blue eyes alight with humor. It came as a relief to her that he wasn't going to try to back out, but she didn't see what the big hurry was.

"Half the day's practically gone already," she pointed out, bracing her hands on either side of him and raising up even further.

Zeke consulted his watch.

"Hmmm—must be the short half. It's not quite nine-thirty." He made a production of shaking his wrist. "But then this isn't a Rolex. Maybe you should check your time."

Honey tried to look reproving but ended up laughing instead. "You're one of the least cooperative men I've ever run into," she accused, levering herself up so that she could climb down to the floor, where she stood with her hands on her hips, surveying him. "I was going to suggest that you show me a little more of your 'planet' today, and then we could go to the Greenbrier tomorrow." Or maybe the next day. She was in no hurry.

Zeke sat up on the edge of the bed. Honey saw that the humor had died out in his face and was replaced by thoughtfulness. She concluded morosely that he was mentally framing a tactful refusal.

"All right. We'll stay here today. I'll show you around the county." He was obviously liking the idea better as he became accustomed to it. The trace of humor returned to his eyes as he glanced from her to a khaki heap near her feet that was her shorts. "We'd better see to getting you some proper hiking attire first, though. Some jeans and a long-sleeved shirt." His expression grew more concentrated. "What about those canvas shoes you were wearing yesterday? What happened to them?"

"I threw them away," Honey admitted ruefully and then added only half-jokingly, "Zeke, I didn't necessarily mean you had to show me around your habitat on foot."

"You wanted to see my 'planet,'" Zeke insisted firmly. "Well, I'm going to show it to you, and some of the places can only be reached by foot."

Honey didn't offer any further objection. They got dressed and then drove to Oak Hill, a bustling, prosperous town complete with its share of national fast-food franchises. Honey was outfitted with sturdy denim jeans, a red plaid shirt, and a pair of inexpensive running shoes, all of which Zeke paid for. The fact that she didn't recognize a single brand somehow added to the novelty and the fun.

Today the noise of riding in the Jeep didn't interfere with conversation at all. They shouted back and forth, becoming more relaxed all the time so that they could joke about almost anything, including themselves and their situation. Honey was amazed at first at Zeke's store of information and then increasingly amused as he bombarded her with facts and figures about every hamlet they drove through.

"Where are we going, anyway?" she asked at one point when they were winding along an incredibly narrow and steep mountain road, driving slowly enough to make conversation possible almost in a normal tone of voice.

"We'll park the Jeep at Fayette Station. The Fayette Station bridge is the small bridge we floated under yesterday. From there we'll hike through the woods to Kaymoor. That's one of the old abandoned mining towns—"

"Why don't you tell me a little about its history?" Honey put in sweetly and grinned at him when he shot a quick look over at her.

"Since you're interested, I will," he retorted, grinning back at her, and promptly launched into a summary of Kaymoor's history that lasted the ten minutes it took them to reach their destination. Fayette Station seemed to be just a stretch of road with dense woods on either side where a lot of other people had parked vans and four-wheel-drive vehicles. When Zeke turned off the engine, though, Honey could hear the rush of water nearby.

"This is a take-out station for private individuals who

use their own rafts or kayaks," Zeke explained and then looked threateningly at her when she giggled.

"I was about to ask what all these cars are doing here," she teased, "but then I knew you'd probably tell me anyway."

Zeke shook his head. "The young woman has no respect for knowledge. You do realize there's a quiz later on?" he warned, leaning over toward her with the intention of kissing the impish smile off her lips.

Honey raised her eyebrows. "A quiz? I hope it's going to be an oral one. I was always good at oral quizzes."

"I'll just bet you were." Zeke kissed her hard and then became so ensnared by soft, responsive lips that he couldn't find the right moment to stop. He was breathing fast when he finally pulled his lips free of hers. "Take that," he said with husky irony.

"I love the sample question, Professor McCade," Honey mocked him unsteadily. "This is one test I'm really looking forward to."

"I'm beginning to wonder how I could ever give up teaching." Zeke opened the door of the Jeep and climbed out. "Now, class, if you'll follow me—"

Zeke had been determined at the outset, when he agreed to show Honey more of the life he currently chose to live, to be himself. By the end of the day, he knew she would be as bored with him, the 'real' Zeke McCade, as she was by the rural countryside and the pokey little villages and towns. The problem was that Zeke found he enjoyed having Honey along with him so much that the thought of her being bored with him became less and less tolerable. He was quiet as they climbed up through the woods to what remained of Kaymoor.

"Aren't you going to tell me about what these old buildings were used for?" Honey demanded, looking around and feeling a strange eeriness. Zeke noted her little shiver and was ridiculously pleased that she might be feeling the sense of the past that he always felt when he came up to Kaymoor.

"I'm sure I would tell you all about them," he said ruefully, "whether you were interested or not." They were standing several feet apart, facing the crumbling row of old coke ovens Zeke knew he would, sooner or later, point out as unusual because there were two rows of them, side by side.

Honey moved up close to him and hugged him around the waist. "But I am interested." Seeing his frankly skeptical look, she added with convincing honesty, "I probably wouldn't be ordinarily. But it intrigues me that you find it all so utterly fascinating. I love to listen to you talk, and then all of a sudden I realize I am interested."

Zeke put his arms loosely around her, linking his hands at the small of her back. "I do find this place where we're standing fascinating, Honey. To me this is more than just a collection of derelict old structures. I look around and with the help of all the old photographs and documents, the historical accounts and the recollections of people I've talked with, it all comes alive for me. I can see it the way it was, see the people who lived here, hear them talk, watch them sweat and strain and work." He shrugged helplessly. "It's more interesting to me to hike into the woods and see a place like Kaymoor than to take in a big hit play on Broadway and go to a fancy restaurant afterward."

"You've done that?"

He nodded.

The point he was making was clear to Honey. His

preference for mining ghost towns over the more glamorous type of diversion she presumably enjoyed was yet another proof of how unsuited they were to each other. Honey couldn't honestly say he was wrong and yet it felt so right to be standing there in the quiet woods in the midst of a lot of spooky old buildings with Zeke's arms around her.

"So you're weird. Now, tell me about Kaymoor," she ordered confidently.

And Zeke did exactly that.

By the time they got back to the Jeep, Honey was conscious of hunger pangs. Glancing at her watch, she noted that it was well past noon.

"No wonder I'm hungry," she commented with surprise. "Look at what time it is."

"Time goes by fast when you're having a good time," Zeke joked self-consciously. Damn, he'd talked her ears off again.

"Zeke, I really am having a good time," Honey told him earnestly when they had both climbed into the Jeep. She laid her hand on top of his on the steering wheel.

"So am I." He turned his hand under hers to capture it and bring it up to his lips. Then he rested it on his thigh, smoothing out the fingers and giving a little squeeze, before he started the Jeep.

Honey left her hand there, loving the casual intimacy even more than the tactile pleasure of hard muscle and sinew working smoothly beneath her palm and fingers as he lifted his leg to brake and then lowered it to accelerate again. *If only my friends could see me now!* she thought with amusement, bouncing up and down when the Jeep would hit a bump or hole in the road. Anyone who knew her would go into stitches at the notion of Honey Drake riding over mountain roads in a muddy, noisy Jeep, wearing unknown brands of clothing bought in a discount department store.

And she'd never felt happier in her life! That was the wonder of it.

"Where're we going now?" she shouted over at him, not really caring.

The young, reckless quality of her voice hit upon an old memory inside Zeke. He looked quickly sideways at her and was sharply aware of the transformation she'd undergone the past twenty-four hours. Here was a new Honey more dangerous than the other two, the innocent nineteen-year-old sex bombshell or the poised, mature woman whose utter perfection had made disappointment rise inside him yesterday when he saw her standing by the Greenbrier limousine. The woman beside him sent out a warm glow of femininity that wrapped around him and seeped pleasurably through his breast until it reached some inner core and touched off a sweet, lurching pain. He'd had the same kind of sensation several times before in his lifetime, most memorably when he was very young—usually during holidays—when everything seemed "too good." At such times the excess of pleasure caused a poignance similar to pain. This hardly seemed a situation to warrant such intensity, and it took him uneasily by surprise.

"I thought we'd have a late lunch up at Hawk's Nest Lodge," he shouted in reply. "The food's just ordinary fare, I'm afraid, but the view might be the best in the whole state of West Virginia."

Honey found that he was right on both counts. The food at the Hawk's Nest Lodge was plain, and the view through the outer plate glass wall of the small restaurant was spectacular, looking down on the New River Gorge with wooded mountains rising in tiers in the

background. There was the sense of depth and vastness
that could never quite be captured in a photograph.

Since it was past the popular lunch hours, they had
their choice of several vacant tables near the floor-to-
ceiling windows. Honey ordered a hamburger and then
sat back with a little contented sigh, gazing down at the
gorge, far below. The only way to get down to the little
marina at the bottom, with its colorful paddleboats,
tiny from this distance, was to take the tram just
outside the lodge.

"This is wonderful," she declared happily. "This
view makes me almost believe your West Virginia
license plate slogan: *Almost Heaven.*" Feeling his eyes
rest briefly upon her, Honey knew that her sense of
euphoria wasn't caused solely by the view. She looked
at him, a broad smile breaking across her face. "Now,
aren't you going to tell me a little about Hawk's Nest?"

Zeke told her with his eyes what he'd like to do that
particular moment, and it had nothing to do with
talking at all. He'd like to punish her for her cheekiness
with a spanking, kiss her good and hard, and then take
it from there. As he rested his arms on the table and
leaned across it toward her, he saw her lips part and her
breath come faster.

"Remember," she teased suggestively, "we have that
test coming up later on. Tonight, wasn't it?"

"I think we'd better reschedule it to an earlier time,
don't you?" he countered, reaching across and touching her soft bottom lip with his forefinger.

"I think so," she agreed quickly and then watched his
face with a devilish glint in her eyes while she flicked
her tongue out and wet the tip of his finger.

Zeke drew his hand away and sat back abruptly, no
match for her in provocation, not in a public place like
this one. He was ready to forget lunch and drive the

most direct route back to his cabin, where he could make love to her again. Hell, if this weren't such a small area where everybody knew everybody, he'd rent a room here at the lodge.

Two park rangers walked into the restaurant and greeted Zeke by name, helping to restore his common sense. Then the waitress came with their order, and the sight and smell of the food reminded him that he was hungry. Still, the whole time that he ate and did his part in carrying on the conversation, Zeke was aware of the sexual tension in his groin, only temporarily subdued.

A flash of color caught his attention as they were finishing lunch. He glanced out and watched a bright red tram car arrive at the top of its steep ascent.

"Want to ride the tram down to the bottom?" he felt obligated to ask and then added quickly, before she could answer, "Say no." His grin was sheepish but honest.

"No," she said promptly. "I wouldn't like to ride the tram, not today."

They held hands walking out to the Jeep. When they reached it, Zeke took her into his arms and kissed her, right there in the parking lot. He didn't care if somebody who knew him was watching.

"I just can't seem to get enough of you," he told her unsteadily when he had finally managed to pull his lips free of the intoxicating sweetness of hers. "It's getting to the point that I don't want to venture too far away from a bed."

"Right now, we seem much too far," Honey murmured in heartfelt agreement.

"You've charged up my sex drive," Zeke teased her when they had climbed into the Jeep. "Until you came along, I was living quite contentedly in the woods, like a scholar monk."

"Some monk," Honey gibed fondly.

Suddenly the question that formulated itself in his mind was hanging there in the air between them, taking them both by surprise and then leaving them open to a flood of other emotions. Zeke hadn't expected to need to know if she slept with a lot of men, and he definitely hadn't expected to feel jealous as hell at the very notion that there'd been any other man at all, besides himself.

Honey was pleased that his interest in her private life was obviously more than just curiosity. But at the same time, she was a little hurt that explanations were even necessary. That was silly, since she couldn't really expect him to know intuitively that she hadn't been acting typically when she stayed behind with him yesterday on a spur-of-the-moment invitation.

"Divorce affects different people different ways," she said carefully. "In my case, having a husband who needed to have affairs with other women didn't exactly boost my general opinion of men or my own self-image." She studied her hands in her lap, as though concerned that the nail polish on several nails was chipped. Then she clasped the hands around one knee and met Zeke's gaze, her chin high. The expression in his eyes totally disarmed her. She had expected apology and perhaps a touch of pity. Instead there was self-disgust and anger. Zeke was furious at himself as well as at the bastard of a husband who had caused her humiliation and pain.

"Don't look like that," Honey begged humbly. She grimaced. "It was perfectly natural, under the circumstances, for you to be curious and mean of me to try to make you feel guilty by association, simply because you're a man. To answer the question you haven't even asked, I don't go in for bed-hopping." She smiled wanly. "I actually tried to right after the divorce, in a kind of childish effort to get even with Phil, but I just ended up feeling cheap and compromised."

Zeke leaned a little sideways toward her and held his right hand in front of her, palm up. Honey looked from his eyes to the hand and then placed one of her own on top of it, expecting a kind of symbolic handshake to mark the end of the discussion. Instead Zeke brought the captured hand to his breast and held it over his heart. He felt rotten about what had just happened. There was the strong sense of having let her down.

"Want to change your mind and ride the tram?" he asked dryly.

Honey smiled, relieved that the tension was dispelled. Once again they were two people having a wonderful time together in the here and now. Life wasn't something serious caught in a vise between yesterday and tomorrow.

"No, I don't want to change my mind." She wrinkled up her nose at him. "Not about anything that's happened to me since about ten-thirty yesterday morning."

Zeke drove them back to his cabin, uneasily aware of an urgency that was more than a suppressed sex need. When they made love, he broke his own established ground rules and took possession of her body almost immediately. He wanted to bring them both to that mindless merger when they clung to each other in a kind of sublime desperation and cried out with the pain and ecstasy as they took the plunge from the pinnacle of sensation outward into the void of oblivion. He wanted to feel in her body and hear in her voice that explosion of joy that turned him into the most powerful and the most humbly grateful of giants.

Afterward, as before, Honey was secretly amazed at her utter abandon during the height of lovemaking. For the first time, she mentioned it.

"You turn me into a wild woman, Zeke. I think that whenever we make love, you're the river guide, not the history professor." She hesitated, shy at completing her whimsical thought. "Has it occurred to you that making love feels a lot like going through a rapid?"

"I used to think that making love was the closest thing to going through a major rapid, like the Double Z," Zeke confessed wryly. "The last couple of days I've revised that opinion."

Honey's head popped up from his shoulder so that she could look smilingly into his face. "What a compliment from a man!" she mocked lightly. "It's like being told you're almost as good as making that ninety-mile run for a touchdown back in college!"

Zeke lifted his brows skeptically as though to say he didn't know if he could go *that* far and then laughed aloud when she scowled in pretended indignation.

Honey would have been perfectly willing to stay right there in the bed, joking and talking until the urge to make love built up again, but she began to sense a contained restlessness in Zeke and guessed the probable reason for it aloud.

"You probably have work to do in that study of yours, don't you?" His thoughtful expression made no denial. "Well, don't let me stop you. I have things to do myself." With this lazy declaration, she languidly got up out of bed and stretched, pleasantly aware of his eyes on her.

"What sort of 'things'?"

"First on the list is a shower. Then I thought I'd make use of your washer and dryer—that is, if you have a washer and dryer."

Zeke sat up, his face doubtful. Why would she want to do laundry when tomorrow she'd be back at the Greenbrier, where surely she had a whole closet full of clean clothes?

"Sure. The laundry room is right off the kitchen. I'll show you, but—"

"It's okay," she cut in briskly. "I can find it. You just run along to your tape recorder and your old papers and photographs." She came over to give him a little peck on the lips before strolling out of the room, on her way to take the shower she'd mentioned.

Zeke drew in a deep breath and looked around his normally tidy bedroom. Her handbag lay over on the dresser along with a little zippered makeup bag, the latter open with items spilling out of it. The closet doors were open, and he could see the pink outfit hanging there in the middle of his sober college professor's attire. Her new jeans, red shirt, and running shoes he'd bought her earlier in the day were strewn over the floor, along with his own clothes. The khaki shorts and white blouse were draped across the back of the chair. He could hear the shower running in the bathroom.

How powerful was the sense of her presence in the room where he slept each night and yet the physical evidence could be cleared away, as it would be tomorrow morning, in just a matter of a minute or two. There would be no pink among the camel tans and grays in his closet, no feminine clutter on the dresser next to his plain hairbrush, no lacy froth of underwear sharing the floorspace near the bed along with his dark cotton briefs. It was the invisible, lingering evidence provided by his memory that Zeke was wondering about. How long would that be there?

Undoubtedly a long time, perhaps as long as he lived here in this cabin. Even so, it was no cause for concern.

He stored his clothing in this room, slept and dreamed here. That was all. The thought of sharing it for some time with Honey's ghost was kind of nice.

Zeke wasn't in the room when Honey returned, wearing a towel. She stood in the middle of the room, looking around, absorbing the quiet in the cabin, which wasn't emptiness now as it had been this morning. Zeke was up front, in those two rooms in the old part of the house, probably deeply immersed in the past by now, reading some old document or journal or listening to some aged person's recollections of his or her life recorded on tape.

Honey had never seen Zeke in his study, but she could clearly visualize him in her mind and the picture she saw brought a little smile to her lips. He would be sprawled comfortably in the chair behind the massive old desk and there would be that absent look of concentration on his face as though he were looking at a mental television screen, seeing people and scenes out of the past, listening to voices and sounds characteristic of a bygone era. She'd seen that expression on his face several times today when he all but forgot she was there.

How wonderful it must be to have that kind of all-absorbing interest. She could almost envy him. Surprisingly, she didn't even resent his having left her to her own devices, but set about her chores contentedly.

While her shorts, underwear, and the original blouse she'd worn from the Greenbrier were being washed, she straightened the room, reflecting with a little grin that its orderliness had undergone considerable deterioration since her arrival. By the time she had finished, her clean clothes were ready to be transferred to the dryer. Until they were dry, she would simply have to put off getting dressed, since she had no other under-wear on hand.

Impulsively Honey eyed Zeke's laundry basket of dirty clothes. Maybe she should wash them for him. Of course, he was used to doing such tasks for himself, but maybe it would be nice for a change to have someone do it for him. Honey was bending over to pick up the basket when she stopped and straightened up again, shocked at the question that had popped out of no-where into her head: *If you stayed, what would you do with yourself when Zeke was busy in his study?*

What had made her even entertain such a thought? She wasn't going to stay here with Zeke. For one thing, he would never go for the idea. Would he? And even if he should be willing, she couldn't see herself living in this environment.

Honey stood there in a kind of trance, watching her clothes through the glass door of the dryer as they went round and round. She thought of all the little towns and hamlets she and Zeke had passed through that day, connected by narrow mountain roads with only here and there a lonely cabin or house trailer, thought of the people she'd glimpsed along the way or seen and heard at closer quarters in the store at Oak Hill and later at the restaurant up at Hawk's Nest. Plain, down-to-earth people. What would it be like to live among them? The idea was strange.

Oh, it had been a wonderful day. She'd taken pleasure in the lush greenery and the fresh mountain air she was drawing into her lungs, shaken her head in amusement along with Zeke at the "gift shops" appear-ing around bends in the roads at the most unexpected times, offering incredible collections of junk manufac-tured in Taiwan or Hong Kong, enjoyed virtually every minute of Zeke's company. But how would she get along in his habitat when he wasn't at her side?

Glumly Honey opened the door of the dryer, determined that both her blouse, a light permanent-press blend, and her underwear were dry, took them out, and then went to get dressed, leaving the lone pair of shorts to continue drying.

During this time Zeke's concentration hadn't been total. He had been aware of the quiet sounds at the back of the cabin. At first he had been expecting her almost at any time to make an exploratory trip up to his study, whose door he had left just barely ajar. To leave it wide open would have seemed an invitation he wasn't sure at all he wanted to extend; to have closed it might have been a rebuff. When she didn't come, he relaxed and discovered a sense of pleasure in knowing that she was there in the cabin, moving about on her own, performing her tasks. When the sounds ceased, he went looking for her.

Chapter Seven

Zeke experienced a ridiculous little spurt of panic when he couldn't find Honey anywhere in the back of the house. The damp towel in the bathroom was the only indication that she'd taken a shower. The bedroom had been returned to its spartan order. He took some reassurance in the one tangible sign of her presence, the supple leather handbag lying on the bureau, which presumably now held the little zippered makeup bag and its contents. Obeying impulse, Zeke opened the closet doors, noted the pink knit outfit still hanging in the same place and left the doors open.

"Honey?" he called out on his way through the kitchen to check the laundry room. "Where are you hiding?" Faintly he heard her voice answering him.

"Out here, Zeke," Honey called over her shoulder and sat half-turned, waiting for him to open the door from the laundry room to the tiny back stoop. She had stepped outside fifteen or twenty minutes earlier and been lulled into sitting down on the top step and listening to the sounds of birds carrying on the business of their lives in accompaniment to the quiet splash of water.

"What are you doing out here?" Zeke stuck his head out and took a quick look at her before he stepped out onto the stoop. To his surprise she didn't appear to be irritated, bored, or restless, and he'd fully expected to be greeted with some composite of those states of mind.

"Just thinking." Honey smiled up at him, amused and intrigued at the expression on his face, a mixture of caution, relief, and simple gladness.

"Thinking about what?" Zeke dropped down next to her on the step, pleasurably stirred by the sight and smell of her. She looked dainty and crisply clean in white blouse and jeans, the combination bringing together the sophisticated woman who'd arrived in the limousine yesterday and the fun-loving companion who'd let him outfit her in a discount store for a tramp through the woods. He could tell that she'd made light, expert use of the makeup that had been spilling over the top of his bureau, but, to his deep satisfaction, she didn't have that "perfect" look he'd found so disturbing yesterday. Perhaps it was because her hair was still damp.

"About you," Honey replied idly and then couldn't keep her smile from broadening at the flicker of surprise in his face.

"No wonder you look so relaxed, as though you're about to fall asleep," he quipped dryly. "No problems figuring out how to work the washer and dryer?" He touched the sleeve of her blouse lightly with his fingertips.

Honey eyed him for a moment with raised brows.

"You mean you aren't even the least bit curious? I'm not even going to get the standard penny offer for my thoughts?"

"Of course, I'm curious."

She waited again, but apparently his rather blunt admission was all the questioning she was going to get.

"Well, then, I'll tell you. I was wondering what your plans are for your career. Do you intend to go back to teaching in a university after you've finished your research project here and finished expanding your dissertation into a book?"

Zeke took note of her faintly nettled tone as he slumped forward, leaning his elbows on his knees. His gaze was directed outward at the woods behind the cabin as he answered as honestly as he could.

"I don't exactly intend to do that, not at this point in time, but I probably will."

He looked around at her to verify what he had expected: it wasn't answer enough. He sighed gently and waded into further explanation. "It's probably inevitable that I'll go back to teaching. That's the most likely means for someone with my academic credentials to earn a livelihood and not one that I find especially distasteful, even though I don't find it especially appealing, either. I'm much happier doing what I'm doing right now than I was teaching, although teaching had its satisfactions, too. Now and again there was that rare student who had some interest other than credit for the course."

Zeke eyed her hopefully and then shrugged when he saw that she still wasn't satisfied. It was all the answer he had, right now, anyway.

"You mean you have no definite plans beyond what you're doing right now?"

He shook his head firmly. "None at all, I promise you. Now you can understand—"

Honey didn't give him the chance to elaborate on what his lack of definite plans should help her to understand. She broke in to pursue her own line of thoughts.

"How long is it going to take you to finish what you're working on now?"

"You mean how long can I 'afford' not to go back to teaching?"

Honey felt her face grow warm under his shrewd gaze, but she didn't back down.

"If that's the way you want to put it."

Zeke's wry little half smile came as a relief, since it indicated that he wasn't offended by her prying into what was clearly none of her business.

"I should be able to live as I'm living now for a couple of years. That should be time enough. By then, I should have finished both the oral history study and the book and will probably be ready for a change. Either I will go back to teaching or something else will turn up." He stopped, watching the concentration grow on her face. "What?" he demanded lightly.

"Your book—maybe it will be successful, you know, the way some nonfiction books are. Maybe you should even be thinking ahead to promoting it. Your publisher could arrange for you to be a guest on TV talk shows, that sort of thing. Well, why not?" she put in sharply, reacting to the deepening patience on Zeke's face. "Don't you have any confidence in your own book? Don't you think it'll be good?"

Zeke was not about to be pushed into a silly, heated exchange. "Yes, I do think it'll be good. And I hope it will be favorably received among those who have an interest in its subject matter. Possibly it might even enjoy a limited regional popularity. But without any doubt, a book on the history of coal mining and lumbering in West Virginia is not destined to show up on the best-seller lists, nor is its author going to be sought after as a guest on television talk shows. Sorry, Honey, but there's no big success story in the offing here. I'll never be rich or famous, and it doesn't matter a bit, doesn't change a thing. This is still the right life for me, even if it wouldn't suit most people.''

Honey pursed her lips rebelliously.

"It might be enough for you now, Zeke, but will it always be enough? Don't you ever get lonely living all by yourself? Don't you ever think it might be nice to have someone to share your life with? One of these days you might wake up and realize that history isn't enough—''

Zeke cut off the torrent of words he didn't want to hear by leaning over and pressing his lips against hers and then pulling them away with an exaggerated smack. "It isn't enough right this second," he declared good-humoredly, "but do we really have to talk about it?" He slid his arm around her and drew her close against him while he kissed her again, more lingeringly this time. What had been initiated primarily as a means to end a pointless discussion quickly became something else entirely as his breathing quickened in response to her nearness and he felt himself being immersed in her sweetness.

"You see what I mean?" Honey managed to put in between kisses. "For someone who doesn't ever intend to get married, you certainly do seem to enjoy loving." As if proving her point, Zeke claimed her lips again, but Honey clung to her idea and advanced it breathlessly at the next break. "I guess you think you can just go out and pick up some unsuspecting woman and bring her home for a day or two to satisfy your male appetite."

"Sure sounds like a good idea," Zeke joked huskily. Privately he was amazed at the extent of his "appetite" where she was concerned. "Maybe I should go back to being a river guide, on an occasional basis, anyway. I could let all the outfitters know I will guide for them, free of charge, whenever they have a group of mixed company from one of the classier resorts, most notably the Greenbrier. I'll lure the most beautiful woman in the group back here to my cabin, make love to her until she's so hopelessly smitten that she insists on giving me a luxury, expense-paid holiday. Sound good?"

"Sounds familiar."

Even as she made this mock-serious retort and then smiled with him at his foolishness, Honey knew he was deliberately evading a serious discussion of his life. She might have persisted in her questions if she hadn't been so uneasy with her own motives for asking them. Why should she want Zeke to be anything but happy with the life he had chosen?

"You know, there's a certain amount of danger in your plan," she teased. "You may develop a taste for luxury. What will you do during the winter months when there's no rafting to bring in new female prey?"

Zeke hugged her closer and pressed his cheek against her hair. "I don't know about developing a taste for luxury, but I do know I'm becoming quite addicted to the taste of Honey, capital H."

His words hit a chord of reminiscence inside Honey, who sighed softly and nestled closer against his chest. "Oh, Zeke, that reminds me of something I hadn't thought of in years. My dad used to call me Honey-With-A-Capital-H."

Zeke suffered another attack of that sensation he'd had earlier in the day, of the moment's being too good. Once again the excess of pleasure was impossible to explain under the circumstances, and he was uneasy with his emotion.

"Speaking of your father, did his marriage that was such a trauma for you work out?"

"Yes, it did. It worked out beautifully. Dad and Bev are very happy together. I'm so glad I didn't succeed in spoiling things for Dad."

Zeke was relieved to feel the poignance inside him ease away as Honey responded to his prompting and got quite involved in telling him about her father. After a while they went inside the cabin and made a leisurely process of preparing dinner and eating it. Zeke kept the conversation light and playful and managed to push aside any thought of how empty these back rooms of the cabin, where he performed the everyday tasks of living, were going to be when she was gone.

The next morning he awoke early and considered getting up very quietly so as not to disturb her and going to his study. But instead he just lay there, watching her sleep, feeling her bare thigh warm against his. When her eyes opened unexpectedly, there was no opportunity for him to mask whatever unguarded emotions might be there in his face for her to read.

"You look so serious," Honey murmured sleepily, raising a hand to his face and gently stroking along his beard-stubbled cheek. "What are you thinking about?"

Zeke managed a grin. "Of course, I look serious. I'm wondering what the hell I'm going to pack to wear at the Greenbrier. I don't want to embarrass you by looking like a resident hick."

Honey smiled drowsily, closed her eyes again, and snuggled up close to him. "Don't be silly. Your clothes will be fine. If you need something you don't have for tennis or golf or riding, there are excellent shops right on the premises. I'll buy you whatever you need. You're my guest, remember, just like I've been your guest here. No arguments."

"Who's arguing?" Zeke wisecracked, sounding a little hollow to his own ears. "I just can't wait to get started, that's all."

It was a lie, of course. He wasn't looking forward to going to the Greenbrier with her, and yet he intended to live up to his promise. For one thing, he simply lacked the guts to do what he should do: deliver her safely and drive off. He couldn't resist the allure of spending a little more time with her. Besides that, he thought it would come home to both of them even more dramatically in her ambiance than here, in his own habitat, that despite their attraction to each other, they were entirely unsuited and should not get any more deeply involved. The thought of not seeing her again was already painful to Zeke.

Honey's thinking was drastically different from Zeke's and entirely optimistic. She just knew the two of them were going to have a great time at the Greenbrier. Zeke would see how false some of his notions were about the kind of people who could afford to vacation there. As good-looking and clever and well-educated as he was, he would fit in fine and realize their worlds were not as incompatible as he claimed. But it would be better for her to let him make this discovery for himself.

So neither of them confided his or her real thoughts to the other. They joined in a lighthearted conspiracy to pretend that no future lurked beyond the present. On the drive to White Sulphur Springs they talked and laughed over the noise of the Jeep, two people utterly delighted in each other's company, enjoying the passage between his world and hers.

But on their arrival at the Greenbrier, Zeke fell silent, growing more intimidated by the minute and more fiercely resentful of his own reaction to the pervasive atmosphere of wealth and privilege. Once he had turned into the main entrance between sedate white-painted brick pillars and entered the lovely, perfectly tended grounds, the engine of the Jeep seemed to grow steadily louder and intrusive. The gaiety in Honey's voice sounded forced to his ears as minutes later a huge white-columned building loomed into view and she announced, "That's the main hotel. Just follow this street around to the right. It'll take us to the front lobby."

"Some place," Zeke said somberly, taking in the formal gardens and immaculate grounds. Under the large portico at the front entrance, he pulled the Jeep up behind a Silver Cloud Rolls and switched off the key, feeling more conspicuous than he'd ever felt before in his life. Two limousines were unloading passengers and luggage. One of the uniformed bellmen glanced over in the direction of the Jeep as Zeke and Honey climbed out.

"Please leave your keys in the car, sir," he called out with routine courtesy.

Zeke had taken his keys out. He dropped them onto the seat and reached through the open window for his suitcase, but Honey stopped him before he could lift it out.

"Don't bother with that," she told him casually. "Someone will park your car and bring your luggage in. We can just go on in and get you registered."

Zeke's face plainly told her his feelings, even though

he didn't argue. It was damned silly in his opinion to have someone else park his car and carry in his one suitcase when he was well able to take care of both tasks himself, being neither old nor infirm. Filled with misgivings, he followed behind her and entered a spacious, high-ceilinged foyer tiled in huge squares of black-and-white marble, flooded with light through lovely tall windows, and elegantly furnished with wing-backed chairs. Broad shallow marble stairs in the center led down to a lower level while flanking stair-cases on each side led upward. Zeke glanced up at the higher landing to his right and read the discreet, black-lettered sign on a little stand requesting that only those with proper attire should use the upper, main lobby.

"Honey—" He reached out and grasped her by the shoulder as she started to move toward the steps leading down to the mezzanine. She stopped and looked back with good-natured questioning, her un-awareness making matters doubly hard for him. "Honey, I don't think I can go through with this after all," he said apologetically. "This place is a bit much. I just don't see any point—"

Honey was making a little face at him. "Don't be silly. You'll get used to it. Come on." She took his hand and pulled him toward the shallow marble stairs with their gleaming brass balustrades. "You promised—you can't back out now."

Zeke had little choice but to let himself be drawn along and gradually he lost the sense of being conspicu-ous. The registration area of the lower lobby was crawling with people who didn't look particularly im-pressive, and Honey acted as though she were at least part owner of the place. She made short work of getting him registered as her guest. By then their bellman had arrived for instructions and arranged to meet them up in the main lobby, where he would take them to Zeke's room, located in the north wing.

"Are you sure we're properly attired for the main lobby?" Zeke demurred ironically as he mounted the marble stairs beside her.

"Of course, we are, silly," she dismissed smilingly. "You can get by wearing anything but shorts and a bathing suit, and I've seen people breeze through in those, too."

While they paused up in the main lobby, waiting for the bellman, Zeke had an opportunity to look around and take in the mammoth dimensions which were accentuated by an incredibly bold decorating scheme. The main "lobby" was actually a whole series of huge, connected rooms with lofty ceilings and great, high windows that seemed to bring the lovely outdoors right inside. The floor was an oversized checkerboard of polished black-and-white marble squares. The colors used in upholstery and draperies were gaily flamboyant, bright reds and yellows and greens. The prints and stripes were on the same grand scale as the dimensions of the rooms themselves. It was all so unabashedly lavish that Zeke felt a grin of disbelief spreading across his face.

"Isn't it great?" Honey demanded happily. "Can you imagine how big this looked to me when I was just a little kid?" The bellman had joined them now and was leading the way toward the adjoining room. Zeke couldn't fail to notice that Honey seemed largely oblivious to the man's uniformed presence while Zeke himself was strongly aware of the absurdity of the situation. He could be carrying his own suitcase and surely he and Honey together were intelligent enough to locate the room, even in this monstrous bulk of a building.

"This place is just reeking with history, but unfortunately I can't remember much of it," Honey confessed ruefully, after a fruitless attempt to dredge some facts and figures out of memory. "I do seem to recall that the decorating scheme, which dates back to the forties, was the work of a big New York society decorator . . . hm, what was her name? Dorothy Draper, that was it! Her theory was that people come to a spa to let go and enjoy themselves. Therefore, the atmosphere should be a drastic change from what they're used to in their homes, gay and festive, not dignified and restful."

"Sounds like a perfectly logical theory to me," Zeke offered agreeably. He was appreciative of her transparent effort to appeal to his interest in history.

In the elevator Zeke was once again strongly conscious of the presence of the bellman and would have exchanged some pleasantry with the man if the latter had so much as allowed eye contact, but he stolidly fixed his gaze on the floor numbers lighted in turn over the door, evidently content as was Honey with the pretense that he was invisible.

After the opulence of the public rooms downstairs, the corridor down which the bellman led them would have seemed like any corridor in a large, old-fashioned hotel except that this one had garish, clashing wallpaper and carpet that, combined with the subdued lighting, gave a sense of claustrophobia. When they arrived at last at Zeke's room, it came as a pleasant surprise to him. Located in a corner overlooking the formal gardens fronting the North Wing portico, it was bright with natural light, cheerful, and homey. The solid, old-fashioned furnishings, painted glossy white, were graceful but not at all pretentious, and the room itself was smaller than those in high-priced chain hotels. The bathroom had huge, dated porcelain fixtures and a sober black-and-white marble floor in one-inch tiles.

"Nice," Zeke approved, relaxing once the bellman had been tipped and gone away, leaving Zeke and Honey alone.

"I told you that you'd like it here," Honey chided fondly, coming over to him and hugging him around the waist. "I just wish now I hadn't agreed to share a cottage, but, of course, I didn't know. . . ." She lifted her face for his kiss. "It might be awkward for the others to explain to their children why 'Aunt Honey' is bringing a man friend back to share her bedroom, and, besides, we will have more privacy here."

Zeke knew the situation and agreed. He hadn't come here to socialize with Honey's friends but to be with her. Besides, now that he was here and had seen the place, it would be reassuring to know that he had this snug little corner in the huge hotel complex where he could come and feel comfortable being Zeke McCade.

"Now I'm going to leave you while you unpack and go and change clothes." After another kiss, Honey pulled away. "When you're finished, you can walk over to the cottage on South Carolina Row. Where's your map? I'll show you."

After she was gone, Zeke didn't begin unpacking at once. He stood with his hands in his pockets looking around the room for several seconds, wondering how in the hell he'd ever agreed to this. Then he walked over to one of the windows and surveyed the scene below. Big circular beds ablaze with russet blooms. Marigolds? People coming and going on the brick walkways, many of them dressed in tennis clothes and carrying racquets.

The familiar dark green limousines pulling up to pick up or discharge passengers, many of them golfers in their bright prints and plaids with color-coordinated visors. Apparently there was limousine service to wherever one wanted to go.

Zeke's attention narrowed as Honey emerged and became a part of the leisurely bustle. Today she was attired in her Greenbrier outfit, the tan shorts, white blouse, and leather sandals, her handbag strap slung over one shoulder. Striding purposefully along the brick walkway curving to her right through the garden, she looked absolutely in her element, even before she waved to a couple approaching the hotel, carrying tennis racquets. Zeke watched her until she was no longer in sight and then turned abruptly away from the window, feeling bleak and alone and irritable at himself. "Fool," he muttered aloud.

It didn't take long to unpack. He hadn't come planning to stay more than a day or two. When he'd finished, taking up only a small space in the huge closet out in the foyer and only one of the ample drawers in the bureau, he picked up a dark green folder from the little desk in the corner and settled down in one of the two cushioned arm chairs to look through it, finding what he'd been seeking almost at once. A discreet leaflet entitled TARIFF SCHEDULE had all the prices listed inside. As he glanced through it, Zeke whistled his amazement. He'd known the Greenbrier was expensive, but not this expensive. Did Honey realize how much her little holiday was costing her? She'd always come with her father before and hadn't had to pay.

Zeke folded the leaflet and stuck it into his shirt pocket, intending to show it to her, and then turned his attention to the other information in the folder, includ-

ing a pamphlet on the historical background of the
Greenbrier. Anyone watching him would have found
the play of expressions on his face interesting as he read
through the pamphlet, automatically storing away the
facts and names in his memory. He grunted cynically at
the statement that the Greenbrier had done quite well
during the depression of the 1930s, since many of its
wealthy patrons found it cheaper to take up residence
there than to maintain expensive summer estates. His
eyebrows lifted in interest at the information that
German and Japanese diplomats had been interned
there at the hotel in the winter of 1941–1942, and he
looked pleased at the realization that this very room he
was sitting in had been used as a hospital room from
1942 until the end of the war, during which time the
U.S. government owned the Greenbrier and operated
it as a military hospital.

By the time he'd read through the pamphlet, Zeke
felt better about being at the Greenbrier. Even a
sketchy knowledge of the history of the old spa made it
less intimidating for him in the present. He could now
look upon it as a place of historical interest and not just
the pleasure ground of a wealthy class of people with
whom he had little in common.

Putting the folder aside, Zeke left the secure little
haven of his room and went to find Honey. Along the
way, nobody paid him any special attention whatever, a
fact which caused him some private amusement. Apparently it didn't show that he was a total outsider.

Zeke took pleasure in his surroundings as he walked
through the central park area with its graceful old oak
trees and neatly clipped lawn and then turned right to
pass in front of a line of detached cottages called
Baltimore Row and then the next group, Tansas Row,

before coming to South Carolina Row. Thanks to the pamphlet on the Greenbrier's historical heritage, he knew that the cottages dated back to the 1800s and had housed the aristocratic southern families who came each summer not only for the healing properties of the spring water but also for the social atmosphere.

The cool spacious front porches of the cottages would have been abuzz with southern cadences in the afternoons and the tinkle of ice as young ladies and gentlemen sipped sweet minty punch heavily spiced with bourbon while they flirted away the hours before the evening ball. Today, more than a hundred years later, the front porch of South Carolina A, shaded by a red-and-white striped awning like the rest of its mates on South Carolina Row, was unoccupied. As he climbed the steps up to the porch, Honey appeared at once in an open door at the far end.

"So you found me. Come on down here and I'll show you my room," she invited.

Zeke saw that she had changed into pale yellow slacks with a matching top in a crinkly material. Her hair was done in the sleek, turned-under style again and her makeup was subtly perfect, but the warmth in her dark eyes and the eagerness in her smile reassured him that her reversion to the Honey of three days ago was only exterior. When he put his arms around her, she stepped into them and pressed close without any hesitation, tilting her head a little backward for his kiss, which developed into more than a casual greeting. Anyone passing by and seeing them in the open doorway, totally oblivious to the scrutiny of the outside world, might have guessed from the urgency of their embrace that they were lovers coming together after a long absence, not a mere thirty minutes' separation.

Finally they managed to find a stopping point, but stood there close together, faces a few inches apart, smiling at each other.

"It's been such a long time," Zeke joked unsteadily. "Good to see you again."

Honey's smile broadened as she drew in a much-needed gulp of air. "It's so good to see you," she said softly. Framing his face in her hands, she pressed her lips to his in a quick kiss and then turned sideways in his arms, drawing him inside her room. "I'm so glad you're here, Zeke," she declared happily. "Here" meaning, of course, not just here in her room, but at the Greenbrier with her, sharing her world, her life.

Zeke glanced around her room, which was a little larger than his own but furnished with the same simple elegance, floral-printed draperies and bright red upholstery on the armchairs giving a splash of cheerful color.

"What's this with the single beds anyway?" he inquired dubiously, eyeing hers with their varnished mahogany headboards. The two in his own room were four-posters with tall, carved posts painted glossy white. "Does the Greenbrier have something against two people sharing a bed?"

Honey shrugged laughingly. "I've never given it a thought before." She snuggled closer to Zeke. "This will be my first time here to share a bed with a man. The smaller the better."

The sound of voices from outside made them both come to the realization simultaneously that they weren't alone in the world. Honey slipped free of his encircling arm and went over quickly to ease the door leading onto the porch quietly shut.

"That's Susan and her two daughters, Sarah and Serena," she whispered, tiptoeing back to Zeke. "Sit down," she urged, pointing to one of the two armchairs. "They probably won't be here long, and Susan doesn't know I'm back yet."

They sat like conspirators, listening to the sounds in the old cottage and grinning at each other until the coast was clear again.

"You're not putting off telling your friends that I'm here, are you?" There was a note of seriousness beneath the teasing in Zeke's voice.

"Of course, I'm not! I just don't want to share you until I have to. That's all." Honey's face was as indignant as her voice, convincing Zeke that she was being truthful with him.

"Where were we when we were interrupted?" He pretended to be probing his memory. "Ah, yes, I believe we were discussing the subject of twin beds at the Greenbrier. . . ." He wiggled his eyebrows Groucho Marx–style and eyed the two beds with a lascivious expression that made her giggle appreciatively.

"Sex. That's all you men think about." It was hard to sound cross and smile at the same time. "Now, what would you like to do this afternoon? No, seriously," she admonished when he went through the Groucho Marx routine again. "It's early. We can do just about anything you want to do. It's such a glorious day. Would you like to play golf or tennis?" The rueful apology on Zeke's face was answer enough. Before he could speak, she rushed on, giving him additional options. "We could go horseback riding, too. I haven't done that in ages. There are miles of bridle paths and some sensational views. Or swimming—what about swimming?"

Zeke smiled in response to the frankly wheedling tone of her voice. Settling back in his chair, he crossed his left ankle over his right knee.

"I never promised you it would be easy to entertain me," he teased lightly. Earlier when he had read through the lengthy list of diversions offered by the Greenbrier, he'd known they would be having this discussion sooner or later. "I grew up playing all the usual 'middle-class' sports—baseball, basketball, football. There wasn't a single tennis court in the whole town and the closest golf course was a private one owned by a country club in the next county. In college I tried playing tennis a few times, but never could get interested in batting a little ball back and forth across a net." He shrugged philosophically. "Sorry, Honey, but you've got yourself a guy here who never learned to appreciate leisure-class sports." *A guy who obviously didn't fit into your world.* Zeke didn't think it was necessary to finish the thought that was clear to both of them. Under her thoughtful gaze, he discovered that he was sorry, purely on her behalf. If he didn't watch himself, he'd be offering to take tennis and golf lessons!

"I can understand why golf and tennis wouldn't appeal to you," Honey said reflectively. "They probably seem awfully tame in comparison to white water rafting."

The little note of admiration took Zeke so utterly by surprise that he stared at her while he came forward in his chair, planting both feet firmly on the carpeted floor. Abruptly he gave his head a little shake.

"That's not it at all, Honey. Don't go making me into some macho adventurer type because I'm not. The reason I don't play tennis or golf or have any interest in learning them is that I don't have the background—"

"Don't be silly!" Honey scoffed, waving aside his explanation. "Lots of perfectly ordinary people play tennis and golf. Besides, it doesn't matter a bit to me whether you ever pick up a tennis racquet or a golf club. It's much too nice a day to sit here and argue. Why don't we go for a walk around the grounds and just let inspiration strike? You'll want to see the old spring house and taste the sulphur water. I can warn you it's awful!" She made a little disdainful face and then brightened at a new idea. "Then there's the Presidents' Cottage, which is a museum. You probably want to look through it."

Zeke smiled as he rose from his chair and held out a hand to her. "I thought you'd never ask."

Honey took his hand in both of hers and squeezed it as she grinned back at him. Mingled relief and gladness welled up inside her as she willingly let Zeke draw her closer to him for a brief, tender kiss that she sensed he offered to signal a momentary truce. In her mind there was no need for a truce, since she refused to see herself in an adversarial position. The battle between them was all in Zeke's mind as was his perception of them as separated by serious differences.

Zeke had very mixed feelings about the outcome of the exchange, which he had known to be inevitable almost from the moment he agreed to come with Honey to the Greenbrier. On the one hand, he found Honey's refusal to face up to facts both flattering and endearing. He was almost tempted to let himself believe that the disparities in background and values *weren't* significant, but the realist in him wouldn't be bribed by wishful thinking into agreement.

"A walk is an excellent idea," he declared cheerfully as they set out for the spring house. "Walking is such a universal exercise."

Honey laced her fingers a little tighter in his and met his glance with a smiling expression that told him more eloquently than words her feelings of that moment. She didn't care if walking were universal or rare. It was delightful being in his company. His presence added a wholly new element to her appreciation of familiar surroundings, and it amused her no end that in such a short time he already knew more about Greenbrier landmarks than she did herself.

"Isn't it pretty?" she mused as they approached the lovely little spring house, with its green copper-domed roof supported by white columns. "The bronze statue at the top is some mythical goddess—I forget who."

"Hygeia," Zeke supplied promptly. "Goddess of health."

"If you say so," Honey teased, regarding him with raised brows. "Did you recognize her from past association or just make an educated guess?"

Zeke loftily ignored her question. "A gift from Stephen Henderson, the wealthy New Orleans planter who built for his own use the cottage that was later to be known as the Presidents' Cottage because so many United States presidents spent their summers there."

"You took the words right out of my mouth. Whose tour is this, anyway?" Honey led the way down to the sunken floor of the spring house and filled a paper cup with water from the fountain. "Here, smarty pants. I suppose you know you shouldn't drink too much of this foul-tasting stuff because it has the effect of a laxative."

"Purgative," Zeke corrected, supplying the term people of the previous century would have used. He ducked his head as though expecting her to douse him with the contents of the tiny paper cone. When she just wrinkled her nose at him, he took the cone and drank a sip. "God, that is awful. It tastes like—"

"Sulphur," they both spoke in unison and then succumbed to gales of laughter that brought tears to their eyes. If someone had asked them what was so funny, they'd have been hard put to give a plausible answer.

"Well, shall we proceed to the Presidents' Cottage?" Zeke prompted when their mirth had finally subsided.

"Why not? I can't wait to hear all about it."

"Not a word. I promise."

"Don't promise. I couldn't bear to witness such human pain."

"You're right. I take the promise back."

Laughing and sparring, they crossed the lush green lawn to an austere white-colonnaded building, holding hands. It was the last place Honey would have chosen, on her own, to spend such a glorious afternoon at the Greenbrier, and she was sure she had never been this happy before in her life.

Chapter Eight

There was no way Honey could avoid spending at least part of the evening with her old friends and their spouses.

"I promised we'd meet the others for drinks in the Old White Club after dinner," she explained apologetically to Zeke when she went up to his room a little past seven, dressed for dinner. "At least we won't be eating with them. They'd already made reservations in the Tavern Room for eight-thirty, and I told them that was too late for us. We'd both be starving by then, since we didn't really have lunch." They'd stopped on the way to the Greenbrier and eaten a mid-morning meal at some little country diner.

"We're not having dinner in the Tavern Room, are we?" Zeke demanded so sternly that Honey eyed him in puzzlement.

"Why, no. I thought we'd eat in the regular dining room tonight, if that's okay with you."

She watched him stride over to the bureau and pick up the creased "Schedule of Tariffs" he hadn't gotten around to discussing with her that afternoon.

"Have you ever taken a look at this?" he asked soberly, holding it out to her. "Do you know how much extra it costs, above and beyond the room cost, which includes breakfast and dinner, to eat in the other restaurants besides the regular dining room? And every single thing you do at this place costs extra. There're fees for tennis, golf, horseback riding—I'm surprised you don't have to pay for a dip in the pool or a sip of water at the spring house. I hope you can afford these prices, Honey, because as you can see, these few days are costing you a small fortune."

Honey dutifully looked at the card and then up at Zeke, somewhat at a loss as to how to handle the situation tactfully.

"It's just for a few days so it really won't be that much. If it'll make you feel better," she added quickly, "we really don't have to eat in the other restaurants, although I did want us to have the lunch buffet down at the Golf Club. I hear it's really outstanding."

"You're telling me you can afford to pay those prices," Zeke said soberly.

Honey made a face at the card she held as though it were responsible for the troublesome discussion and then walked over to drop it into the trash can.

"I can't remember asking you whether you could afford supplies for breakfast or clothes for me to wear on our hike into the woods," she pointed out mildly. "Yes, I can afford a few days here at the Greenbrier. It's all just a matter of perspective, Zeke. If I decided I wanted to come here, I would come and enjoy myself even if I were spending the balance in my bank account. I just don't look upon all *this*—" she gestured with both hands to take in the room and the outside environs with all those additional fees he had mentioned "—as extravagant the way you do. Please. Enjoy yourself and don't worry about the cost, or you're going to spoil everything for us."

"I won't mention another word," Zeke promised so grimly that Honey couldn't hold back a smile. "I'll enjoy myself if it kills me," he added ruefully.

"That's all I ask," she retorted softly, coming up to him and putting her arms around his neck. "Just that and a kiss. You look so handsome dressed up in a jacket and tie." She wasn't just being diplomatic with that last compliment. In her eyes, at least, he was going to be the best-looking man at dinner tonight. The navy jacket, which he wore as casually as he wore his plaid flannel shirts, accentuated the breadth of his shoulders. He seemed somehow taller and perhaps even more noticeably male in refined dress than he had been in jeans and sweatshirt back at the cabin.

Zeke just barely touched his lips to hers. "I'll mess up your lipstick," he protested gruffly, suffering some unavoidable pangs of male pride over the discussion he had just forced upon them, which reasserted that he could never afford her life-style, never afford her. When she had shown up minutes ago, she looked like she had stepped right off the page of a fashion magazine in a misty green dress of telltale simplicity and pearls. He had been overwhelmed by her chic and sophistication and yet so stirred by her femininity that he had to suppress the urge to take off the lovely wrappings and make love to her on one of the single beds in the room she was paying for. He'd wondered again what the hell he was doing there and resolved to return to his own element as soon as possible.

"The lipstick can be fixed," she coaxed, wetting her

lips with the tip of her tongue and then uttering a little moan of satisfaction when her provocation had the desired effect and Zeke crushed her mouth with his.

"Thank you," she murmured dreamily a minute or so later when reluctantly he lifted his head.

Zeke eyed her skeptically. "Why do you 'thank' me?"

"For messing up my lipstick."

They grinned at her deliberate foolishness, glad to be freed of all the unwanted restraints imposed upon them by differences and conscious only of the simple joy they found in each other's company, for whatever inexplicable reasons.

"Wait till you see yourself," Zeke warned, chuckling. "I did make quite a mess of it, but you asked for it."

Honey giggled. "Wait till you see yourself."

Together they moved over to the bureau and side by side inspected themselves and each other in the mirror. Zeke licked at the pink smear on his lips and then smacked.

"Not bad. Tastes pretty good . . . like Honey."

Honey met his mirrored gaze and was warmed all the way through by its intimate message. Taking a tissue in her hand, she turned to the solid flesh-and-blood man and gently wiped away her lipstick from his mouth. It took all her willpower not to say aloud what trembled in her heart, thrilling and scaring her at the same time: *Zeke McCade, I think I love you.* The time definitely wasn't right, and she needed to be sure before she spoke.

When she had finished, Zeke took the tissue and performed the same service for her, taking obvious enjoyment in the casual intimacy of the situation. Now that he had discovered for himself how touchable she still was beneath the gloss and finery, the urge to make love to her was a powerful one.

"Before you repair the damage . . ." He took a brief, deep kiss and then held her by the shoulders while he stepped back. "Better not take your time," he warned softly.

Honey understood perfectly the hazards of delay, but fought hard not to give in to temptation because she knew that if they made love now, they would spend the rest of the evening there in Zeke's room. While the prospect was an alluring one, it wasn't what she wanted the evening to be for them. Suddenly it was dawning clear to her exactly what she hoped to gain during their time together at the Greenbrier, and that purpose wouldn't be served by closeting themselves in Zeke's room. She wanted Zeke to see for himself that they could be right for each other in this environment—her environment, at least in Zeke's mind—as well as in any other.

"I really am starving. Aren't you?"

The tentative note drew a tolerant smile from Zeke, who understood that it was prompted by the desire not to offend him.

"Starving."

Dining in Colonial Hall was a formal, leisurely experience. One could rely upon superb food, faultless service, and an elegant setting. With the glitter of great chandeliers suspended from high ceilings and mellow strains of cello, violin, and grand piano from the chamber music ensemble, the background elements for romance were there to intensify the pleasure a man and a woman could feel in each other's company.

For Honey the first part of the evening she had planned turned out to be pure magic. She was beautiful and Zeke was handsome. In the midst of a multitude of other handsomely dressed diners, they were alone, their table an island for two. The sense of intimacy was paradoxically both relaxing and stimulating, making every sensory pleasure razor sharp. To Honey's delight, Zeke seemed unreservedly appreciative of their gracious surroundings, gave no hint of feeling out of place, made no mention of the price of such luxury.

"Would you like to have wine with dinner?" she asked with extreme casualness when they were looking over the evening's menu.

Alert to every nuance, Zeke looked up curiously. "Sure. That is, if you would like to."

"Why, yes, I would. I had just noticed that you don't seem to drink anything alcoholic." He had automatically turned down their waiter's offer of a before-dinner cocktail.

Zeke gave a little nod of comprehension and then grinned good-naturedly. "No, I'm not a reformed alcoholic. Lately I've gotten out of the habit of drinking, which was always pretty much a social habit with me, anyway. Except for a cold beer on a hot day, I'd never think of drinking alone. I really don't miss it, but, yes, a bottle of wine with dinner sounds nice." He turned his attention back to the menu. "I'm getting hungrier by the minute, but with choices like these, it's not going to be easy to decide. This is some menu."

Honey was as pleased as though he had complimented her personally. "I'm thinking of having either the leg of lamb or the roast duckling," she offered complacently.

They both settled on the leg of lamb, served with spoon bread and tarragon sauce. For the appetizer course, they had smoked salmon and vichyssoise for the soup selection. Zeke approved each course of the seven-course meal, but he declared that the lamb was undoubtedly the best he had ever eaten. While Honey managed to get down a few mouthfuls of lemon sherbet dessert, Zeke savored every mouthful of a rich pecan tart.

"Wonderful food," he said contentedly, sitting back to sip a second cup of coffee. "If I lived in the area, I'm afraid I'd have to save my pennies and splurge on a meal here occasionally."

Honey beamed but managed not to speak aloud her delight at this admission from Zeke that he could easily enjoy the finer, and more expensive, pleasures of life. After dinner they went for a leisurely walk out on the grounds, as lovely by night as by day, lighted by the moon and by hidden floodlights in the flower beds and shrubbery. Mellowed by the wine and the good food and utterly content with Zeke's company, Honey was torn when he asked if she really wanted to join the others for drinks, but the evening was working out so perfectly, just as she had wanted it to be, that she reluctantly said yes. Her friends would be hurt if they didn't at least have one drink with them.

The one drink turned into much more than that. The others had had cocktails before dinner as well as several bottles of wine and were in a convivial mood, welcoming Zeke into their company as though he were an old friend, too. Honey had already informed them of his real occupation, and at first the conversation centered on him. He seemed thoroughly relaxed answering their questions and exchanging banter.

It's going so well, just as I knew it would, Honey kept telling herself the first hour, and even through part of the second hour, when she had begun to look forward to the time when she and Zeke could break away. But he appeared to be enjoying himself thoroughly, drinking bourbon and water on the rocks, one after another, talking, laughing, dancing to music by the Populaires, not just with Honey but with DeeDee, Susan, and Amy Lou. The sight of another woman in his arms was anything but pleasurable to Honey, and it seemed to her that he was holding them much too close.

"If you're hoping to make me jealous, you're certainly succeeding," she told him very late in the evening when he was dancing with her. Vaguely she was aware that despite the effort it took to pronounce each word, her speech was still slurred. Taking a deep breath, she closed her eyes and was immediately hit by a wave of dizziness that made her lose step with the music. Zeke stopped, holding her tighter to steady both of them.

"You okay?"

"I think I'm drunk," she confessed apologetically, tightening her arms around his neck. It didn't matter the least to her that they were standing in one place on the dance floor, holding each other.

"I know damn well I'm drunk," he retorted cheerfully.

The distance from the Old White Club through the labyrinth of corridors, lobbies, elevator, and more corridors seemed endless to Honey. She would never have made it to Zeke's room if he hadn't half-supported and half-carried her, in spite of being not too steady on his feet himself.

In his room they managed, with difficulty, to get Honey undressed and into one of the single beds.

"Oh, I get so dizzy whenever I close my eyes," she wailed complainingly. "Why do people get drunk? It's such a stupid thing to do! Why did we stay there all evening? I kept wanting to leave, but you never would say anything!"

If talking hadn't seemed at that moment a huge and futile effort, Zeke would have replied that he hadn't wanted to have a drink with her friends in the first place. It had been her idea, and he had thought it her place to indicate when she wanted to leave. Instead he got out of his clothes after a lot of fumbling with buttons and zipper and fell down on the other bed, letting out a long groan and then muttering a curse word when he realized he had left the lights on and would have to muster the energy to get up again. Some of the fog in his head cleared as he identified the sounds coming from Honey's bed as sobs. Wearily he pushed himself up and looked over at her.

"What's wrong, sweetheart?" Carefully he negotiated the distance between the beds and lay down next to her. "Don't cry. It'll be all right," he crooned, gathering her close against him and fighting without much success the thick fog easing around his brain.

"It's all my fault," Honey whimpered. "All my fault." On this note of self-blame, she fell asleep, emitting a little half sob now and then that was lost in the sound of Zeke's deep labored breathing.

The next morning when she awoke, she was alone in the bed. Her mouth was bitter and dry and her skull felt like a tight-stretched drum being cruelly pounded with a giant hammer.

"God," came the low, anguished moan from the other bed.

Very gingerly Honey eased herself up on her elbows and rotated her head, an inch at a time, to look over at Zeke. He groaned again and then managed a wan grin as he met her gaze.

"You feel as rotten as I do?"

"Worse," she said tonelessly, noting with compassion the dark circles under his eyes and his pasty, unhealthy color. It was her fault that he looked like that. "Zeke, I'm sorry," she said in a miserable little voice.

He shook his head and then winced at the shooting pain. "No need to feel sorry."

"But I am," she went on sorrowfully. "If only I hadn't insisted on having a drink with the others. I was just so determined that you would have a good time." She paused and sighed gloomily. "I'll bet you didn't, did you? I'll bet you were bored stiff and that's probably why you drank too much."

Zeke wiped a hand across his face, summoned his courage, and sat up on the edge of the bed. He looked down at himself with mild interest and noticed that he still wore his dark cotton briefs and one sock.

"I couldn't tell you if I was bored or had a wonderful time," he said bluntly. "Isn't that the whole purpose behind getting bombed out of your mind? You don't know whether you're bored or interested, or whether you're boring or interesting, for that matter. It sure as hell doesn't matter one way or the other this morning, does it?" Realizing how cross he sounded, he tried to muster a conciliatory smile, which he was fairly certain looked more like a grimace in his present state.

"We didn't make love or even sleep together," Honey lamented.

Zeke tried the grin again and found that it felt less like a painful contortion. "We did sleep in the same bed part of the night—the part before I rolled off onto the floor. But it's pretty definite that we didn't make love. An excessive amount of alcohol doesn't work too well as an aphrodisiac."

While he was in the shower, Honey called room service and ordered coffee and orange juice to be sent up immediately and then breakfast an hour later. The coffee and orange juice arrived while she was in the shower. Feeling somewhat restored, she wandered out into the bedroom wrapped in a bath towel and sipped a glass of orange juice.

"Guess what just occurred to me?" she inquired cheerfully. "I don't have any clothes here except what I had on last night, and I can hardly traipse over to the cottage wearing that, looking like 'the morning after.'"

Zeke was looking considerably more like himself. He had already started in on the coffee.

"In a little bit I can walk over to the cottage," he offered. "You'll just have to give me some very detailed description of what you want me to bring back."

Honey gave the matter some thought. "Maybe I'll just call the shop downstairs and see what they have in my size. That'll be simpler. I'm thinking that by ten-thirty we both might be up to taking the tour of the hotel." The expression on Zeke's face brought a flood of dismay. "Zeke, you are staying at least today! You just got here yesterday!"

Zeke sighed. It was damned hard for him to say no to her under any circumstances, but out of the question when they both were hung over and sharing this sense of human frailty.

"Okay. I'll stay today, but that's all. Tomorrow I leave. Is that a deal?"

Honey decided not to push her luck. She would take the extra time he'd granted them and trust that his mind could be changed later. If they could salvage some enjoyment out of the day, despite hangovers, and then have a wonderful evening together, an evening that would include making love and not any excessive drinking, surely he'd want to stay at least another day.

After a leisurely breakfast they both felt on the way back to normal health. Dressed in a snappy navy-and-kelly-green outfit sent up from the shop downstairs, with espadrilles from the neighboring shoe shop across the way, she was ready to face the world outside. Down in the formal lobby, a group of guests were already assembled, waiting for the tour of the main hotel, which today was not being conducted, as was usual, by the social director, because she was on vacation. Taking her place was the Greenbrier historian, a pleasant, witty man of about forty.

What happened before Honey's eyes was so inevitable that she wondered why she didn't see the outcome sooner. It was only a matter of time before Zeke drew attention to himself with the knowledgable questions that he asked and his responses to the answers. By the time the tour had ended, the two historians were thoroughly engrossed in their own private exchange and Zeke had been issued a warm invitation to pursue the discussion of Greenbrier history in the historian's office and look at some very interesting items in the archives.

"Of course, I don't mind," Honey lied in a hollow voice.

It was a long, miserable day. She refused several invitations that might have helped the time to pass because she didn't want Zeke to come looking for her and find her gone. Besides, she didn't feel physically up to vigorous exercise like tennis or horseback riding.

When Zeke finally came to the cottage on South Carolina Row in the late afternoon, Honey was out on the shaded front porch on a wicker chaise longue, a magazine in her lap. The sight of him walking along with a spring in his step only deepened the disgruntlement she would try her hardest not to reveal to him.

"Have a good day?" she called out as he approached within hearing distance.

Detecting the forced cheer, Zeke didn't answer until he had bounded up the steps to the porch. One glance at her face told him the effort it was causing her to look bright and interested.

"I had a very interesting day. What about you?" He walked across the porch to the chaise longue and perched on the space she made for him by her legs.

"My day was fine." Under his steady gaze Honey gave up the pretence and grimaced. "No, it wasn't fine. It was boring. I missed you. But I'm glad you enjoyed yourself," she added quickly as he looked apologetic.

"It was rotten etiquette, I know, for me to go off without you for half the day, when, after all, I'm your guest. But you'd probably have been even more bored if you'd been there. And I didn't think there was any danger of your not being entertained."

Honey was sorry she'd put a damper on his good mood. She tried to undo the damage and soothe away his guilt, even while she took advantage of it.

"Normally I'd have been too busy to miss you," she protested lightly. "With a hangover, I just felt a little below par, that's all. But since you did ignore me most of the day, you'll have to stay tomorrow and make up for it."

The expression on Zeke's face didn't tell her much, but she sensed as he moved over to a cushioned wicker armchair that he was putting a little distance between them while he sorted out his reaction. She prepared herself for resistance, but not for flat refusal, and it hit her hard, much harder than she'd have thought.

"No, I can't stay tomorrow, Honey. I have to get back. Despite the fact that I don't punch a time clock, I have work to do, important work." His expression grew reflective. "Today helped me realize just how fortunate I am to be doing what I want to do, the way *I* think it should be done. I wouldn't trade places with Bob, for all the perks of being the Greenbrier historian."

"Why not? I would imagine that he's doing some of the same things you are. Collecting old photographs and memorabilia, talking to people about bygone eras." Honey's voice was sharp with her deep disappointment that Zeke obviously didn't want to stay longer and spend more time with her. Ironically, it had crossed her mind during the tour that morning that Zeke was qualified for the Greenbrier historian's job and there must be others like it, in attractive settings.

"He is," Zeke agreed earnestly. "I'm not belittling his work or him. He's doing a good job with a fascinating subject, but I wouldn't be comfortable with a situation where I was merely expected to add new pages to a glamorous legend. I see the Greenbrier historian as a glorified PR man."

What he was saying was utterly reasonable, but Honey clung to her opposition as though her very life depended on making him see that his attitude was narrow. Somehow his view of the Greenbrier historian's job was a judgment of the Greenbrier itself and of her. She had to defend all three.

"Remember when you took me into your cabin the first time and told me about what the original rooms were used for. You said you loved the idea of living in a place where former generations of people had lived. You liked the idea of human continuity. Well, you can't deny that you feel that here at the Greenbrier, Zeke. My God, everywhere you walk, there've been hundreds, no, thousands, of footsteps in that same place before you. If you didn't have such a bias against people with money, you'd appreciate the fact that the owners of the Greenbrier care about its history and make every effort to preserve tradition!"

Zeke had listened carefully to every word, growing more puzzled by the moment at her aggressive tone. He failed to see how he could have offended her personally by his comments, but he must have.

"You're right," he agreed. "One has to be grateful that there apparently is still a profit motive in continuing the Greenbrier's tradition as a place of relaxation for the rich, but—"

Whatever he had been about to say was totally forgotten as Honey's face crumpled unexpectedly into an expression of abject misery. Right before his eyes, her lips began to quaver, and tears welled up into her eyes and spilled over to form wet paths down her cheeks.

"Hey, what's wrong? Did I say something—" He got up and went quickly over to her, dropping to his knees beside the chaise longue.

Honey turned her face aside, wiping viciously at the tears, which had come upon her with such force and unexpectedness that she hadn't been able to keep them back. Suddenly everything had begun to look so hopeless. She was crying about a ruined evening the night before, a ruined day, a ruined future that she didn't have a prayer of salvaging.

"You didn't say anything to bring on this stupid sob scene, Zeke," she gulped angrily, despising herself for her weakness, but unable, nonetheless, to stop the flow of tears. "I—I'm just su—such a fool, that's all!"

As Zeke put his arms around her and gathered her close against his chest, nothing else seemed important in the world except consoling her. "Tell me why you're crying," he begged gently. Deep down, he already knew. The moment he had known was inevitable had come prematurely.

Honey leaned against him, desperately needing his strength. Waves of despair washed through her, one after another, rubbing abrasively over the ache of misery located right in the center of her chest.

"It's just so unfair, Zeke." She gulped into his shoulder so that the words were muffled. "I can't help being me, and you can't help being you. You've probably been right all along when you said we weren't right for each other, and yet—" She had to stop a few seconds and cope with the contractions of her throat muscles that played havoc with speech. "I just can't stand the thought—"

"I know, I know," he said in a low, heavy voice, tightening his arms around her as though resisting the reality that brought them such sadness.

"Why, Zeke? Why did we have to—to feel this way about each other if—"

"I don't know, Honey, I really don't. But it just wouldn't work, sweetheart. Now, please, don't cry." There was a note of real desperation in the plea. It was tearing Zeke apart to see her so vulnerable and unhappy. He wished that it was in his power to say healing words and make promises that would open up the future like an eastern sky flushed with the sunrise. But, God help him, none of that was in his power, and Zeke McCade was an honest man. All he could offer her was a sadness as deep as her own and a savage resentment that fate could be so cruel as to awaken longings that couldn't be satisfied.

Something about their combined misery was oddly heartening to Honey. She lifted her face away from the warmth of his shoulder and then pushed away from him so that she could look into his face.

"What would it hurt to give it a try, Zeke? No, wait, listen to me! Please. I'm willing to try to fit into your life, if you'll agree to let me." Zeke was closing his eyes to shut out the sight of her pleading, tearstained face, shaking his head.

"It won't work, Honey. You know it won't work."

"No, I don't know! All I know is that I can't stand the thought of having you drive off and leave me here alone tomorrow! Can you stand that thought, Zeke?" She waited tensely, not daring to breathe, while he opened his eyes and looked at her, his silence an affirmative answer that gave her the courage she needed to continue.

"It's too late to play it safe, Zeke. We should have thought of that days ago when you asked me to stay with you instead of coming back here to the Greenbrier with the others, and I stayed. Just think what we would have missed if I hadn't. You don't regret what we've had together so far, do you?"

"You know I don't."

Honey disregarded the quiet accusation that she wasn't playing fair. She slipped her arms up around Zeke's neck, ready to go for broke.

"What do you think, Zeke? Is it worth taking the risk?" she pleaded softly. "The worst that could happen is that it won't work. Isn't some time together better than none? I'm not saying that we have to get married. We could try living together for a few months and see how it works out, couldn't we?"

Zeke shook his head despairingly, not because he was going to hold out for what he knew was best, but because he wasn't.

"What are you going to do with yourself while I'm buried under a pile of old documents and photographs in my study? You'll be bored stiff in two days, Honey."

Honey tightened her arms around his neck and kissed him, hope blooming inside. His very phrasing of his protest encouraged her to think she'd won her case. "You underestimate my resources," she chided and then kissed him again, moving her mouth lingeringly on his and then taking nibbling tastes of first his top lip and then the fuller bottom lip until he was kissing her back hungrily, his hands caressing her back and shoulders so possessively that she knew without a doubt that he'd given in, despite his reservations. Only then did she realize how frightened she had been that she wouldn't be able to make him agree to give them a chance together. The enormous relief brought on a fresh onslaught of tears, of which Zeke was unaware until he tasted the saltiness and drew back to eye her with sharp concern.

"What's wrong?"

Honey drew a long, unsteady breath and smiled her reassurance. "I'm just so happy, that's all. So happy." She bumped her nose against his. "Would you rather check out and go back to your cabin tonight, or wait until tomorrow morning?"

"No big hurry," Zeke replied with gruff tenderness. He framed her face in his hands and gently swiped at the wetness on her cheeks with his thumbs. "We still have to try out those single beds. Hmmm?" He pressed his lips against hers in a kiss that quickly deepened from playfulness into passion. They were both breathing fast when their lips reluctantly parted.

"Yours or mine," Honey prompted softly, her head thrown back provocatively. "Single beds, I mean."

Zeke scooped her up in his arms and stood up.

"Yours now. Mine later," he declared on the way to her bedroom door.

"Hmmmm. Four beds all together. We're going to be busy. Maybe we'll have to skip dinner."

Zeke stood her on her feet and pushed open the door.

"Ha, not a chance. I'm not leaving the Greenbrier without one more feast like the one we had last night."

Honey ambled inside the room, her arms crossed over her chest, pretending to pout. It wasn't easy when she was bursting with happiness. "That's the real reason you want to stay tonight, isn't it? To get another good meal."

Zeke shut the door and locked it, then walked over to the interior door that opened into the cottage parlor and locked it, too.

"The price I'm paying per day for a room and two meals, I intend to get full benefit," he announced deliberately, coming toward Honey. "I am paying my own bill, you know. I had every intention of doing so from the beginning."

Honey opened her mouth, read the determination on his face, and then said nothing, smiling instead and holding her hands out to him. The one really crucial issue had been settled. That was all that really mattered.

Chapter Nine

"I guess a single bed is big enough," Honey murmured contentedly after they had made love and were lying close in each other's arms. She was filled with such utter certainty that the future would work out for them that she was compelled to probe a little into Zeke's feelings. "I guess we should have guessed after that first time we made love that we had something special going between us, shouldn't we?"

At first Zeke's hand caressing the bare planes of her back was answer enough, but then she wanted verbal confirmation. "You do think there is something special between us, don't you, Zeke?" She raised up far enough to look into his face.

The hint of anxiousness in her query brought a smile of reassurance to Zeke's lips that didn't erase the gravity from his eyes. "Of course, I do. Whatever it is, it was there ten years ago for me." He raised a hand to her face, which was all eager attention, and lightly traced each delicate feature.

"Why do you look so serious, then?" she chided. "Look on the bright side. We can do this—" She kissed him on the mouth, rubbing the peaks of her breasts provocatively across his chest. "Any time we want, morning, noon or night."

Zeke closed his arms around her and drew her down on top of him, pressing her head against his shoulder. He held her tight, so that she couldn't move.

"I don't mean to look serious, Honey. It's just that I can't imagine your fitting into my life, not for any length of time. We can't make love all the time." Honey's squirming efforts to free herself expressed her protest. Zeke held her prisoner against him long enough for him to finish what he wanted to say.

"Right now, it's a novel idea for you to live in the boondocks in a mountain cabin, but that novelty won't last long. I just don't want to build up hopes and dreams that can't come true. That's all." Zeke loosened his hold and Honey's head immediately popped up.

"But, Zeke, you've said yourself you don't even intend to live the rest of your life in a mountain cabin!" she pointed out with a touch of impatience.

"True, but I also have problems imagining you living contentedly in a modest professor's house in some university town." His expression became ruefully apologetic as Honey's face mirrored her hurt and disappointment that his own view of their future was so pessimistic. "I'm not being critical in the least," he added urgently. "There's no reason in the world you should want to live a life stripped of luxury and glamour. I'm just being honest with you, that's all." He forced a cheerful expression. "But you're right, I should look on the bright side. Right now I'm thinking about a shower for two and then . . ."

"I know what you're thinking about—dinner!" Honey's joking accusation was a little halfhearted and her smile a little wan, but the droop in spirits didn't last long. She would just have to let time prove to Zeke that he was wrong. Although she'd suggested a living arrangement on a trial basis, just to get him to agree, deep down Honey knew she was making a permanent choice in Zeke. How could a woman be so lucky as to find a man like him and then give him up?

Two weeks later she recalled the conversation in precise detail as she stood in the kitchen of Zeke's mountain cabin and dawdled over wiping the few dishes and pieces of cutlery from their lunch. Much as she hated to admit it, Zeke had been right. Honey was bored to death most of the time when she wasn't with Zeke. And she knew he wasn't spending nearly as much time on his work as he had before.

There wasn't enough housework and laundry to keep her busy, not with just the two of them, and Zeke refused to let her do everything, insisting that he hadn't brought her home with him to be a maid or housekeeper. This afternoon she faced a stretch of several hours with nothing, absolutely nothing, to do except somehow entertain herself. The cabin was clean, the laundry basket empty, the pantry well stocked with food. What was she going to do?

In the city there had always been shopping and friends to call, but she didn't have any friends here, didn't actually know anyone except Zeke. As for shopping, she'd made several excursions into Oak Hill the first week and bought a "mountain" wardrobe consisting mostly of jeans, gingham shirts, and practical

shoes. That left reading, watching television, or sitting
and watching the hands of a clock as possible ways to
while away the time.

The television set was located in the sitting room next
to Zeke's study. Honey wouldn't have wanted to risk
disturbing him. Besides, daytime television had no
appeal and the reception was terrible anyway. As for
reading, she didn't have anything on hand and was
probably too restless to sit still, even if she had.

As she hung the damp dish towel on a bar to dry,
Honey made up her mind. She simply had to go
somewhere and do something this afternoon, or she'd
be a basket case by the time Zeke emerged from his
study. Taking the keys to the Jeep, she eased quietly out
of the cabin, leaving a note on the kitchen table: *Back
by five. Love, Honey.*

She thought about the note as she started the Jeep
and backed it around. Her fingers had faltered over
that next-to-the-last word, *love*. Strange that she and
Zeke were so intimate and "loving" in their daily
relationship, and yet neither of them came out and said
to the other, *I love you*. Why was that? Perhaps it was
just unnecessary to voice what was obvious. They did
love each other. Or at least Honey was sure she loved
Zeke. Somehow his not voicing his feelings put a
restraint on her so that she couldn't voice hers.

From inside his study Zeke heard the Jeep engine
roar to life. He stopped mid-sentence and sat there
behind his desk, looking off into space, the expression
on his face an odd mixture of pleasure and sadness. The
pleasure rose from the reminder of Honey's presence
and the knowledge that she would be there later this
afternoon when he had finished with his work for the
day. The sadness came from the awareness that she
would soon run out of chores to fill her time, grow

bored with dull repetition and the lack of social stimulation in a rural environment.

He'd do whatever he could to keep her. He'd take off as much time as he could. They could drive into Charleston and stay overnight, have dinner, see a movie or a play. Charleston was a far cry from New York City, but it would look like a thriving metropolis after the likes of Thurmond and Oak Hill.

Or maybe he should work doubly hard and try to finish up the oral history study so that they could move on somewhere else. It would take a lot longer, but he could work on expanding his dissertation into a book while he taught classes in a university. Perhaps he should put out feelers for a teaching post in a large northern university, or perhaps one out west. Honey might like California. . . .

The sound of the Jeep died away. Zeke sat there for long minutes, exploring a hundred possibilities and listening to the silence of the cabin. Was there really any way he could keep her? Wasn't he only fooling himself? It took considerable effort to force his attention back to the half-composed sentence on the page before him and pick up his broken train of thought.

As far as Honey knew, she was just driving aimlessly. When she realized she was quite near the base station of White Water Adventurers, she followed a blind impulse and drove straight there. The parking lot was full, but there was nobody moving about outside this time of day. The guides would all be on the river with rafting parties.

The New River . . . that's where it had all started with Honey and Zeke, ten years earlier. As she sat in the parked Jeep, Honey smiled, remembering her adolescent encounter with a stubborn young man with piercingly honest blue eyes that said exactly what he was thinking. Zeke had been right in his initial summation of her character that first day: She had definitely been a willful spoiled brat, determined to have her way at all costs, utterly lacking in consideration for other people.

Was Zeke also right about her now? Was her boredom and restlessness after only two weeks at the cabin proof that she was too shallow and pampered to be content living an ordinary, middle-class life? She was afraid the answer was yes if such a life didn't offer a little more stimulation than household duties and waiting for Zeke to have time for her.

Heaving a discouraged sigh, Honey got out of the Jeep and walked inside the base station, having no purpose whatever in mind except to kill some time. Maybe she'd have a Coke and chat with whoever was on duty.

It seemed that nobody was on duty. The big combination shop and snack bar was empty. Honey wandered around, shaking her head in disapproval at the general untidiness of the place. At the far end, through an open door into an office, she glimpsed a young brunette woman working at a desk. The young woman looked up with a distracted frown as Honey paused in the doorway.

"Can I help you?"

Honey had seen with a quick glance around the office that it didn't look in much better shape than the outside. There was clutter everywhere and not a sign of a modern office machine like a copier or a computer. Open in front of the sole occupant of the office was the old-fashioned kind of ledger for handwritten entries.

"Hi. I thought I might stop in and have a Coke, but it looks like you're all alone here and busy."

The brunette threw down her pencil and blew out a

noisy sigh. "I'll be more than glad to stop, believe me. I don't halfway know what I'm doing anyway." She got up and came around the desk so that Honey could see that she wore faded jeans with her scoop-necked knit top and leather moccasins on her feet. She swept by Honey and led her toward the snack bar, talking nonstop.

"Sally, Lee's wife, used to take care of all the book work, and I took care of things out here. He's supposed to be trying to get somebody to do the books, and the guides are all supposed to be pitching in and helping in the shop and snack bar." She snorted her opinion of how well that plan was working, snatched a paper cup, filled it with ice, and jammed it under the Coke spout, all with one practiced movement. "Here you go. By the way, I'm Rose. Who are you? I don't remember seeing you around."

Honey swung herself up on a stool and took a sip of Coke to forestall an answer. If she were going to live with Zeke, she couldn't just hide out in the woods. People would have to know.

"Glad to meet you, Rose. I'm Honey Drake. I've just moved here from New York."

Rose had poured herself a Coke and was in the process of taking a sip, eyeing Honey over the rim. Her eyes widened as she lowered the cup. "Honey Drake. I remember that name. You're the one who called and insisted on having Zeke McCade as your guide. . . ." She nodded so wisely that Honey knew there was no need to worry about letting out the news that she was living with Zeke. Obviously the staff around the White Water base station was already informed.

"You were coming over from the Greenbrier with a group of old friends, weren't you?" Rose looked morose as she asked that purely hypothetical question. "I don't guess you have any background in keeping books and would be interested in a job."

Honey looked sympathetic. "No, I'm afraid I haven't done any bookkeeping." Her gaze drifted over toward the shop area with its crowded racks of clothing. "This would be more in my line of interest out here." She'd never worked in any kind of clothing shop or department, but she'd done her share of shopping in the best of them. In her present mood, it might feel good to tackle a mess like that, where the slightest improvement would stand out.

Honey had already noticed in her shopping during the past two weeks that the merchants in this area seemed to give little regard to attractive display, but here there wasn't even any concern for simple convenience. She'd learned that for herself looking for an outfit while she was waiting for Zeke a few weeks before, the day her whole life was about to change.

Rose leaned her elbows on the counter and followed Honey's critical gaze. "The guides just unpack the new shipments and jam it all into the racks, wherever they can find room. Then when all those college kids come swarming in looking for their size, they just make things worse." Rose sighed philosophically and straightened up. "If you didn't mind taking a temporary job, I could ask Lee about hiring you to work out here until he could find someone to do the books," she offered helpfully.

"I'm not really looking for a job," Honey replied quickly. "Not one with regular hours, anyway." It would be good to have a place to go to kill time when Zeke was busy, but when he wasn't busy, she wanted to spend every minute with him.

Rose looked so comprehending that Honey suspected her answer had been entirely transparent to the other woman. "I'm sure Lee would let you work by the hour, whenever you wanted to. And he'd probably pay you more than minimum wage, too. He's that kind of guy, even when he's in a bind the way he is now."

Honey probed her memory, remembering that Zeke had said he'd guided their party several weeks ago because his friend Lee Baxter needed the money. As far as she could recall, he hadn't elaborated. Before she could phrase a tactful question, Rose had already taken note of her puzzled expression and volunteered a summary of the recent tragic circumstances in Lee Baxter's life, his wife's lengthy illness and death, leaving him not only grief-stricken but burdened with huge medical bills.

"It nearly killed Lee, losing her," Rose mused sadly. "More than anything, I think he wishes he could get away, go somewhere and start over fresh. It makes all of us who worked here under Sally feel bad to see the business sliding the way it is. We're all crazy about Lee, but he just isn't the type to run a business. The first part of the season we didn't have enough brochures because he hadn't thought to order them. Anybody who happens to answer the phone takes reservations, and some of them have gotten fouled up. That makes for unhappy customers and can ruin an outfitting company's reputation. It's just really too bad."

"Why doesn't he sell out?"

"He would, to the right kind of person. You see, even though Sally was the business brains, Lee put a lot of himself into White Water, too. His feelings about white-water rafting are about the same as some people's religion."

Honey nodded thoughtfully. "You're saying that he would only want to turn the business over to someone who shared his feelings." *Somebody like Zeke.*

"That's exactly it." Rose looked inquiringly at Honey's Coke cup. "You want another Coke? No? Well, I guess I'd better get back to the books." She nodded over in the direction of the shop and shrugged. "If you got the time and want to do something with that, go ahead. Like I said, I'm sure Lee'd be glad to pay you."

Rose went back into the office without charging Honey for the Coke. It apparently didn't bother her to leave a stranger unattended with all the stock in the shop and the cash register. Honey sat there a minute or two, bemused, mulling over the conversation. *Why not?* she asked herself, sliding off the stool. It would give her something useful to do this afternoon if she straightened this place up and probably earn her Zeke's good opinion, since Lee was Zeke's friend and apparently was a guy who could use a helping hand right now.

Once she'd begun, Honey realized the job was bigger than she had thought. Two hours later when she glanced at her watch and saw that it was time for her to think about getting back to the cabin, she wasn't even halfway through, partly because she'd decided not just to straighten the racks of clothing but to rearrange the whole shop area. That had meant emptying racks completely in order to move them. She also wanted to talk to Lee Baxter about displaying some individual outfits on the walls, above eye level. The rough cedar planks would make a terrific background. She'd seen the same display technique used in smart ski shops.

"I have to go now," she told Rose, who was still laboring in the office, the same worried frown creasing her forehead. "I'll be back tomorrow, but right now I can't say what time. Maybe Lee will be around, and I can talk to him."

Rose had that look of cosmic acceptance that Honey

suspected was the key to her general outlook on life. "Sure thing. See you tomorrow."

Zeke had finished working but was still in his study when the Jeep drove up to the cabin. He'd been sitting there, glancing at his watch and wondering where Honey had been gone all afternoon. When the cabin door opened, he called out, "Hi. Welcome home," and then got up and moved swiftly to the door of his study to cut her off before she could come in.

"Hi." Even as she smiled at him, Honey took note that he casually pulled the study door almost closed behind him. He always left it like that, just slightly ajar, and he'd never invited her inside.

"I was beginning to get a little worried." Zeke glanced meaningfully at his watch. "You didn't have trouble with the Jeep, did you?"

Honey shook her head, smiling, and came to him, conscious of the gladness spreading through her in anticipation of his touch and his presence through the evening ahead. Together they would prepare and enjoy a leisurely dinner, talk, laugh, make love later on and sleep together, warm and close, in Zeke's bed. For hours he would be hers.

"The Jeep was fine," she declared, meeting him in the middle of the room and moving with consummate naturalness into his arms.

There was nothing remotely casual about Zeke's kiss. From its depth and intensity, Honey might have been gone for days or weeks rather than for several hours.

"I missed you," he told her as though some explanation of his fervor were necessary.

"Good." Honey gave his cheek a tender, playful little pat. "I missed you, too, for a few minutes, anyway."

Zeke's curiosity grew stronger.

"Where did you go this afternoon?"

Honey drew back and assumed a mock-indignant expression. "Do I have to account for every minute of the time I'm not with you?" she demanded, and then smiled. "Come on back to the kitchen, and I'll tell you everything. I could use a cup of coffee after a hard afternoon's work."

"Work?" Zeke echoed, following behind her.

He listened to her account of her afternoon without interrupting her. It was one of Zeke's appealing traits, Honey thought, this rare ability he had to listen. He was surprised, as she'd expected him to be, and amused by her lightly entertaining depiction of herself struggling with great armloads of T-shirts and sweat pants, but he wasn't pleased as she had assumed he would be. He just grew more and more thoughtful toward the end. Honey thought that maybe the mention of Lee Baxter's troubles might have touched off the serious mood.

"Do you think it might be the best thing for Lee to sell White Water?" she asked gently.

"Hard to say what's best for somebody else." Zeke saw surprise flash across Honey's face at the faint irony in his tone and realized he must have sounded pretty callous. He just didn't think he was in any position to give anybody advice about doing the "best thing," especially Lee. Since the last time the two men had talked, Zeke's whole life had changed. He could understand far better now Lee's devastating loss because Zeke himself now had someone important to lose. Not only did he dread that time farther along when Honey would leave him, every time she left the cabin he found himself worrying that something would happen to her

"Lee will have to figure out what's best for him." Zeke pushed his chair back and stood with his hands braced on the table, leaning toward Honey, who adjusted very quickly to the change of routine she read in his eyes.

"Aren't you hungry?" It wasn't a question at all, but an invitation. She was leaning toward him, lips softening in readiness for his kiss. Their lips met, clung sweetly, and parted, only to come together again at a slightly different angle. "Very hungry," Zeke whispered, and sampled every curve of her lips, taking the softness between his own in leisurely tastes and welcoming delightful confrontations with the tip of her tongue.

It became a delicious kind of torture for Honey. He wasn't touching her anywhere with his hands, and her body had come alive with demands for its own share of attention. Without taking her lips from his, Honey rose from her chair and placed her hands flat on the table, too, so that their fingertips just barely touched. When this preparatory move still didn't bring any suggestion that they move to the bedroom, she made the suggestion herself.

"Why don't we go to the bedroom?"

Zeke pulled back a little, letting her see the desire in his eyes, mixed with a glint of humor. "When I'm hungry, I don't go to the bedroom," he said suggestively. "I go to the kitchen." He straightened up and under her amazed observation, matter-of-factly took off his clothes. Naked and quite magnificently aroused, he backed up and sat down in his chair.

"Hungry?" he prompted with bold, blatant sexuality.

Honey just looked at him measuringly for a moment and then sashayed around the corner of the table, swaying her hips. The novelty of the whole situation was titillating to both of them and the humor they shared only sharpened the sexual attraction.

Honey stopped in front of him and unsnapped the waistband of her jeans. Zeke moved her hands and took over. The jeans were tight, so that when he tugged them down over her hips, her panties were dragged down, too. After she had kicked off her shoes and stepped out of both jeans and panties, with his help, she stood there still wearing her shirt, whose long shirttails fell provocatively short of providing modesty.

"No, not yet," Zeke said, stopping her when her hands went to the top button. He slid his hands up under the shirttails and caressed her waist and hips before he slid around and fondled her buttocks. Sinking his fingers into them, he uttered a combination sigh and groan.

"Did I ever mention what a sweet bottom you have? I can still see those leopard spots. . . ." The tone of his voice was sensual devastation in itself, but Honey's legs turned to rubber when Zeke leaned forward and pressed his lips to her feminine triangle.

Feeling her lurch weakly forward, he quickly grasped her by the waist and pulled her astraddle him with a cautioning, "Easy. No, not yet. Not yet, sweetheart." Honey quite desperately wanted the deep penetration he was denying her, but she contented herself with moving her hips and deriving a kind of agonizing pleasure from the intimacy of their position while Zeke unbuttoned her shirt and took it off, exposing her breasts with the restrained eagerness of a man unwrapping a treasure.

For Zeke the sound of Honey's voice speaking his name, telling him of the exquisite, unbearable pleasure he was bringing her, was like background music unerringly right for the occasion. As he caressed her breasts with his hands and adored them with his mouth and tongue, he carried in his mind's eye the picture of their perfection and counted himself the luckiest of all men to be who and where he was at that moment. Surely a man didn't come closer than this to heaven on earth.

When her urgency and his own were too great to ignore any longer, Zeke raised his head, after a lingering kiss for each hardened peak, an amused smile on his face. Through her haze of passion, Honey eyed him questioningly. This struck her as an odd time for humor.

"What's funny?" she demanded with a little writhing movement of her hips that made Zeke catch his breath. For good measure, she made the same movement again.

Zeke looked down and felt a primitive thrill at the bold spread of her legs and her readiness to receive him. His voice was absent and yet intent as he grasped her by the waist and lifted her upward.

"That making love to you is heaven—" Honey had been helping, guiding his tumescence with caressing fingertips. On the final word the coupling was complete. Zeke lowered her and definition became a sensory reality that knocked the breath right out of both of them. Honey froze for a long moment, her head thrown back and her face contorted with the piercing pleasure of taking him deep inside her. It seemed that she would never ask for more, but eventually one of them made a movement and started them again on that spiral upward to higher and higher planes of stimulation leading finally to devastation and then sweet, languid satisfaction.

Spent, Honey lay cuddled against him, arms around his neck and face resting on his shoulder. "You're right," she murmured. "Making love is like heaven, but with a little bit of hell mixed in, don't you think? Especially when the pleasure starts to end," she added, bemused.

"So in this case, heaven doesn't last forever," Zeke retorted dryly. *Nothing lasts forever.* The thought came unbidden, slipping upon him cruelly when he was highly vulnerable. He tightened his arms around Honey as though his embrace could ward off unrelenting reality and then spanked her lightly on the buttocks. "Now that you've had your fun, I suppose you want your dinner."

Honey straightened up and looked at him with serious eyes. She had felt the shadow darken his soul, sensed the compulsoriness in the embrace, heard the false note behind his heartiness, and could guess from the context what sort of thought had gone through his mind.

"Zeke, it's true that nothing on earth is permanent," she said gently, touching his face lovingly. "There are no assurances, but people can still make each other promises they'll make every effort to keep, short of accident or death."

Zeke was sure that he would never love her more than he did at that moment. She looked so grave and concerned for him. It was a powerful temptation to take her cue and lead them into exchanging words of commitment, but he resisted it, for her sake as well as for his own.

"Personally, I think people should be very careful about making promises, Honey. Or at least long-term promises that don't take into account the possibility and probability of change." He smiled with forced humor. "Have you ever thought that divorce might not be such an embittering process if people hadn't made such impossible promises to begin with? The marriage vows should be made more flexible: 'I take this man as my husband until he gains more than twenty pounds, loses his hair, and keeps me awake nights snoring.'"

He saw from Honey's face that she was neither amused nor fooled. She was disappointed, hurt, and a little angry. The last was Zeke's salvation. He didn't try to hold her as she climbed off his lap.

"In other words, Zeke, you don't intend to make me any promises, and you're not interested in hearing any I want to make. Isn't that what you're really telling me?" Honey held his eye for only a moment and then started picking up her clothes. She was afraid if she hung around, discussing the matter, she might turn into the quintessential hurt female and start crying.

It was a very bad moment for Zeke. To make up for the hurt he had caused her, he'd have been willing to promise her just about anything. It wasn't the part about his making promises that bothered him. He just didn't want her to make any that would later cause him bitterness and her guilt. To say as much to her now would only make matters worse.

"Don't you think it's a little early in our relationship to start making promises?" he cajoled, unashamedly imploring her to give him this out.

Honey sighed. "Yes, I guess you're right." He was still sitting in the chair but leaning forward with his elbows on his knees, not looking at her directly so that she couldn't read in his eyes whatever he wasn't saying. "We've actually only known each other a short while. There's one promise, though, that I'll insist you make me or else I'll leave right now." As she'd intended, that brought his gaze to her quickly. She held his eyes, not allowing him to look away. "I want you to promise that if you get tired of me and want me to leave, you'll tell me."

Relief, tenderness, bitter amusement all flitted across his face and were present in some measure in his prompt reply.

"I can promise you that."

But those piercingly direct blue eyes that had sized Honey up within seconds of meeting her ten years ago now made a far more binding promise, the kind he had just declared people shouldn't make to each other. *Never, my darling, will I ever grow tired of you.*

Honey was satisfied with what hadn't been said, at least for the time being. "Good. Promises or no promises, the only way you'll ever get rid of me is to kick me out. Now that that's settled, I'm going to take a shower. Care to join me?"

Zeke was badly in need of a few minutes to himself. "Why don't I get dinner started? Then you can take over while I shower."

Honey accepted that plan without argument, and the evening progressed harmoniously with neither of them referring to the conversation about promises. The subject of White Water Adventurers and Lee Baxter did come up again, though, since they both were fresh in Honey's mind.

"How much would you think Lee's business is worth?" she asked Zeke over dinner.

"I really couldn't say, but quite a lot. For one thing, he owns the land the base station's built on."

"How much is 'a lot'?" Honey persisted. "Are we talking fifty thousand, half a million, or what?"

"I have no idea," Zeke replied indifferently. The dollar-and-cent value of his friend's business was a subject that had never aroused any curiosity, nor had

he any reason to speculate upon it now. "Just 'a lot.'"
He smiled teasingly. "To me that's any sum with more
than four digits. Why all this interest, anyway? Thinking of buying Lee out?"

"Don't be silly!" Honey scoffed. "I wouldn't know
the first thing about running a company like that.
Besides, even if I wanted to buy him out and could
afford to, according to Rose he wouldn't sell to somebody like me."

Zeke's mildly surprised expression made Honey realize she had gone to unnecessary lengths to deny what
hadn't been a serious suggestion at all.

"I was just curious, that's all," she added defen-
sively.

A thoughtful frown creased Zeke's forehead.

"I would hate to see Lee sell out right now, when any
decision he makes would be emotional. In a year he
might feel entirely different. After he comes to terms
with his grief over Sally, he might realize how much
White Water means to him, because he and Sally built
it up together."

"But that wouldn't change the matter of his not
having any business ability, would it?" Honey pointed
out quickly. "I wouldn't think he could be happy seeing
what they had built together go downhill."

"You're right." Zeke's shrug said eloquently that he
was concerned for his friend, but didn't have the
answers.

"Maybe what he needs is a partner, or even a good
business manager."

Zeke didn't want to pursue the conversation any
further since well-intentioned speculations about solutions to Lee's problems were pointless. Lee had to live
his own life, just as Zeke had to live his.

"How would you like to spend a couple of days in

Charleston? We could drive there tomorrow, stay overnight, and come back the following afternoon—not a good idea?" The plan obviously had little appeal for her. After the initial surprise, she was just hearing him out patiently, almost reprovingly.

"No, it's not a good idea," Honey replied firmly. "You have work to do, and I don't have to be entertained. Besides, I already have plans for tomorrow."

Zeke appreciated the unselfishness inplicit in her refusal, but it didn't put his mind to rest. "Plans?" he probed skeptically. "What sort of plans?"

"I told Rose I'd come back tomorrow and finish up the job I started." Honey's expression became absorbed as mentally she picked up where she had left off rearranging the shop area at the base station. "It may take more than another day. . . ."

She came back to the present to find Zeke regarding her with tender amusement, but the anxiety was still there, far back in the clear blue depths of his eyes.

"Please. Don't worry about me, Zeke," she implored softly. "You do your work and let me take care of me. Okay?"

He winked and nodded.

"Okay."

Honey grinned impishly. "Sounds like a promise to me."

Zeke grinned back at her then, and they looked at each other, sharing that recurring sense of wonder at the simple joy they found in each other's company.

"Damned if it doesn't."

Chapter Ten

$\mathscr{L}$ee Baxter walked in the next afternoon just as Honey was arriving at that satisfying state of mind when the success of a project seems certain, even when the end isn't in sight. She had finally settled upon an overall arrangement of the clothing racks and had them in place. Now she was deciding what clothes would go where and putting like items in order according to size.

"Say, that looks nice. Real nice," a male voice drawled, and she looked around, knowing at once that she was about to meet Lee Baxter.

"Thanks," Honey replied, pleased.

They sized each other up frankly. Honey was predisposed to like Lee, since he was Zeke's friend, but she felt at once the force of the personality that drew people to Lee Baxter. Grief was stamped on his weathered features, but the gray eyes were open and friendly and utterly without guile or judgment. He was totally relaxed in his demeanor, without any hint of male swagger, and yet managed to radiate the untamed spirit that had made him a white-water legend. Honey was captivated and understood at once the loyalty that kept Rose slaving away at a hopeless task.

"You're Lee Baxter," she said, coming forward with her right hand outstretched. "I'm Honey Drake."

Lee took her hand in a hearty grip that hinted of his strength. "Glad to meet you, Honey. How's my old buddy, Zeke?" His gaze was openly complimentary and not at all subtle in expressing his opinion that his "buddy" was a lucky man.

Honey wasn't in the least offended by his directness.

"Zeke's fine. He's told me a lot about you." She looked Lee straight in the eye and followed his example, saying exactly what was in her mind. "I'm sorry about your wife."

He just nodded, sadness eclipsing his spirit. Honey couldn't have been more achingly sympathetic if she'd known Lee all her life instead of having met him mere minutes ago. She was grateful that Rose, having heard the voices, chose that time to emerge from the office.

"Oh, good. It's you, Lee. Isn't Honey doing a dynamite job out here?"

Lee gave his unqualified approval of what she had already done and gave her carte blanche to make any other changes she thought might improve the place.

"You just keep track of your own hours, and I'll pay you whatever you think is fair," he told her.

Honey started to protest that she didn't want to be paid for what she had done, and, even if she did, he shouldn't be so trusting, but Rose caught her eye and philosophically shook her head as if to say Honey might as well save her breath.

What had begun as an afternoon's clean-up project turned into a week's work, and then Honey found herself tackling the office and the stockroom. Sales picked up so dramatically that she and Rose decided they should order more of certain items. Keeping the racks orderly and replenished wasn't time-consuming in itself, just a matter of an hour or two each day. But the more time Honey spent at the base station, the more she found to do.

One day as she parked the Jeep in the parking lot, it occurred to her that she'd been coming there four or five days a week for a month. She and Zeke had been living together for six weeks. It was about time, she realized, to get her personal affairs in order. She still had her apartment in New York filled with possessions, including the huge wardrobe she'd deemed a necessity when she lived there. She wouldn't need all the gowns, furs, jewelry, and fashionable accessories now. It came as an interesting revelation to Honey that the thought of ridding herself of most of what she owned brought little more than a twinge of regret. She was happier than she'd ever been before in her entire life, and material things had come to have little importance.

Zeke noticed Honey's distraction that evening. "Why so quiet?" he asked. "What are you thinking about?"

She smiled and gave him a vague answer. "Oh, about things that wouldn't interest you at all. Clothes, furniture, jewelry." It was the truth. She had been building up an inventory in her mind all day, deciding what she should keep and what she should sell or give away to charity.

Before Zeke was able to suppress a stir of premonition at her cryptic words, she was dropping on him the bombshell that he had known would be coming in time.

"I have to go to New York for a few days."

Honey had deliberated long and hard about whether

to tell Zeke what she intended to do in New York and decided not to. Memory of that conversation about promises a month ago was still vivid in her mind, and even though she had more proof every day that Zeke loved her, he still had never told her as much in words and never made even the most casual assumptions of permanency in their relationship. There was no mention of "next month" or "next year." Any number of times Honey had been right on the brink of asking him point-blank if he thought eventually he'd want to marry her, but something held her back, perhaps silly pride, perhaps the fear of getting an answer that would spoil a status quo that was idyllic when taken just as it was.

Now, seeing the stark dismay on Zeke's face when she announced her intention to go to New York, she changed her mind, but treated the whole matter casually, as though Zeke wouldn't be surprised that she was burning bridges, so to speak, and returning to him with permanency in mind.

"Don't look so upset, darling. I won't be gone any longer than I have to. It's silly to keep paying rent on that big, expensive apartment when I'm not living there anymore. I'll have to check on the lease agreement and decide what to do with all the furniture and artwork." She grimaced with distaste. "I suppose I really should contact Phil and see if he wants any of it." She saw that her explanation hadn't made Zeke look any more reassured, just bleakly resigned. "I am coming back," she added emphatically. "That is, unless you tell me not to. That was our promise, remember?"

"You know I want you to come back." Zeke's reply had an odd restraint because he was thinking about what he felt he had to say next, knowing that he could so easily be misunderstood. "But, Honey, I'm not sure it would be wise—" He stopped, hearing how stiff he sounded, and picked up again, in a forced, casual tone. "You shouldn't be in a big hurry to get rid of things you must have wanted, in the first place, things that have brought you enjoyment. Later on, you might wish you had them back again." Zeke's courage gave out on him and he abandoned the warning against haste that had been halfhearted at best. God knows he wanted her to dispose of all those material and emotional investments in another life that hadn't included him.

Honey understood all too well what Zeke was saying. It was essentially what he had been saying from the first: They were too unsuited to each other for their relationship to last. *Don't burn your bridges because you'll end up having to build them again.* It hurt that everything she had said and done and been during the past month and a half hadn't convinced him, but the fact remained that she loved him too much to let his lack of faith sway her.

"One of these days, Zeke, you're going to have to gamble on believing in me, you know," she told him in a small, proud tone.

"For God's sake, Honey, *believing* in you has nothing to do with it!" Exasperated, Zeke ran a hand roughly across his face and felt his own inner tremor of fear. "Just forget what I said. Please. Do whatever you think is best and come back as soon as you can. I'm going to miss you like hell."

Honey resisted a little as he took her into his arms, but not for long. She loved and needed him too much to hold back anything, despite the pain his reservations caused her. It would just take time to prove him wrong, and perhaps a very long time.

Zeke was aware of the desperate quality in his

lovemaking that night. Honey's return to New York brought a whole host of fears. Once she was back in her milieu, would life here with him in the West Virginia mountains seem impossibly dull? She'd get together with her friends for luncheons and dinners at fancy restaurants, go out to the theater and to nightclubs, feel again the frenetic pulse and excitement of big-city life. She'd realize, wouldn't she, how important the glitter and glamour of her old life was to her?

If that weren't threat enough to torment him, there had been the mention of making contact with her ex-husband. What if the old spark of attraction was still there between them, and they both realized they'd made a mistake? Honey might look at her husband with new eyes now that she had lived with Zeke. She might appreciate a worldly polish and ambition and success in measurable terms like money and power.

Dear God, what would I do if she didn't come back? He'd thought he was keeping himself prepared for the time when she would be gone for good and he would be alone again, but with the first real possibility that the time might have come, he felt himself cringing with dread at the mouth of an abyss. Even if she came back from this trip to New York, he would continue to live with this fear based on inevitability until the worst finally happened.

Honey lay in Zeke's arms that night and felt his inner turmoil, knowing that it was futile to address his fears with words. The best thing for her to do was just carry out her plans and then come back here and face him with the idea that had taken shape and been steadily growing the past weeks. To mention it now, in his negative state of mind, would be a big mistake.

Zeke saw Honey off at the airport in Charleston. He

felt utterly abandoned as her plane took off and soared up into the sky. For a crazy, panicky few seconds, he seriously considered buying a ticket on the next plane headed for New York and following right behind her. Once he'd suppressed that impulse for the insanity that it was, he welcomed the numb resignation that made his movements mechanical as he walked out of the airport to the Jeep in the parking lot and drove back home. *It's a relief,* he told himself, *for the worst to go ahead and happen.*

Honey had done her best that morning to treat her return to New York casually. When the time came to board the plane and leave Zeke behind, there had been a wrenching sense of separation she wasn't able to overcome until the jet had attained its cruising altitude and the flight attendants were serving beverages. Honey sipped a glass of orange juice and resolutely worked on compiling a list of the possessions she would have to contend with when she arrived in New York.

It wasn't as simple as she'd thought to close down her old life. Once she was there and the news got around, people made claims upon her time. Some of them, like her father and Bev and certain friends of long standing, were people she needed and wanted to see. The city itself, even in stifling hot August weather, presented temptations.

"It's taking longer than I thought," Honey apologized cheerfully to Zeke on the telephone and then launched into a narrative of her activities that made his heart feel huge and heavy in his chest. He tried to sound matter-of-fact when she demanded to know what he'd been doing and he told her he'd been rafting on the Gauley River with Lee and some of the guides and doing a lot of fieldwork tracking down old-timers and getting their stories on tape. What he didn't tell her was that he stayed away from the cabin as much as possible because he found its emptiness unbearable.

"Sounds like you're getting along just fine without me," Honey accused. "Don't you miss me at all?"

"I miss you a lot."

Honey waited and was both disappointed and a little irked that he didn't speak the lover's words she wanted to hear, telling her of the empty spot beside him in his bed, in his life, in his heart. What he did say a minute or so later took her totally by surprise.

"I've been thinking of coming up to New York. I was there just once, a few years ago, but I didn't know a real insider like you, to show me around. . . ."

Honey didn't know what to say and for several seconds said nothing, until the silence had grown heavy. She didn't for a moment think that Zeke had the time, money, or inclination to come to New York and do some sightseeing. Why did he want to come? Did he have some crazy idea in his head that here on her old home territory she'd see what he'd been so sure she'd comprehend for herself at the Greenbrier: the fundamental differences that separated them?

"I'd love to show you New York some time, Zeke," she told him awkwardly, "but the weather's ungodly hot and humid this time of year. Actually, nothing much is going on now, either, and I only expect to be here a few more days. If you don't mind, I'd rather rush back to West Virginia as soon as I can and see you there."

"You're right. It's probably not a good idea at all," he agreed tonelessly.

"Zeke, you do know that I'd love to have your company here—"

"Sure, Honey. I know that." Zeke didn't know

anything of the kind. She seemed a million miles away from him, and despite what she said, and no doubt believed herself, something told him that he had lost her. The suggestion about going to New York was nothing more than half-cocked desperation or maybe it had been a test. She didn't want him to come.

The telephone conversation scared Honey with its lack of communication. In any really important exchange with Zeke, she depended on being able to read in his face, and especially in his eyes, all those things he wasn't saying. He couldn't have stopped loving her in a week, but maybe he had decided he preferred living the solitary kind of life he had found perfectly to his liking before she moved in with him.

The impulse was strong to call him back and put the question to him directly, but in the end she lacked the courage, and it frightened her even more to think that absence from Zeke might be eroding her confidence in the basic soundness of their relationship. She had to hurry up and conclude taking care of her affairs, return to West Virginia and work things out with Zeke, face to face. Talking on the telephone wouldn't do.

When three days passed and Honey didn't call again, Zeke tried to call her and got a recorded message that the number he had dialed was no longer in service. With fingers that trembled, he dialed the number again and subjected himself to a repetition of the bored, impersonal voice.

Two possibilities presented themselves to him. Honey had gone back to New York with the intention of letting her apartment go. Of course, she would also have her telephone disconnected. But why hadn't he heard from her during the past three days? Surely she would let him know if she was leaving New York and on her way back to him. Had she changed her mind about coming back, as he'd expected she would all along, and requested another telephone number so that he couldn't reach her?

Zeke knew that his loneliness had led him into paranoia and that there was no way he could determine the explanation for the recorded message or for Honey's silence until he could talk to her. He also knew that he couldn't sit there in the cabin for hours on end, vacillating between hope and despair. Somehow he had to get a respite.

Honey tried to call Zeke from her motel room that evening to tell him that she was on her way home. Disappointment welled inside her as the phone rang and rang and there was no answer. After she hung up, she sat there on the side of her bed, besieged by one emotion after another as she progressed from worry that something might be wrong with Zeke to suspicion that he was out somewhere enjoying himself without her, perhaps even with other female company. The faces of several of the girls who worked at White Water Adventurers flashed across her mind and made irrational jealousy curl like a vicious spiral in her breast. They had made no secret of their admiration of Zeke or of their opinion that she was fortunate to be his woman.

Realizing that she was reacting stupidly to the one simple fact that Zeke was not home to answer his telephone, Honey quelled her totally unfounded suspicions and went to bed. Tomorrow she would be with him after what seemed like an interminable separation. They would talk and get everything out in the open. In her mind's eye, she could see his smile and the wry amusement on his face when she confessed tonight's jealous imaginings.

But then when she tried his number early the next morning, before starting out again, and there was still no answer, it seemed conclusive that Zeke had spent the night somewhere else besides the cabin. *Where?* All Honey's worry, suspicion, and jealousy came flooding back, but the worry was foremost. She was afraid that he might have had an accident or fallen ill.

The only person she could think of to call was Lee Baxter. He would know if Zeke were lying sick or injured in a hospital, and if he had no such dreaded news to tell her and hadn't seen Zeke the past couple of days, Honey would urge Lee to drive out to the cabin and check on Zeke.

Lee didn't answer his phone either. Frustrated, Honey banged the receiver down, wondering what she should do next. She could sit there for hours on the telephone trying to track down Zeke's whereabouts and determine if he was safe. Or she could get on the road and not waste a moment getting to him. She decided on the latter since she wouldn't be able to do anything for Zeke at this distance, no matter what his condition happened to be. Probably there was some simple explanation of his absence from the cabin and nothing at all was wrong.

Honey was glad that she had pushed herself the previous day and driven two-thirds of the six-hundred-mile distance between New York and Thurmond. Taking into account mountain roads, she should arrive at the cabin, driving the sporty little compact car she had just purchased, by mid-afternoon. That was time enough to imagine a thousand mishaps that might have befallen Zeke. She had to stop for fuel only once and tried the number at the cabin again. There was still no answer.

At the appearance of familiar landmarks that told Honey she was just minutes away now from her destination, the anxiety she'd been suppressing for hours gripped her in its vise. Horrible images flashed through her mind: Zeke injured and bleeding; Zeke unconscious; Zeke in some faceless woman's arms. Turning finally onto the narrow, rutted road that led to the cabin, Honey drove faster than she should have, gripping the wheel tight and hanging on as the little car jolted along. When it shot into the clearing, Honey had to step hard on the brake to keep from colliding with Lee Baxter's bright red van, parked behind Zeke's Jeep.

She'd been expecting emptiness in the parking space in front of the cabin that in her mind would be deserted but was still the first place she had to go, perhaps to find some clue to lead her to Zeke. It came as a shock to see the Jeep parked in its usual place, an indication that its owner was home. After all her worry and panic, there was such a normal feel in the air. The cabin looked as sturdy and timeless as ever, birds fluttered busily in the trees and called to each other against the peaceful background music of the nearby creek. The presence of the red van even seemed routine and ordinary. Once he'd gotten to know Honey and was assured of his welcome, Lee felt free to drop by now and then, as he'd done before. He and Zeke were probably inside, talking over a cup of coffee or a beer.

Slowly Honey got out of the car. After all the hurry and panic to get here, she found herself seized by an odd reluctance. Where had Zeke been last night and part of today? Halfway to the porch, she stopped in mid-step as the door to the cabin burst open and Lee Baxter came out, shaking his head and talking to someone behind him, who turned out not to be Zeke but one of his guides, whom Honey knew only slightly. At the sight of Honey, incredulity flashed across Lee's face, followed swiftly by relief and then wholehearted welcome.

"Honey! You're back!" He walked quickly down the steps and enveloped her in a bear hug. Then he held her back from him and eyed her warmly, a broad grin splitting his face. "You came back after all," he marveled in a pleased voice.

"Of course, I came back. Did Zeke tell you I wasn't going to?" Honey searched his face for clues as to what was going on. Her uncertainty deepened when Lee exchanged glances with the guide, who had come to a stop behind him and stood quietly. "Lee, what's going on?" Honey asked sharply. "Is Zeke all right?"

Lee's smile had turned mysterious.

"He's not exactly all right, but I think he'll probably make it now that you're here." He gave Honey's shoulder a pat as he walked around her, headed for the van. "Better go check on the big lug," he advised cheerfully over his shoulder.

Honey heard the two men's chuckles behind her as she climbed the steps. Inside the front door, she paused, hearing the van start up outside and then drive away. There was silence inside the cabin.

"Zeke?" she called out tentatively.

No answer.

With growing puzzlement, she walked to the door of his study, looked in and saw that he wasn't there. "Zeke?" she called out again, heading toward the back of the house. This time she thought she heard some sound. It seemed to be coming from the direction of the bedroom.

In the doorway of the bedroom, Honey stopped and stared, realizing what the sound had been as Zeke groaned again, a prone, inert figure lying across the unmade bed, fully clothed except for his shoes, which Honey guessed that the other two men had removed. The room reeked of the smell of liquor. Now Honey understood the knowing look exchanged between Lee and his guide and the reason for their chuckles as they took their departure.

Zeke was dead drunk!

Speaking his name again, in a scolding tone this time, Honey went over to the bed and climbed up on it next to him. Grasping one shoulder in both hands, she tried to roll him over and couldn't. He was too heavy to budge.

"Zeke! Wake up! It's me, Honey. I'm back!" She shook him, but his only response was another deep moan. "You idiot, why have you done this?" she implored softly and lay down next to him, one arm hugging him across the shoulders. For a long time she lay that way, listening to his deep, labored breathing. It was so good just to know that he was whole and well except for the terrific hangover he undoubtedly would have.

After a while, Honey got up and went out to the kitchen to make a pot of coffee. While the coffee was dripping, she wet a washcloth with cold water in the bathroom and came back into the bedroom, thinking that she might be able to rouse Zeke from his alcoholic stupor, but it was hopeless. She soon gave up and left him alone, deciding that she would have a cup of coffee and then bring in her belongings from the car. Sooner or later, Zeke would sober up.

When she brought two suitcases into the bedroom a half hour later, Zeke had rolled over onto his back but was still deep in his drunken sleep. Honey put both suitcases down and stood in front of the open closet, assessing the amount of available space for hanging her clothes. There wouldn't be enough room for everything but she could just unpack the things she thought she would be needing.

Honey was humming a little tune to herself and taking her time as she worked, her back to the bed. Suddenly it occurred to her that Zeke wasn't breathing audibly anymore. She looked around and saw that he was awake and staring at her with a wild expression as though she were some kind of apparition.

"Well, hello. You've finally decided to wake up and welcome me home." She dropped the blouse she was holding and approached the bed, her movements calm like her voice, as though he were a patient she didn't want to scare.

"It's really you. You're here." Zeke's voice was gravelly and unconvinced. He lay very still, staring at her as though not daring to let himself blink for fear she would vanish in that split instant he didn't hold her in his vision.

"Of course, I'm here." Honey perched on the bed next to him, smoothed his hair back from his forehead and dropped a little kiss on the place she had cleared, knowing that his head was probably throbbing and pounding. "You knew I would be back as soon as I could, didn't you?"

When she straightened, Zeke had his eyes closed. He kept them closed while he muttered dully, between clenched teeth, "Your phone was disconnected . . . tried to call you but . . . disconnected."

"Of course, my phone was disconnected," Honey chided in a nurse-soothing-patient voice. "I'd have no use for a telephone without an apartment, now, would

I? Poor Zeke, you've put yourself through all this for nothing. I told you I was coming back, just like I've told you lots of other things, but you just never would believe me, would you?''

"God, what a stupid bastard—" Zeke turned his face aside, feeling like the lowest species of life. He knew he had to look and smell as bad as he felt, and he wasn't at all sure he'd live. He was ashamed to have her find him like this. Somehow he had to get himself up out of this bed and clean up.

"Don't call the man I love names," Honey ordered tenderly, caressing his beard-stubbled face.

Zeke reached up and captured her hand and held it against his cheek, still keeping his head turned aside. He drew in and expelled a deep, shuddering breath and then had to clench his teeth against a groan. "You came back." The pain and humble wonder in the low, gravelly voice brought the prickle of tears to Honey's eyes.

"What you need, Zeke McCade, is about a gallon of black coffee and an ice-cold shower," she scolded huskily. "I can't believe that the minute I leave you on your own, you go off on a binge with the boys. Now, up with you!"

It took superhuman will on Zeke's part to drag himself up out of the bed, fight the nausea and weakness, endure the dizziness and the shooting pains in his head. Even worse was the humiliation of having Honey see him with so little command of his own body that she had to undress him, help him to the shower on his rubbery legs and then wash him while he braced himself against the wall, gritting his teeth to keep from uttering over and over like a pathetic recording how sorry and ashamed he was.

After the shower he felt clearer in the head, and

stronger. With a towel wrapped around his waist, he managed to walk out to the kitchen on his own power, sat propped at the table, and got down several cups of black coffee with grim-jawed determination, knowing that it was touch and go whether the bitter liquid would stay down. Only when his stomach eased its convulsions did he trust himself to talk.

"Some homecoming," he said heavily and then seemed to ponder his own words. "How did you get here? I hope I'm not going to wake up any minute and find out I was hallucinating." His lips barely moved in a wan effort at a smile. "That's what I thought, you know, when I opened my eyes and saw you, an angel in triplicate."

Out of consideration for his feelings, Honey had been hiding her amusement over the comic elements of the situation. Now she took advantage of the excuse to smile.

"In triplicate?"

Zeke nodded very carefully, mindful of his head. It seemed important to clear up some of the mundane questions first. "Did you fly to Charleston and drive a rented car here?"

"No, I drove down from New York. I bought a car there before I left. I hadn't really needed to own one before. It's so much more convenient in the city to get about by taxi or limousine and just lease a car when you need one, but I thought it would be better if I had my own transportation here. After all, there'll be lots of times when you'll be needing the Jeep." She stopped and examined him approvingly. His face had more healthy color now and his eyes were losing the unaccustomed dullness. "You're definitely looking more like a man who might live. Are you feeling better?"

"Physically I feel better, but I think the embarrassment is terminal."

The wry tone of voice was so normal and the elaborations of the answer in his eyes so complex that Honey felt her pulse quicken in a manner very unbecoming to a nurse or an angel of mercy. Zeke was seeming less like a patient every second, less in need of compassion. He was a man, the man she loved.

"Why be embarrassed? We've seen each other in that condition before, at the Greenbrier, remember?" Honey reached across the table to squeeze his hands and then got up briskly, needing to dispel the faint beginnings of sexual tension that would have to wait. "What you need now is some food in your stomach— something light," she added soothingly when the healthy color in Zeke's face ebbed at the very thought of eating.

Zeke braced his hands on the table, in preparation for heaving himself up out of the chair, and then found that standing up wasn't the major endeavor he thought it might have been. He stood experimentally, as though checking out all the normal processes such as breathing up at that altitude, and then relaxed a little with his success and smiled sheepishly.

"I'm not sure at this point whether I'll ever eat again, but dressing myself does seem like a definite possibility." He came around the table to where she stood and took her into his arms. Honey hugged him hard, feeling that she had really come home.

"I love you, Zeke," she told him, the words coming with the utmost naturalness out of the intense happiness inside her. "I missed you so much."

"God, I missed you, too, sweetheart," he told her with heartfelt gruffness, rubbing his cheekbone against her hair and holding her tighter against him as though the contact of their bodies made strength flow into him. "I'm sorry as hell you had to find me like you did. What a homecoming." He sighed regretfully. "A classic case of insecurity, I guess, but I convinced myself you weren't coming back. All along I expected you to realize at some point that this wasn't the life for you. When you said you had to go to New York, I thought, 'This is it. She'll get back there and be drawn back into her old life.' When we talked on the phone and you were obviously having a wonderful time, my worst fears seemed confirmed."

"I was having a good time," Honey admitted honestly and turned her face into his shoulder to press her lips to his warm, hard flesh. "But that didn't change the fact that I missed you terribly and wanted to get back here as soon as I could. Part of this is my fault. I should have called you back that same night you mentioned coming up to New York and gotten things straight then and there, but I was scared."

Zeke pulled back to look at her face. "Scared?"

"Yes, scared. You were so strange on the phone, so distant. I couldn't *see* you to figure out what was really in your mind. I thought that maybe you liked having the cabin all to yourself again . . . that maybe you really didn't want me to come back. That's the reason I didn't call you back that night or call you again before I left New York. I wanted to hurry on back and talk to you face-to-face." She could see that he was deeply skeptical and also that he was tiring of standing up, supporting her weight. "Zeke, don't you think you'd better sit down?"

He acquiesced grimly by pulling out a chair and dropping down into it. Honey let him draw her down onto his lap.

"How could you possibly think that?" he asked,

picking up the conversation precisely at the place it had been interrupted. His doubt wasn't for her honesty, but for her reasoning process. "Why would I have suggested coming to New York if I wanted to break off with you? You had to know I couldn't really afford the time or the money."

"Yes, I did know that," Honey agreed, caressing the tendons in his neck with her fingertips. He briefly closed his eyes, giving himself over to her touch, but then his attention was back on her explanation as she continued. "I thought you had some notion of proving how wrong we were for each other. That was your reason for coming with me to the Greenbrier, wasn't it?" She smiled to see how startled he was by her shrewd perception.

"I knew that's what you had in mind, but your plan completely backfired on you, Zeke. It would have backfired in New York, too, because there isn't a place on the earth I wouldn't enjoy more if you were there with me. You're intelligent and fun and good-looking, even with a hangover—" She paused to pat his unshaven cheeks, amused at the chagrin in his eyes. "I'd be proud to let the whole world know that Honey Drake loves Zeke McCade." She pressed her cheek against the beard-stubbled roughness of his.

"We're going to be very happy, Zeke," she promised him softly. "You're going to get over this feeling that any second spoiled little Honey will get bored and flit away to some other playground. You're going to start believing in 'us' so much that you'll tell me the way you feel inside, that you love me very much and want to marry me and someday have a family." He was absolutely still. Honey pulled back to look into his face and was immensely reassured by what she saw. His eyes were amused, brilliant with all those emotions she'd insisted he was going to declare, and very happy.

"I am?"

"You are," she declared with false bravado and then waited with hope written on her face.

Zeke reached up and rubbed his cheek, his expression ruefully apologetic. "This is hardly the way a man imagines it will be when he tells a woman he wants her to be his wife," he said, sighing.

"Life is not always perfect." Honey's rejoinder was quick and teasing, but her eyes were still hopeful. As certain as she was of Zeke's feelings, she still wanted him to say it all aloud. It was the recognition of her need that made Zeke overcome his own very real self-consciousness.

"Here goes, then." He cleared his throat and then dropped the whole pretense of lightness, speaking simply and looking into her eyes. "I love you, Honey, very much. I have for a very long time. I think I started loving you on that first rafting trip and just picked up ten years later. There's nothing that I'd like better than to be your husband. I'd do everything in my power to make you happy." He closed his arms around her, turning his head aside, but Honey struggled, crying out, "No! No!"

Pushing back, she held him by the shoulders and looked fiercely into his face, seeing his surprise and uncertainty.

"I want to hear the rest, Zeke," she told him firmly. "Tell me."

He held her gaze a long moment and then made the slightest nodding movement. "Okay. I don't want to have reservations, but I do. When I said just now that I'd do anything in my power to make you happy, meant that, and I know that you'd make the s promise to me and mean it, too. But as much as we humans can love someone else, Honey, we still have to be true to ourselves, to our own unique talents, interests, needs. It seems to me that you're giving up too much—"

"I'm giving up nothing!" Honey broke in impatiently. "And gaining everything! Zeke, I get goosebumps when I stop and think how totally unlikely it was that I would ever 'find' you again. It was meant to be. There's simply no other explanation. DeeDee might not have run into Guy in a shopping center in Chicago, the idea of a Greenbrier reunion might never have occurred to anybody, DeeDee might not have been able to reach me, I could have had plans or stuck by my original reaction and refused, you might have been a thousand miles away from Fayette County. . . ." Honey stopped and shook her head at all the possibilities. "It's just incredible that everything came together, don't you see?"

Zeke's expression said that he did see. "The element of chance does tease the mind," he mused. "But there was more than chance. There was memory involved, yours and mine. I'm still amazed that after ten years, you recalled the name of White Water Adventurers and a guide you'd known only a day."

Honey was nodding eagerly. "And once I'd dredged you up out of my memory, I was obsessed with the idea that you had to still be here and would be our guide again. Thank God you didn't have an interview set up ~~~ some hundred-year-old coal miner for the day of ~~~ing trip!"

~~~de a little grunting sound of denial. "Noth-
~~~d would have kept me from guiding your
~~~hen Lee came here and brought up
~~~mber the odd feeling that struck me.

It was as though I'd been waiting for ten years, fully expecting that I would see you again some day, but not even knowing all that time that I was waiting."

They looked at each other, sharing wonder at the unpredictable workings of fate and the mysterious chemistry of human relationships.

"It is going to work, Zeke," Honey told him softly. "I promise you that. It'll take some effort and a lot of understanding, but it's going to work. You're going to go right on being the kind of historian you're meant to be, and I—" She hesitated, gathering up her courage.

"What about you, Honey?" Zeke prompted, still not totally convinced. "What are you going to do to satisfy Honey while I'm busy being a historian?"

"I thought you'd never ask," she declared flippantly. "It's something I've been meaning to talk to you about. I'm thinking quite seriously of going into business. Not on my own, but with a partner, Lee Baxter, to be exact. He needs help badly. He also needs money to pay medical bills, and I have some money. Think he'd be interested?" She waited anxiously, not just for his answer but for his general reaction.

Zeke's initial surprise had faded fast. From every angle that he looked at it, her idea seemed a good one.

"I think he'll be very interested. He might as well be, if you've made up your mind."

The humorous gleam in his eyes brought a sheepish smile to Honey's lips. "I pretty well have made up my mind," she admitted. "It seems like a good idea for everybody concerned. Lee's business won't go down the tubes while he's trying to put his life together again, you can track down your old miners and lumberjacks and poke around in your ghost towns without worrying about me, and I'll have somewhere to go and something challenging to do." She looked thoughtful. "I need to start finding out about computers and book-keeping programs right away. I may even have to take some courses—" She wrinkled up her nose at Zeke, who was watching her with interest and amusement. "You're going to be surprised at what a terrific businesswoman I turn out to be," she warned him jokingly.

"I don't think I'll be surprised at all," he denied seriously. "You're intelligent, very determined, and a natural leader. I'm quite sure you're capable of doing anything at all that you set your mind to doing."

"Do you think that, Zeke?" Honey framed his face in her hands and kissed him tenderly on the mouth. "Thanks for your vote of confidence. It means a lot to me. Less than two months ago, there was nothing I wanted to do. Nothing seemed worth doing. Life seemed like one big boring disappointment. And now all that's changed, because of you." She started to kiss him again, but stopped when he pulled back.

"I need to go and shave," he told her.

It was the unspoken message in his eyes that really got her attention.

"Are you sure you feel up to it?" she asked doubtfully.

He raised his eyebrows, pretending to misunderstand. "Shaving's not that vigorous. Besides, you can help, can't you?"

Honey got up off his lap. "I'd love to help."

She actually did help him shave. It turned into a giggly, lighthearted procedure and then Zeke evicted her from the bathroom while he brushed his teeth. Honey straightened the bed, took off her clothes, and was lying there waiting for Zeke when he came in, minus the towel.

"We don't have to make love," she told him as he got in bed beside her and she turned into his arms. "It's enough just to be here and have you hold me." He didn't answer. She felt him growing and hardening against her. Her voice had a breathless, distracted sound as she talked on happily.

"You should have seen the faces of my friends when I told them I was moving to West Virginia. 'Really, Honey, West Virginia!' I told them I couldn't wait to get back and apply for my own license plate. *ALMOST HEAVEN* . . . that slogan's perfect for the way I feel about my life right now, Zeke." She caught her breath as Zeke moved and she felt the full-blown evidence of his arousal. His hands were moving over her, bringing to life delicious sensations.

"Nothing in life's ever perfect. . . ." Her voice drifted off as she fell back unresistingly so that he could lower his lips to her neck and then slowly find his way down to her breasts, whose peaks were hardened and aching. *Except this!* she thought as he kissed her breasts and then took them by turns into his mouth. She moaned softly with her pleasure and arched her back, letting her thighs part to welcome the stroking presence of his hand. *Except this!* she thought again as he discovered her readiness.

The distinction between a state of near-perfection and sublimity was lost for Honey as Zeke joined his body to hers. The universe consisted of nothing other than their union, with its gradations of intense pleasure. It was like leaping from one plateau of heaven to the next, higher, higher, higher, right up to the perilous, topmost part, then poising there for the space of a cry of reckless joy that for Honey was twofold. Along with the unbearable exhilaration of reaching so high was the sweet knowledge that afterward they would make the descent together, back to earth where, true enough, life wasn't perfect. At best, it was "almost heaven." In her own case, she wouldn't dream of asking for more.

WIN

a fabulous $50,000 diamond jewelry collection

ENTER

by filling out the coupon below and mailing it by September 30, 1985

Send entries to:

U.S.
Silhouette Diamond Sweepstakes
P.O. Box 779
Madison Square Station
New York, NY 10159

Canada
Silhouette Diamond Sweepstakes
Suite 191
238 Davenport Road
Toronto, Ontario M5R 1J6

SILHOUETTE DIAMOND SWEEPSTAKES
ENTRY FORM

☐ Mrs.   ☐ Miss   ☐ Ms   ☐ Mr.

NAME   (please print)

ADDRESS   APT. #

CITY

STATE/(PROV.)

ZIP/(POSTAL CODE)

RTD-A-1

RULES FOR SILHOUETTE DIAMOND SWEEPSTAKES

OFFICIAL RULES—NO PURCHASE NECESSARY

1. Silhouette Diamond Sweepstakes is open to Canadian (except Quebec) and United States residents 18 years or older at the time of entry. Employees and immediate families of the publishers of Silhouette, their affiliates, retailers, distributors, printers, agencies and RONALD SMILEY INC. are excluded.

2. To enter, print your name and address on the official entry form or on a 3″ x 5″ slip of paper. You may enter as often as you choose, but each envelope must contain only one entry. Mail entries first class in Canada to Silhouette Diamond Sweepstakes, Suite 191, 238 Davenport Road, Toronto, Ontario M5R 1J6. In the United States, mail to Silhouette Diamond Sweepstakes, P.O. Box 779, Madison Square Station, New York, NY 10159. Entries must be postmarked between February 1 and September 30, 1985. Silhouette is not responsible for lost, late or misdirected mail.

3. First Prize of diamond jewelry, consisting of a necklace, ring, bracelet and earrings will be awarded. Approximate retail value is $50,000 U.S./$62,500 Canadian. Second Prize of 100 Silhouette Home Reader Service Subscriptions will be awarded. Approximate retail value of each is $162.00 U.S./$180.00 Canadian. No substitution, duplication, cash redemption or transfer of prizes will be permitted. Odds of winning depend upon the number of valid entries received. One prize to a family or household. Income taxes, other taxes and insurance on First Prize are the sole responsibility of the winners.

4. Winners will be selected under the supervision of RONALD SMILEY INC., an independent judging organization whose decisions are final, by random drawings from valid entries postmarked by September 30, 1985, and received no later than October 7, 1985. Entry in this sweepstakes indicates your awareness of the Official Rules. Winners who are residents of Canada must answer correctly a time-related arithmetical skill-testing question to qualify. First Prize winner will be notified by certified mail and must submit an Affidavit of Compliance within 10 days of notification. Returned Affidavits or prizes that are refused or undeliverable will result in alternative names being randomly drawn. Winners may be asked for use of their name and photo at no additional compensation.

5. For a First Prize winner list, send a stamped self-addressed envelope postmarked by September 30, 1985. In Canada, mail to Silhouette Diamond Contest Winner, Suite 309, 238 Davenport Road, Toronto, Ontario M5R 1J6. In the United States, mail to Silhouette Diamond Contest Winner, P.O. Box 182, Bowling Green Station, New York, NY 10274. This offer will appear in Silhouette publications and at participating retailers. Offer void in Quebec and subject to all Federal, Provincial, State and Municipal laws and regulations and wherever prohibited or restricted by law.

SDR-A-1

She fought for a bold future
until she could no longer
ignore the...

ECHO OF THUNDER

MAURA SEGER

Author of **Eye of the Storm**

ECHO OF THUNDER is the love story of James
Callahan and Alexis Brockton, who forge a union
that must withstand the pressures of their own
desires and the challenge of building a new television
empire.

Author Maura Seger's writing has been described by
Romantic Times as having a "superb blend of
historical perspective, exciting romance and a deep
and abiding passion for the human soul."

**Available at your favorite
retail outlet in SEPTEMBER.**

Silhouette Special Edition

COMING NEXT MONTH

ONE MAN'S ART—Nora Roberts
To Genevieve Grandeau, love meant giving, sharing...trusting.
Grant Campbell was a loner. Could he, would he, allow
himself to be drawn into the life of this beautiful socialite?

THE CUTTING EDGE—Linda Howard
Brett Rutland's search for an embezzler brought Tessa Conway
into his life. For the first time, Brett was falling in love...until
his heart's desire became his prime suspect.

SECOND GENERATION—Roslyn MacDonald
Hollywood had taught costume designer Deanna Monroe that
there was no such thing as instant love. But Rick seemed to
defy Hollywood law, and Deanna was too charmed to realize
she could be heading for heartbreak.

EARTH AND FIRE—Jennifer West
Chalon Karras had once fallen in love with and married a rich
older man. Now Chalon was filled with grief over his sudden
death, and guilt at her growing passion for his dangerously
handsome son.

JUST ANOTHER PRETTY FACE—Elaine Camp
They met while working together on a film shot on location in
Egypt. Among the pyramids, assistant director Savanna Collier
and actor Teague Harris discovered the passion that made
Hollywood infamous, and treacherous.

MIDNIGHT SUN—Lisa Jackson
Because of a bitter family feud Ashley Stephens and Trevor
Daniels had tried to deny the flaming passion between them for
eight long years, but even fiery hatred couldn't keep them apart
forever.

AVAILABLE THIS MONTH

ALMOST HEAVEN
Carole Halston

REMEBER THE DREAMS
Christine Flynn

TEARS IN THE RAIN
Pamela Wallace

WATER DANCER
Jillian Blake

SWEET BURNING
Sandi Shane

THAT SPECIAL SUNDAY
Maggi Charles

HER FORBIDDEN BRIDEGROOM

Susan Fox

DISCARD

DISCARD

DISCARD

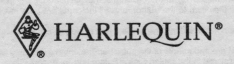

HARLEQUIN®

TORONTO • NEW YORK • LONDON
AMSTERDAM • PARIS • SYDNEY • HAMBURG
STOCKHOLM • ATHENS • TOKYO • MILAN • MADRID
PRAGUE • WARSAW • BUDAPEST • AUCKLAND

ISBN 0-373-03717-1

HER FORBIDDEN BRIDEGROOM

First North American Publication 2002.

CHAPTER ONE

LORNA FARRELL would never forget the last time she'd seen Mitch Ellery. She'd been nineteen then. Now, five years later, the memory of that terrible day hung suspended in time, burned so deeply into her heart that it could have happened twenty minutes ago.

The certain knowledge that she would—perhaps in a matter of moments—come face-to-face with Mitch Ellery again caused her memory of him to go bright as lightning. She discreetly brushed at the sheen of cold perspiration on her forehead, dismayed by the slight tremor of her hand.

Lorna had faced trauma and hard times before, so she knew how to steel herself against them and survive. This time, though, she would face calamity knowing she deserved what happened next. Her sense of responsibility was too exacting for her to ignore the heavy load of guilt, hence the reason for the sick dread in her chest and the tremor of her hand.

She glanced cautiously at the young brunette who stood next to her in the elevator. Barely three years younger than Lorna's own twenty-four, Kendra Jackson was blissfully unaware of Lorna's anguish.

As the silent car rocketed them to the twentieth floor of the San Antonio office building, Lorna studied Kendra's pretty profile. Emotion stung her eyes, but she continued to stare, alert to any sign that her scrutiny had been detected. It could very well be that these moments with Kendra would be her last.

Once Mitch Ellery found out she'd had such close contact with his stepsister, he would likely speak to her boss, if not also to the police. And the good job she'd worked so relentlessly hard to get would not only be gone, but the circumstances of her firing might ensure great difficulty in securing another.

Kendra Jackson. Now the fiancée of her boss, John Owen; the young woman who'd persistently undermined Lorna's aloof distance, even to the extent of having her boss put Lorna at her disposal for small tasks and favors. Kendra had seemed to set out to make Lorna a friend and minor confidant, and Lorna had been trapped by Kendra's friendly persistence. The fact that Kendra had commandeered her time and attention had been a bittersweet joy that Lorna had faithfully kept to herself.

Because Kendra Jackson was a young woman too happy and carefree and in love—and too naïve about the secrets and selfish motives of others—to be aware that the very efficient Miss Farrell, whose time and attention she apparently coveted, was actually her half sister.

And therein lay the reason for Lorna's guilt. She'd known who her sister was the moment she'd heard her name six months ago. To then see her walk into the office three weeks later to meet her new beau for lunch had been both thrill and torture.

Because Lorna could never allow her sister to know who she was. Their mother had wanted nothing to do with the out-of-wedlock daughter she'd given birth to, and she'd not only made that crystal clear five years ago, she'd followed it up by sending her stepson, Mitch Ellery, to hunt Lorna down and give her wishes emphasis.

Though at first he'd restated it all with a gruff kind of tact, the no-nonsense glitter in his dark eyes and the rocky sternness of his harsh face had given his quiet words the impact of a sledgehammer.

It hadn't mattered to Mitch Ellery that she'd been as shocked as her mother had been by the surprise meeting at the ritzy San Antonio restaurant where Doris Jackson Ellery had been having lunch with him and his father. The unstable friend who'd arranged it all had been nowhere to be found by the time Mitch had caught up with Lorna later that afternoon.

Lorna had been intimidated enough by his sudden arrival at her one-room apartment that she'd defended herself by telling him the truth: that her well-meaning but misguided friend had arranged the surprise, that she'd been as shocked and horrified as her mother had been.

Lorna had watched his hard expression darken as she'd vowed to him that she wouldn't for the world have vetoed her mother's choice and approached her in such a public manner.

The explanation and sincere apology she'd made hadn't mattered a whit to Mitch Ellery. Though he'd started out with her quietly and sternly, once she'd said all that, his deep voice had lowered to a growl and the scorn on his rugged face had cut her to the quick.

He'd told her bluntly that he thought she was lying, not only about her friend arranging the meeting, but about even suggesting that she could truly be Doris Ellery's daughter. He'd hinted that it was her own stability that was in question before he'd declared her an inept opportunist using a cruel claim to extort money from a wealthy family. On his way out of her tiny apartment, he'd threatened to inform the police if any of them ever heard from her again.

She'd been devastated by that, devastated by the notion that her mother had apparently lied about having an out-of-wedlock child that she'd given up years ago, and mortified to be thought a liar herself.

Not that Lorna was unsympathetic to the plight of her mother. Doris Jackson Ellery was barely forty by now, so she must have given birth to Lorna when she was only sixteen years old. No doubt the circumstances of her out-of-wedlock pregnancy and the act of giving up her child for adoption had been troubling enough for Doris to go through.

Lorna completely understood that her mother must have surely meant to put that time in her life behind her and to possibly forget it had ever happened. Which was an indication to Lorna that her birth and the circumstances surrounding it must have been traumatic.

Though Doris had married Kendra's father two years after she'd given up her first child and had many years later married the much older Jake Ellery, the respectable upscale lifestyle she lived now no doubt made her leery of the scandal that might be associated with giving up an out-of-wedlock child, should it become public knowledge. Not everyone had a liberal outlook on such things. And since Doris had obviously kept it a secret from the Ellerys, they might all have considered a belated revelation of the truth a betrayal of trust.

The Ellery family was an old one in the oil and ranching community, and their sterling reputation was no doubt paramount. Kendra herself had been a member of that family for years, and if there was ever a proper young lady, it was Kendra, who clearly had been brought up with strict traditional morals and taught to behave in a respectable manner.

Lorna was acutely aware of how important respectability was. She'd worked hard for her own respectability and the value of having a sterling reputation with no hint of moral failure attached to it was worth everything to her.

But it would all come crashing down now, her respectability would be sullied and her wonderful job humiliatingly snatched away. How else could Mitch Ellery take this situation that she'd allowed to go on because she'd wanted to keep her job and couldn't bring herself to hurt Kendra's feelings?

One look at Lorna and he'd know that the Miss Farrell he'd surely heard about was Miss *Lorna* Farrell. *That* Lorna Farrell. The Lorna Farrell he'd thought an unstable opportunist and a liar, the Lorna Farrell he'd threatened to turn in to the police.

Just then, Kendra turned her head and Lorna glanced away. The elevator whispered to a halt and Lorna gripped the strap of her handbag in preparation for the doors opening.

As they stepped out, Kendra's sweet voice sent a fresh jolt of alarm across her ragged nerves.

"Why, Lorna...you're shaking!" The younger woman touched her arm and they both halted as the elevator door closed behind them. "Are you all right?"

Lorna gave her a smile she hoped didn't tremble. "I'm fine. I skipped lunch."

"Why didn't you say something?" Kendra went on, and her genuine concern gave Lorna's heart a poignant nudge. "We could have grabbed something to eat while we were out."

"I wasn't hungry, and I'm still not." Lorna made herself smile gently at her sister. "You've had days like that lately, haven't you? When you're too excited about the wedding and too busy with plans to think about food, so you forget to eat until you get shaky?''

Kendra, despite her carefree manner, was slow to lose her concern. And that touched Lorna again.

''If you're sure? You've been working hard lately, and I've been running you all over San Antonio. Maybe you should take a couple days off. You've more than earned the time.''

Lorna shook her head. ''I love to work and I love the challenge. I'll have all weekend to rest up and recharge, but—'' she paused as they started to walk along the hallway to the open office doors ''—I really need to get back to work. Your fiancé gave me a raft of correspondence this morning that I need to finish by five o'clock. I've got an apple at my desk to tide me over.''

Kendra's expression lightened to uncertainty as they walked along and she searched Lorna's tense features. Then she smiled. ''All right. Thanks for all your help, but don't work too hard.''

''Hard work is good for the soul,'' she said as they walked past the wide doorway into the office.

As she said it, Lorna touched her sister's arm. Not only was it a silent thanks for her concern and meant as a reassurance to the younger woman, but it was also a heartfelt need to indulge what might be her last opportunity to do so.

If she could think of an excuse for a business errand that would take her to another floor of the building, perhaps she could delay the inevitable.

Perhaps it was still possible to contact Mr. Ellery privately, confess what she'd done, and explain her dilemma. Perhaps he'd take more kindly to that than an out-of-the-blue surprise.

Why hadn't she done that months ago? Why hadn't she been more sensible before things had gone so far?

She'd just glanced forward as they walked deeper into the large outer office when she noticed the big man who slowly rose from one of the wide sofas across from her desk.

Kendra saw him then too, because she called out, "Mitch! You're early! I'm so sorry you had to wait."

And then Kendra was walking to her stepbrother, outpacing Lorna who'd suddenly faltered at the sight of the tall, rugged man whose dark gaze lanced into hers and now cut over her like sharp blades.

Terror gripped her, but she tried mightily to glance away from him and walk calmly to her desk. She'd hoped she could somehow avoid a formal introduction, but she'd known from the moment Kendra had announced ten minutes ago that Mitch Ellery was picking her up that her chances were nil. The best she could do was to wrap herself in the aloof composure that few people other than Kendra and a handful of friends had managed to breach.

Lorna had no more than put her handbag into her desk drawer and casually reached over to press the button on her computer screen when Kendra got her attention.

"Lorna?"

Lorna made herself glance Kendra's way and forced a faint smile as her sister approached the desk with Mitch Ellery at her side. Ever the proper, accommodating employee, Lorna stepped around the desk for the dreaded introduction.

"This is my stepbrother, Mitch Ellery," Kendra began, and Lorna shifted her gaze to meet the fiery darkness in his eyes. "Mitch, this is Lorna Farrell."

Lorna's heart shot to her throat and pounded painfully. Three hard beats and she jerkily extended her icy hand. Three more hard beats as she waited for disaster.

The dizzying thought—that putting out a hand to Mitch Ellery was no less risky than putting her hand into the mouth of a ferocious beast—threatened her waning courage.

But then his hand came up and took hers. The callused strength in his fingers could have crushed hers with one casual flex, but his firm grip was as gentle as his skin was hot and work-hardened.

As he'd been that day years ago, he was dressed in a black suit, and his boots carried a muted shine. The suit was in keeping with his millionaire taste, but his callused hand, black boots and the pearl-gray Stetson he'd left on the sofa were proof that beneath his millionaire oilman look, he was a rancher.

And not only a rancher who ruled over a small

empire but, from the rough feel of his palm, an everyday cowboy who sweated and bled and dirtied his hands to keep it his.

Long seconds stretched longer as they stared at each other, their hands clasped together as if neither of them could risk letting go just yet.

The hot bolts of feeling that radiated through her from the engulfing strength of his hand arrowed straight to every deeply primal, feminine place in her body and set off a series of quivering earthquakes.

Mitch's voice was low and his drawl pronounced. "A pleasure, Miz Farrell."

His fingers tightened ever so slightly, prompting her to stammer out a half choked, "Mr. Ellery, nice to m-meet you. Miss Jackson has mentioned you warmly."

Mentioned you warmly? Warmly? Mortification scorched her face. Mitch's dark gaze seemed to flicker then and the quiet rage she saw in his rocky expression eased. She continued to stare into his eyes, searching for some bit of mercy. The hint of reprieve was there, but she knew better than to take it as anything less than a momentary one.

And she was right, because she suddenly understood he wouldn't confront her now. He'd never do it in front of Kendra. That meant he'd come after her as he had years ago. But this time their meeting would end differently. What she'd done by not rebuffing Kendra or quitting her job ensured that.

security guard. When she arrived in the lobby, her gentle smile and soft "good night" prompted the guard to step ahead of her to chivalrously open the door before he once again locked up for the night.

Her head began to pound once she reached the nearly empty parking lot where she'd left her car that morning. Trying hard to resign herself to the idea that Mitch Ellery might already have found her apartment and taken up a convenient place to keep watch for her, she started her car and drove out of the lot to the post office, then home.

There was no point in hoping for another reprieve or even a delay. The suspense of waiting even a few hours was already more than she could tolerate. She'd known this day was coming for months. She should have contacted Mitch Ellery long ago, but selfishness was the real reason she hadn't.

Through Kendra, she'd got a taste of family that she'd hungered for since childhood, and she hadn't had enough character to keep from taking it. And since the notion of family and home and belonging were the sweetest and most sacred things in the world to her, it made sense that those small tastes and rare glimpses of what mattered most would come at a steep price.

Now it was time to pay for those treasures in whatever coin Mitch Ellery decreed. Though she knew the payment was certain to devastate her, she'd pay quickly and, because she was guilty, she wouldn't complain.

As she finally turned onto her street then pulled into the driveway between her building and the next one, she resisted the urge to glance around for unfamiliar vehicles. She made it all the way inside to her apartment before she heard the buzzer sound from the call box outside the front door of the small lobby downstairs.

The simultaneous knock on her apartment door came before she could cross to the tiny foyer and press the button on the intercom. Rattled, Lorna belatedly recognized the knock and gratefully opened the door.

Melanie Parker, her closest friend, greeted her with a wide smile that vanished the moment she glimpsed Lorna's pale face.

"What's wrong?"

Lorna let out a nervous breath. "I'm so glad you're home. I need a favor."

The buzzer on the call box sounded again and Lorna reached to grip Melanie's hand. "You remember Mitch Ellery?"

Mellie's pretty face showed her alarm. "Oh, no, Lorna. What can I do?"

Lorna felt the sting of grateful tears. Though Melanie knew she'd silently indulged her craving to spend time with her sister, Mellie had never made more than a couple of remarks to caution Lorna about the risk. She'd kept her disapproval mostly to herself because Melanie Parker, more than anyone, understood. But Mellie knew as much as Lorna did what Mitch's arrival now meant.

"If he comes up," Lorna said shakily, "I'd like you to check on me in a few minutes. Just a quick phone call, you don't need to come over."

Melanie was distressed by that. "Do you think he'd hurt you? Could he become violent?"

God, she hadn't thought of that, but she doubted it. She shook her head.

"He's very angry, but I don't think he'd hurt me. Not like that. I'm probably overreacting."

The buzzer on the call box sounded again and Lorna urged Melanie back into the hall.

"I can't make him wait, Mel. Please. Call me in...twenty minutes?"

"That long?"

"Twenty minutes," Lorna repeated and tried for a smile, suddenly feeling guilty for worrying her friend. "It'll be all right."

Melanie nodded, though she didn't look convinced as she backed toward her apartment door across the hall. Lorna let her door close, then reached to press the intercom button before Mitch could ring again. If she was very, very lucky, the person downstairs would not be Mitch Ellery.

Her soft, "Yes," sounded strained.

Mitch's gravelly voice was curt. "This the right apartment?" He'd apparently recognized her voice.

No proper greeting, no "Is this Lorna Farrell?" no "May I please come in?" No acknowledgment that she had a choice in whether she buzzed him into the building or not. Almost as if the only thing that had made him pause from charging in like an angry bull was the need to make certain he'd be charging into the right apartment.

On the other hand, building security was sometimes lax. He could have waited until another tenant came along to slip past the locked door. The fact that he hadn't was at least honest and some indication of a sense of propriety, if not also fair play.

Her soft, "Yes," was resigned. She hesitated a moment, then pressed the button that would release the lock downstairs and let him pass into the lobby.

Real fear surged then. This was it. And, as she'd sensed, Mitch Ellery was about to charge in like a bull. Far too soon he'd cleared the stairs and she heard him striding down the hall. The cadence of his heavy boot heels was a confirmation that he was angry and would charge in. The relentless sound of his long stride coming so quickly near cranked her dread up at least a thousand notches.

She didn't think her nerves could take the sound of him pounding on her door, so she reached out to open it.

CHAPTER TWO

AT THE sight of Lorna Farrell standing so primly at the open door, Mitch stifled the same private shock he'd felt when she'd walked into John Owen's office with Kendra.

Lorna Farrell was slim and petite. Her dark head of glossy, shoulder-length hair curved under, her eyes were large and deeply blue, and her facial features were fine and delicate enough for a Renaissance portrait. The resemblance between her and Kendra was unmistakable.

Five years had smoothed out her features and turned her into a beauty. She had polish now, class, and the poise of a queen. But what she had by the bucketful was a resemblance to Kendra she'd not had five years before. No doubt it was now that stronger resemblance that had made her think she could engineer another try at Doris.

Mitch might even have given her some leeway had she simply tried to contact Doris again. His stepmother had finally confided that she'd given up a child for adoption years ago, but she'd denied the possibility that Lorna Farrell could be that child. A simple blood test might have thwarted Miss Farrell a second time. Surely she knew how easily she could be proved a liar if someone called her bluff.

But instead of inflicting herself directly on Doris, she'd managed to wedge herself into Kendra's life. That alone undermined her in his eyes. In the past few hours, he'd found out that Lorna had worked for John Owen long before Kendra had become engaged to him, but she'd had no business befriending Kendra, no business at all crossing the line as far as she had.

Kendra was a sweet, naïve child-woman. Strong-willed, a little spoiled, but blinded by the optimism and generosity of youth. She hadn't yet learned that the world was full of liars and opportunists. She hadn't been bitten by the bitter truth that jealous people would do their damnedest to knock her down for having money or that the greedy ones would play her for a fool to get a piece of it.

Lorna Farrell's slick intrusion into Kendra's confidence marked her as the second kind. And though Mitch had long thought his stepsister needed to wise up to the ways of the world, he was determined that Lorna Farrell wouldn't be the one to educate her.

Lorna didn't speak and neither did he as he strode through the open door into her apartment.

Lorna had done much better for herself these past five years than the cramped one-room apartment she'd had back then. These rooms were painted bright white, and the furniture was tasteful blend of nice pieces, though probably second hand. She liked color and she liked interesting little accents, like the whimsical caricature of a gangly palomino pony with inch-long eyelashes that stood almost a foot tall on the floor in front of an antique bookcase lined with hardcover and paperback books.

The dove gray sofa was plush and artfully scattered with old-fashioned needlework pillows. There were a few inexpensive but tasteful paintings on the walls and she had a fondness for dark tables with delicate legs. The dining room had a bowl of vivid silk flowers in the middle of the table, and every surface throughout the two rooms he could see were polished to a deep luster.

Everything was neat and orderly without a single thing out of place. Was this the rigid care of a woman who'd only recently come up in the world and appreciated that enough to take religious care of everything? Or was she an opportunist who liked to have nice things and by such diligent care demonstrated not only a lust for material possessions but a hunger for more and even better?

Because he was so suspicious of her, he discounted the idea that she kept her things so neat and orderly because it was an admirable habit.

He didn't bother to take off his Stetson. Though it was polite to do so and expected indoors, he didn't intend to pay her the compliment. He heard the tremor in her voice and sent her a surly glance.

"Would you like to sit down, Mr. Ellery? Can I get you something? Coffee? A s-soda?"

He watched color flash across her cheekbones at the small stutter and took note of the way she gripped her slim fingers together. He detected the tremor she clearly tried to suppress in the faint vibration of her shoulders beneath her suit jacket.

"I didn't come to be sociable, Miz Farrell. Your pretty manners are wasted on me."

Now he saw the color vanish from her cheekbones, confirming the notion that she was as completely intimidated by him as she'd been five years ago, and thus would be easy to manage.

He lifted his hand to his chest, frowned at the small start she gave at the movement, then slipped his fingers into his suit pocket to remove the check. He held it out so she could see the amount.

Her deeply blue eyes dropped automatically to the digits. There was a spark of something then. Surprise? Or was it a flash of pain?

"Give Owens two weeks notice, then quit," he told her brusquely. "This should hold you over until you can find another job. If you leave San Antonio to take a job, I'll give you double that amount. Every year up to five years, I'll leave a matching check for that double amount in an account with my attorney. Every year up to five years that you stay out of San Antonio and have no contact with Kendra, the attorney will transfer that yearly amount into whatever out of town bank account you choose."

Mitch paused because she appeared to sway. He

hardened his heart to that show of shock because it was more likely shock that he'd given her what she'd wanted so easily. And from the amount on the check, she could surely see that multiples of that kind of money, if carefully handled, would soothe the sharper edges of her lust for riches for a long time to come. He went on.

"After five years, the money deal expires. By then there'll be a record of every transaction. If you approach Kendra again, we'll have a money trail to take you to court for extortion."

"How dare you?"

The words were choked and Lorna's stormy gaze came up to his. She'd stood stiffly before, but now she looked so rigid that movement might make her bones crackle.

Mitch lowered the check and tossed it dismissively to a lamp table.

"How dare *you*, Miz Farrell? Trading on the resemblance you didn't have five years ago to worm your way into an innocent kid's life. You aren't Doris Ellery's long-lost anything. If you say one word to Kendra, we'll press charges, petition the courts for a blood test, and when it comes up a nomatch, you'll have an arrest record and very likely a conviction."

He paused to let that sink in. Her face had gone bright red now and she was shaking. He kept his low voice harsh.

"Choose a happy life, Miz Farrell. Take the

money and leave town. You're beautiful, you're obviously clever, and you've got taste. Find some rich old boy and hold out for a ring and a date.''

"Get out." Her voice trembled as hard as she did now.

"I meant every word, darlin'. Every single word. And you're bright enough to know I can make it happen."

"Get out."

Lorna gave the two words separate emphasis. No matter how foolish she'd been, no matter how long she'd let the situation with Kendra go on, she wouldn't tolerate this. So much for Mitch Ellery's propriety and sense of fair play. He was trying to bully her into a setup. She was so outraged over it that she felt faint. Dark dots were swimming in her vision and her eyes felt on fire. Her whole body felt scorched.

And still he made no move to leave, just stood there like a column of granite. The hostility that radiated from him in waves was so intimidating that it magnified her hurt and the fury she felt.

She almost wished he had roughed her up. Anything, even that, would have been better than the brutal sting of his insult, not to mention the sheer menace of a man so much larger and stronger than she. The top of her head barely came to his shoulders. If he'd roughed her up, she could have dialed 911.

But she was helpless against this. She had no

doubt that he had the will and the means to frame her for extorting money from him, though she'd die before she took a single cent from anyone.

Mitch Ellery was a bully, but suddenly none of it mattered. None of it mattered because the emotions of these past few months, the old hurts and traumas that had been stirred up and the horror of this confrontation, seemed to have short-circuited her body.

The two-bite breakfast she'd caught on the run, the lunch she'd forgotten, the uneaten apple she'd carried home from the office, suddenly conspired with all the rest and she felt an odd lethargy as the dots swam faster and multiplied.

Panicked, she tried to reach the nearest chair. She'd no more than taken a wobbly step and sensed Mitch Ellery's sudden move when the world went black.

Mitch had hesitated to reach for Lorna because he thought she was faking a faint. And then he'd caught her a second too late because she'd wilted so fast and gone so boneless that even catching her arm hadn't prevented her temple from grazing the corner of the coffee table.

He'd gathered her up and placed her on the sofa, but her small body was so rag-doll limp that it was amazingly hard to manage, though she weighed almost nothing.

A pink welt marked her right temple and already the skin beneath it was staring to swell. Shock jolted him. She hadn't flinched when she'd hit, and as he tested the delicate skin next to the swelling, not even a hint of reaction showed in her lashes.

Hell. She hadn't hit the table hard enough to be knocked out, so the lady had well and truly fainted. An alien feeling of guilt punched him in the gut. Remorse made him pick up one of her limp hands and chafe it between his palms.

"Miz Farrell," he growled. "One of us is gonna be damned upset if you don't come around quick."

Mitch gritted his teeth for admitting that much. He patted the back of her still hand and when that got him nothing, he lightly tapped her pale cheek. Her glorious black lashes lay closed and motionless, and he felt another arrow of concern.

Gently laying her hand on her small waist, he rose to find the bathroom. Once there, he grabbed an artfully folded washcloth from a white basket on the counter and wet it beneath a jet of cold water in the sink.

Squeezing the excess water from it, he stalked back to the living room. Now her lashes spasmed and he sat down by her hip on the edge of the sofa cushion. He touched the cool, damp cloth to her cheek and was rewarded when she weakly turned her head to escape the sensation.

Mitch lifted the cloth to gently press it against her other cheek before he realized he'd picked up her hand again. Her fingers tightened on his, but her grip was weak.

His own low words, ''Come on, darlin', come on back,'' startled him.

Perhaps it was the remorse he felt, perhaps it was the simple compassion he had for any injured creature that accounted for the uncommon tenderness he felt suddenly. Or perhaps it was Lorna's sharp resemblance to his stepsister. Whatever the reason, feeling tender toward Lorna Farrell was not quite the anathema it should have been.

And when she made a soft sound of protest and brought up her other small hand to ward him off, he felt like a brute.

Mitch allowed her to brace her hand against his chest while he pressed the cool cloth softly against the welt. She winced at the pressure and sucked in a breath, then struggled to move her head away.

''Lay still.''

His tone was harsher than he'd meant, and he was privately horrified when he saw wetness spring onto her lashes. He forced his voice to soften so much it was almost a rasp.

''Let me take care of this, darlin'.''

The fact that he'd repeated the endearment in a sincere way was a fresh shock. But she responded to it by going still. Her wet lashes opened and those blue, blue eyes focused mistrustfully on his face. He could see her fear and she lay completely still, as if she was afraid to move.

The guilt that made him feel was sharp and uncomfortable, and his gaze shied briefly from her wary study before he brought it back to say something that would let her know he meant her no harm.

"Looks like I scared you into a faint. You hit the coffee table before I could catch you."

Confusion darkened the blue of her pretty eyes, but mistrust lingered in the mix. His pride was choking him, but he added a quiet, "I apologize."

Mitch couldn't maintain eye contact with her, so he lifted the cloth and inspected the small welt. "I'll get you some ice for that."

Her soft, "No," made him pause and he looked down at her. "You have to leave."

Despite her fear, she was rallying. Her refusal nettled his sense of responsibility. "Not till I'm sure you're okay."

She came right back with, "I don't need your help."

"How do you know that? Do you keel over in a faint so often it's a routine?"

"I never faint."

He gave a short bark of laughter and she jerked as if startled. Her eyes darkened again with wariness. Mitch ignored her reaction and leaned closer for emphasis.

"Well you just fainted, Miz Farrell. Write it in your diary."

She seemed to fumble a moment for an answer to that. "I ha-haven't eaten today."

That nettled him again. "You out of money till payday?"

Color surged into her cheeks. "I have plenty of money. I was too busy to be hungry."

Lorna wouldn't confess to him that the months of worry about her increasing contact with Kendra had affected her appetite.

Mitch came to his feet and loomed over her. "I'll put some ice in this cloth, then I'll see what you've got to eat around this place."

He strode away and she sat up in alarm. She cautiously touched her temple, but felt only a faint bit of pain. Sitting up had made her dizzy, but she turned to put her feet on the floor, determined to intercept Mitch and force him to leave.

And why wouldn't he just leave? His orders and threats had been traumatic enough, but now she couldn't get rid of him. And his concern confused her. He'd spoken to her earlier as if she was dirt under his feet, so his concern now was not only a shock, it was deeply suspicious.

Pride wouldn't permit her to allow someone who hated her and had just tried to lure her into an extortion charge to do kind things for her.

She reached for the check then got up and walked unsteadily to the kitchen. Once she got there, she stopped in the doorway while she waited for her legs to strengthen.

Mitch Ellery was a dark giant in her pristine kitchen. As in the living room, his larger-than-life presence dwarfed everything around him. He'd already loaded the washcloth with ice cubes, but he now had her refrigerator open and was peering inside.

Since she hadn't yet gone grocery shopping as she normally did on Friday nights, the refrigerator was humiliatingly bare. He glanced her way, his face a thundercloud of disapproval.

"No wonder you aren't eating. You've got little more than condiments and a half quart of milk that went out-of-date two days ago."

Lorna crossed the room and plucked the cloth-wrapped ice cubes out of his huge hand to toss them into the sink before she gingerly tucked the check back in his pocket. When she boldly reached between him and the refrigerator to catch the top of the door and crowd him out of the way so she could close it, he caught her hand.

Her wide gaze flew up to his. She gave her hand a testing tug, but he held it fast.

Mitch was so big, so virile, and so powerfully male. The small space in front of the refrigerator was smothering suddenly. The cool air from inside the open door had no impact on the heat between their bodies or the arrows of attraction that peppered her skin and made her feel hot and edgy inside.

His voice was gruff and low and it stroked her someplace deep. "It's a wrongheaded idea, but we'll go to a restaurant."

"No, we won't."

His dark brows lowered in irritation. "You need to eat. We'll get that swelling down, then go."

Lorna yanked at her hand and he released her. "I wouldn't cross the street with you." Her chin went up the smallest bit. "And I believe I'll call your bluff about that blood test, Mr. Ellery. Since you're obviously a take-over artist, you can make the appointment and I'll be there."

His eyes suddenly glittered with temper and she felt herself sway.

"And I'll call *your* bluff, Miz Farrell. You'll have that blood test. But right now, I'll call your other bluff."

With that, he leaned close. She managed a half step back before he swept her up in his arms as if she was no bigger than a small child. The quick movement made her head spin, and she reflexively gripped his wide shoulders. He seemed to sense he'd made her dizzy, so he didn't move right away to carry her out of the kitchen.

He was growling again. "What am I gonna do with you?" His minty breath sent warm puffs of air against her face.

"You can put me down and leave," she got out.

He studied her face, his irritation deepening. "Stubbornness and persistence can get you into all kinds of trouble. As you'll find out if you don't agree to back off with Kendra."

Anger roared through her. "Ditto, Mr. Ellery. Put me down."

"Fat chance." He turned with her and stalked

back into the living room to deposit her on an over-stuffed chair.

The phone jangled on the table next to her. Lorna was mildly surprised that he didn't snatch it up. She reached over and picked up the receiver as he towered in front of her.

Melanie's worried voice came over the line. "Are you all right? I haven't seen him leave."

Lorna glanced up at the rock-faced man who watched her, his dark brows lowered in a surly frown.

She realized then that Mitch Ellery wasn't a handsome man. His features were too rugged and rough. But he had a charisma that made him as magnetic and appealing as men whose features were smoother and more conventionally handsome. Perhaps more so.

Amazed that she'd been distracted by those thoughts, she glanced away from him. "I'm all right and yes, he's still here," she told her friend, then looked up at her unwanted guest as an idea sparked. "But he refuses to leave. If you'll come over with your pepper spray, he might change his mind."

Mitch's expression went thunderous again. Lorna watched as his stern mouth moved to shape a succinct profanity.

Melanie's, "Oh my gosh!" was as fervent as if she'd actually heard the silent word across the phone line. "I'll be right over."

"We'll give him five minutes, then come over."

"And you'll explain why you gave him five more minutes when I get over there, right?"

"Right."

Mel hung up and Lorna reached over to put the receiver in its cradle.

"You need to leave now, Mr. Ellery," she said as she leaned back in the chair and looked up at him. "My friend lives across the hall, she doesn't own a can of pepper spray, but she's fiercely loyal and very protective." She couldn't help a weary smile. "You could very well find yourself on the drive home reeking of either cooking spray, furniture polish or the soap scum remover she might substitute."

"Can she make you a sandwich? Get your blood sugar up?"

The questions were another surprise and hinted that he felt at least a particle of genuine care. And that touched her. Lorna felt her resentment toward him mellow.

"I'm sure she can do better than a simple sandwich. She's a fabulous cook. Which reminds me. She might bring over a wire whisk or a potato masher. Have you ever seen what a wire whisk or a potato masher can do to the average tyrant? They've done all sorts of studies, and the photographs are pretty gruesome."

His formidable expression eased, and she sensed something in his stern personality give way. The faint curve of his harsh mouth was probably as close to a real smile as she'd ever see from him. But if he was truly amused, he didn't remark on it.

"She'll look after you tonight?"

The caring that implied was suddenly painful for her and her faint smile dropped away. "Why on earth would you care?" The words were out before she'd thought them through.

Suddenly he bent down and braced his big fists on the chair arms. His face was very close now and the thrill that whirled over her was shockingly sexual.

"If not for this thing with Kendra, I might have found you...interesting."

It was a blunt admission that shocked her to her toes. She fumbled for a way to answer that.

"And what will you find when the blood test proves that Kendra is my sister?"

Now he was angry again because his expression seemed to turn to stone in front of her. "It won't."

"It will, Mr. Ellery. And when it does, it won't change a single thing, because Doris will never acknowledge it." Saying that out loud sent a flood of old hurt surging up and she felt her eyes sting. She struggled to defy it, her gaze never wavering from the harsh lights in his as she declared, "In fact, unless I miss my guess, Doris will never submit to a blood test herself."

"She will because it'll put an end to you."

She'd made him angry again and saying that was his retaliation. The smile she gave then was not a true smile, it was more of a grimace that eased some of the painful pressure in her heart.

"She sent you here with a check to put an end to me. That's the only end she wants."

He straightened, his dark eyes cutting into hers as if he was measuring her in some way.

"Get something to eat. I'll be in touch."

Lorna didn't respond to that and he reached over to pick up his Stetson from the coffee table. He put it on and tugged down on the brim. It was a cowboy version of goodbye that was almost polite.

"You'll hear from me about the test," he said, his low voice now almost a warning.

"I'll look forward to it," she said. "But don't hold your breath waiting for Doris's consent." She'd nicked his temper again, because his dark eyes glittered with it.

As if he was making a silent declaration, he pulled the folded check out of his jacket pocket, then tossed it to the lamp table out of her easy reach before he turned and strode out of the apartment without a backward glance.

Aggravated about the check but relieved he was gone, Lorna got up and walked to the bathroom. The small swelling was so minor it was almost nonexistent. It was merely a faint graze and would probably be completely healed by morning. Why had he fretted over it as if it was some grave wound?

She heard Melanie call out as she entered the apartment, so she called back, "I'll be out as soon as I change my clothes.'' Lorna stepped into the bedroom and shakily found a pair of jeans and a T-shirt. She gave her mussed hair a quick brushing, then went out to join her friend.

''I was watching at the peephole, so I saw him,'' Melanie reported as Lorna came into the living room. Mellie lifted her light brows and made her green eyes go wide. ''And wow. Kinda like a mix of John Wayne, Tommy Lee Jones and a Minotaur. Not handsome, but…awesome. And, dare I say it? Sexy,'' she declared with a sparkling glance. ''No need to explain the extra five minutes, amiga, but are you all right?''

Lorna laughed at that, suddenly feeling worlds better than she had in ages. She'd survived Mitch Ellery and he'd virtually decreed the blood test that, if nothing else, would prove she wasn't a liar—or at least that she was willing to have her honesty put to a definitive test. Perhaps it was good that he'd left the check. It would feel even better giving it back to him a second time than it had the first.

''I'm fine,'' Lorna said. ''Pretty great, actually. I'll tell you all about it over pizza. You can choose the toppings this time.''

''Sounds good. You want to call or should I?''

''I'll buy, so you can make the call.''

While they waited for their pizza to be delivered, Lorna began to tell her dearest friend almost everything about Mitch Ellery. Almost everything, but the stunning attraction she felt.

Why she suddenly couldn't confess that one thing when she'd confessed nearly everything else in her life to Melanie—was a surprise.

If not for this thing with Kendra, I might have found you...interesting.

It shocked her to realize how tantalizing that was. And how much she'd like to be the focus of his interest.

Mitch's iron-willed protectiveness toward her sister—even though it was aimed at protecting her sister from her—was as much an indication of his character as his formidable personality and his reluctant, kind care when she'd fainted.

Men like Mitch Ellery were all too rare; she'd understood that five years ago. He'd scared her then, and he'd scared her today. But the glimpse of tenderness in him tonight had deeply affected her.

I might have found you...interesting.

What would it have been like to capture his interest? If she'd caught his eye in the usual way women caught men's eyes, what would he have been like? There was a certain rough-edged gallantness about him, and even as they'd shaken hands that day when he was clearly furious to see her, his grip had been gentle. And he'd touched her tonight in the most tender way.

For a man of his size and brute strength, the contrast between his power and his touch was breathtaking. The memory made her skin tingle as it had then. What would it be like to have someone like Mitch Ellery in her life?

Eventually her speculation waned. The truth was, she hadn't got his attention in the usual way. His mission—and he'd made that mission shockingly clear—was to bribe her to leave San Antonio.

A whisper of fresh fear skimmed over her heart. If Doris wouldn't do her part with the blood test, it was certain Mitch would bring some other pressure to bear if she didn't quit her job and clear out.

Wealthy, powerful tyrants like Mitch Ellery had a legion of legal help at their fingertips. And men like him were socially influential. The right word in the right ear could destroy everything she'd worked so hard to get and ruin her chances for good things for a long time to come.

Choose a happy life, Miz Farrell.

The silly half-fantasy about winning his interest suddenly seemed as foolish as it was futile. She must have hit her head harder than she'd thought. By the time her friend had gone home, Lorna was caught in a grip of melancholy that grew so dismal later that she laid in the dark a long time and worried about what more Mitch Ellery could do to force her out of her sister's life.

CHAPTER THREE

LORNA slept in that next morning to make up for her lost sleep. After a late breakfast of cold pizza, she started a load of laundry in the small washer in an alcove of her bathroom. Frustrated that Mitch dominated her thoughts, she threw herself into her Saturday chores before she left the apartment to run errands.

She dropped off clothes at the dry cleaners and picked up the batch she'd left there the Saturday before. A fast trip to Wal-Mart was followed by another to her favorite grocery store to take care of the shopping she'd not had time for on her way home last night. It was midafternoon when she got home.

Living alone and having to carry everything across the mostly full parking lot and up a flight of stairs in one trip was a challenge that was also part of Lorna's normal routine.

After draping her dry cleaning over her arm and carefully gathering up the handles to the various plastic bags that contained her purchases, she made her way across the sun-scorched parking lot to the back door of the building. She'd reached the sidewalk when a big man came around the corner and strode purposely toward her.

Mitch Ellery was dressed like a real cowboy in a blue plaid shirt and denim jeans worn soft. The black Stetson he wore had a more common look than his pearl-gray one, and the black boots he had on today carried the scuff marks of daily wear.

From the stern line of his harsh mouth and the faint scowl that darkened his gaze beneath the hat brim, he looked like he meant business. If he'd been wearing a six-shooter, the black Stetson combined with his tough-guy ruggedness would have made him look like an Old West outlaw.

His dark eyes showed a gleam of disapproval. ''You gotta lazy man's load,'' he said bluntly as he smoothly relieved her of everything but the dry cleaning.

Lorna's quick move to snatch back the bags was quelled by his curt, ''I've got 'em.''

''I haven't invited you in, Mr. Ellery. Nor do I plan to.'' She gave him a stiff smile as she again reached to hook her fingers through the handles of the plastic bags to reclaim them. ''But thanks for the show of chivalry.''

The minute her fingers were laced through the handles, Mitch shifted his grip, managing to neatly trap them. Tiny shocks radiated from his firm hold and her wide gaze flashed up to the glittering darkness in his.

''We can either stand here the rest of the afternoon, or you can invite me in,'' he growled.

''We have nothing to say to each other, so there's

no reason to invite you to do anything but leave.''
Lorna straightened her fingers to tug them free of
the bag handles, but Mitch's grip was too strong.

''You and I need to talk.''

His expression was grim and Lorna sensed a new
threat. ''The only thing I want to hear from you is
the date and time for the blood test.''

''You'll hear from me Monday about that. Right
now, we've got a new problem.''

Lorna did her best to appear unimpressed. She
heard his frustration with her when he added darkly,
''It's about Kendra.''

As if he knew she'd cave in at the mention of
Kendra and a problem, he loosened his grip on her
fingers. Lorna pulled free. ''What about Kendra?
Nothing's happened, has it?''

Now his harsh look eased fractionally. ''No problem beyond a damned fool idea that involves you.
Which is why we'll have a talk. Now.''

Relieved Kendra was all right, Lorna decided that
she'd had enough of his dictates.

''Listen, Mr. Ellery. You might give orders at
your ranch, but you aren't allowed to rule the world.
Whether you have a particle of respect for me or
not, you'll at least go through the verbal motions of
good manners or you'll be invited to go straight to
hell.''

The faint shock that showed on his face for a
space of a second was wiped away by a mighty
frown. He hadn't expected her to stand up to him

and he clearly didn't like it. She'd never in her life spoken to anyone like that, but something in his autocratic manner warned that she'd better learn to or he'd run over her without a second thought.

His expression went stony. The time it took him to swallow his pride and make an effort to frame a proper request seemed insultingly long.

Which sent her temper soaring. "You can either sit my bags on the sidewalk for someone else or you can keep them."

She turned then and dug her key out of her pocket. Since his hostage takeover of her purchases wouldn't work on her, he could decide if he liked the food and the toothpaste and toiletries from Wal-Mart enough to be stuck with them. Hopefully he'd just put down the bags and leave.

"Miss Farrell." His voice was low, and Lorna stopped to glance back. "You must think I've got the manners of a..."

He paused to search her flushed face, as if trying to gauge how far he needed to humble himself. She raised a dark brow and he finished on a growl.

"...a pig."

Stifling a surprised laugh, Lorna came right back with, "If you have any evidence to disprove that, you'd better speak up quick."

Again he seemed to hesitate, but then he spoke, the words coming out as tonelessly as if he were reading them off a cue card.

"My apologies, Miz Farrell. Would you please

consider inviting me inside to discuss a new problem?''

Lorna felt her anger cool, but she was wary of letting him in. ''You'll behave?''

''I surely will.'' His swift answer was proof that he could barely contain his impatience to have the discussion.

The notion that this big bull of a man was knuckling under to her demand for good manners—even if it was difficult for him—made her feel a small bit of power.

Though common sense told her this was only an illusion of cooperation, the secret part of her that had never truly felt valuable or particularly powerful gobbled it up.

''All right. We'll see how things go. But I should warn you that I've got a black belt in screaming down apartment buildings.''

It was meant to lighten things between them, but neither of them smiled. She'd already got the impression that Mitch didn't smile often.

But perhaps the biggest reason neither of them smiled was because they both recognized that her lighthearted remark was an expression of fear and mistrust. Fear and mistrust leached the humor out of most things, at least in her life.

Lorna turned back to the door to unlock it, and Mitch followed her in. They walked up the stairs then down the hall to her apartment in silence. As she'd done downstairs, she held the door open for him as he carried her bags in. He took her purchases to the kitchen while she carried her dry cleaning and handbag to her bedroom to put away. By the time she joined Mitch in the kitchen, he was unloading groceries onto the counter.

Her, "Thank you," were the only words between them until she'd put everything away and disposed of the empty bags. She left the things from Wal-Mart for later, then turned to him and clasped her hands together. She glanced up at his Stetson, so he obliged her silent reminder and took it off.

"Would I again be wasting good manners if I asked what you'd like to drink? The choices are still a soda or coffee. Or a glass of water."

Mitch couldn't seem to keep his gaze from eating her up. Lorna's delectably curved body was virtually perfect. The white cotton blouse she wore over her most interesting curves was still crisp despite the heat, and her jeans carried a crease that let him know she ironed them. As a man who was too macho to wear jeans with a persnickety crease, the feminine fussiness of that tickled him. The plain sandals on her pretty feet revealed neatly clipped toenails painted a soft pink. He'd never been particularly attracted to a woman's feet before, but Lorna's were almost as touchable looking as the rest of her.

He had the sudden urge to grab her up and see if her kisses were as fiery and tantalizing as her personality, and that aggravated him. In view of the complicating developments with Kendra and his

stepmother that day, the urge could prove dangerous. He remembered his manners enough to answer
Lorna's question before he blurted out his purpose
for being here.

"No, thank you. But you go ahead if you want
something."

The small knot she'd made of her fingers got
tighter and she shook her head. "Maybe we should
just move on to what you came here to discuss.
Should we sit down?"

He was too impatient to sit around, so he shook
his head to the offer and baldly stated the problem.
"Kendra's love-struck and she imagines everyone
else ought to be love-struck, too. She thinks there's
chemistry between us that I'd be a fool to ignore."

Lorna looked honestly shocked, and she looked
shocked enough with just the right touch of politely
repressed horror, that his ego took a sting.

"H-how did she get that…idea?" She'd asked it
a little breathlessly, as if it was a complete mystery
to her.

"From the way we looked at each other in the
office and shook hands. And she knows neither of
us is seeing anyone." He couldn't keep from adding,
"Which, by the way, is more personal information
than you should've given."

Lorna glanced away from him and her cheeks col-
ored a bit. She didn't comment on his disapproving
remark, but then, she still looked a little stunned.
"Single people meet all the time and have a reaction

that no one feels compelled to do anything about. Surely she knows that?''

Now her wide gaze shifted back to his. ''And you were so angry and I was so...*horrified* to see you...''

Her voice trailed away, as if she'd suddenly realized what she'd said and how it might sound to him.

She tried a small smile that looked strained. ''No offense, but you know what I mean. I'd only heard ten minutes before that you'd be picking her up and...then there you were, angry. I didn't know what you'd do.''

Her answer mollified him somewhat and he got right to the point of this talk. ''So we'll go out a few times until she's satisfied there's something between us, then you can suddenly dump me for whatever reason you like.''

The kitchen went completely silent for several moments.

''Excuse me?'' Lorna gave her head a faint shake before her eyes narrowed suspiciously on his face.

Mitch couldn't help his terse, ''You heard me.''

She shook her head again, as if she was more certain this time. ''If I heard you right, then the answer's no. No. No, no.''

Now she was shaking her head emphatically, but the smile on her face was more a sign of mortification than humor. She turned to pace to the kitchen sink then stopped to grip the counter as if she needed to hang onto something.

"Why on earth would you come up with something like that? *How* on earth could we possibly date each other?"

She let go of the counter and turned fully toward him before he could answer. "Why not tell her she was mistaken, that I don't appeal to you, that you were just being nice? Or that you were trying to get a reaction from me, but my reaction wasn't what it should have been from a woman you'd consider dating? You told her that or something like that, didn't you?"

"I did not."

Lorna stared at him as he gave each word subtle emphasis. She wasn't certain it was possible to feel more taken by surprise.

"Why not?"

"Because she's got eyes and she's walking around in a romantic haze. Kendra's in love, and she thinks it's so damned wonderful that everyone she cares about should be in love, too."

Lorna couldn't keep looking at him and glanced away. It dawned on her then that a large part of her horror was that she was so strongly attracted to Mitch, despite his harsher qualities. Keeping in close company with him would make it impossible to fight her attraction, and pretending to date him could be lethal for someone like her. And then there was the whole thing with Kendra and their mother. She looked at him.

"Doris doesn't know about Kendra's matchmaking, does she?"

"Kendra talked about it at breakfast. Going on and on about you and I meeting in the office yesterday, how it was so romantic and sweet and...cute." His stern face showed faint disgust at repeating those words. "So Doris knows."

Lorna caught what he'd left out. "Doris knows and you talked to her privately about this scheme, didn't you?"

"I did."

"What did she say?"

Lorna shouldn't have asked that question, because she knew that hearing anything Doris might have said about her would be devastating. Doris had given her up as an infant, but she'd also refused to claim her that other time long ago, years before their shocking introduction in the restaurant. Lorna closed her heart to that memory because she couldn't bear to think about that other time.

"She suggested that it might be better to pick up on Kendra's assumption and give dating a shot, but then to have things between you and I not work out later. Kendra's loyal to me and she'd naturally turn cool to someone she thought did me wrong or hurt me in some way. Lots of love affairs don't pan out and ours would be just another one that goes flat quick."

He paused and seemed to fight a silent war between being harsh with her and being...less harsh.

"It's an alternative solution if you won't quit your
job. It'd solve the problem of how to keep you from
getting too involved in Kendra's life, and you'd look
a lot less like friend material."

"So I get to be the bad guy." The notion made
her sick. It meant she wouldn't even have Kendra's
regard. Knowing that this faked dating idea was
Doris's was particularly painful.

Could she honestly face knowing that her sister
would think she was an awful person, or worse, a
cruel one? Because that's what Doris's plan was calculated to do. And she'd sent Mitch to pressure her
into spoiling Kendra's good opinion of her forever.

As if he'd sensed some of what she was thinking,
Mitch went utterly grim. "You need to remember
that her other solutions aren't as kind to you."

The sickness she felt mingled with dread. "What
other solutions, the legal ones?"

He stayed silent and sparked her temper.

"Then tell Doris to bring them on, cowboy. I'll
find a lawyer of my own and compel her to have a
blood test."

Lorna managed to bite her tongue before she said
the rest: that both she and Doris already knew the
truth, so a blood test wasn't necessary, though it
would be a dandy legal defense that Doris would
never provoke because she wouldn't be able to
hoodwink anyone once the test results were known.

Mitch's voice went low. "If you take Doris on in court, you'll be up against the caliber of legal talent Ellery money can buy."

The reluctant attraction she felt toward Mitch suffered only a moment's disappointment. Of course he'd say that, it was the truth. Though she didn't think much of him for throwing the weight of the Ellery name around, she sensed it was not a regular thing with him. And he was doing it now to protect people he cared about.

No one with any kind of power or money had ever gone to war to protect her. There had never been a Mitch Ellery in her life, and she couldn't help the sudden hunger to have someone like him be her faithful protector, however much she hated being his target now.

The tension between them was sharp, but her anger toward his high-handedness waned fast in light of what her mother planned.

In spite of Doris's rejection and dishonesty, Lorna wasn't certain even now if she resented her mother enough to reveal to Mitch precisely how she knew Doris was her biological mother. If she did, Doris's good relationship with the daughter she wanted and with Mitch, could be irreparably harmed. On the other hand, Mitch was probably too loyal to Doris to believe Lorna anyway, so it was wiser to keep quiet.

Lorna let out the breath she'd been holding and

glanced away a moment to collect her thoughts before she looked over at him again.

"Look, I think this is all an overreaction," she said quietly, suddenly exhausted by it all. "I swear to you that I will never tell Kendra who I am. You can trust me to keep silent because if I'd wanted to tell her, I could have done it months ago."

She paused to get a careful grip on herself because saying the rest would make her emotional and she was struggling to show none of it. "I know Doris wants nothing to do with me, so I'd never put Kendra in a position like that or say anything that would taint her relationship with her mother. I give you my word."

The laser intensity of Mitch's gaze made her feel cut up and invaded, but she tolerated it because she hoped he could somehow tell that she was trustworthy.

"Please, Mr. Ellery, go back to your ranch and forget all this. I'm willing to find better excuses to keep Kendra from drafting me for small things and, since Doris has already nominated me to be the villain, I'll find some way to discourage Kendra's attention."

"How?"

She shook her head helplessly, hating the thought of hurting Kendra, even in a small way. "I don't know how exactly. She's sensitive and I don't want her feelings hurt any more than you do. But she's also sensitive enough to take a hint with subtle things.''

"Name those.'' He was relentless when it came to protecting her sister, and she couldn't help another ache of envy.

"I don't know.'' Lorna shrugged wearily. "I could plead a headache, tell her I'd like to leave the office early so I don't have extra time. Something.''

"Why didn't you do those things months ago?''

The question made her feel choked. "That's too…personal to talk about with you. But if family means as much to you as it seems to, I'm sure you can figure it out.''

She lifted a hand to comb her fingers into her hair and ruthlessly pull it back in a rare show of restlessness before she realized what she was doing and made herself stop.

She couldn't bear the stern scrutiny of solemn dark eyes that missed nothing so she looked away.

"Please, go home now. I'll keep my silence and my word. I'll also very gently begin to distance myself from your stepsister.''

She held her breath again, waiting for some signal that he would now leave.

"Kendra expects you and I to join her and John for dinner tonight.''

He said it as if it was a done deal. Lorna looked at him, baffled that he'd not given up on the dating charade even after what she'd just promised. There

was absolutely no reason for either of them to consider following through on that bizarre idea.

"Besides the fact that the date-and-dump idea is
crazy, not to mention dishonest, surely Kendra
doesn't think it's proper for me to double date with
my boss?" It was another sign of Kendra's youthful
openness and naiveté that both frustrated and
touched her.

"I told her the same thing. But you and I will
show up later on the dance floor. Twenty minutes,
tops. After tonight, she won't need to know more of
the story between us than hearing that we date. Two
weeks of that, then you can break it off. I'll be un-
derstandably cranky and closemouthed about it, and
she'll draw a loyal conclusion and act accordingly."

Lorna shook her head again. "I can't believe
you're serious about this."

Mitch's dark look turned tough and no-nonsense.
"Kendra's a sweet, tenderhearted kid. I won't have
her feelings hurt by excuses she'll see through.
She'll be sensitive to the idea that you've turned
cool to her, so you can't be the one to do it."

He hesitated, and she saw a faint hint of discomfort before he added, "Better for her to do it to you
later."

Better for her to do it to you.

The picture of Kendra's face when that happened
flashed in her brain and pummeled her heart. It took
her several agonizing seconds to recover.

"I think...you'd better leave now."

"Dress up tonight," he ordered brusquely. "I'll come for you at eight."

Her frustration with him peaked. "Didn't you hear anything I said? There's no way in the world this could work. Whatever you and Doris think of me, I'm not a good enough actress to pretend a romantic interest in someone so awf—in—in you."

Now his dark eyes glittered with the softened insult. "You won't have to pretend," he drawled. "I see it every time you look at me."

Embarrassment made her face go hot and she scrambled to deny the charge. "What conceit! I'm not certain which of your flaws should go at the top of what's become a lengthy list, but right now conceit and hubris could arm wrestle for the spot."

A stunning flash of amusement slanted his hard mouth, though his dark eyes glowed like black diamonds.

"Go dancing with me tonight."

She caught a hint that the dictate was personal. That going with him tonight was not part of a charade, but something he wanted for himself. The impression shocked her, and she instantly dismissed it.

"No." She'd made it sound firm and absolute.

Mitch put on his Stetson and tugged it down to a rakish angle that matched the glitter in his eyes. His voice was a growl and dealt her another quick shock.

"Suffer conceit at eight o'clock, or hubris at eight-fifteen."

His gaze dropped from her flushed face and wandered down the front of her to her feet before it leaped up to blaze into hers.

"And while you're at it, put on something cut low that's short enough to show some leg. I like my women sexy."

Lorna was so utterly stunned and so furious those next seconds that she couldn't piece together words strong enough or foul enough to say to him. By the time her shock faded and she could find her tongue, Mitch was gone.

She stomped around the apartment for the next half hour, so frustrated and stirred up that if she'd been a man she would have gone after Mitch Ellery and punched that conceited grin so far off his arrogant face that he'd have to drive to Waco to get it back.

CHAPTER FOUR

THAT night, Mitch was eager to get to Lorna's place. The drive to San Antonio had never seemed so long. He always looked forward to female company, but he'd never felt such keen anticipation.

He'd thought about Lorna all day, particularly after he'd left her delightfully speechless in her apartment that afternoon. He mentally reviewed every second he'd spent with her, reexamined every word she'd spoken, every expression, every nuance. The only dishonest thing she'd said was when she'd tried to deny she was attracted to him. She'd been caught flat-footed with that, but her reaction had given him clues to compare to everything else.

And he couldn't forget that Lorna was completely uncowed by the threat of a blood test. It was hard to believe she had anything to hide when she was so eager to have it done. That he now believed Lorna to be genuinely decent and her story credible, severely undermined the notion that she was an opportunist out to swindle either Doris or Kendra.

Besides, a true gold digger who was about to be thwarted in one area would have compensated for that loss by zeroing in on the dating scheme in hopes of somehow snagging herself a generous lover, if not a wealthy husband.

The initial reports from the private investigator he'd hired seemed to confirm the things he'd already sensed about Lorna's character. Though an investigator could only provide so many concrete facts from her past, in the end it was up to him to interpret them. He could be wrong, but if Lorna Farrell was trying to fool anyone, he couldn't see it. He wished he was as confident about his stepmother.

In his mind, you didn't offer bribes for any amount, much less automatically choose to bribe someone with the kind of money Doris had set aside. There were cheaper, more ethical ways to get rid of an opportunist. And if the truth was on your side, you sought protection from the courts.

Mitch was a blunt, straightforward man, so he didn't approve of the things Doris was insisting on. What seemed particularly odd was the dating scheme, though truth to tell, spending time with Lorna wasn't exactly a hardship.

And the nagging notion that Lorna might truly be Doris's daughter troubled him. He couldn't imagine rejecting an opportunity to know his own child, and would have found irresistible even a belated chance to do so.

Since adoption records were difficult if not impossible to get, perhaps Lorna was mistaken. Being mistaken about something didn't make her dishonest. Maybe he could get her to explain her certainty about Doris.

By the time he turned off onto Lorna's street, he stopped himself from speculating further. He'd indulge Doris's wishes for now and wait for the results from the blood test.

Perhaps it was the tightrope he was walking that heightened his anticipation of seeing Lorna again. The forbidden was always a lure, but the truth was he would have been powerfully attracted to Lorna whatever the circumstances.

He liked the qualities he saw in her, and he liked *her*. Lorna was quick-witted and bright. She also had grit and spunk, and the way she'd primly stood up to him made her unique. He was surprised by how much he enjoyed her.

The fact that he had to do a believable job of pretending an attraction to her tonight for Kendra's benefit—without giving into the blood-heating lust he felt—would be both the highlight and the challenge of the evening.

Lorna had finally managed to calm down and once her anger was under control, practicality and common sense reasserted themselves.

She'd known for months that she was courting disaster by allowing Kendra to get close to her when she knew Doris would vehemently object. She'd initially been resigned to the idea that she deserved a consequence for that, but when Mitch had shown up with a check she'd been so outraged that her willingness to suffer a consequence had come to an abrupt end. But everything had gone a little crazy since then, and things promised to get worse if she didn't do something decisive to put a stop to it.

In view of the fact that Kendra would be marrying John Owen, it was probably inevitable that she'd have to quit her job, though she'd lived through enough financial hardships in her life to know she needed to wait for the right one to open up.

Until then, there was still the problem of Kendra. Though Lorna was appalled by Doris's date-and-dump plan, she now saw it as the only way to forestall whatever else Doris might send her way. And, as painful as it was to contemplate, what Mitch had said was true: it was better for Lorna to suffer Kendra's rejection than the other way around.

Kendra was sweet and open and she had a charming innocence life hadn't allowed Lorna. Though these past months she'd been a little frustrated by her sister's sunny naiveté, her driving instinct was to protect Kendra and shield her from hurt.

The blood test would prove who she was to everyone else, but it wouldn't compel Doris to have anything to do with her or to approve a relationship with Kendra. She'd accepted that long ago, but it was entirely possible that Doris's next legal move would be to claim harassment if Lorna didn't remove herself from Kendra's orbit. A biological mother could claim that she was being harassed by a child she'd given up and wanted nothing to do with. It had happened before.

God knew how messy something like that could become. Because of the Ellery name, a harassment lawsuit could end up in the newspapers, and the only sure outcome of that would not only be the damage to Lorna's reputation, but it could taint her prospects for the future family she so highly prized. How many decent men would choose to marry a woman who'd been charged with harassment, and have her bear and raise their children?

Nevertheless, the thought of losing Kendra's regard hurt. If there could ever be a realistic chance that she and Kendra might get to know each other as sisters, Lorna would never consider going through with things tonight. But because Doris would never accept her, she couldn't put Kendra in the middle or risk that Kendra's close relationship with their mother would be damaged.

Mother-daughter relationships were sacred to Lorna. After she'd been put into a series of foster homes after her adoptive parents' deaths when she was eight, she'd been forced to accept the fact that she'd never know a true mother-child relationship again until she had children of her own. When that miracle happened, she'd be devastated if an outsider came between her and her child.

Since she was the outsider this time and needed to take measures for the sake of her sister, Lorna finally gave in and selected a dress from her closet for the date with Mitch.

It was a stylish black one that was as low-cut as her sense of propriety allowed and was also short enough to show her legs to advantage. She wasn't certain it was precisely as low-cut or short or sexy as Mitch Ellery had decreed, but it was certainly tasteful and flattering enough to suit her personal standard or she'd wouldn't have bought it in the first place.

She didn't get many invitations to go dancing, so the opportunity was some consolation. Lots of men seemed allergic to dancing. She'd assumed the high-testosterone ones like Mitch might be more so, but perhaps he was more secure in his machismo than the average male.

Her attraction to Mitch complicated her feelings about everything else. Why on earth was she so wildly excited by the thought of being with him? She'd had plenty of dates, though they all seemed dull and weak compared to Mitch. She'd never been intimate with any of them, and hadn't wanted to be.

But Mitch was something else entirely, and despite his conceit and his colossal nerve, she suddenly wished with all her heart that she'd met him under different circumstances. He was unique in her experience and certainly out of her league sexually, so perhaps it was the sensual peril he represented that accounted for her excitement. Where was her common sense?

When she realized she was taking extra pains with her appearance, she scolded herself for it, then continued anyway.

The moment Lorna opened her door to him and he caught sight of her in the low-cut black dress that was the stuff of classier male fantasies, Mitch was instantly suspicious.

He'd half expected her to defiantly meet him at the door in the white blouse and jeans she'd had on that afternoon, but the sexy dress and the glamorous way she'd swept her dark hair up and left a few sleek strands to dangle in saucy squiggles made him wonder if she'd decided to have a try at his wallet.

But if she was a gold digger, he couldn't see it in the somber blue of her eyes as she let him in. And she gripped the check he'd left there the night before in nervous fingers. She didn't waste time getting to the point and held it out to him.

"I won't keep this," she said stiffly, and when he made no move to take the check, she pushed it closer. "Please. Either take it back and keep it, or I'll run it down the garbage disposal. I don't want Ellery money of any amount, so if there's something to pay for tonight, I'll pay for my own."

He took the check, folded it and slid it into his jacket pocket. "Nice speech."

She gripped her hands together in front of her and he could tell she was working up to something. "I have another speech."

He reached for her arm. "Give it to me in the car."

Lorna eased back to prevent him from rushing her out. "I've decided to find another job as soon as possible," she said quietly. "I only ask that you give me a reasonable length of time to find something comparable to what I have now. The moment I do, I'll put in my two-week notice."

He gave her a narrow look. "Good choice, but you're talking a month, maybe longer."

"I know, and that can't be helped. It looks better to a prospective employer when there's no employment gap."

"You should have done this months ago."

Now he saw the spark of resentment in her eyes, but she gave him a restrained, "Perhaps. However, in view of my promise to you now to find another job, we don't need to go through with this charade. I won't take a job away from San Antonio, but with any employer other than John Owen, I'm sure Kendra won't feel free to ask for my time during working hours."

"What about after working hours?"

Lorna shook her head. "That's never been a problem, and it won't be after I switch jobs because I won't allow it. Shallow friendships come and go. It will be a drift-away sort of thing."

"The dating idea has a shorter shelf life," he pointed out, "so we'll go ahead with a convincing performance, then see how it plays." He started to reach for her arm again to hurry her along, but she again stepped back.

"I don't think it's wise to go through with this."

"Wise or not, Kendra's expecting us."

Now his formidable frown eased a fraction and she saw his stern mouth curve slightly. The cagey look in his dark eyes hinted at a devilment that caught her off balance.

"But maybe you're right. We could cancel tonight and it could still be effective. She could get the idea tomorrow morning that things got so out of hand before we could leave your apartment that I spent the night."

Her cheeks instantly turned a deep red that spread up to her hairline and sent a flush downward to the soft skin between the deep V of her dress. Her blue eyes went stormy. "There's no way on earth she'd ever think that of me."

"A picture's worth a thousand words," he drawled. "Especially if I show up at breakfast in the suit I left the ranch in tonight, unshaven, with my tie in my jacket pocket. It's been known to happen."

Lorna felt her face go hotter as his outrageous words impacted her. "You'd do that to me?"

Mitch's smile eased to a serious line. "After seeing you in that dress, I half hope it'd be the truth."

Things felt intimate between them suddenly. Lorna's anger with him was not nearly as strong as it should have been because the peculiar shiver that went through the deepest parts of her made her legs feel a little weak, and that confused her. How could she respond with anything but outrage to what he'd said?

The glittering heat in his eyes stroked her insides and his deep voice went rough. "You look so...beautiful. I don't like the reason we're together tonight, but I'm not sorry to be here."

The blunt compliment was a new shock and sapped a little more of her anger. His candor did something odd to her, and she was suddenly afraid she might actually start to like him more than was prudent. There was no good future for her in any of this, and she needed to remember that.

"Please, Mr. Ellery—"

"Mitch. It's too late to be formal, Lorna."

"Please, Mitch. Don't do this."

He glanced away from her briefly and she took hope in the hint of discomfort. When his dark gaze came back to her, it was somehow softer.

"I won't drag you to the nightclub, but I think Doris will be more reassured if you do."

Lorna thought instantly of a potential harassment charge and what it could mean to her. Like it or not, she was trapped. Worse, she'd trapped herself and now felt pressured by her mother's aversion to her. If she'd quit her job months ago or contacted Mitch and explained her dilemma, perhaps they wouldn't be here tonight and she wouldn't be in this fix, flirting with disaster.

Because it would be flirting with disaster to pretend to be romantically interested in Mitch. If she hadn't been attracted to him at all, the pretense Doris wanted wouldn't be so perilous.

But she was attracted to Mitch, deeply attracted. Though he was tough and intimidating, she couldn't forget the tender side he'd demonstrated last night. And though she wouldn't have believed it of him, beneath his harsh exterior he was showing a surprising sense of humor that was almost playful. She liked that so much.

He was also one of the few men who seemed neither intimidated by her reserve nor put off by her aloofness. The fact that he seemed to enjoy the small verbal battles they'd had so far and was intelligent enough to catch her by surprise with some of them, was enormously appealing to a woman who'd often been disappointed in other, more predictable men.

But if she hadn't also sensed the integrity beneath Mitch's tough exterior, she wouldn't consider having a thing to do with him tonight. In spite of his outrageous threat about showing up at breakfast like a sexual conqueror, she'd also sensed he was too honorable to ever do it unless it was the truth. And even then, if he had any respect for the woman he'd been with, he wouldn't flaunt it. Only weak or immature men needed to do that.

She'd got another glimpse of the character behind his rugged face when he'd told her he wouldn't drag her to the nightclub. The soft regret in his dark eyes had made her instantly trust him.

"All right," she said quietly. "But I think this is a mistake."

"Maybe so."

Mitch reached out and touched her cheek. It was just a tiny brush of the back of his finger, but it sent a lightning bolt of energy through her that shot to her toes. One side of his stern mouth quirked.

"Smile at me, lady," he said gruffly, "and enjoy yourself tonight. You might as well."

Lorna stared up at him, very nearly mesmerized. Why did it have to be Mitch Ellery whose touch affected her so strongly? Why did she look into those dark, dark eyes and sense that this man could have been much more to her than an adversary?

Nothing could come of this, however much she suddenly hoped it would, so why was she letting him get to her like this? Somehow she had to get hold of her emotions because Mitch Ellery was even more off limits for her than Kendra.

She pulled her gaze away, silently picked up her tiny beaded handbag, then walked out the door when he opened it for her. The possessive hand he placed at the back of her waist was a huge distraction from her dismal feelings.

Mentally she was comparing him to every other date she'd ever had. They hadn't even reached his car yet, and he'd already made the others seem clumsy and vaguely repellent. She told herself it was Mitch's age, since he was older than the other men she'd dated. He was probably over thirty, though his ruggedness made it difficult to guess precisely what his age was.

He did cowboy work, which was often dangerous and always demanding, and his maturity and confidence made him a standout compared to her other dates. And despite the rough outdoor work he did and his earthy masculinity, his every move seemed suave and sophisticated and just as natural for him.

When they reached his car, he tripped the power locks on the door, then opened it to smoothly see her seated. She couldn't help staring as he walked around the front of the car, waited a beat for a break in traffic, then came to the driver's door and got in. He quickly started the engine, buckled up, then eased the big car into the street.

The silence between them was peaceful, but she sensed the thread of delicate tension between them that seemed firmly attached to her insides. She was aware of every move he made, so she glanced his way to see his big hand move with easy competence on the wheel before her gaze dropped to stare at the one that rested casually on his thigh. She had to make a determined effort to stop ogling him and face the windshield.

Mitch's low voice brought her attention back.

"Given the fact that your adoption records were sealed, what makes you think you're Doris's daughter?"

Lorna heard the genuine curiosity in his mild tone, but the question put her squarely on the spot.

It was not a story he should hear from her, and it wasn't a story she thought she could repeat to him without becoming emotional.

Besides, it wasn't right to injure Doris's relationship with her stepson. From what Lorna now sensed about Mitch Ellery, telling him the whole story might gain her an ally, but it might also diminish Doris in his eyes and strain their relationship. And something like that would affect Kendra, who would surely be able to sense something amiss between her mother and stepbrother.

Lorna would soon be out of their lives. It wasn't fair to any of the Ellerys for her to expose something they'd all have to live with after she was gone.

Even if she told Mitch a tiny part of it to satisfy his curiosity, instinct told her it wouldn't stop there. Mitch had money and if he was the kind of man she sensed he was, he'd already hired someone to look into her background. He could make hay with the tidbit she might give him and he'd find out too much.

Better not to reveal anything of that horrifying time when she'd been eight years old. Better to keep that door closed, for Doris and Kendra, and for her. And now that she'd agreed to quit her job and go through with this dating sham, there was no longer a reason to bother with the blood test.

"We've passed the point for that question," she said quietly, careful to keep her voice even and businesslike. "I've promised that I will exit Kendra's life. I've not only agreed to quit my job, but I'm cooperating with this bizarre plan to date you then break your heart.'' She gave a small shrug that made him momentarily glance her way.

She met his stern gaze. "So even a blood test has become unnecessary. Since I'm not a very public person and we don't move in the same social circles, I doubt any of the Ellerys will hear from me again.''

His dark gaze drilled into hers longer than was prudent, considering he was driving, but then he faced forward. His profile was harsh and his rough voice was terse as he concluded, ''Then you don't know for a fact.''

"No comment.''

He glanced at her so suddenly that he caught her off guard. She jerked her gaze from his but not before she saw the glitter in his dark eyes that showed both anger and perception.

The car moved smoothly along and Lorna tried to relax. She could feel his speculation and that he glanced her way from time to time. Her nerves seemed impossible to calm and she jerked a little when he spoke.

"Like to know what I think?''

The gravelly sound of his voice was soothing, but his question was not. She gripped her fingers together on her lap but didn't look at him. They were stopped at a red light, so she watched the pedestrians in the crosswalk.

"No, not particularly.'' She did look at him then.

"No offense, but what you think and what I think won't affect the outcome of any of this."

"Maybe not." His dark eyes were all over her face as if he was searching for something very small and hard to see. She had to look away from such close scrutiny.

"The light's changed." She got out, hoping he'd just get them to wherever they were going so they could put in their twenty minutes and leave.

She held her breath until he eased the car into the intersection, then relaxed the tiniest bit when the car picked up speed. But that tiny bit of relaxation vanished when he went on.

"I'll tell you what I think anyway."

Her, "I'm not surprised," was not as prickly as it should have been, and came out sounding faintly amused. But then, he did amuse her somewhat. He was a blunt, out-with-it kind of man, and he was also a minor tyrant used to having his own way. Very likely he was a despot, but instinct told her he was a benevolent despot to those he loved. After all, he must love his stepsister and probably his stepmother, because he was apparently ready to do whatever it took to protect them.

Mitch expelled a long breath that ended on a soft chuckle and she sensed that her retort had pleased him in some way. Or perhaps it was a sound of male weariness. Most men didn't know what to make of her comments from time to time. Mitch might not either, but he seemed to enjoy them.

Which was another dismal hint that there might have been something important between them if not for everything else. She looked over at him and saw the faint smile that softened his profile as he spoke his mind.

"I don't think you're a liar or a hustler."

She felt her brows go high with surprise. "Thank you very much."

"You don't seem unstable or delusional."

"My goodness," she said dryly, "such sweeping praise. I must get your name on my résumé as a character reference."

To her utter surprise, he reached over to take her hand. The move had seemed spontaneous and it shocked her to see that his big hand nearly swallowed hers up. And his grip was gentle. Firm enough to keep her from pulling away, but wonderfully gentle. And that gentleness sent such a huge wave of emotion through her that she felt her eyes sting. What was wrong with her?

Mitch did a very casual turn of the steering wheel and pulled the car into a huge parking lot. He drove up one of the parking lanes straight for the door of the nightspot.

Evidently he'd said all he'd meant to say about what he thought when he'd listed her "qualities." But she didn't understand why he'd reached for her hand and held it so warmly. Almost...affectionately.

Her emotions had been running the gamut for months over Kendra, and they'd become particularly intense since yesterday over her encounters with Mitch. Surely that was the reason his gentle grip was having such an emotional effect on her.

Someday very soon, this emotional roller coaster would come to a stop and she could go back to her quiet, humdrum life and an occasional date with safe, low-key men who took her to dinner and later gave her damp, unimpressive kisses, then seemed irritated or crushed when she didn't invite them past the front door of her building. The pang she felt at the thought made her eyes sting worse.

Lorna was grateful for the distraction when Mitch brought the big car to a stop in front of the nightclub and released her hand to get out. He handed a bill to a valet, then came around to open her door. Resigned, Lorna picked up her handbag and got out.

She looked up briefly into Mitch's face, saw the no-nonsense set of his mouth and felt a bit of comfort. This was as grim a duty for him as it was for her. She wouldn't truly have to pretend to be attracted to him, but she would have to keep the brakes on that attraction. That was the grim part for her.

It was probably a tougher prospect for him to pretend to be attracted to her, in spite of what he'd said last night about finding her interesting. The things he'd said tonight were probably no more personal than any red-blooded man's attraction toward a female who didn't have to go around with a bag over her head.

As she saw it, Mitch's performance had to look more realistic to Kendra than hers did, because he'd have to seem convincingly let down and disappointed later when their fling "went flat." Probably those glimmers she'd seen had been his attempt to either warm up to his role or an effort to get the response he thought he needed to get out of her.

Satisfied that she'd accounted for everything between them, at least on his side, Lorna had taken a step toward the door before Mitch caught her elbow and fell into step beside her to tuck her hand in the crook of his arm.

"Make it look good," he growled, and he was, of course, right. It was wise to look like a couple from the moment they arrived, whether they thought Kendra was watching or not.

But it was insane to enjoy it so much that your heart went wild with excitement and impossible hope, and you suddenly couldn't wait to be in his arms, pressed up against the most sexy, dynamic, masculine body you'd ever laid eyes on.

When they stepped inside the crowded nightspot and Mitch shifted his arm to wrap it around her and pull her tightly against his side, Lorna's heart truly went crazy, and suddenly the only coherent thought in her giddy brain was *yippie-ky-iay!*

CHAPTER FIVE

TREMBLING from the effect of Mitch's arm wrapped so wonderfully tight around her, Lorna was suddenly certain that tonight would be one of the biggest emotional mistakes of her life.

Mitch didn't bother to find them a table. He managed to easily navigate the crowd, his big body both bulldozer and shield for her. And when they stepped onto the dance floor and he turned toward her, he relieved her of the tiny handbag to put it into his jacket pocket for safekeeping. The gesture startled a brief smile out of her, but without missing a beat, Mitch caught her hand, slid his arm around her waist, then pulled her against him.

The sudden, full contact from chest to knee was like coming in contact with a wall of heat and electricity. It was amazing she wasn't knocked off her feet or burned to a crisp. Her legs went embarrassingly weak, and she peered up at him uneasily, afraid he would detect her response. Neither of them were dancing yet.

Mitch's dark gaze was focused on hers like a searchlight. She couldn't bear to look into his eyes and feel his hard body against hers at the same time, so her gaze dropped to stare at the turquoise ornament that secured his string tie. But then the subtle scent of his musky aftershave flooded her senses and her blood thickened and grew sweet with what could only be her first true taste of lust.

"Twenty minutes is either not enough or about nineteen minutes too long," he said gruffly. "You feel even better in my arms than I thought you would."

The blunt remark sent heat over her face. Why would he say something like that to her? As if he'd thought about having her in his arms. As if he'd looked forward to it. As if he'd been eager...

She tried to pull back, but the steely arm around her waist didn't allow her to escape full contact with him. They still weren't dancing.

"We should find a table," she told him, feeling a little shaky.

"There don't seem to be any, so we need to dance."

At the soft order, she looked up. Even in the dim lighting she could see the fire in his dark eyes. "Dance with me," he said, still gruff.

But her knees were weak and she tingled everywhere. The self-consciousness she should have felt—that she usually felt—was gone, pushed away by the intimate cocoon that seemed to have enveloped them in a heavy haze of sensuality. Even the sound of the country ballad that had been so loud just seconds ago was muted. Mitch smiled down at her—a faint smile, but a smile nonetheless—and she saw the blatant gleam of lust in his eyes.

Her gaze flinched away and Mitch started them in the slow dance. His every move was steady and certain, and her idiot body melted more tightly against him. His fingers tightened gently on hers and she felt the hand at her back slide down and linger a bit more boldly lower than she'd allowed any other man's hand to rest.

The shivery cascade of feeling that went over her from scalp to toe turned hot and pooled deep. Desperate to counteract the sensation, Lorna tried to think of something to distract them both. "Do you see Kendra?"

She looked up and was again snared by the warm gleam in Mitch's eyes.

"Not yet. Why?"

"The whole point is for her to see us together," she said, then glanced away to see for herself.

"It won't look right if she sees either of us searching the crowd for her," he pointed out.

"I didn't mean that we should make it obvious."

"You're nervous."

The gravely pronouncement was completely accurate. "Why wouldn't I be?" She hesitated then added, "We shouldn't be doing this."

"Maybe not, but like I said, I'm not sorry to be here."

Lorna made herself stare at his shoulder. "If that's meant as a compliment, you need to know it's not. Unless what you mean to say is that you haven't been out dancing in a long time, so that wasn't a personal comment.''

"Why not?"

"You seem to be a reasonably intelligent man. I'm sure you can figure it out.''

She felt the slight tightening of his fingers on hers and the subtle flex of the hand that rested just short of too low on her back, and was prompted to look up at him. She saw the somber study he made of her face and couldn't escape the quiet probe of his gaze.

"I realize you're the one who'll pay the biggest price, and I regret that. More than you know.''

The understanding in his eyes—the sudden hint of bleakness there—made her like him even more and she was compelled to put a stop to it.

"I'm thirsty. Could we get something to drink?''

Mitch stopped dancing right away but kept her hand in his as he led her through the dancers. The ballad had stopped and the band began to tune up for a rollicking number that began just as they reached the edge of the dance floor.

The bar was crowded but Mitch found a bar stool near the end of the long counter and gallantly helped her up on the high perch. He angled in between her and the next patron but kept a proprietary hand at her back. He glanced at her to prompt her request, raised dark brows at her choice of a double "anything,'' then signaled the bartender and ordered two whiskeys.

He leaned closer to her when the bartender moved away to get the drinks. "I didn't picture you a fan of hard liquor.''

"I've never had hard liquor in my life.''

A slow half smile softened his rugged face. "If that was meant as a compliment, you need to know it's not,'' he said, repeating her earlier words. "I don't like to think that I've driven a teetotaler to drink.''

Now that he'd repeated her words, something playful in her made her answer with the question he'd asked her. "Why not?''

"You seem to be a reasonably intelligent lady. I'm sure you can figure it out.'' His eyes were dancing with that, as if he enjoyed the small bit of banter. It was incredibly flattering that he remembered her every word. And it was some sort of consolation, because she doubted very much that she'd forget a single word he'd spoken to her. Ever. Which was something else that made her feel melancholy about the situation.

"How big is your ranch?'' she asked, then caught herself. She'd meant to change the subject and get him to talk about something normal, but she suddenly doubted he'd consider questions about his ranch appropriate, not when it was probably one of the largest in the area. She'd already got the strong hint that he jealously guarded Ellery property and wealth enough to be vigilant against potential gold diggers.

And, sure enough, some of the dancing light went out of his eyes. "Big enough that you can't ride a horse across it in a single day."

She glanced away from him, grateful that the bartender was setting their drinks in front of them. Mitch moved his hand from her back to reach into a pocket for his wallet. Lorna picked up her drink while he selected a bill that he tossed on the bar. She couldn't relax, particularly once the wallet was put away and Mitch's hand returned to her back.

Then she remembered that she'd said she'd pay for her own things that night. She set down her drink without a taste, then asked for her handbag.

Mitch pulled it out of his pocket and handed it over. She took it with a soft thanks, then promptly opened it to pull out a bill that was half the amount of the one he'd paid with.

"Put your money away," he groused, but she ignored the order and discreetly tucked the bill in his jacket pocket.

"I said I'd pay for my own." She looked up to make eye contact. "And the question about your ranch was to make polite conversation. I wasn't trying to figure out how much you're worth so I could make a play for you."

"I could be generous both in bed and out with the right lover."

The blunt surprise of that took her breath away,

and her feelings for him began to frost over. "I don't take lovers."

"You didn't drink hard liquor before tonight, either. What's changed?"

Frustrated that she was worse off with him in the bar than she'd been in his arms on the dance floor, she faced forward and reached gamely for her drink. Anticipating the bite and burn of the drink, she lifted the glass and cautiously sipped.

And choked a little anyway. Her eyes watered as if she'd turned on a fountain. She grabbed for the napkin and pressed it beneath one eye and then the other before she forced herself to take another sip.

Mitch's low chuckle sounded at her ear and she felt the warm gust of his breath on her cheek. "Tryin' to drown what's eatin' you?"

Her raspy, half-choked "Yes" made him chuckle again. Angry and frustrated and feeling idiotic and trapped, she forced down the entire drink, then shakily set the glass on the bar and pressed the napkin harshly against her mouth. She wasn't certain an X ray would be able to detect what was left of her scorched esophagus and stomach. But her stomach was probably still there because now it was pitching wildly with nausea. Lorna didn't move to so much as breathe as she waited desperately, praying for the nausea to calm before she added a truly humiliating calamity to the events of the evening.

Mitch's hand slid up her back and closed warmly

around her shoulder as he leaned closer. "You all right?"

She dared a small nod, relieved when her stomach didn't object. She couldn't look at him, though his face was only a finger space or so from hers.

"I think maybe something to dilute that would be good," she croaked. "A soda or glass of ice water."

Mitch chuckled again and she felt hopelessly foolish. He quickly ordered her a Sprite, and she fumbled with her handbag for a couple of dollars to pay for it. She'd barely opened the catch before he smoothly plucked it from her fingers, snapped it closed, then whipped it back into his jacket pocket.

"You're too stubborn, Lorna Dean Farrell. And I believe you about the ranch."

"Then please stop testing me. I thought you'd concluded I wasn't a gold digger. And, for your information, not every woman who makes less money than you do covets your fortune. Besides, even a gold digger would think twice about facing a dragon to get his treasure, so you're reasonably safe."

His use of her full name dawned and she finally looked at him. "How soon did you hire the private investigator?"

"The minute I took Kendra home Friday and could get to a phone."

The Sprite was delivered and paid for, so she reached for the glass. "And what information did your money get you?"

He didn't hesitate. "Lorna Dean Farrell, middle

name the same as her adopted mother's maiden name. Quiet, well-behaved, six foster placements.''

''You got access to my juvenile records?'' She searched his face warily. ''Is that legal?''

''Want to hear more?''

Suddenly heartsore and embarrassed, she shook her head. ''No. Never mind.''

Mitch leaned his forearm on the bar to loom close again. ''All right, but there's something I'd like to know.''

He was so close that she could feel his breath on her face. Her gaze was trapped in the solemn grip of his.

''Something your investigator overlooked?''

He smiled faintly then, but didn't answer directly. ''I hope you learned enough about horses from those backyard ponies you used to ride at one of your placements to enjoy the picnic at the creek. Since you're coming out to the ranch tomorrow.''

Any hope she'd had about her privacy was well and truly dashed if he'd found out those kinds of details about her foster placements. She couldn't help being impressed by the resourcefulness of whomever Mitch had hired. The fact that she'd done nothing dastardly in her past kept her from resenting the intrusion. At least there was some payoff for having been a ''good girl'' growing up, though she'd never imagined it would pay off quite like this.

She gave her head a decisive shake. ''I can't go to your ranch. Not ever.''

"Kendra will never believe I could fall for a woman I wouldn't bring out to the ranch."

Hurt rose high and she faced forward to sip a last bit of the Sprite before she set it down. And then she abruptly turned away from the bar and slid off the high stool to leave.

Mitch was immediately at her side, but she shrugged away from his hand and led the way past the tables into the main room of the big club to make a beeline for the door. Mitch smoothly took her arm, but before she could pull away a second time, she caught sight of Kendra at one of the tables, waving madly to get their attention.

As if the evening hadn't gone dismal enough, now she had to face Kendra. And worse, they had to pretend they were a happy couple. Lorna's distaste for this scheme was already sharp, but she pasted a neutral smile on her face as Mitch urged her in Kendra's direction.

"Oh, Lorna, you look so elegant and sophisticated," Kendra declared over the sound of the country band. "The two of you make the perfect couple."

Kendra fairly radiated happiness and approval. She reached for Lorna's free hand to give it a squeeze before she turned her enthusiastic smile on Mitch. "Isn't she gorgeous?"

Lorna felt acutely uncomfortable, but Kendra seemed oblivious to it.

"That she is," Mitch answered.

Self-conscious, Lorna nodded a wordless greeting to her boss, and John nodded back a hello to her before Kendra went on with a cheery, "Why don't the two of you join us? We could go someplace quieter if you'd like."

Lorna automatically shook her head to that and Mitch answered almost simultaneously. "No thanks, sis. We're off to a late supper."

"You *are* bringing her out to the ranch tomorrow, aren't you?"

Lorna cringed inwardly and Mitch chuckled. "For a *private* picnic. No kid stepsisters, no spies."

Kendra crossed her heart with her finger. "I wouldn't dream of intruding on a romantic courtship in its tender beginnings."

John Owen spoke up. "I've got plans for Kendra tomorrow that will keep her out of harm's way."

"I'd appreciate that," Mitch told him. "I learned my lesson years ago with her."

Kendra's face reddened. "That was a long time ago, Mitch."

"And I've got a long memory. I doubt the young lady ever completely recovered from the shock of discovering that a certain fourteen-year-old brat and her friends had just witnessed the awkward start of her first attempt at seduction."

Kendra gave an embarrassed laugh. "I outgrew that stage long ago."

Mitch gave his stepsister a mock stern look. "I seem to recall another time about two years ago—"

Kendra laughingly grabbed his jacket to give it a silencing tug. "All right, you've made your point. I'll leave you and Lorna in complete privacy. No interference."

"That's right. John'll see to it this time." Mitch nodded to John and said to him, "I'll owe you."

John grinned. "Just the fact that you never paid her back in kind when I started coming around is enough for me."

Lorna stood by, listening to the conversation, impatient to be gone. Her head was swimming with the loud music and the shouting to be heard over the noise. She wanted nothing more than to escape this and get out in the fresh air and quiet. And to find some way to cancel Mitch's plans for a picnic at his ranch tomorrow.

Because she could never go to his ranch. Doris lived there, and the very last thing she wanted was to ever come face to face with her mother again. Surely Mitch was bright enough to understand that without her spelling it out.

Finally, finally, Kendra let them escape the crowd and the noise and her enthusiastic matchmaking. To Lorna's dismay, her head was swimming worse in the hot, calm air outside the nightclub. The heels she'd bought to go with the dress suddenly seemed precariously high and perilous to walk in, but now that Kendra wasn't around to see, she let go of Mitch's arm to walk on her own.

She did fine the first three steps, then managed to

catch the sharp point of her heel in a sidewalk crack. Only Mitch's quick reflexes saved her from more than an awkward falter.

Her belated, "Ooops," was followed by a spontaneous giggle as she clutched his arm and carefully extricated the narrow heel. Mitch signaled the valet for his car, then gave her his full attention.

"Are you tipsy?" The look in his dark gaze said yes, but Lorna shook her head.

And felt the pavement tilt. Mitch turned fully toward her to catch her other arm.

"We'll get some food into you. It'll soak up some of that booze."

The giggly feeling undermined her. "I am not drunk."

"No more than you weigh, that double was probably enough to pickle you."

"I'm not pickled, either," she told him, and a bit more of the giggly feeling died down, though the world still felt tilted and whirly. "I want to go straight home."

"Not until you've had something to eat."

A flash of angry frustration made the world shift a little more dramatically, but she managed to defy the sensation and make a coherent point.

"We agreed to twenty minutes on the dance floor. Kendra's seen us together, and she's assumed we're an item. Mission accomplished, I'm going home." Where hopefully she could think of some way to avoid going to Mitch's ranch tomorrow. Some way he couldn't pressure her out of.

"We weren't on the dance floor longer than five minutes and I already know it'll take me most of a steak dinner to persuade you to come to the ranch tomorrow. So we'll go for that late supper."

Frustration killed off the last of the giggly feeling. Her temper shot high and she glared up at him. She wasn't aware that she'd grabbed onto the lapel of his jacket as Kendra had done to emphasize her words.

"Look, Mr. Ellery, as I pointed out to you earlier today, you aren't allowed to rule the w—"

Lorna broke off what she'd been trying to say when Mitch's hand closed warmly over her fist and made her realize she'd been yanking on his lapel.

"Please, Lorna, have supper with me," he said, his low voice a quiet rasp. "I'm hungry, the cook'll be in bed long before I can get home, and I hate to eat alone."

Lorna stared, transfixed. There it was again, that compelling switch from tyrant to gentle persuader. The sincerity she saw in his dark eyes kept her from scorning the slightly pitiable picture he'd painted of a solitary man going home to a barren ranch kitchen or eating a late, lonely meal in a restaurant while surrounded by couples out on the town.

Her frustration with him eased into a kind of excited misery as she felt herself succumb to the inevitable. Before she completely lost her will, she tried a last, "Please, Mitch, this is foolish."

He gently lifted her hand off his lapel to kiss her knuckles. The sight of his stern mouth shaping into a loosely puckered line to press lingeringly against her skin was erotic, and the scorching waves that rushed through her made her ache for much, much more.

"Might be the most enjoyable foolishness we've ever had, Lorna Dean," he drawled. His eyes were so somber. Even though the brim of his Stetson shaded his gaze from the dim light of the parking lot, she could see his sincerity and it touched her. "I don't think I want to pass up a single second with you."

And then his firm lips pressed tenderly against her knuckles again, lingered again, and she was pierced by the deepest longing she'd ever felt in her life. Slowly he lifted his head, his gaze never breaking contact with hers. She was so shamefully susceptible to him, to this. The urge to cry came from a place so deep and lonely and lost inside her that she was incapable of speech. She only barely managed to keep the burning fullness in her eyes from spilling over as she tried to hold back.

This man was the one she'd been waiting for. Every instinct she'd had about him until now had hinted at it, but suddenly the knowledge was burning brightly in her brain and in her heart. The sad, sad knowledge that nothing but heartache could ever come from spending time with him was quite possibly the deepest of her life.

Though she'd long ago learned the ability to not show tears and was confident of her ability to do so, it was a miracle she managed not to cry. The corners of her mouth felt as heavy as her heart but she made herself give them a trembling little lift.

"It's no fun to go to bed hungry, I guess." Though she'd been able to smile when she said the words, they sounded melancholy to her. She saw the gleam of perception that flashed into his eyes and made herself give a laugh to distract him. "You poor, poor Texas millionaire. I suppose a hamburger drive-though wouldn't do, would it?"

She pulled her hand from his to make the sensations stop. "Or do you ultra rich Texas boys even know what a drive-through hamburger joint is, outside of your stock portfolio?"

The silence that followed her question was about a half dozen quick heartbeats too long. Lorna couldn't breathe, but widened her smile as she waited for him to say something that would signal that she'd managed to make him doubt whatever he might have seen of her sad feelings just now.

But all he said was, "The car's here," and she was grateful for the excuse to glance away from him to see the valet get out and rush around to open the passenger door for her. Lorna quickly got in and buckled up while Mitch tipped the valet and strode to his side of the car.

Neither of them spoke as Mitch drove slowly through the crowded lot then out into the street.

"So what's the decision, Lorna? Will you go to supper with me?"

Lorna had a last moment of sanity that ebbed so quickly it was as if it had never happened. Her soft, "All right," came out on a tide of surrender, but when she sneaked a look at Mitch's profile, it was grim.

As if he'd sensed her scrutiny, he glanced her way. He reached for her hand and gripped it gently before he faced forward again and continued to drive. Lorna looked down at their clasped hands, and couldn't seem to resist placing her free hand over his. She did it tentatively at first, felt the firm tightening of his fingers on hers that signaled his approval, then gave in and let her hand settle comfortably.

Her feelings for Mitch were far too strong, but for one of the rare times of her life, she was able to push away the sense of doom and impending heartache. And because it was already too late for her and she might never feel like this again, she simply allowed her fragile, sweet feelings to swell into a few small blooms.

CHAPTER SIX

As IF he too was caught up in the same relentless sense of inevitability that she was, Mitch was as pleasant and solicitous as if he were truly courting her. Once they'd ordered steak dinners in a small, out-of-the way place Lorna had never been to, they managed to chat on a wide range of subjects from weather to politics.

The conversation was easy and relaxed, but Lorna was cautious and less forthcoming than Mitch was. He had blunt, firm opinions that were entertaining and he was wonderfully well-read. He would probably be at ease and knowledgeable enough to carry on thoughtful conversations with anyone, and that was another enormous attraction for her.

They'd just finished their meal and sat back with coffee, when Mitch asked her what she'd consider a dream job, then listened attentively when she'd lied her heart out.

She couldn't confess to him that her idea of a dream job was to be a wife and have a home and raise children, so she'd made light of his question, giving him a lengthy list of glamorous careers before she'd turned the question back on him. What would he do with his life if he'd had no family ranch and oil wells, if he suddenly had no fortune?

"Anything with outdoor work and horses," he answered without hesitation.

"Macho to the core," she commented, not truly surprised. She couldn't picture him in an office day in and day out for the rest of his life. "Would you have to be rich or could you be a regular mortal with a mortgage and a modest way of life?"

"Money isn't everything, but I'd want to make enough of it to raise and educate a family. Maybe buy my wife something nice from time to time."

Until then, the conversation between them had been fairly mundane, as if they'd both reached an unspoken agreement that prohibited serious personal talk. Lorna had given a frivolous job list, but the moment she heard that, she felt her heart sink at least a mile. Family was her secret goal, the goal she'd waited most of her life to achieve. To hear Mitch declare his job preferences and then to seriously specify that the goal of his income was to raise and educate a family made him even more desirable to her.

But the remark he'd put on the end, *Maybe buy my wife something nice from time to time* seemed intensely personal and directed squarely at her.

Mitch's loyalty and protectiveness toward his stepsister and stepmother had already made her envious. To hear this made her envy worse. Perhaps she'd mistaken what he'd said about his "wife," and her wrong interpretation was nothing more than wishful thinking.

Most of the men she'd dated were caught up in careers. They seemed so unsettled and immature, so focused on material things that home and children were distant considerations. Lorna took none of those men seriously.

But she took Mitch Ellery seriously. Too seriously.

"Did I say something wrong?"

Mitch's low voice made her face go a little hot but she made herself give a neutral smile. "A lot of men focus on their careers or money. Your answer hinted that your priorities are family and children."

"*Wife* and children," he corrected. The calm study he made of her tense features was slow and thorough. She felt transparent and it was an effort to keep her expression from giving her away. She couldn't respond to his correction, and she didn't need to as he went on, as if driving home the point.

"I've sowed my wild oats, Lorna. I'm nearly thirty-three. Past time to start the search for a wife and plan for the next generation of Ellery kids. And since I was an only child, I want more than one."

Lorna hastily lifted her coffee cup and had a sip while she tried to think of a way to answer that. Her heart was reeling, but she managed an awkward smile. "Perhaps your wife will have something to say about that."

Play the
"LAS VEGAS"
GAME

Play the "**LAS VEGAS**" Game

and get

3 FREE GIFTS!

FREE!
No Obligation to Buy!
No Purchase Necessary!

Play the
"LAS VEGAS" Game

YES! I have pulled back the 3 tabs. Please send me all the free Harlequin Romance® books and the gift for which I qualify. I understand that I am under no obligation to purchase any books, as explained on the back and opposite page.

386 HDL DNYG   186 HDL DNYR

FIRST NAME	LAST NAME

ADDRESS

APT.#	CITY

STATE/PROV.	ZIP/POSTAL CODE

(H-R-09/02)

7	7	7	**GET 2 FREE BOOKS & A FREE MYSTERY GIFT!**
✽	✽	✽	**GET 2 FREE BOOKS!**
🍒	🍒	🍒	**GET 1 FREE BOOK!**
🔔	🔔	🔔	**TRY AGAIN!**

DETACH AND MAIL TODAY

The Harlequin Reader Service® — Here's how it works:

Accepting your 2 free books and gift places you under no obligation to buy anything. You may keep the books and gift and return the shipping statement marked "cancel." If you do not cancel, about a month later we'll send you 6 additional novels and bill you just $3.34 each in the U.S., or $3.80 each in Canada, plus 25¢ shipping & handling per book and applicable taxes if any.* That's the complete price and — compared to cover prices of $3.99 each in the U.S. and $4.50 each in Canada — it's quite a bargain! You may cancel at any time, but if you choose to continue, every month we'll send you 6 more books, which you may either purchase at the discount price or return to us and cancel your subscription.

*Terms and prices subject to change without notice. Sales tax applicable in N.Y. Canadian residents will be charged applicable provincial taxes and GST.

"She won't be my wife if we can't agree on the number."

The mood between them had grown heavy. With just a few blunt words, they were suddenly on a deeper level, and going deeper as quickly as a big rock dropped in a pond.

How about four children, Mr. Ellery, she wanted to say. *Or better yet, a half dozen?*

Dark-haired children with dark eyes, and at least a couple with blue eyes. Happy, healthy, protected children who'd never lack love and security, who'd never be able to imagine being unwanted or neglected or given back.

And maybe one or two more who were true castaways. Children like her who'd been orphaned and whose extended families hadn't wanted to take them in. Rejected children who had no one, who were hungry to belong and starved for love. Abandoned children who craved adoption. At least two of that kind, maybe more than two.

Lorna couldn't say that, but her heart was suddenly shouting it and she longed to know what Mitch might have said if she'd had the courage to say it out loud.

Thankfully the waitress brought the check and Mitch handed her a large bill to cover the meal along with a hefty tip. Lorna was profoundly grateful the deep mood between them had been disrupted. They'd run out of shallow, safe topics and from here on, there was no subject that couldn't somehow turn back on her to nick her heart or inflame her hope. Now that the meal was over and paid for, they could leave the restaurant and end the evening.

She slid her chair back slightly as if preparing to leave, then rested her hand on her handbag. Mitch's gaze shifted to take note of her small signals, but he didn't respond to them.

"What about you?" Mitch asked, his gaze sharp on her flushed face. "Do you want kids?"

Her low, "Yes," was followed by a desperate prayer for a way to change the subject. She didn't want him to pursue anything to do with family or children, but he was suddenly dogged on the subject.

"Will you want to keep your full-time career and be a part-time modern mommy or are you old-fashioned enough to chuck a work life and stay home to raise your kids?"

He'd asked a genuine question and because he had, it was clear he expected a genuine answer. But it was long past time to stop the direction the conversation had taken. Answering his question with another question was the only thing she could think to do.

"Will you still be a full-time rancher going out to ride the range from dawn to dusk while your little woman stays at the house taking care of your children?"

Lorna's gaze held his, though the glimmer in his eyes probed deep into hers.

"You aren't comfortable with personal questions."

He'd said it as a statement of fact, but one that subtly compelled a response. So she'd give him one.

"Think about our situation," she said at last. "Your questions and mine shouldn't be personal, and neither should our answers to each other." She was drawn deeper into the intensity in his gaze, and her voice grew softer. "There's no reason for you and I to know anything about each other beyond basic recognition so we can avoid contact. Which is why this dating sham is such a waste of everyone's time."

It relieved her to get it all out, to reestablish some sort of boundary between them, though it made her feel faintly sick to think that theirs would always be a cross-to-the-other-side-of-the-street relationship instead of what her heart told her it might have been.

"And speaking of which," she added, desperate to draw a firmer line between them, "I said I'd pay my own way tonight. I'll reimburse you for my half of supper when we get to the car."

"So you're anxious to change the subject from husbands and wives and raising kids," he said, ignoring her declaration about paying him back. The pent-up breath she'd been holding eased out then caught when he went on. "Then we'll discuss what needs to happen tomorrow."

He went on briskly as if they'd already agreed. "I'll pick you up at eight, drive you to the ranch.

We'll take a couple horses out, have our picnic at the creek, but the heat'll probably send us to the house by one o'clock. I'll show you around so Kendra has a chance to see us together, then have you back in San Antonio by five, six at the latest.''

Dismay made her fumble her handbag off the table into her lap where she gripped it, more desperate than ever to leave and put an end to the evening. She shook her head.

"I can't go to your ranch.''

"Kendra won't buy a minute of tonight if you don't go to the ranch tomorrow.''

"I can't go to your ranch.''

"Why not?''

She saw the look in his dark eyes that told her he'd already guessed, but the sternness on his face told her he expected her to say it.

And why not? Why shouldn't she answer him? Resentment roared up, and she realized it wasn't resentment toward him so much as it was resentment toward Doris. She lifted her chin slightly and hoped the look in her eyes was more cold than injured.

"I never want to see Doris again, and we both know the feeling is mutual.''

"You won't see Doris tomorrow,'' he said calmly. "She'll be gone long before you get to the ranch and she won't be back until late tomorrow night.''

"The less I know about Doris, the easier all this is to…live with.''

"Ellery Ranch belongs solely to me."

Lorna shook her head. "She lives there now, it's been her home for years—"

"Forget that Doris lives there. I live there, Lorna, it's my home."

The reminder was no consolation. And the way he said it, as if he wanted her to think of it as *his* home, somehow implied that the fact should be significant to her. As if he was taking her to his home for reasons of his own that were personal—and that his personal reasons for doing so should also be hers. And just as personal.

If anything, spending time on Mitch's ranch and in his home would only give her more to remember about him later.

This time, she didn't wait for him to take the hint that she wanted to leave. She simply stood up, paused a moment for him to rise, then started toward the door as he fell into step beside her and slid his arm around her waist.

It was a reasonable thing for a gentleman to do on a date, but it only increased her torture. Her body fitted easily against his, and she loved the warm, protected feeling he gave her.

Her attraction to Mitch had been expanding by the second, and having his arm around her made her feel hot and excited inside. She'd rarely had sexual feelings and urges until tonight, but she was drowning in them now.

The moment they got to his car and she got in,

she quickly got out her small wallet. While he walked around the car to his side, she tucked a couple of bills for her half of their meal above his sun visor. Mitch got in, started the car, then noticed the corners of the two bills. He didn't comment and to her relief, he didn't try to give them back.

Lorna managed to weather the silent ride home. When Mitch pulled to the curb in front of her building, she gave him a hasty thanks for the evening. She'd reached for her seat belt release the moment he switched off the engine, but he caught her hand before she could open her door.

"You're in a rush, Lorna."

Her quick glance at him, and her nearly breathless, "It's late," was met with a faint smile from him.

"Is this the way you want the night to end?"

The question kicked her heart into a faster rhythm. But then, part of her reaction was because she was reading the heat that had come into his dark eyes. Surely he didn't mean to kiss her.

Her voice was husky with the fear and yearning she felt. "If you're talking about what I think you are, then…please don't."

"Dress for riding tomorrow. If you don't have boots or a hat, I'll find some for you."

The order was both a relief and an aggravation. A relief because she'd managed to give him a refusal that he'd apparently accepted, but a new aggravation, because he was so relentless on the subject of the picnic at his ranch.

"I can't come to your ranch."

His big thumb chafed gently against the back of her hand, and his voice was low and surprisingly soft. "We have an agreement."

She felt the tendrils of that wrap around her insides. "Don't bully me." Somehow, instead of sounding outraged, her voice carried a hint of faint pain.

His stern expression eased. "Let me take you riding tomorrow. The creek's cool and shady, the food'll be good, it'll be a beautiful day—"

"And every second of it will be dishonest and a lie," she cut in, but even then she couldn't make the words sound as forceful as she'd meant.

Mitch's grip tightened on hers and she saw the heat in his eyes flare higher as he leaned swiftly toward her.

"Not every second," he said in that lightning fast moment before his mouth landed on hers.

His firm lips dealt hers a soft concussion and somehow sealed them to his before she could either draw back or turn her head. Just that suddenly fire flashed through her and sent sweetness shimmering through every nerve in her body.

She wasn't aware that her hand had lifted until her fingers touched his lean cheek. By then a small sliver of sanity quivered to life and she drew back.

The kiss couldn't have lasted more than a handful

of seconds, but she was scorched with it and her breath was coming as quickly as if she'd been deprived of air for several moments. Her body was wild with chaos and her brain was frantic.

"Please, Lorna Dean. Come to the ranch with me tomorrow."

She stared at him, overwhelmed by the seductive timbre of his voice and the sincerity in his dark eyes. The way he called her Lorna Dean was so mystifyingly persuasive that she couldn't seem to resist.

Her half-choked, "All right," was barely audible, and she felt her heart shake with fear and excitement and self-disgust. When had she become so spineless?

Lorna fled the car abruptly, rushing so quickly to the front door of her building that Mitch was only halfway up the sidewalk by the time she let herself in. She glanced out the glass door to see him come to a halt, watched a moment more as he touched the brim of his Stetson in farewell, then felt teary as she watched him turn and walk back to his car.

Surely it was her imagination that the big man moved a little slower than normal, as if he was just the tiniest bit reluctant to leave. Surely it was her imagination again when he reached his car door and looked over the roof of the vehicle to stare at her for several pulse-pounding moments before he got in.

It was no one's imagination that she stood there like a forlorn fool and watched him drive off until the red taillights of his car merged into the late traffic then disappeared in the distance.

Once Lorna reached the sanctuary of her apartment, she flew to her bedroom to get out of the dress and hang it up. Her body and heart were still in an uproar over Mitch's kiss. The flurry of activity as she undressed, took her hair down and ruthlessly combed it out, was meant to impose some feeling of normalcy and routine. But not even removing her makeup and taking a quick shower did more than emphasize the notion that she'd been profoundly affected.

It hadn't only been the kiss, it was everything about the past two days. From the moment she'd walked into the office the day before and seen Mitch, her heart had come to life.

It was as if these past few years she'd been biding her time, working hard to bring herself up in the world while she waited for the one man who was special enough to be the flesh and blood version of the ideal she'd held in her heart. An ideal comprised of a specific set of qualities that had seemed more and more fanciful and unrealistic as time had gone by. Until Mitch had appeared and given them substance.

Surely she was mistaken. The qualities she'd seen in Mitch had to be nothing more than a trick, a willing delusion conjured up by a lonely heart that had grown too impatient, a heart too easily distracted by feminine excitement and attraction to see clearly.

Lorna stepped out of the shower and vigorously toweled herself dry before she wrapped up in a light-weight robe. Her reflection in the steam-misted mirror was large-eyed and haunted, so she turned away to step into her bedroom.

As she walked to the kitchen for a soda, she heard Melanie's distinctive knock and went to her door to open it.

Melanie held up a folded sheet of paper to explain her presence. Because Mellie had been out all day, Lorna had slipped the note under her door earlier that evening, and no doubt her friend was wild with curiosity.

"You went dancing with Mitch Ellery?"

"Unfortunately, yes." She gave her friend a weary smile. "And now I need someone to talk some sense into me. Or maybe knock me in the head."

"So you've fallen for him."

Lorna stepped back and her friend walked inside. They got sodas from the refrigerator and went to the living room.

"Your note said you'd explain later, so I've been waiting in suspense all evening." They both chose a place to sit and Mellie leaned forward eagerly to hear the story.

Lorna quickly filled her in on everything, from the dating sham Doris wanted to her agreement to go to the Ellery Ranch for the day tomorrow.

Mellie sat silent for several minutes, then gave her

a sympathetic glance. "So I take it from the utter misery in your eyes that you think Mitch Ellery is the most exciting male ever born to a woman, and you're completely smitten."

Lorna had already set aside her soda to prop her cheek on her hand. "It's probably just infatuation. A crush. Falling in love so quick is never true love, is it?" She lowered her hand and looked at her friend hopefully. "At least it's not the kind of love that's real or that lasts. Right?"

Mellie gave her a quiet smile. "Never in all the time I've known you have you ever used the word love to define your feelings about a date."

Lorna abruptly stood and began to pace, too restless and stirred up to sit still. "A truly interesting man was bound to come along sometime," she said, struggling to sound philosophical. "Maybe it's because he's the first one to truly get my attention."

She stopped pacing to turn back to her friend. "Better yet, maybe the reason he's so appealing is because he's the one man who's romantically off limits."

The conclusion didn't so much as nudge the edge of the truth, and Lorna was privately dismayed.

"Except you aren't self destructive," Mellie pointed out, underscoring the notion that Mitch being off limits had nothing to do with her impossible feelings for him. "And why is he off limits?"

The question amazed Lorna because it was so

monumentally obvious. "Oh, please, Mel, you know. Because of Doris. And Kendra."

"But they're his stepfamily. Doris is still young. She'll probably remarry and make her life someplace else. And Kendra is getting married and moving to San Antonio. Your Mr. Ellery will soon be on his own. Besides, I doubt a man like him needs anyone's permission to either choose the woman he wants to see or to marry her." She grinned then. "I've only seen him through the peephole in my door and I can tell that much."

Lorna's heart leaped with hope but she shook her head adamantly. "The three of them are very close, Mel. And family seems to mean a lot to him. He wouldn't let his relationship with Doris and Kendra fade away, and he wouldn't let an outsider spoil it. They'll probably stay close forever."

Melanie's face showed instant regret. "I'm sorry. I forget sometimes that all families aren't as faithless as ours were."

The word "faithless" was an understatement. When Melanie's divorced mother had died, her father's new wife and children hadn't wanted her in their lives, so he'd given up his parental rights. In Lorna's case, her adoptive parents' families hadn't seen her as a legitimate member of the family so none of them had wanted to take her in.

Mellie gave Lorna a perceptive look. "And that's part of the attraction for you, isn't it? First he comes charging in to fend you off to protect his stepsister, then he lets his stepmother manipulate him into this fake dating thing so you won't have to hurt Kendra's feelings to end your friendship with her.''

Mellie smiled sadly. ''And you're thinking, if he'd be so indulgent and protective with his step-family, what would he do for a wife and children of his own?''

Lorna felt her heart drag lower. ''That's probably what this is, Mel,'' she said, suddenly choked with emotion. ''I'm sure it is.''

Mellie appeared to think about it, then nodded. ''Yes, that's probably all it is. Men like Mitch are your Achilles' heel and mine, so…I'm sure it couldn't possibly have anything to do with him also being intense and macho and…hot.''

Melanie had said this last part deadpan, and Lorna couldn't help the quick smile that burst up. ''Well, yes, I suppose that might be part of it, too.''

They both laughed then and the dismal mood lifted a little before Melanie went on.

''I don't know Doris and I don't want to say anything to get your hopes up, but I think this dating thing is more than it seems. She's up to something, and maybe it's something good.''

The brief moment of lightness fled. Lorna glanced away from her friend, panicked by how much she longed for that to be true. ''No, it's not good, not any of it,'' she said quickly. ''Doris has no hidden agenda. At least none that will benefit me in any way.''

Besides, Doris's idea of "something good" would be if Lorna didn't exist. It wasn't a self-pitying thought so much as it was a proven fact of life.

"You don't think Doris is curious about you?"

Lorna began to pace again, pitifully tantalized by the notion, despite her certainty about Doris's feelings—or lack of feelings—for her. That Doris would be curious about her wasn't even a remote possibility, not in light of her mother's past actions. Besides, Doris could satisfy any curiosity she might have through private investigators, and Mitch had already hired a good one.

"Doris was a royal no-show in my life," she said grimly, suddenly desperate to dash the small bit of hope that flickered feebly despite her determination to ignore it. "She wants nothing to do with me."

"Then I'm sorry I suggested it. If Doris is like my dad, then she's not worth a moment's consideration."

Lorna stopped pacing to touch her friend's shoulder in silent sympathy. At least she'd never known Doris. Mellie had lived with her father and his new family a while before he'd given her up. Lorna considered that an even bigger betrayal than the ones she'd suffered.

"The world is the way it is, Mellie," she said quietly, "however much we hope it's not."

Mellie tried for a small smile of agreement that

was more of a grimace. ''So that brings us back to Mitch Ellery.''

''What I feel for him is hopeless, Mel, and it seems to get worse by the second.''

Lorna could tell by the way Melanie looked at her what was coming.

''Then don't go near him again, Lorna,'' she said with soft candor. ''Call him and refuse to go tomorrow, then get out early and spend the day someplace away from here to distract yourself from thinking about him.''

Lorna glanced away from her friend, not truly surprised by how much it hurt to think of not seeing Mitch again. Before Lorna could remind her about the dating scheme, Mellie went on as if she had.

''He can tell Kendra that you stood him up without giving him a chance, so the plan works without inflicting any more of this on you. Kendra will be just as disenchanted. I hate that idea, but I'm not sure what else you can do.''

The mental picture of Kendra turning cool to her was again painful and raw. Being ill-thought-of had been a lifelong aversion, but to have her only sister think badly of her forever was too much.

The idea of *immediately* quitting her job to suddenly vanish from Kendra's life surged brightly in her mind. After this perilous evening with Mitch, even the risk of financial hardship was preferable to losing both Kendra's good opinion and an even larger part of her heart to a man she could never have.

Perhaps the dating scheme could be altered, as Mellie had said. Perhaps if she quit her job right away without notice or with very little, Mitch would agree to pretend that their faked romance had fizzled from *his* lack of interest in *her*. There would be no pretense of upset or hurt feelings from either of them, just a low-key parting of the ways with no one at fault.

These next weeks Kendra's wedding plans would be taking more and more of her time and focus. Once Lorna was no longer working for her fiancé, there wouldn't be an opportunity for Kendra to have contact with her, and Lorna would surely fade from Kendra's thoughts.

If she quit her job right away, then going to Ellery Ranch tomorrow wouldn't be critical. The altered plan could be successful without spending the day with Mitch, and perhaps more effective if she did cancel. It might give Kendra the impression that Lorna was not enamored enough of Mitch to see him again so soon. No one but her would have to know that wasn't the truth.

Relief began to trickle through her then. The kind of love that was the real thing never happened in the miniscule length of time she'd already spent with Mitch. If she could stop seeing him now, these impossible feelings could die a quick, natural death. In a couple of weeks, she'd be able to look back on

these two days and see them as nothing more than
the silly time she'd overreacted to a man because
she'd been emotionally stirred up about things that
had nothing to do with him.

Hadn't losing her adoptive parents and being
shuttled from one foster home to another taught her
something about letting go and moving on? She
wasn't exactly a novice when it came to adjusting
to new places and new people.

And wasn't willingly giving up her job and walking away from Kendra and Mitch something she
could initiate and control? If she were the one to
take charge and make things happen this time, surely
it would be far less traumatic than the heartbreak
forced by sudden fate and the peculiar whims and
mysteries of a government foster system.

Lorna was able to hang onto her feeling of relief
long enough to disclose her plan to Melanie. Once
Mel had gone home, she called Information for the
main phone number at Ellery Ranch.

Before she could lose her nerve, she tapped out
the number, then waited in suspense as she counted
the rings. Though Mitch couldn't have had time to
drive all the way home yet, she assumed there was
a messaging system after a certain hour so people
at the house wouldn't be disturbed by a late phone
call.

To her horror the phone was answered, not by a
recorded message but by a female voice. The sharp

leap of her heart told her instantly that it was Doris who'd picked up the telephone.

"Hello?"

Several sickening moments went by as Lorna desperately tried to speak.

"Hello?"

"Please e-excuse me for phoning so late, but I was wondering if I might leave a message for Mr. Ellery?" Lorna cringed at the timid tremor in her voice, and heartily wished she'd just hung up the phone without speaking.

The long, long silence that followed her question confirmed the notion that it was indeed Doris who'd picked up the phone. And just as Lorna had somehow recognized the soft sound of her mother's cultured voice, she sensed instantly that Doris had recognized hers.

"With whom am I speaking?"

The imperious question made her shaking knees go weak and Lorna sank down on the sofa to answer. She tried to inject a firmness into her voice that she hoped telegraphed some sort of poise and confidence.

"This is Ms. Farrell. I'd very much appreciate if you'd have Mr. Ellery phone me in the morning before he leaves for San Antonio. He won't need to worry about calling me early because I need to cancel our plans for tomorrow."

Lorna pressed her fist against her lips, mortified

that the words had come out in a shaky, breathless rush. So much for pretending to be unaffected.

The silence on the line then went even longer, and Lorna felt every excruciating second. At last the woman spoke, and left Lorna no doubt that it was indeed Doris.

"I hope you won't do that."

Doris's stern tone made Lorna feel like a child who'd misbehaved. Or one that was being warned. White-hot anger boiled up from old heartaches and she began to shake. It was a new struggle to keep her voice even. "Would you please give him the message?"

Again the long silence that made her heart pound until she could stand it no longer. Her soft, "Thank you," before she quietly hung up the phone was the only polite way she could think of to deal with it. Somehow she'd managed not to give in to the anger she felt. It alarmed her to realize how much she wanted to strike at Doris and rile her.

Lorna went to bed then, heartsick. Everything she thought she'd dealt with and overcome now seemed to be nothing more than self-delusion. She still felt raw inside and ached to the point of tears, but she refused to cry. She'd made herself stop crying over Doris a long time ago.

But then the focus of that raw ache shifted to Mitch, and she again tried to convince herself that her feelings for him weren't really what they seemed to be. She laid in the dark a long time doing that. It was a miracle she fell asleep at all.

CHAPTER SEVEN

THERE was no early phone call from Mitch. Lorna realized then that she shouldn't have expected one. Mitch was dogged on the subject of her visit to his ranch, and it was entirely possible that Doris hadn't passed on her message.

Mellie's words kept coming back to her. *You don't think Doris is curious about you?* The question thumped at her heart and got her out of bed by 6:00 a.m.

Grimly she dressed for the day and struggled with Mellie's question. She'd given up on Doris years ago, and it upset her to realize there was even a whisper of hope left. Doris couldn't possibly be curious about her now, not in any good way. The only curiosity she might have at this late date would be a curiosity about any weaknesses or flaws Lorna might have. Ones that could be used against her.

By seven, Lorna decided to take Melanie's suggestion to leave her apartment for the day. She'd just got her few essentials transferred from her beaded handbag into the one she normally carried when she heard the knock at her door.

She knew instantly from the brisk, masculine sound that it was Mitch. Somehow he'd gotten into her building without using the call box outside the front lobby.

Just the thought of seeing him again sent a shaft of anxiety through her. And excitement. Quick, sweeping and intense, it shot her heart into a wild rhythm. She couldn't possibly spend the day with Mitch and yet the only thing she wanted suddenly was one more day with him.

Oh God, she was such a fool. She was crazy about a man she had no business even speaking to. The crushing knowledge—that she couldn't bear to refuse any opportunity to see Mitch or be with him again—gave her heart another wild jolt. She had to fight this.

Lorna shakily set her handbag on the small table in the entryway and stood staring at her apartment door holding her breath. The knock came a second time and she made herself turn away.

I doubt a man like him needs anyone's permission to either choose the woman he wants to date…or to marry her…

Whether Melanie's estimation of Mitch's forceful personality was accurate or not, it was excruciatingly unhelpful to remember it now when he was standing outside her door waiting for her to let him in.

Even forcing herself to remember her friend's other words, *Then don't go near him again,* was enough to squelch her craving, particularly since this time she'd have a whole day. A long day at his ranch that she already knew would fly by like a span of minutes just because she was with him.

Lorna gripped her hands together in silent agony as she counted the seconds. The silence outside her door weighed heavily on her heart. Would he give up? She strained to hear the sound of his retreating boot steps, but there was nothing.

Until she heard a soft papery scrape and glanced over her shoulder in time to see the edge of a business card peep out from under her door.

The urge to pick it up was unbearable in the waiting silence, but she stayed where she was. Perhaps he'd concluded that she'd stood him up and had slipped his business card under the door to let her know he'd been here. Perhaps he'd leave now.

But he knocked a third time, only it was softer and slower. In her foolishness she imagined it sounded like a last, sad entreaty because he knew she was standing near the door.

Her barely audible, ''Oh, damn,'' was thick with self-disgust. She moved quietly toward the door to at least look at the small bit of paper. Once she'd given in that far, it was even harder to stop. Just enough of the card showed for her to read a large *Pr,* and she was lost. She leaned down to pull it from beneath the door and straightened to read the rest.

Pretty please, Lorna Dean.

The almost childlike plea was diabolical. Emotion from some old, sweet time that she'd put out of her mind years ago surged up to tease fond memories of her adoptive parents.

Lorna Dean? Where's my girl?

Lorna Dean. The special endearment her daddy called out when he'd come in from ranch work at the end of each day. Sweaty and cheerful and loud, her father would boom out, *Ermalene? Where's my woman?* Then he'd go right on with, *Lorna Dean? Where's my girl?*

Ermalene and Lorna Dean. Her mother's name had been Erma, but her daddy had added *lene* to her name to make it a silly double-rhyme with Lorna's. The sharp memory of her bighearted, exuberant daddy and his artless poetry struck her heart hard.

No one had ever called her Lorna Dean but him, and the fact that Mitch had called her by that same name more than once and had now written it in his curt scrawl affected her profoundly. Feelings of home and terrible loss and deep hunger welled up and she felt her eyes sting.

She pinched the bridge of her nose and fought to stop the memories and force the tears back. She hesitated a moment more to slip the card into the small shallow drawer of the entry table like a stolen treasure she was compelled to hoard.

As if she was no longer in control of herself, she reached for the doorknob. She hesitated again as a last bit of sanity tried to stir. That was the moment she accepted that she wasn't strong enough to deny herself this one last day of craziness. Not even the doom she felt about how things with Mitch would have to end was enough to make her give up this last chance, not until she had to. And not when it was already too late. Resigned, she opened the door.

Mitch had casually leaned his shoulder against the door frame, but now he straightened to tower in front of her. He held a glorious bouquet of flowers in a beautiful crystal vase that she knew at a glance was far more costly than the functional ones sold in most flower shops. No two flowers or colors of the bouquet were the same, and the heady scent of so many blooms seemed to engulf them both in heavy sweetness.

The somber look in Mitch's dark eyes pierced deep. "It seemed more *efficient* to tag along when someone came in downstairs."

"No, it wasn't," she said shakily. "You just didn't trust me to answer the buzzer."

"And I was right," he said as he pressed the bouquet toward her.

Flustered by the sharp pleasure of his presence, Lorna reached to take the flowers. Her soft, "Thank you, they're...beautiful," was self-conscious.

"Do I get to come in?"

Heat flashed into her face and she stepped aside in a wordless invitation for him to enter. "I need to put these somewhere."

She turned away to rush into the living room, terribly aware that Mitch followed at a calm pace. He tossed his black Stetson to a chair then stood watching as she set the vase in the middle of the coffee table.

Lorna lingered over the flowers to toy with a delicate bloom or two as she delayed looking at him. "You're early," she managed to say.

"I was hoping to get you to reconsider coming home with me today."

"Because Doris wanted you to," she concluded hoarsely.

"I would have been here anyway, whatever Doris wanted."

Lorna looked at him then, searching his stern expression for the truth. He was so big and rugged looking. He wore a blue striped shirt that emphasized his wide shoulders and strong arms, and jeans that were just old enough to have learned to be faithful to the muscular lines of his long, powerful legs. His big boots carried a muted shine. There was not so much as a flicker of insincerity about him and she couldn't maintain contact with the grave look in his dark eyes.

She wanted to order him to not speak to her like that, as if this was something much more personal for him than part of an act for Kendra's benefit. But saying something to discourage those kinds of remarks was tantamount to confessing that she was vulnerable to them.

Besides, since she hadn't spoken to him since last night, she still had to tell him about her idea to revise the dating scheme, even though she'd already lost the battle with herself. In spite of that, if she could make a case for the idea, surely he'd change his mind and his cancellation would stop her head-long rush to disaster. She made herself come right out with it.

"I called you because I thought it best to cancel today. I'd hoped to spare you the long drive in." She saw resistance in the hard line of his mouth, but rushed on anyway. "You could tell Kendra that I wasn't interested in your ranch—"

"You don't trust yourself with me for a whole day, do you?"

The blunt question made her heart jump and she fumbled for believable comeback. Mitch went on before she could.

"You're afraid you won't be able to keep your hands off me for eight, maybe ten hours." The con-ceited grin he gave her then was male arrogance at it's most potent. "And because that must be the case, then the answer is no, I won't cancel today. I'd be crazy to."

The chagrin she felt sent a telling heat to her cheeks but she struggled to think of a way to deny it. In truth, her heart had revved with excitement because he was teasing her, almost chiding her for trying to hide her attraction to him, when it was clear that he welcomed it. And possibly felt the same about her.

"Perhaps it would let a little of the hot air out of

your conceit if I came along today and proved just how easy it is to keep my hands to myself.''

His dark eyes glittered and she realized with dismay that her smart comeback had as much as issued a dare. ''Oh, yes, ma'am, you do that. Put me in my place and teach me a lesson overdue. Yes, ma'am.''

His conceited grin eased away and she felt the lightning stroke of his masculine intensity pierce her like an expertly aimed arrow. There was a harsh tension in the air that was like the heavy silence before a clap of thunder. The attraction between them was unmistakable and it suddenly seemed far more powerful than either of them.

She could see the edginess in his eyes and realized that in spite of what he'd just said about refusing to cancel the plan, he was waiting for her to officially relent. That was as tantalizing as it was reassuring.

''I'll have to change into something for the ranch.''

Now a smile angled his mouth. ''If you don't have boots or a hat—''

''I've got both.''

''Good.''

Lorna turned away to walk to her bedroom, closing the door silently behind her before she leaned back against it and tried to get her breath. This was such a wrong, wrong thing to do. It was stupid and careless and self-destructive.

And so infernally exciting that she practically ran to her closet to change.

It surprised Lorna that they'd flown to the ranch in the small Cessna Mitch owned. "So we don't burn up so much time on the road," he'd told her on the way to the small airport they'd taken off from.

The view of Ellery Ranch from the air was thrilling. Mitch pointed out landmarks and boundaries before he banked the plane to head to the airstrip and hangar that was situated a mile east of the ranch headquarters.

The view of his home from the ground was even more impressive than from the air. The house was a rambling two-and-a-half story Victorian with a veranda to encircle it and a massive patio in back with a jewel-bright pool that was overhung by shady trees.

The tour he gave her indoors wasn't at all necessary, but he ignored her tactful attempt to decline. The last stop was his office in the large den on the main floor where he invited her to take a glass of tea from the serving tray the housekeeper had left for them. While she did, he glanced through some papers that had stacked up in the tray beneath his fax machine.

A phone call interrupted so Lorna took her tea through the sliding glass door to the back veranda and patio to give Mitch privacy.

She'd no more than found a shady place to sit and

put her tea on a side table, when she heard the light clatter of puppy paws on the other side of the patio.

Mitch hung up the phone and watched as more pages scrolled out of the fax machine. He picked them up and began to read, a heaviness in his gut. His investigator had found out more about Lorna and as he read through the report, the heaviness he felt rose into his chest and began to burn.

The sound of laughter from outside made him glance through the sliding door to see that Lorna had attracted the attention of the Kelpie pups who'd wandered up from the barns. He paused a minute to watch as they jumped around her legs while she tried to give each one attention.

In seconds, she was sitting on the paving stones and the excited pups were all over her. Her attempt to get them to calm down was a complete failure as the pups jumped and licked and yipped around her.

Her childlike glee over the pups had banished her reserve. The sad lights that seemed to glow persistently in her eyes were gone as she giggled delightedly and struggled to corral all four puppies in her arms at once while trying to prevent them from licking her face. She almost succeeded but none of the squirming pups would settle down.

Somehow she got to her feet and walked back to the bench where she could sit above the fray. The puppies' wiggly bodies made for slow progress, but she made it at last and Mitch continued to watch as the stark details of the report whirled in his thoughts and he grappled with their impact.

Apparently neither the Farrells or the Deans had considered Lorna a full member of either family, and the shocking truth of that had been exposed by the sudden deaths of Robert and Erma Farrell. From the look of it, there'd been enough brothers and sisters between the two families, so one of them could have taken Lorna in and raised her. No one had.

Because Lorna hadn't been blood kin, none of them had felt an obligation to her. According to the investigator, it couldn't have been because she was a troublesome child. And even if she had been, how troublesome could an eight-year-old have been?

The burning heaviness in his chest churned into anger and he yanked open a desk drawer to shove the fax pages inside and snap it closed before he locked it.

Maybe the real question was, how heartless did you have to be to send away a grief-stricken, orphaned child and condemn her young life to years of government foster care?

The investigator was digging for more, but Mitch wasn't certain how much more he needed to know, since he'd already found out enough basics to be satisfied that Lorna wasn't a threat. He knew instinctively that it would hurt Lorna's pride if she caught any hint that he'd found out about the Farrells and the Deans, so it was better to get his anger under control before she could detect it. She was already on guard with him because she wasn't sure what to expect today, and she was too perceptive to miss much.

Amazingly she'd gotten the puppies to calm down and they crowded adoringly around her feet as she lavished each one with attention. She was so gentle and open with them and so comfortable and patient with their antics. Her reserve, her wariness and the way she'd tried to keep a stiff distance with him in spite of her attraction, was a bleak contrast that took on a deeper meaning now that he had an explanation for it.

Lorna could have been bitter, she could have been an insatiable victim who thought the world owed her or been full of self-pity, but she'd obviously not fallen prey to those things. She'd worked hard to make an independent life for herself. It shamed him now to have thought for a second that her nice apartment and the obvious good care she'd taken of it was anything less honorable than the grateful behavior of a woman with neat habits and high standards. It was clear that if she had a lust for more of anything, it would never be possessions.

Lorna had a refinement he doubted she'd learned while being shuttled from foster home to foster home. She was a lady, even under the gentle assault of a small hoard of rambunctious pups. But her reserve with him, her refusal to come face-to-face with Doris, and the melancholy he'd sensed when she was quiet, were the only lingering evidence of the abandonment and rejection she'd suffered.

And what about Doris's reaction to her five years ago when she'd shown up in that restaurant? He'd been guilty of adding to Lorna's hurt when he'd gone after her to warn her away from further contact with Doris. He regretted even more the bribe and the empty threat about an extortion charge. And now there was the dating scheme Doris wanted.

He'd known from the start that if everything went the way Doris hoped, Lorna would come out the loser. He'd been uneasy about that initially, but he wasn't certain anymore that the scheme would turn out exactly the way his stepmother hoped. Particularly after last night.

Lorna glanced toward the sliding doors and shaded her eyes with both hands to look in at him. He couldn't count the number of times he'd seen Kendra shade her eyes that same way, and he felt a new tenderness. If he wasn't staring at the biological daughter of Doris Jackson Ellery, then Kendra wasn't hers, either.

The pups yipped protests to reclaim Lorna's attention but she gave them all a round of pats as she got to her feet and reached over to get her glass of tea. She made her way carefully to the slider and he walked over to open it for her.

His gentle order to the puppies to stay back distracted them for the brief second it took Lorna to squeeze through the opening into the den. Mitch had to block the slim passage with his boot so he could ease the door shut after her.

"I need to wash up before we go riding," she said to him, her face still glowing from her play with the pups. She glanced through the glass at the wiggly animals as a couple of them whined pitifully at her.

As if she couldn't resist, she reached toward them and they scrambled to throw themselves against the glass to get to her. One puppy hit the door hard and gave a piping yelp.

"Oh, no!" Lorna drew back abruptly, then reached for the door as if to intervene.

Mitch chuckled. "He's fine, Lorna. They're just in love. I'll have someone corral them so they aren't tempted to follow us."

"I started something, didn't I?" she remarked as she straightened.

"More than you know."

Her blue, blue gaze shot up to his and he felt the connection like a touch. But then he saw the reserve she'd lost so briefly with the pups snap fully into place.

"I'll just go get cleaned up."

"We'll head for the stables when you're done," he said, still watching her wariness and reserve shutter everything lighthearted he'd just seen.

Lorna left the den in search of a bathroom and he followed her to the hall to walk to the kitchen to wait.

*   *   *

Lorna loved the ride, despite the growing heat of late morning. The bay mare Mitch had selected for her was well trained, and in no time at all the big horse felt natural beneath her. Though she'd lived on a ranch until she was eight then later during a foster placement, she was still pretty much a novice rider when it came to full-size horses. The pony her daddy had given her and the ponies on the acreage she'd lived on during another placement were vastly different in temperament and size from Mitch's quarter horses. Nevertheless, Mitch did no more than give her a couple of reminders about safety and posture, and she was glad of his lack of criticism.

He was the perfect host and it felt good to be with him. He was obviously proud of his ranch, and she deeply envied the fact that generations of Ellerys had lived on this land and would continue to live on it. His family history was proof that most people had grown up his way rather than hers, and she got a fresh sense that someday she'd find a place to belong and a family of her own to be part of.

But in spite of her effort to ignore it, a subtle sensuality flowed naturally between them like an ever-deepening current. She saw it in every look Mitch gave her and felt it in every word they spoke to each other. And whenever they shared the slightest casual touch, the longing inside her surged.

The fact that they still had most of the day left kept her in a state of constant vigilance because she couldn't allow those warm looks and wonderful touches to become anything more, however much she wanted them to.

The quiet heat in Mitch's gaze and the tension that was building steadily higher between them made it difficult to remain aloof. She had to keep reminding herself that if she could keep Mitch at arm's length, perhaps she wouldn't add to the personal devastation she was sure to have later once the dating sham had run its course.

The tree-lined creek they finally stopped at was low enough to wade in, and the shallow banks were sandy. There was a picnic table in the shade and a bright red cooler sat on top of it.

Mitch dismounted easily, but Lorna's legs were so stiff that it was almost impossible to get her leg over the back of the saddle. Mitch stopped her before she'd got too far into the process.

"Whoa there," he said gruffly as he stepped over to her, "try it the other way."

Lorna settled back into the saddle to look down at him. "What other way?"

"Swing your leg forward over the saddle horn."

She managed to lift her right leg to awkwardly guide it over the front of the saddle and her horse's neck, but once both legs were on the same side of the horse, her left boot had twisted the stirrup so she was stuck. Mitch easily freed her, but without the stirrup to stand in she started an abrupt slide to the ground.

Mitch caught her waist to both slow her and guide a safe descent. And of course her hands landed on his hard shoulders while the front of her body lightly skimmed the length of his.

The sensual friction of the contact scorched her insides like lava. She let go of his shoulders the moment her boots touched the ground, but her legs refused to take her weight. Startled, she grabbed for Mitch's forearms but it was his firm grip on her waist that kept her from landing in a heap at his feet.

Mitch chuckled. "Thought you were going to keep your hands to yourself today."

Lorna's head snapped up and she saw the gleam of orneriness in his eyes. "I think a certain rancher set me up for this one," she said, secretly dismayed at the breathlessness in her voice.

"Only because a certain tenderfoot forgot what a horseback ride can do to a pair of city girl legs," he drawled. The hard muscle beneath her fingers and palms only heightened her awareness of his superior strength, and the lavalike heat inside her began to simmer.

"We haven't been riding that long."

"Long enough. When you get your legs back, you might want to walk off the weakness."

Lorna realized then that her legs might also have been weakened by something far more debilitating than a horseback ride. They were still lightly touching each other from chest to knee. The solid feel of

Mitch's hard forearms and the steady energy of his incredible body heat were making her go weaker by the second. With her back so close to the side of her horse there was no way for her to put distance between them. Much more of this and she'd melt into a puddle on the ground.

Lorna moved her hands to the hard wall of his chest to maintain what space she could and she glanced away with faked nonchalance. "I'm okay now," she said softly, and waited tensely for Mitch to let her go.

Thankfully he did and he reached for the reins of her horse. She hobbled out of the way to walk around a bit and looked on as he tied the reins to the saddle horn. He led the animal a few steps and, to her astonishment, gave the mare a slap on the rump that sent her trotting off through the stand of trees to the open land beyond.

Her shocked, "Hey—" was cut off as she watched him reach for his sorrel gelding and do the same. "What are you—"

The gelding sprinted away and Mitch turned back to her. One side of his mouth quirked up.

"Your eyes are as big as dinner plates, Lorna Dean. Look into the trees, a little to your right."

Lorna almost didn't trust him enough to look away. Because she didn't, she sent only a fleeting glance in that direction then did a double-take when what she'd glimpsed registered. A black pickup was parked in the shade. A couple of tree trunks had blocked part of her view of it, and the shade was dark enough in that spot that the parked truck wasn't obvious.

"Thought your legs would have more than enough riding for one day by now," he said, "so we'll take the pickup home when it's time. We're only about a mile and a half west of the house."

"What about the horses?

"The horses'll go right to the stable and one of the men'll take care of them."

A little ashamed of her overreaction, Lorna glanced his way to see his cocky grin.

"So you think I'm up to no good, huh?"

Lorna felt acute embarrassment and rubbed her palms nervously on her jeans. "I guess so. I apologize."

He chuckled again and turned to walk to the picnic table. "Don't bother with an apology," he called back to her. "You were right."

The full second it took his words to register gave them an added punch that startled a small "ha" of laughter out of her before she could catch it. Thank God he was too far away from her to hear the small sound.

Growing warm in the hot sun nearer the creek, she hobbled after Mitch into the line of deep shade, more on edge than ever.

CHAPTER EIGHT

LORNA'S legs had gotten stronger walking those few feet to the table, and the stiffness was easing. Now that she was in the shade, she pulled off her Stetson and set it on one of the bench seats next to where Mitch had moved the cooler. He was spreading a heavy, red-checked tablecloth on the weathered wood.

"There's a waterless hand soap in a wad of napkins on the other side of the cooler," he told her. "Help yourself to a soda."

Lorna used the antibacterial soap then chose a soda and opened it to have a cold drink. Mitch waited until she'd slaked some of her thirst.

"Hungry yet?"

"Starved."

Together they inspected the contents of the cooler, helping themselves to servings from several small containers. There was an assortment of cold salads and three different kinds of sandwich wedges with thick meat fillings. Mitch informed her that they'd have dessert at the house later, so they took what they meant to eat, then left the rest inside the cooler.

Mitch suggested they sit on top of the table as

they would have if they'd spread the tablecloth on the ground, and Lorna appreciated the bit of extra height as they looked out over the creek and ate.

"You've enjoyed yourself so far, haven't you?" Mitch asked after they'd eaten in silence for a while.

Lorna had been savoring the steady gurgle and rush of the stream and the sound of birds around them as much as she'd savored the food. Because Mitch had made no more sexy remarks, she'd let down her guard. The peacefulness around them had soothed her and she was relaxing more by the moment.

"Yes," she admitted, "very much." She debated briefly, then added, "My daddy had a ranch. I'm sure it wasn't as massive as this one, but I thought it was the biggest in Texas. I'd forgotten all the smells and sounds, the barns, the creeks, the animals, the vastness." She smiled, and felt a calm and contentment she hadn't had for a long time. "It's wonderfully quiet and soothing out here. I'd forgotten that, too."

"So you liked living on a ranch," he said as he finished with his food and leaned back to set his plate on the cooler on the other bench seat behind the table.

"I loved it. Of course, I wasn't big enough to do anything very useful, but I loved being outdoors and having the run of the place." The sweet feelings those memories caused made her forget to be more reserved with him.

"I had a black pony named Pepper and a yellow mixed breed dog named Flash. We found lots of things to do and lots of things we shouldn't."

Lorna glanced at Mitch, saw the curiosity in his eyes and was instantly self-conscious. She looked away. She'd just told him things about her childhood that she'd rarely spoken of to anyone, and she shouldn't have done that. Not with him.

Coming to the ranch had brought back so many things and they seemed clearer in her heart than she'd allowed them to be for years. And once she'd relaxed, her heart began to succumb to the sweet feelings that she associated exclusively with the happy part of her childhood, when her mother and father had still been alive.

Her life had been idyllic then. Over the years, her memories had grown hazy, but today they were surprisingly detailed and were affecting her so deeply that it felt natural to talk about them. Since her play with the puppies, the tour of the ranch headquarters and the ride to the creek, she'd been thinking of Pepper and Flash in particular.

She heard the smile in Mitch's voice. "Pepper and Flash. Did you name them by their personalities?"

It would be awkward to evade a simple question about something she'd brought up, so she started cautiously.

"My daddy helped me name them, and yes, he believed in naming animals according to their personalities. He was very good with animals, especially small ones and any that were hurt or sick.''

''What about your mama?''

Since she'd mentioned her father, it wouldn't feel right to neglect telling him about her mother, but she tried to keep it brief.

''Mama was very proper and quiet, a total lady. Since my daddy was big and cheerful and liked to laugh, they were almost complete opposites, but they were devoted to each other.'' *And to me.*

Lorna went silent then, a little appalled, not only because she'd told Mitch this much but because of the swift rise of emotion that suddenly felt too powerful to conceal.

Desperate to distract herself, she got out a shaky, ''What about your parents?'' before she turned to set her empty plate behind them with Mitch's on the cooler. ''If you don't mind telling a little about them.'' She didn't look at him.

''My father was a stern man who hardly ever cracked a smile. When something amused him, it was usually something ironic. He married my mama when he was almost forty. She was beautiful and fragile and she passed away about the time I started first grade. He took it hard and didn't remarry for years after that.''

Mitch stopped and Lorna got the distinct impression that he'd done so to avoid bringing up Doris's name, though his next question made her more uncomfortable than a mention of Doris.

"Was your daddy still ranching when he passed away?"

It was natural for him to ask that since as a rancher himself, he'd likely wonder about it. She had to be careful with this answer, too.

"Yes. But the ranch was heavily into debt, so it had to be sold."

That should have cut off the subject, but she glanced Mitch's way in time to catch the gleam of interest in his eyes. Her heart sank a little so she looked away and was only faintly aware that she'd started rubbing her palms on the thighs of her jeans.

She'd never believed her father had been in that much debt, but she'd been eight years old at the time so it was possible such things had been kept from her.

One of her father's older brothers had been his executor, and he'd been in charge of everything, including her. Since he'd turned her over to foster care within weeks of her parents' deaths and virtually abandoned her instead of offering her a home or persuading someone else in one of the two large families to take her in, she'd always suspected him of something shady in connection with the ranch. Particularly since he'd been the one to buy it later.

But it was too late to do anything about it now, even if she'd had the resources to pursue it. Unfortunately she'd had no one like Mitch Ellery around at the time to look out for her interests. She was certain that was a large part of her foolish attraction to him. A man like Mitch would never have allowed a child to suffer the incredible loss she had.

She didn't want him to ask any more questions about the ranch because if she evaded them now as she had to, she'd stir up too much interest. And if he looked too far into her past, he'd surely stumble across the kind of information that might lead him straight to Doris's part in that horrifying time. Though it might be a long-delayed comeupance for Doris, Kendra wouldn't deserve the fallout.

More uneasy by the moment with the tense silence between them, Lorna lifted a hand to check the large barrette she'd used to put her hair up as she casually asked, "Will Kendra be home in time to know I was here?"

Giving a verbal reminder about why she was really here was better than to allow the conversation go on as it had.

"Nice try," Mitch said mildly. "But today stopped being about Kendra or Doris last night when I pulled you into my arms on that dance floor."

Startled, Lorna's gaze flew to his. Before she realized what he was doing, he'd laid down full-length on his side behind her on the long table and had propped himself up on one elbow. She twisted around to keep a wary eye on him, but eased closer to the edge of the table as if prepared to flee.

Mitch calmly watched her as he removed his hat and dropped it to the bench at her feet before he settled back with his head propped on a big fist. The thickening tension between them flowed like a river of sensual peril.

''Since last night,'' he went on lazily, ''all I've been able to think about is how to get that close to you again.''

The declaration gave her a soft jolt and she felt her heart begin to pound. His masculinity reached out for her and her blood heated and began to pool down low. There'd be no more questions about the past because Mitch had shifted his focus to something much more personally dangerous for her.

Lorna couldn't seem to take her eyes off him. It was as if he was hypnotizing her and she was rapidly losing her will to snap out of it. It dawned on her that this was some sort of sexual showdown and he had more control over it than she did. Wary of that, she prudently started to move off the table, but he gently caught her arm to keep her close.

She had to make this stop. He had no business toying with her like this, not when the emotional stakes for her were so high. ''Maybe you can separate animal urges from this situation, but I can't.''

''All right, Lorna Dean,'' he said reasonably. ''I'm sure you've wound up for a dandy speech along the lines of 'You're-nothing-but-a-sex-obsessed-male-beast.' Go ahead with it now and I'll take a bow after you finish.''

Her face went hot with frustration and she was suddenly furious with him. She made a move to free her arm and he released her instantly.

"What on earth is wrong with you? Why can't you understand that all your loaded remarks and flirtations aren't welcome?"

"Why can't you see that there's a point to all those loaded remarks and flirtations?" he returned, his calm tone riling her even more.

"Oh please," she burst out with uncharacteristic scorn, "what point could there be? Unless you're that desperate for another notch on your bedpost."

He smiled faintly but his gaze was serious. "There aren't as many notches as you think, Lorna. I'm not some hormone-crazed kid."

Lorna was trembling now but it suddenly struck her that she wasn't trying to douse his sexual ambitions as much as she was trying to douse her own. She felt like a traitor to her own common sense. "Then stop acting like one," she said, a little desperate now. "Kendra can't see us out here, so there's no reason for you to talk like that or do some of the things you do, unless you're looking for some cheap thrill to pass the time. And I *won't* be part of that."

His faint smile eased away. "You're fighting this pretty hard, aren't you?" A ghost of a grin came back. "Can't say when I've had a bigger compliment, but you really ought to kiss me now and get it over with."

The suggestion was so outrageous and tantalizing that her mouth went dry. Her fury abruptly faltered and her voice was a little choked.

"I thought you understood what this would cost me. You said you did."

A tenderness came into his eyes. "You don't have much faith in the power of love to win out, do you?"

She was stunned by that. It was a shocking conclusion for him to have come to in such a brief time. What had his investigator found out? On the other hand, perhaps she was more transparent than she wanted to think. Either way, what he'd said about love wasn't some vague hint, it was blatant. And dangerous for someone like her. She couldn't afford that kind of hope and she was compelled to put a stop to it.

"Love isn't what we're talking about," she said in a low, fierce voice, "and you know it."

"How do we know if we don't follow this down the road a while?"

So what he was really after was some kind of sexual test drive that had nothing to do with love. This wasn't the first time a man had suggested that to her, but it was the first time she'd ever been vulnerable to the suggestion.

As frustrated with herself as she was with him, her anger went cosmic. "Spare me the good ole boy verbal seductions."

"So I've advanced from loaded remarks to verbal seductions." His voice lowered to a gentle drawl, and she caught an inkling of sexy deviltry in his eyes. "Then come kiss me."

The arrogance of that was the last straw. Why should she be the only one tortured by something she couldn't have? He might not be so cavalier about all this if the stakes for him were a little higher.

And since he was waiting to take a bow for the title of "sex-obsessed male beast," then it would be richly deserved justice if she could inflame his beastly appetites then send him home as empty and aching as she felt.

She was too angry and inexperienced to recognize the peril, and she was too stirred up to realize she was overreacting because of the powerful sexual feelings in herself that she couldn't acknowledge. So she did the unthinkable.

Lorna barely noticed the stiffness in her legs as she rose to move across the table and kiss him full on the mouth. As she did, she nudged him to his back, determined to give him such a wanton, fiery kiss that he'd go crazy for her.

Though she knew women who did that to men were foolish and low-class, perhaps he'd think twice next time about toying with her when there was absolutely no hope for anything permanent between them

In those first seconds of the kiss, Lorna used everything she'd ever learned or read about to give him the most erotic kiss she was capable of. She felt the first small flare of victory when his big hands came up and his arms closed fiercely around her.

But that small flare of victory went out like a
match tossed in water the moment she suddenly
found herself on her back, at the mercy of the most
carnal and demanding kiss of her life.

Lorna felt herself melt into the table as deep heat
bubbled through her to set her insides on fire. She'd
never experienced anything like this and she was
helpless beneath a vastly more diabolical expertise
than she'd ever known existed.

And then Mitch's hand began to move on her,
efficiently dispensing with the buttons on her shirt
and beginning an invasion as skilled and overwhelming as anything he'd already done with his
lips.

She was the one who'd gone wild and she reveled
in it, following feminine instinct to both respond and
to initiate more. She'd lost her mind and her body
loved it.

By the time Mitch finally broke off the kiss, she
was shaking and starved for air, and she lay boneless
and utterly powerless as the shock of what she'd
done began to impact her. She'd never in her life
lost control like that, and the maddening fact that
she was eager to have it happen again made her feel
even more a traitor to common sense.

A hot tear of defeat streaked from her eye to her
ear, but instead of completely withdrawing, Mitch's
talented mouth nibbled at her neck, then moved ever
downward like a dictator parading his army over
conquered ground.

"You win." The sound of her own whisper was little more than a mild surprise to her dazed senses. She'd already surrendered to the devastation ahead, so she guessed it would cost her only a little more of her shredded pride to admit it.

"It's not win or lose, Lorna," he said gruffly, then lifted his head to stare down at her with an intensity that she felt all the way to her soul.

She slipped up a hand and touched his lean cheek, still too hungry for more to resist savoring the feel of his skin. He leaned down and gave her such a tender kiss that she ached with the sweetness of it until he drew back.

"I think we'd better finish this at the house."

The words caused no more than a small pang of regret. What was he supposed to think after the way she'd kissed him? Because he'd so expertly turned the tables on her, she had no illusions about teaching him anything. She certainly had no illusions about being able to resist whatever intimacies he might have in mind once they got to the house, because now she wanted them as much as he did.

Mitch eased back and pulled her into a sitting position. But instead of leaving her on her own to button up and put herself back together, she endured the tender pleasure of watching him button her blouse and retrieve her lost barrette.

They both prepared for the ride to the house in silence. Mitch quickly folded the tablecloth and stowed it in the cooler while Lorna tucked in her shirttail and found her hat. She avoided looking his way until she heard a low growl and looked up in time to see him reach under the table for his Stetson.

When he pulled it out, Lorna saw the reason for his growl and gasped. The crown of the big hat had been comically crushed down. She must have stepped on it when she'd climbed onto the table, and she felt torn between mortification and laughter.

Mitch turned dark eyes on her that were glittering with amusement, but he said nothing. His lips curved faintly as he placed his big fist inside the hat, gave it a small punch to poke it back into shape, then put it on and tugged the brim low.

Lorna managed to keep a straight face and give what she hoped was a suitable impression of regret. "I'm sorry. I must have stepped on it when I..."

A fit of giggles burst up and she had to bite her lips to keep them from gurgling out.

Mitch saw that and his dark eyes flared with silent laughter but he kept his expression stoic as he reached for the cooler and lifted it to one shoulder.

"Never mess with a man's hat," he said with a mock severity that was calculated to make her lose control of her giggles. "And *do not ever* step on it to climb all over a man, even when you mean to kiss the daylights outta him."

The exaggerated nonsense of that gave her heart a sparkling lift, but Lorna managed to keep a straight face until Mitch passed her.

His only comment then was, "Let's get movin',"

and then a barely heard, "Hat-masher," but it was enough to finally set loose a stream of nearly hysterical giggles as the tension and the longing and the emotion of these past three days rushed out from a lonely heart that still couldn't think of a way for any of this to end happily.

Lorna managed to get control of herself by the time they were in the truck to head back to the ranch house. Mitch reached across the big seat to coax her against his side, and she leaned into him wearily, absorbing the heat and the feel and the musky scent of his body so she could imprint it on her heart.

Very soon now, she'd have to file all this away in that lonely little place where she'd stored all her other sweet memories of loved ones and places she'd never see again. And someday her memories of Mitch would grow hazy, just like the other ones.

How many days or weeks or years that would take wasn't nearly as important now as her sudden greed to create as many memories as she could for however much time she had left with him.

The tenderness Mitch felt for Lorna was unlike anything he'd ever felt in his life. He'd pushed her at the creek until he'd felt like a brute, but he'd been compelled to shake her out of that damnable reserve. Then she'd gotten so riled at him that she'd kissed him after all, and they'd both lost control.

He'd felt it the moment the dam of passion in her had broke to thunder over him, and he'd reveled in her response. And he'd been a heartbeat short of making her completely his right there by the creek. Now that his head was clearing a little more, he realized even more how shattering that would have been to her pride. A woman like Lorna wouldn't be able to cope with full intimacy without the security of marriage, not without paying a heavy emotional price.

The quiet devastation in her sad eyes afterward had got him by the heart, but he should have expected that. She was a woman who truly didn't believe in love for herself and was terrified to make a serious try for it, though it was obvious to him now that she craved love like she craved her next breath.

She was nestled against his side as if she'd begun to feel at least some trust toward him, but he was the last one to believe the fragile feeling had any sort of permanence. And because Doris and Kendra literally stood between them, there was every chance that none of these first feelings would survive the week for either of them.

Maybe Lorna was right. Maybe he should have left her alone. Mitch leaned down a little to press a soft kiss against the dark silk of her hair in a secret apology. She'd left it loose and it still smelled of shampoo. His lips lingered, savoring the rich sensation as he brooded about the risk.

Three days wasn't long enough to know anything for sure, but then, how long did it take to know whether you wanted to take a chance on something that showed promise? Or on someone?

When they reached the house, Mitch hefted the cooler to his shoulder and they walked hand in hand to the back patio, past the pool, then stepped into the air-conditioned chill and silence of the big house.

Lorna knew the moment they walked inside that something was different. There was another quality to the big house that hadn't been there earlier, a formidable presence that sent anxiety swimming through her like a poisoned stream. Lorna glanced uneasily at Mitch as he set the cooler on the floor.

"I thought you said Doris wouldn't be home until long after I was gone?"

"That was the plan," he said, as he straightened. His brow furrowed. "What makes you think she's here?"

They heard the sound of high heels on the wood flooring in the hall and Lorna panicked. She started to turn in an instinct to flee, but Mitch gently caught her arm and pulled her close.

His deep voice was a calming rasp as he took hold of her waist and she braced her hands against his chest. "There's no reason for you to be afraid of this," he told her. "Her plans must have changed, but today won't be like that time in the restaurant." His grip tightened. "You've done everything she's wanted, Lorna, so she'd be a fool to put any of it in jeopardy."

Distracted by mounting anxiety, Lorna looked up, amazed to realize what Mitch had said. He was reminding her she had at least some protection against Doris, and his very reminder was a form of protection in itself. He gave her the impression that he was more on her side than Doris's, but that couldn't be right. She must be mistaken. And how could he be so certain of Doris?

She had no time to ponder the question because the steady, light tap of high heels changed pitch as Doris stepped into the tiled kitchen and came to an abrupt halt.

Lorna glanced her way and couldn't help that she stared as she struggled to blank her expression and brace herself for disaster. She watched, frozen, as Doris's blue gaze took note of the way Mitch was holding her. Doris didn't look her in the eye and barely let her gaze linger more than a scant second on Lorna's face.

Doris offered a faintly polite smile that was fixed on neither of them yet coolly included them both. There was a brisk, imperious quality to her gently cultured voice.

"Mitch? Would you mind making the introduction?"

CHAPTER NINE

WOULD you mind making the introduction?

The hypocrisy of that incensed Lorna. She managed to keep her voice soft. "I think we know who all the players are, Mrs. Ellery. We don't need a dress rehearsal."

It ranked as one of the nerviest things she'd ever said to a parental figure in her life, and Lorna clenched her teeth together to keep herself silent. Doris was no parent to her, so she should feel no guilt over challenging her pretense. Lorna hated that she felt guilty anyway.

Doris's gaze shifted to finally meet hers and sharpened, then lowered briefly to again take note of Mitch's grip on Lorna's waist before it shifted to Mitch.

"I'd like to have a private word with Miss Farrell, Mitch."

Everything in Lorna went on full alert and icy anxiety crackled through her blood as Doris went on briskly. "In the den, if that's all right with you?"

Lorna wasn't looking at Mitch to see his reaction. She couldn't seem to look away from the rigid set of her mother's face. It seemed to take forever before Mitch answered.

"I reckon that's up to Lorna."

Lorna saw the flicker of surprise in Doris's eyes and it dawned on her that what Mitch had just said had again offered her a protection of sorts. It stunned Lorna that he would do that, and it was clear Doris hadn't expected it, either.

Doris's rigid expression appeared to falter as she offered a more conciliatory, "Of course," before she looked at Lorna, again just missing a direct connection with Lorna's gaze.

Lorna felt the pressure of Doris's expectation and bitterness surged up. She eased away from Mitch as she said, "I'd rather not." She took a shaky breath as she fought against giving in to the urge to rile Doris and shake a little more of her regal poise.

"I'm not a threat to you, Mrs. Ellery, or to your daughter. And now that I've visited Mitch's ranch and we have at least one witness to that, I'd like to go back to San Antonio now."

Doris's lips parted as if she'd started to veto the idea, but then she appeared to change her mind. "As you wish. But I'd like some assurance that you'll be back on Friday for the barbecue. It's our Fourth of July celebration and a yearly tradition on Ellery Ranch. Kendra would naturally expect an appearance by Mitch's current love interest."

Lorna needed no other reminder of her place in the scheme of things. Whatever had happened between her and Mitch at the creek, she was still little more than a minor player in his stepmother's dating charade. The fact that he hadn't yet mentioned the barbecue on Friday made her think that perhaps he'd counted on things being finished between them by then. Maybe he'd already decided that the road they should "follow a while" would reach its dead end by then.

"I don't know if that will be necessary," Lorna got out, suddenly caught in the acid grip of old hurts and resentments that were too caustic to contain. It was all she could do to struggle for a scrap of civility.

"I'm giving John Owen notice tomorrow, then I'm taking off the rest of the week and all of the next in vacation days. I'll make certain Kendra can't contact me and, who knows? Perhaps Mitch will meet a new love interest at the barbecue to soothe his broken heart."

It gave Lorna remarkably little satisfaction to see the instant devastation in her mother's eyes as her face went pale. Doris gave Mitch a distressed look and a hasty, "May I see you in the den?"

A wave of dizziness came over Lorna as she realized that Doris's devastation and distress were solely the result of an unexpected veto of the date-and-dump plan. She'd dreaded ever coming face-to-face with her mother again, and because she'd been caught by surprise by this, there'd been no time to shore up her self-control.

And now that Doris was about to whisk Mitch away, most likely to persuade him to somehow bully or sweet talk her into compliance again, Lorna couldn't seem to restrain herself. The urge to give Doris an unwanted glimpse of the pain she'd caused was so overpowering that Lorna struck out.

"I think of it as the 'What shall we do with Lorna' meeting," she said quietly, and she paused until she had Doris's full attention.

"There've been quite a few of those in the past, and I never liked the decisions that resulted. I'd rather not be anywhere in the vicinity for yours, so I ask that you save it for later when Mitch comes back from taking me to San Antonio.

"Besides which, I'm feeling very bitter and very bitchy right now, and if I stay around much longer, I think we're all in danger of discovering what abominable manners I'm capable of."

Lorna's insides were churning with a volatile mix of pain and fury, and such agonizing regret for her spiteful words that she was nauseous. She hadn't known she was capable of such venom and the discovery caused her the deepest shame of her life. What little pride she had left was all that kept her from giving in to the confusing need to apologize and make amends. Doris might deserve her venom, but Lorna's main shame was that she'd lowered herself to give Doris a taste of it.

And of course, Mitch had witnessed it and heard every evil word. She'd been aware of his stony presence beside her the entire time and she didn't dare peek now to see his reaction. Was his iron silence responsible for the crashing roar in her ears and the sick dread that was going over her in waves?

Surely that was the reason for her impulse to apologize. It couldn't possibly be because of her unwilling compassion for the haunted shock in Doris's eyes and the way her mother appeared to sway.

Lorna got out a choked, "I'll just go get my things and wash up," before she walked out of the kitchen into the hall, taking a few moments to get her handbag from the den before she found a downstairs bathroom and locked herself in.

Her shaking legs buckled and she dropped her handbag to go to her knees in front of the pedestal sink, pressing her forehead against the cool porcelain while she took deep breaths and tried to cope with the awful things she'd said.

"God forgive me, God forgive me," she panted soundlessly, so deeply submerged in guilt that she was smothered by it.

Until now, she'd been the one wronged, the one who bore no blame. But the bit of vengeance she'd taken on Doris had somehow put a stain on her soul that was eating her tender conscience alive.

Bitter tears of confusion boiled up from it all, and she reached up defiantly to turn on the cold water tap. She couldn't go to pieces here, of all places, so she pulled herself up and bent over the sink, dashing her hot face with cold water as she made the monumental effort to compose herself until she could make good her escape.

"Mitch, if you can't get her to stay today, you *must* get her to come to the barbecue," Doris whispered urgently the moment Lorna was out of earshot.

"I gave my word she wouldn't have to see you today. Why are you here?"

"I've obviously upset her."

Something in the way Doris ignored his question alerted him. "You care about that?"

His question registered on the distress in her eyes and he watched as his unshakable stepmother began to twist her elegant hands together in an uncharacteristic sign of upset. The fact that the gesture was one he'd seen Lorna do—with the same distracted finger-bending twists—underscored the trait and made it appear familial.

In the silence, they both heard the snap of the bathroom door latch down the hall, then the telling click of the lock. The sound appeared to further rattle Doris and she pressed him again.

"Please, Mitch. Find some way to keep her here today. At least until Kendra gets home. There's something—"

"I think she's had enough of this charade. I know I have."

Mitch's harsh tone dealt Doris a new shock. The stepson she'd respected and admired and had come to love as a trusted friend had never looked at her like that.

Despite their relatively close age—he was only eight years or so younger than she was—he'd never treated her as anything less than his father's wife, and therefore he'd accorded her all the respect and deference he might have if she'd been twenty years his elder.

But his stony look now and the laser probe of his hard gaze was something only a bit less intimidating than that of an employer pulling rank on an employee who'd stepped so far out of line that they were in danger of being fired.

Doris had feared seeing that look from his late father and now that Ben was gone, she'd feared to see it in Mitch. Because she had so much ugliness and selfishness to hide, she'd always been terrified of discovery, alert to any signal that her biggest failings had been discovered. And, as she'd been with his father, she'd always been terrified to lose not only Mitch's respect but also his affection and loyalty.

But now her greatest personal fear was coming to pass, and even though she knew that what was ahead was inevitable, she was still struggling to somehow hold back the disaster until she could find some way to begin making amends. She'd worried that it was only a matter of time until someone with means and motivation looked into the past, but she'd hoped to somehow continue to live her charmed life in relative peace.

Then Kendra herself had innocently set something in motion, and now Lorna had unwittingly advanced the process. The sense of justice that had secretly flayed Doris's soul for years recognized the rightness of Lorna being the one to unknowingly bring this all to fruition, but her fear of losing everything she held dear made her want to somehow escape one last time.

Lorna was the key to it all, and now that Doris had finally found the courage to approach her, it looked as if her last chance to make amends was over before she could truly begin. She'd bungled this badly.

Mitch's stern voice got her attention again and made her realize she'd slipped away into her panicked thoughts and missed what he'd been saying. "What?"

"I said, what have you done?"

What have you done? Doris reeled with the question.

What have you done?

The small word "you" pinned the wrong completely on her, precisely where it belonged, unerringly landing it like a bomb on a target. Doris reached for Mitch's big hands and squeezed them madly as she tried to start.

"I...I made some mistakes, Mitch." She stopped and tears began to slide in hot trails down her beautiful face. "Oh God, no. Not mistakes...

"No." She shook her head adamantly. "A mistake is buying a dress that's the wrong color, or when you misspell a word and have to erase or start over. What I did was no mistake."

Mitch held Doris's cold hands and felt something inside him clench. Doris got control of herself then and looked up at him, the look in her eyes as haunted as any he'd ever seen.

"It was a sin, Mitch. A sin. What I did to Lorna Farrell sixteen years ago was a sin. I thought it was the right thing to do at the time, I thought it was the only way I could keep Kendra and somehow escape that nightmare, but I never should have done it, Mitch. Never."

A coldness went over him. Sixteen years ago, Lorna would have been eight years old. And when Lorna'd been eight, her adoptive parents had been killed.

"I'm so tired of being afraid someone will find out. First your father when he was alive, and now you and Kendra. But I finally have the courage to tell the two of you about it, Mitch. I deserve whatever happens next."

The truth struck him then. "Lorna knows it all, doesn't she?"

Doris's tears came harder then and she struggled to speak. "She knows some of it, but she doesn't know why. Maybe it would give her a little comfort to know why, and maybe I'm tired of living with the guilt and I want someone to forgive me, I don't know anymore. But I do know that if Lorna leaves here today she'll never come back and she'll never let me near her again. Help me make her stay, I must talk to her. Please, Mitch. It's the last thing I'll ever ask of you.''

Doris was too distraught to notice the movement just outside the kitchen in the hall. Kendra had gotten home and stood in the doorway, her teary gaze fixed on her mother. John stood in silent disapproval just behind her.

When Kendra spoke, Doris jerked and glanced fearfully toward her youngest daughter. ''It'll be all right, Mama. If Mitch can't get Lorna to stay, I will. She'll listen to you, I know she will.''

The magnitude of what Kendra was saying impacted Mitch and he suddenly realized what was going on. When Kendra's gaze lifted to his, he suddenly saw a worldliness and a knowledge that told him his naïve little stepsister was not half as naïve and innocent of the ways of the world as he'd believed.

The anger that made him feel would likely not hold a candle to the outrage Lorna would feel. And yes, he agreed now that Lorna should stay. It would be best to get everything out in the open once and for all.

Mitch released Doris and strode to the hall, not sparing his stepsister a glance as he passed her and she rushed to her mother. When he reached the small bathroom, the door was open and the light was off. There was no sign of Lorna in the den. She wasn't the kind of person who wandered around in other people's houses, so he went out the front door then around the side of the house.

He found her sitting with her Stetson and handbag at the far back corner of the veranda. She wouldn't have been visible from the front when Kendra and John had arrived, but she'd probably heard John's car.

The Kelpie pups had found her but, as if they were alert to her quiet mood, they'd crowded around her in silent sympathy, content to just let her sit with her arms loosely around them and her fingers gently rubbing their soft coats.

Lorna looked up at him, then away. "I behaved badly in there. I apologize."

"Doris admitted some surprising things after you went out. Both she and Kendra have some confessions to make and a lot of explaining to do if you're ready to hear them out." He'd been blunt to spare her the suspense, but he'd expected her to refuse and to demand that he take her back to San Antonio. He'd do it without question if she chose that because he thought she was owed that much.

But she nodded somberly and looked down at the puppies. "Now that I've been thinking about it all, I realize something was going on. I'm just not sure I want to know what it was. I doubt any of it matters now."

Mitch picked up one of the pups and sat down next to her. "It might matter very much. Doris says you know about it, but you don't know why. Looks like it's been eating her a while. If you've wanted answers for things, this might be the time.''

''I won't put up with having her play on my sympathy, and I don't want to hear a litany of excuses,'' she said, still weary in the aftermath of her own emotional upset and terrified of more. ''I've discovered I'm not quite the paragon of compassion and tolerance and proper behavior that I thought I was.''

''You don't have to be.''

Lorna looked at him briefly to see the truth of that then turned her attention back to the pups while she struggled with the tantalizing question of how much she wanted to know. The risk of even more emotional turmoil was too high for her to immediately rush right back in and ask for more.

It was a long time before she could bring herself to give Doris another chance.

By the time Lorna and Mitch joined Kendra and Doris in the living room, John was just leaving. Lorna knew her boss well enough to know he was angry. Possibly furious. Kendra looked distressed, but neither Kendra nor John referred to the tension between them beyond his announcement that he was going back to San Antonio. His surprising offer of a ride made Lorna feel even more uneasy about what was going on.

Mitch spoke up. ''I can fly Lorna home when she's ready.''

John managed a polite goodbye to them all, but he was reserved with Kendra to the point of rudeness before he went out the door and they all went into the living room to find places to sit.

Lorna had kept hold of her handbag and Stetson, quietly declining an offer to put them away until she was ready to leave. There was something about all this that made her feel she should be prepared to flee, and something unsettling that made her want to keep familiar possessions close by. Now that she'd agreed to this, the tension on Doris's and Kendra's faces made her even more uneasy. They both looked as if they'd been crying, and Lorna tried to ignore that.

She turned down the offer of an iced tea, wanting to get this over with. Mitch sat near her on the sofa, and Doris and Kendra chose wing chairs on the other side of the huge glass-topped coffee table.

Doris gently cleared her throat and looked at Lorna. This time she made eye contact, and Lorna was unwillingly touched by the impression of shame she read in Doris.

The details and events Doris outlined about her adolescence were surprisingly blunt and told without much emotion, and when she told the details of her actions as an adult, she was unsparing of herself and her motives.

Doris had grown up poor, with an alcoholic mother and a father who'd slapped them both around. Starved for a bit of tenderness and love, she'd been too naïve to realize she'd gotten pregnant from a single sexual encounter with a neighbor boy in the back seat of his car. She'd been months into her pregnancy when her mother's suspicions and a hasty trip to a doctor had confirmed the truth.

Young Doris's life had gotten desperately worse after that, until a beating from her father had landed her in a charity hospital. Robert and Erma Farrell found out about her situation, and in exchange for allowing them to adopt Lorna, they'd paid all her expenses, including rent on a tiny apartment and a generous allowance until Doris was through high school.

Terrified to be on her own in the world, Doris had married the first boy who'd asked when she was eighteen. But the abuse she'd thought she'd escaped returned with a vengeance and escalated with her young husband. After enduring six years of it, she'd tried to seek a divorce when her husband's abuse began to include Kendra.

By the time Lorna's adoptive parents had been killed, Doris had been in a vicious custody battle for her youngest daughter, and she'd been too terrified her ex-husband would find out about Lorna and use it against her to even consider reclaiming her. And even after she'd won custody of Kendra and they were safe, she'd been poor, so she'd taken comfort in the notion that beautiful little Lorna had surely been adopted by an intact family.

She'd worked hard to make a good life for herself and Kendra, then met Ben Ellery and fell in love. Ben had been an honorable man with high standards of right and wrong, duty and family.

She'd been so afraid of losing her grand opportunity for love and an escape from lack for her and

Kendra that she'd worried Ben would disapprove of the fact that she'd given up a child. She'd been certain he wouldn't forgive her if he knew she'd sacrificed one daughter to save the other when she'd also failed to look for her orphaned child and reclaim her once her life improved.

Particularly since she'd never sought Ben's help when they'd decided to marry. It would been a simple matter for a man with his money and influence, but Doris had been too afraid of jeopardizing her new rich life to ask. And the longer she'd waited, the more impossible it became.

So she'd kept silent until that day five years ago in the restaurant when, in front of both Ben and Mitch, Lorna's former friend had introduced her as the child Doris had given up. Panicked, Doris had denied it and though Ben had initially shown signs of doubting her, he'd soon relented and taken Doris at her word.

It had been another reprieve for Doris until that past Friday when Mitch had discovered Lorna's friendship with Kendra.

Doris had been frustrated by Lorna's refusal to accept money. In some ways, it had been her way of somehow giving Lorna a financial compensation for the past. Then she'd been shocked by Kendra's suggestion to Mitch about dating Lorna, but she'd seen the potential in taking Kendra's idea seriously.

It was just after she'd persuaded Mitch to go along with the dating scheme that she'd begun to let herself wonder what Lorna was like. If Lorna didn't want money, what could she want?

That was also when she'd caught on to what Kendra was trying to do and realized that perhaps bringing Lorna closer to their family and somehow mending things with her was not only inevitable but something she wanted to do.

Which was why Doris had come home today earlier than expected. She'd meant to begin the process directly, but then she'd handled it poorly and now admitted she'd probably done far more harm than good.

Lorna didn't comment on that. As if to spare Lorna the pressure of doing so, Kendra made a start at her own explanation and dropped a bombshell.

She started with that day in the restaurant five years ago. Kendra had been having lunch with her family but had excused herself to go speak to friend in another part of the restaurant. On her way back to their table, she'd got near enough to overhear what was going on and had slipped behind a large fernery to hear the rest.

She'd sensed her mother's upset was too deep for the claim of a long-lost child to be a lie. Kendra had pondered the incident those next years, then used her own money to look into the claim after Ben's death a year ago.

Once she'd become convinced Lorna might truly be her sister, Kendra had arranged to meet John Owen at a party in hope of dating him so she could meet Lorna. The happy consequence of that was that she'd fallen in love with John.

Impatient with waiting for an accidental meeting between Lorna and Mitch that she could exploit,

Kendra arranged for Mitch to pick her up in John's office where he'd be sure to meet Lorna. If Lorna could be drawn close to Doris through Mitch, Kendra was certain Doris wouldn't be able to resist accepting Lorna at long last.

After all, Doris had been a wonderful mother to her, and Kendra hadn't been able to accept that her mother could refuse her own child. And the more Kendra had found out about Lorna's upbringing, the more guilt she'd felt for being the child who'd had an easy, charmed life.

When the confessions were finished, Lorna was too drained to react. The things that had caused her a lifetime of hurt and abandonment had been explained, yet both Doris and Kendra had used that lifetime of hurt and abandonment to manipulate her.

No one spoke as Lorna sat silently and tried to absorb it all. She glanced Mitch's way and saw his stony expression. He disapproved of what Doris and Kendra had done, there was no mistaking the dark turbulence in his eyes. She wished her own feelings and thoughts about it all could be that clear-cut.

After several minutes, her soft, "I can't sort through this now," was the only thing she was truly capable of.

The old resentments had been diffused in a way that made her feel off-kilter. But the new resentment she felt about being manipulated by Kendra, whom she'd though so innocent and in need of protection, was sharp.

And Doris had done her share of manipulating as well. In essence, they'd both led her along, playing on her deepest needs to move her in the ways they wanted in order to manipulate each other.

The fact that they'd had reasons that might ultimately help satisfy her craving for family didn't seem worthy of merit yet, and she couldn't bring herself to declare an unqualified trust in people who'd taken their own sweet time being honest with her.

Her words to them were quiet. "I'd like to go home. I don't want to decide right now how I feel about either of you. If I had to make a snap judgment, I don't think you'd be very happy with what I'd have to say."

She gave a sad smile. "Of course, I was part of the dating charade, so I guess I've got no right to feel too self-righteous."

She'd said that without looking at anyone. When she finished she stood, taking her handbag and hat with her as she walked out of the room. Mitch followed her as they went out the back to his pickup and drove to the airstrip.

CHAPTER TEN

LORNA might have a family that she was getting to know but she'd apparently lost Mitch, and she didn't understand why.

He'd flown her back to San Antonio on Sunday afternoon then taken her to a steakhouse on the way home. He'd accepted her silence and the fact that she didn't appear to want much conversation, but he'd been sweetly determined to see her fed.

She'd loved that he was so patient with her. Mitch had a gift for making her feel cared for, and she'd been moved to tears because his gentle care had had seemed genuinely heartfelt. She got the distinct impression that Mitch was the kind of man who was capable of spoiling the woman he loved and that made her feel even more emotional.

After they'd got to her apartment from the steakhouse, he'd spied a deck of playing cards on a bookcase and coaxed her into a few hands. He'd lifted her spirits and got her to laugh, but when it was time for him to go home, he'd boldly walked across the hall and drafted Melanie to look in on her.

Melanie had been all eyes during the quick introduction Lorna had been prompted to make between her minor tyrant and her best friend, then Mellie had given them a few minutes of privacy before Mitch left so they could say goodbye.

The tender kiss he'd given her was long and so incredible that Lorna was terrified she'd ask him to stay the night. Thankfully she'd managed to keep the impulse to herself. After all, they both had a lot to think about. It would have been foolish to complicate things even more with greater intimacy.

And realistically, they'd only been around each other for three days. Though each hour of that time now felt like years, she'd managed to cling to her common sense.

Once everything calmed down and her emotions settled in a few days or weeks, she might recognize this past weekend as a romantic mirage fueled by the intensity of the situation and an infatuation that could only be fleeting. She didn't believe in love at first sight, not really. Her head knew that for a fact, though at the moment her heart wasn't at all convinced.

Now she wished she hadn't let Mitch leave Sunday night. He'd called her each day to see how she was doing, but he'd not come to San Antonio to see her. And although he'd warned her he'd probably not see her until the barbecue on Friday, she began to worry about the real reason he'd stayed away.

Was this a way for him to distance himself from her? Or was he truly giving her time with Kendra and Doris to get to know them a bit? She'd recov-

ered almost right away from her upset with Doris
and Kendra, and it had felt right to forgive them and
to wholeheartedly make a fresh start. But the fresh
beginning she had with them somehow seemed to
underscore Mitch's absence and give it a sad sig-
nificance.

After all, her status with his stepfamily had
changed. Since she'd been accepted by Kendra and
Doris, there'd be more serious consequences to any
romantic involvement that might develop between
them from here on.

Unless Mitch's attraction to her had been entirely
sexual. Since that kind of relationship would be
awkward under their new circumstances, Mitch
might be rethinking the kind of relationship he
wanted to have with her. If he wanted one with her
at all beyond that of stepsister.

Doris and Kendra came to San Antonio and Lorna
had spent Tuesday with them, since she'd taken a
week of her vacation time after all. It was a huge
adjustment getting used to each other but Lorna had
begun to feel more at ease with them both by the
end of that day. Because Doris had decided to move
back to San Antonio, they invited Lorna along when
they went house hunting on Wednesday.

The only sad part of that was that Kendra was
planning to move to San Antonio with Doris because John and Kendra had put their wedding plans
on hold. John had been upset by Kendra's machi-

nations and he'd thought they both needed to spend time apart to think about things and reassess.

Kendra was trying to be optimistic, but she fully accepted that she'd done the wrong thing and that John was right to suspend things between them for now.

In view of all that, it looked as if Doris and Kendra would soon not be a daily part of Mitch's life on Ellery Ranch. And because the ranch was too far away from San Antonio to make an easy commute possible, perhaps Lorna's opportunities to see Mitch from here on were few.

The irony of finally being accepted into her family was that her family was now going through an upheaval. It might have been easier to cope with everything had she been the only change, but there seemed to be a huge chain-reaction going on and the best Lorna could do was hope that things would stabilize soon. And that she'd be able to find out and accept what might be ahead for her with Mitch.

By afternoon on the day of the barbecue, Lorna and Melanie set out for Ellery Ranch. Melanie had also been invited to the festivities, and they'd both packed bags to stay overnight in case they were too tired to drive back to San Antonio after the fireworks.

It seemed to take forever to get there, and once they'd arrived, the driveway and the grounds around the headquarters were already starting to fill up with cars and pickups. After they changed out of their jeans and T-shirts into the sundresses they'd brought, Kendra took Melanie to show her around and Doris immediately began introducing Lorna to her friends. Doris didn't announce anything along the lines of, "This is my daughter," but Lorna realized several of Doris's friends had already heard all about it, and whoever hadn't heard was sure to hear the gossip by the end of the day.

She'd been eager to see Mitch again, but the fact that he'd not been close by when she'd first arrived was a huge disappointment. And possibly another indication that he was keeping a distance from her for a reason.

Kendra sought her out then, a smile of excitement on her face. "John's here, and we've worked things out." She took hold of Lorna's hands and rushed on with, "I've been waiting to ask this, and now I can't wait any longer. I'd like you be my maid of honor. Would you please, Lorna?"

"I'd love to," Lorna said, pleased. "Does your mother know?"

"*Our* mother, Lorna. You need to get used to saying it that way. And yes, that was one of the first things mama suggested to me once we'd talked everything out, but I'd already decided on that weeks ago and, come hell or high water," she chattered excitedly, "I was going to somehow do it. Which was why I needed to hurry your introduction to Mitch. It's only four months until the wedding you know, and there were only so many explanations I could keep making for the reason that John had a best man and three groomsmen while I had three bridesmaids but no maid of honor.''

Kendra squeezed her hands again. ''But I've given up plotting and scheming and trying to get my way.'' Kendra's gaze caught on someone behind Lorna and her smile widened. ''Isn't that right, Mitch?''

The big hands that settled warmly on Lorna's waist from behind sent a hard charge of excitement through her. She felt the heat as Mitch leaned down and kissed her cheek as she started to turn her head to look at him.

''John's smart to get you to promise that before the wedding. Might give him an even chance of keeping you in line.''

Kendra grinned at that. ''I'm growing up, Mitch. I'll keep *myself* in line.''

''You do that, sis. And go easy on the matchmaking. Just because you had one success doesn't mean you won't make a royal mess of the next one.''

Lorna felt a trickle of hope but kept it carefully to herself. Melanie's attention was distracted by one of the other guests and Mitch turned Lorna to face him.

''You got out here quicker than I expected. Sorry I wasn't here to be a better host.''

''You must be pretty busy.'' She paused to glance around at the tables that were set out across the patio, and the country band that was setting up just outside the den. Several children and a few adults were making use of the pool. The growing crowd of milling people had started choosing places to sit, as if the delicious smell of barbecued beef had made them eager to start the meal.

"This is a huge party," she said. "I wasn't expecting so many people. The house was already crowded."

"It's a big turnout, bigger this year," he said and she caught an inkling of something in the way he'd put it, then chided herself for wishful thinking. It had only been a week ago today that she'd walked into the office and Kendra had introduced them.

And it had been days since they'd seen each other. Even if they'd spent the whole week together, it was too soon for love pledges, and far too soon to seriously contemplate anything permanent between them. Her mind shied away from the word "marriage."

Mitch took her around, introducing her to people she hadn't met and keeping a proprietary hand at her waist the whole time. It was nearly six by the time all the food was set out and everyone began to line up to fill their plates.

The barbecued beef was tender and there must have been every kind of sweet or tangy summer salad on the tables along with steaming ear corn and icy cold, sliced vegetables. It was a feast with dozens of cookies and an assortment of sheet cakes and pies that took up two tables of their own.

By the time most of the food had been cleared away, the depleted desert tables had been reduced to one and moved to the verandah for nibbling. Another table with ice-filled chests of soft drinks and a huge punch bowl had been set at the edge of the patio next to the veranda rail. Several of the men were walking around with beer, and Lorna spied a couple of shiny kegs off to one side that were quite popular. A handful of teenagers had now taken over the pool and had a game of pool volleyball going.

The country band began to tune up as a few tables and most of the chairs were moved to ring one side of the patio and wooden dance floor that had been set up on the lawn. The long shade of evening had begun to cool the air. White fairy lights went on in the trees and the band started with a ballad.

They danced the first dance together and the male heat of Mitch's body established instant dominion over hers. His dark gaze glittered down at her and she read the blatant message there. Until now, he'd been playing the gallant host who had time for everyone and made sure each guest felt welcome and comfortable.

But the message in his eyes was entirely for her and the sensual warning in it made her heart race and her blood go heavy and sweet.

''How're you gettin' along with your mother and sister?''

The bit of common conversation made her try to still the rapid pounding of her heart. Although she probably shouldn't have, she'd expected him to talk about something else. Something teasing and maybe sexy. He seemed to enjoy that almost as much as she did. To be honest, she'd been craving a few "loaded remarks" and flirtations, but he hadn't made a single one.

"We're getting along fine. It's a huge adjustment to make, but wonderful."

"Doris is as excited as a kid with a new best friend. All she talks about is you, your apartment, how independent and smart you are. How sensible and beautiful. Kendra thinks you're the best thing since lipstick and the Neiman Marcus catalog. You agreed to be her matron of honor?"

Lorna smiled tolerantly at the soft surprise of that, because he'd got it wrong. She felt the impact of his male charm in the small mistake. "A matron of honor is a married woman," she said gently. "You mean maid of honor."

"I'm familiar with wedding terms. Do you mind if we go inside?" he asked, instantly distracting her from the spike of excitement his comment caused. "I've got a confession or two of my own to make now that things have calmed down."

Lorna's excitement rose, but she was careful to conceal it. The kind of confession she most wanted to hear from him was unrealistic and far too fanciful, but she sensed he was moving along toward a goal, and that made her excitement worse. Once again, her common sense was being short-circuited.

Lorna walked with him into the busy kitchen then down the hall to the den. He closed the door when they walked in, but he didn't bother to close the heavy drapes on the sliding doors. Because the band was just outside, the only privacy they'd have was that their conversation couldn't be heard. Which meant that she was letting herself become excited for nothing.

Luckily the band's amplifiers were faced away or it would have been too loud in the room for comfortable conversation. Mitch invited her to sit down in one of the wing chairs while he went to his desk. She noticed that he pulled out a key to unlock a desk drawer. He took out a thick file of papers and brought them around to the front of the desk.

Lorna rested her elbows on the arms of the wing chair and laced her fingers together. Mitch eased back against the desk, his long legs stretched toward her in the space between them. It was obvious that he would hand her the file, but he didn't just yet.

"I'll make this confession short," he said. "You know I hired an investigator. That was a week ago. Most of this he dug up by Sunday. I intended to stop the process, but then you mentioned your daddy's ranch."

Lorna felt tense suddenly over that bit of information, but Mitch went on before she could dwell on it.

"There's enough in this file already to hint that your daddy's brother was up to no good. If you say the word, we'll see what else can be dug up. If there's enough to nail him, we'll see if anything can be done about it."

The complete surprise of that disoriented her a little. And as she'd known, Mitch's aggressive protectiveness toward people he cared about was one of the things that had so drawn her to him. The fact that he seemed to have designated her as one of the people he cared about gave her heart a sweet lift.

"I don't have the kind of resources to undertake something like that. Even if I did, I'm not sure I want to. Compared to everything else back then, the loss of that ranch was…minimal."

"You don't want revenge?"

Lorna released a pent-up breath and glanced away to consider it before she shook her head and looked at him. "If I started taking revenge for everything I didn't like in my life back then, what would be the result? My life now would revolve around that, and I want happier things than to dig around in the past looking for trouble."

She missed the faint gleam of satisfaction in his eyes as she went on. "That doesn't mean that as an adult I would just lay down and let myself be run over if something else came along."

"Oh, no, ma'am, I doubt you would," he said, then chuckled as if he were tickled by that. "You can either take this file and keep it or you can destroy it. It belongs to you now.'' He handed it over.

Lorna started to take it, then froze. ''I don't want to look at it tonight,'' she said, then lowered her hand. ''If you wouldn't mind keeping it locked away until I'm ready to go home, I'd rather do that. I don't think it's wise to leave it lying around.''

''You can do whatever you want,'' he said, then stood and walked around the desk to lock the file in the drawer. When he'd pocketed the key, he came back around the desk and leaned back against it to fix her with a solemn glance.

''You still haven't told me whether you're willing to overlook or maybe even forgive that I dug around in your past. I intruded on your privacy, Miz Farrell.'' His confession was sincere, that was plain. ''Anything else I want to know, I'll ask you. Even then, you can either tell me what you want or tell me to mind my own business.''

Lorna felt the pleasure of that and gave him a slight smile. ''I understood why you did it. Under the circumstances, yes. I'm willing to overlook it this time and I won't hold it against you.''

Mitch changed the subject so suddenly then that it took her a moment to follow.

''I see you remembered.''

He smiled at her look of confusion. His dark eyes lowered to move almost caressingly over the soft blue sundress. The deep V ended where propriety dictated, but she supposed a man would find it enticing. The crisp, fitted bodice with its tiny spaghetti straps ended in a drawstring waist before the skirt flared out and ended a good four inches above her knees. The white sandals she wore with it had small heels that enhanced the feminine line of her legs.

His voice went low. "You remembered that I like little dresses like that. Cut low and worn short enough to show some leg. Hundred-proof sexy. And I'm not the only country boy who's been gawking at the scenery.

"So thank you, Lorna Dean. I appreciate you takin' my personal tastes into account when you dress up."

Lorna couldn't keep back a small smile, but she didn't know whether to be amused with him or self-conscious.

Before she could decide, he came out with a blunt, "How many kids do you want?"

The question landed on her emotions like a fireball of electricity. Her heart went wild and she felt sweet tendrils of joy begin to unfurl. She tried mightily to suppress them, but his next remark weakened the effort.

"I told you I couldn't marry a woman unless we agreed on the number."

Lorna glanced toward the sliding glass door as if she'd just remembered that she needed to control her reaction. There were too many people close by who could simply look in.

"How many, Lorna Dean?"

She looked at him and answered softly. "As many as—six? And maybe one or two of those could be...adopted."

Mitch crossed his arms over his chest and appeared to give that serious consideration. "Six is a good number. And kids are kids, any kind of kids are fine. We can love 'em all. But won't that be a burden to a career?"

She saw in his eyes that he already knew her answer. "I've wanted a family all my life," she said, straining to speak calmly, "a traditional one. I'll stay at home, but my husband will also have to make our children a priority."

"Your husband will probably have to devote at least a few hours a day to keeping a roof over your head and theirs," he pointed out. "But I know he'll not only make your kids a priority, he'll make *you* a priority. A big one."

Her growing joy made her dare a breathless, "I didn't know you predicted the future. H-how long have you been doing that?"

"About a week. Every time I look into your pretty eyes I see it. But here's fair warning: Whatever I have to do to get you to marry me, I'll do."

But he'd not made a single move toward her and she again glanced toward the glass door. Now that the sun was going down, the light in the room highlighted them like a movie screen.

She looked at him again and was struck by the

tender sincerity in his gaze. Still, she was compelled to remind them both, "It's only been eight days."

Mitch smiled and stood to walk over to the sliding door. Excitement made her heart race with sweet anticipation as he steadily pulled the cord to close the drapes. Lorna felt her eyes go large as he walked back to her and bent down to brace his big fists on her chair arms. Her body trembled with his nearness and his warm breath gusted lightly on her upturned face.

"I've known for a long time what I want," he said, his voice nearly a growl. "I know what to look for, but I'd never seen it before you."

The tender kiss he pressed on her lips then made her lift her hands to place her palms on his lean cheeks. He drew back just enough to move his fist off the chair arm and reach into his shirt pocket. He made a bit more space between them to hold up a gold ring with a large diamond. A ring of rubies encircled the diamond and as Lorna stared at it, stunned, he went down on his knee in front of her chair and gently took her left hand.

"If you don't like this ring, you can have any other ring you want."

"It's beautiful," she said hoarsely. "Perfect."

Mitch smiled at her dazed expression. "I can't put it on until you give me your answer, Lorna. Pretty please, Lorna Dean, I love you. Come live with me and let's make the beautiful life I see every time I look at you."

"I love you," she said, almost too choked with emotion to speak, "I love you so much. Yes."

A small tear streaked happily down her cheek.

Mitch slipped the ring on, then leaned toward her to seize her lips with a soft kiss that rapidly escalated into a carnal conflagration.

They were aware only briefly of the applause and cheers outside the closed drapes that were soon drowned out by the country band's rollicking rendition of "Here Comes the Bride."

And later, after Mitch made the formal announcement of their engagement to all of their guests, the fireworks display burst in the night sky like a celestial celebration.

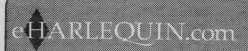

magazine

♥──────────────── **quizzes**

Is he the one? What kind of lover are you? Visit the **Quizzes** area to find out!

♥──────────────── **recipes for romance**

Get scrumptious meal ideas with our **Recipes for Romance**.

♥──────────────── **romantic movies**

Peek at the **Romantic Movies** area to find Top 10 Flicks about First Love, ten Supersexy Movies, and more.

♥──────────────── **royal romance**

Get the latest scoop on your favorite royals in **Royal Romance**.

♥──────────────── **games**

Check out the **Games** pages to find a ton of interactive romantic fun!

♥──────────────── **romantic travel**

In need of a romantic rendezvous? Visit the **Romantic Travel** section for articles and guides.

♥──────────────── **lovescopes**

Are you two compatible? Click your way to the **Lovescopes** area to find out now!

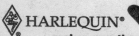

Do you like stories that get *up close and personal?*
Do you long to be loved *truly, madly, deeply...?*

If you're looking for emotionally intense, tantalizingly
tender love stories, stop searching and start reading

Harlequin Romance®

You'll find authors who'll leave you breathless, including:

Liz Fielding

Winner of the 2001 RITA Award for
Best Traditional Romance
(The Best Man and the Bridesmaid)

Day Leclaire

USA Today bestselling author

Leigh Michaels

Bestselling author with 30 million
copies of her books sold worldwide

Renee Roszel

USA Today bestselling author

Margaret Way

Australian star with 80 novels to her credit

Sophie Weston

A fresh British voice and a hot talent!

Don't miss their latest novels, coming soon!

HARLEQUIN®
Makes any time special®

Possibly pregnant!

The possibility of parenthood: for some couples it's a
seemingly impossible dream. For others, it's an
unexpected surprise.... Or perhaps it's a planned
pregnancy that brings a husband and wife closer
together...or turns their marriage upside down?

One thing is for sure, life will never be the same when
they find themselves having a baby...maybe!

This emotionally compelling miniseries from

Harlequin
Romance®

will warm your heart and bring a tear to your eye....

Look out in April for:

THE BABY QUESTION

by

Caroline Anderson

(#3697)

And keep an eye out for pregnancy stories by other
popular authors such as:

Grace Green

Barbara Hannay

Visit us at www.eHarlequin.com

HRMB

HARLEQUIN®
Romance®

**is thrilled to present
a brand-new miniseries
that dares to be different...**

TANGO
Fresh & Flirty...
it takes two to tango!

Exuberant, exciting...emotionally exhilarating!

**These cutting-edge, highly contemporary stories
capture how women in the 21st century *really*
feel about meeting Mr. Right!**

Don't miss:

August:
THE HONEYMOON PRIZE—
Jessica Hart (#3713)

October:
THE FIANCÉ FIX—
Carole Mortimer (#3719)

November:
THE BEDROOM
ASSIGNMENT—
Sophie Weston (#3724)

*And watch for more
TANGO books to come!*

HARLEQUIN®
Makes any time special®